YOHANA

DEBORAH GALILEY

*To Marilyn,
Bless you!
Thanks for inviting me
to speak!
Deborah Galiley*

CAPSTONE FICTION

WATERFORD, VIRGINIA

Yohana

Published in the U.S. by:
Capstone Publishing Group LLC
P.O. Box 8
Waterford, VA 20197

Visit Capstone Fiction at
www.capstonefiction.com

Cover design by David LaPlaca/debest design co.
Cover image © iStockphoto.com/Boris Katsman
Author photo © 2007 by Robert Jeff

Scripture verses are taken from:
The HOLY BIBLE, NEW INTERNATIONAL VERSION®. NIV®.
Copyright © 1973, 1978, 1984 by International Bible Society. Used by
permission of Zondervan. All rights reserved.
The JEWISH NEW TESTAMENT, © 1979, 1989, 1990, 1991 by David
H. Stern, Jewish New Testament Publications. All rights reserved.

ISBN: 978-1-60290-146-9

This book is dedicated to

**the King of kings
and Lord of lords.**

*Your maidservant lifts her eyes to the hills
and eagerly awaits Your return.*

Author's Note

When I first began writing *Yohana*, I was recovering from a hip replacement. I had been through two bouts of breast cancer: the initial outbreak and a reoccurrence in my hip bone. Due to the amount of radiation used, my hip had progressively deteriorated until I finally just went ahead and had the joint replaced. The cancer, however, had miraculously been confined to one spot and had gone away. I knew firsthand of God's healing touch.

Partway through *Yohana*, the breast cancer returned. This time, it ate its way up through my spine and into my neck. Several vertebrae fractured from the insidious tumor. While writing the crucifixion scene, in terrible pain, immobilized in a stiff neck brace, on pain killers, and using a cane, I had a small taste of what Yeshua went through for us. He spoke to me, and promised me healing. I believed Him, despite the medical prognoses and evidence to the contrary.

Today, as I write this, I am cancer-free! My bones, without surgery, have been healed. I am without neck brace, without cane, without pain killers. I have full mobility. I can testify with complete honesty and assurance that God has done this, and it is an awesome thing. He is powerful, indeed!

So, dear reader, enjoy this book. But also realize that its truth is profound and life-changing. The miraculous wasn't just for 2,000 years ago. It's for today, as well.

Who is this...

striding forward in the

greatness of his strength?

<small>ISAIAH 63:1</small>

Your eyes will see

the king in his beauty....

<small>ISAIAH 33:17</small>

ONE

I'll never forget the first time I saw the Rabbi. I had awakened that morning, my hip throbbing with its usual pain, knowing I should go to the Temple as was my sporadic custom. My maid, Rachel, accompanied me. We left the cool interior of the palace and emerged into the cloudless glare of another hot day. Servants and guards alike deferentially made way for me as I inclined my head briefly in recognition.

Once we were past the palace grounds, I breathed easier. Living in close proximity to Herod Antipas was a tense and sometimes overwhelming experience. Like his father before him, he saw the slightest wavering as treachery and was quick to throw formerly trusted friends and allies into prison to be tortured and killed. Often he misread people, which resulted in a fatal mistake for those misunderstood. Too many people over the years had fallen prey to his paranoia. Lately, since he had divorced his first wife and married the beautiful yet wickedly manipulative Herodias, political intrigue increased by tenfold. And it hadn't been lacking before. I found the palace more and more distasteful; a snake pit.

Now we headed east to the Temple grounds. Except for the three great pilgrim feasts each year when the City filled to overflowing, Jerusalem was relatively easy to travel through. For some reason, though, today was wall-to-wall people.

By the time we approached the outskirts of the Temple Mount, the Temple itself towering above us in a dazzling mass of white marble and gold, the crowds surged against us. Everywhere we turned, men, women and children jostled and pushed, struggling to get by.

1

"What is going on today?" I remarked irritably to Rachel. My plan had been to come down, put some money in the Temple treasury, offer up some prayers, and then proceed to the *shuk* for some shopping. All of these unwashed hordes annoyed me.

Rachel looked as dumbfounded as I. "I do not know, my lady," she answered me, shrugging her delicate shoulders. "It is not a feast day. Where are they all coming from?"

"Ask someone," I commanded her.

Haltingly, Rachel pulled at the sleeve of a respectable-looking woman to her right. "Excuse me, madam," she politely said, her natural reticence overcome by my request. "But can you tell us why so many people are at the Temple today?"

"Don't you know?" asked the woman in some surprise.

Rachel shook her head while I strained forward to hear.

"It's the Prophet," said the woman, a hungry look in her eyes. "The Prophet is speaking in the Court of the Gentiles."

Rachel and I looked at each other quizzically. *Who was this prophet?*

The woman turned, impatient to keep going.

"Wait," I shouted after her. She looked back at me. "What is the name of this 'prophet?' " I asked.

"Don't you know?" she said again, amazed at our ignorance. "It's Yeshua ben Yosef. Of Natzeret." And without waiting for a response, she vanished into the crowd.

"Have you heard of him?" I asked Rachel, not pleased at appearing unknowing.

"I've heard rumors, my lady," she said, brow furrowed in concentration. "But I haven't paid much attention to them. Something about an uneducated carpenter's son from the Galil who supposedly heals the sick...."

Heals the sick. Even as she spoke those words my hip began to throb again. I was never one to put much stock in the so-called miracle workers. Many of these charlatans plied their trade in and around Jerusalem, making fantastic sums off a gullible and desperate populace. Still...

I made a spontaneous decision that would irrevocably change my life. "Rachel."

"Yes, my lady?"

"Let's go and listen to this man. I'm curious to see who he is."

"Are you sure, my lady?" Rachel turned horrified eyes to me. We *never* mingled with the common people. I was acting extremely out of character and Rachel knew it.

I had not been entirely convinced that my plan was a good one, but when she questioned it, I felt bound and determined to defend it. "Of course I'm sure," I snapped. "Let's go." I plowed my way through the crowd, pulling rank and staring people down whenever it would help me make progress. The slowness was tedious.

After several minutes spent clearing a path through the vast sea of people, we found ourselves at the entrance to the Court of the Gentiles. This was the large outer boundary of the Temple where anyone was free to go. A square of 750 feet, it was paved with the finest marble. No Gentiles were allowed past here. Further up lay the Court of Women, beyond which I, as a Jewish woman, could not progress. Normally, I would have swept right up to the Court of Women, but not today. Straining to see, I stood on tiptoe; then, as if by some giant invisible hand, the whole assembly seated itself on the ground. It appeared that only I remained standing.

"Can you sit, my lady?" whispered Rachel, crouching, hand at my elbow, ever attentive to my needs.

"Not very well, with this hip." I winced. Already I felt foolish, knowing that I blocked the view of the people behind me. But with everyone else sitting down, I could suddenly see the man who stood at the very front of the assembly. He must have been about fifty meters away. Dressed in the rough garb of the poor working class, dark haired and bearded, he could have passed for any one of a hundred men like him I saw every day on the streets of Jerusalem. It was when he lifted his eyes and looked straight at me that I suddenly and inexplicably felt overcome by an emotion I could not name.

His gaze penetrated the thin veneer of my public persona such that my soul stood exposed. Overcome, I averted my eyes and sank slowly to the ground, unaware until later that the pain in my hip had subsided to the point where it was possible to sit like everyone else.

The man lifted his hands in the air and prayed in a loud voice, "*Baruch Atah Adonai Eloheinu, Melech ha olam,* Blessed are you, O Lord my God, King of the Universe. O my Father, bless the words of my mouth as I speak forth Your truth to Your people. Open their ears that they may understand. In Your holy Name, Amen."

"Amen," echoed the crowd, the word rolling off thousands of tongues like rumbles of thunder, reverberating again and again. All around me, men, women and children settled expectantly on the ground, lifting up faces so that they might catch the Prophet's words as they flowed through the assembly.

3

Despite my customary skepticism, I, too, leaned forward eagerly.

Slowly and clearly, with great projection, the man spoke. "A farmer went out to sow his seed. As he was scattering the seed, some fell along the path, and the birds came and ate it up. Some fell on rocky places, where it did not have much soil. It sprang up quickly, because the soil was shallow. But when the sun came up, the plants were scorched, and they withered because they had no root. Other seed fell among thorns, which grew up and choked the plants. Still other seed fell on good soil, where it produced a crop—a hundred, sixty or thirty times what was sown. He who has ears to hear, let him hear."

What kind of teaching was this? It made no sense! I looked over at Rachel. She met my eyes and shrugged, as if to say, *It was you who wanted to come here. Don't expect me to know what's going on.* All around me I heard murmuring, as people spoke to their neighbors, trying to make sense of what had been said. This man was nothing like the Torah teachers and religious leaders I had seen—and grown to despise—all of my life. He did not hold himself apart from us, contemptuous of the very air we breathed as if being near a woman, a Gentile, or a commoner would contaminate him. His air of authority mixed with humility was a refreshing change. Very different. So different that I didn't know what to make of him.

"Tell us the meaning of this parable, Rabbi," boomed a man's voice from somewhere to my left.

"Those who have ears to hear, let him hear," repeated the Prophet, looking back at all of us with a look of—was that love?—on his face. He waited, then, allowing his words to seep into our dark, cluttered minds. Some faces started to brighten, illumination coming forth. Others turned dark and angry. Scores of people got up and left. If the man saw them go, he gave no sign.

After several minutes, he spoke again. "Listen! The time is short. The Kingdom of Heaven is near. Now is the time to repent. Now is the time to seek out God the Father. Don't look back! Don't wait! Repent of your sins and He will forgive you." With these and many other words, the Prophet encouraged us to follow God. When he finished speaking, he prayed a blessing and dismissed us.

Confused and stiff, I slowly rose from the ground, unsure of what I thought. Just then a man rushed up to the Prophet. His left hand was shriveled, and with his right he reached out beseechingly in a gesture of supplication.

"Help me, Rabbi," he begged. "Help me!"

"What would you like me to do for you?" responded the Prophet, though it seemed obvious to me that he already knew exactly what the man wanted.

"Please, sir," he said earnestly. "If you are willing, heal my hand."

"I am willing," stated the Prophet. Then he reached out and touched the man's left hand and instantly it grew and became healthy, like his right hand.

Amazed, I blinked, not quite sure that I had really seen what my eyes witnessed. Never, *never,* had I known such a thing could be done on this earth! As I stood there in shock, the crowd surged forward. Cries of *Yeshua, heal me! Lord, heal me!* rang out on all sides, the tightly held longings of a desperate people unleashed. At least a dozen men who had sat right under the Prophet's feet sprang up and surrounded him protectively, allowing only one person at a time access to him. I too had a need, but that crowd! I shuddered. I knew that it would be impossible for me to spend hours here, waiting while the Prophet prayed for hundreds of people. Instinctively, I realized that he would not be pleased if I attempted to push my way through ahead of others. There would be another opportunity. Inexplicably confident that I would meet the Prophet, Yeshua, again, I turned to Rachel.

"Let's go."

Dumbly, she nodded, eyes wide as she took in the scene around us. Carefully we threaded our way through the lines of people waiting to be healed and made our way out of the Temple courts and back toward the palace.

❧ ❧

"You did WHAT?" my husband exploded, his normally inscrutable face registering anger and surprise.

"Shhh," I hushed him, pointing toward our closed bedroom door, not wanting news of what I did today spreading throughout the palace before it even completely left my mouth. "Don't be so loud," I cautioned him.

Kuza glanced toward the closed door, opened his mouth, closed it again, and sat down heavily on one of the several elaborately brocaded chairs that graced the room. "Look," he said, quieter this time. "Whatever possessed you to attach yourself to the rabble that follows this pretender?"

"He's no pretender," I corrected, shaking my head. "I tell you that I've never seen anything like it before! I *saw* this fellow's arm restored. It was amazing!" Unexpectedly, my eyes filled up with tears. "Oh, Kuza, this man Yeshua actually *heals* people. What if, what if..." I stopped, unable to continue.

Kuza's face softened. He rose from his chair and came over to me, wrapping his arms around me. "I know how much pain you're in, Yohana. I understand that you would like nothing better than to believe this man can really change that—"

"You understand nothing!" Angrily I shook off his embrace and took a step backwards. "You know nothing of what it's like to be in pain, day after day. To wake up two, three, four times in one night, constantly changing positions and doing everything you can to alleviate some of the stress. To watch yourself worsen every day. To hear the snickering of children because of the lopsided way you walk. To know that it's only a matter of time before..." I would have gone on, but the love on the dear face of my husband stopped me. He didn't deserve this tirade.

"I'm sorry, *motek*," I said wearily, apologetically.

"I'm sorry too." He sighed. "It's not easy for me to see you like this. But surely you know that *he*," meaning Herod, "would not take lightly a member of his household seeking after this man. Don't forget what happened with Yochanan the Immerser," he warned.

"I don't know if I am seeking after him right now," I said, ignoring his last comment. "All I know is that I had an extraordinary experience today and it's changed the way I'm looking at things."

"Well, why don't we both sleep on it, then," suggested my husband mildly. "Tomorrow we can talk some more."

"Yes, tomorrow." Suddenly I was terribly tired. I attempted to smile affectionately at Kuza. "I think I'll go to bed now. Will you be in?"

"In a bit," he answered. "I still have some accounts to go through for today. When I'm done." He reached over and kissed me briefly. "Sleep well, dear Yohie."

"I'll try."

⅌⅌

That night, lying in bed, unable to sleep, many images flashed through my mind. I remembered my childhood, growing up in Jerusalem. I hadn't always lived in a palace, fearful of those around me. Once I lived in a small but beautiful home, hidden in the side of a hill. Orange and lemon trees spread their fragrant perfume over the limestone terraces. Pomegranate trees dropped deep orange blossoms. Brightly colored flowers filled earthen pots, their sun-drenched petals splashing color along the walls of the house. Shoulder-high walls blocked our comings and goings from the prying eyes of anonymous passersby. Fruits, flowers, scented air, hot outside, cool within. Growing up, I was convinced that the Garden of Eden must have closely resembled home.

There were five of us: Abba, Ema, two older brothers, and me. Abba was a spice merchant, often away on buying trips. My earliest memories of him center around homecomings: the pure joy of seeing him again, clasped into big, strong arms, the acrid smells of the road still clinging to his hair, his beard. Laughing eyes crinkled at the corners, kissing me—*ah my little girl, I have missed you!* And then there would always be a special gift, a small piece of inexpensive jewelry, or a little doll, or perhaps a carved wooden animal. How I loved those treasures! Ema would visibly soften. Ema, who sternly disciplined us in his absence, always threatening and chasing us with a stick when we misbehaved, now stood quietly behind Abba, one hand on his shoulder, relief at his presence flooding her face. Now she could relax and be the nurturing mother since he had returned to take up his rightful place as head of the household.

And my brothers. Aharon, the elder. Self-confident, eager, ambitious, well-liked, he was being groomed to take over the family business. When only a young lad of twelve, he had made contacts among his friends' parents, expanding the trade. I adored him, even though he ignored me. Every so often, though, he spoke to me and included me in something he was doing and then I floated on clouds all day.

Caught in the middle between myself and Aharon was the irrepressible Yishai. Sometimes my best friend, often as not my worst enemy, we played and fought our way through the years. Even now, so very many years later, I could clearly see his mischievous grin, bright eyes, and grubby fingernails. Always with a plan, always doing something. I loved him and hated him. Now I missed him terribly.

Sighing deeply, I turned over on my side, thoughts straying back to the man Yeshua. What was it about him that caused me to recollect those hazy, golden years of love and family? He bore no resemblance to any life I had ever known, yet he seemed infinitely familiar. What was it about him? I *did* want to seek him out again. Kuza was right, though. Herod would not be pleased if I became a follower of this man. Well, asking for healing made me no man's follower. Was I intending on asking for healing, then? My sleepless mind ran in circles.

Herod was pleased with less and less these days. Another prophet, Yochanan the Immerser, the one to whom Kuza referred, recently raised his voice against the marriage of Herod and Herodias and now lay rotting in the dungeons below the palace floors. I shivered. I had never seen the dungeons myself but heard enough descriptions of them: filth, darkness, rats and torture, generally leading to a grisly death of some sort. My stomach lurched at the images.

Some months earlier, reports of Yochanan and his ministry of immersing people in the Jordan River south of the City had reached us. Herod always grew alarmed at the prospect of someone gaining any kind of following, and it seemed that more and more people were flocking to Yochanan and calling him a great prophet of God. Herod's approval ratings with the public were at an all-time low due to his marriage to Herodias, so he thought it would pacify the people to go down and be immersed by Yochanan, thereby showing that he identified with Judaism and the common man.

His advisors (the *yes men*, I secretly called them) fell all over themselves assuring him what a spectacular idea this was. Kuza stood out as the only one objecting.

"And why, my dear Kuza, is this a bad idea," casually asked Herod, stroking his chin (he had no beard, like the Romans), eyes shrewd.

I'm very proud of my husband. He held firm. "Because, Your Excellency, this man Yochanan sees only Adonai as his authority. I have heard that he believes himself to be the forerunner of someone of such significance that he refuses to clearly state who that man may be. He may act in a manner which will cause difficulty for you. We cannot depend on his response."

Herod stared thoughtfully at Kuza for several moments while Kuza held his breath. "Maybe," he said vaguely. Then, shaking his head, he snapped his fingers. "Thank you for your advice, but we will proceed with my original plan." Kuza bowed his head in deference and the meeting was adjourned.

So it was that Herod, Herodias, and several members of the court, my husband included, rode camels out to the Judean wilderness one fateful day as if they were on a day trip. When the royal entourage appeared at the desolate section of the Jordan River where Yochanan immersed, the crowds who were already there drew back to let them through in fearful respect. Only Yochanan himself seemed less than awed by their presence.

Kuza told me later that one would have had to search the world over to find a man as different in appearance from Herod as Yochanan. Dressed in a tunic woven from the hair of camels, a leather belt around his waist, hair long, beard shaggy, he looked utterly bizarre to the king and his followers. Apparently, this Yochanan made locusts and wild honey his food. "If Elijah the Prophet had come back to life," said Kuza, "this is how I would have pictured him."

He went on to tell me how Herod and Herodias emerged from their chariot and blithely tripped down to the man of God, sniffing with distaste but determined to seem congenial. Herodias attempted to ooze charm, but it was an effort as she was hot and sweaty and not used to discomfort on any level. But any smile was wiped off her face when she heard the greeting Yochanan gave her husband:

"Have you come to repent then?" he boldly asked, staring at Herod.

"I've come to be immersed with the rest of the people," replied Herod carefully.

"Good," said Yochanan, walking over to Herod and standing within a few feet of him. He was a big man, muscular and hairy. He towered over the tetrarch. "Torah says that it is not lawful for you to have your brother's wife. Repent and be immersed into the Kingdom of Heaven." His voice rang with the truth and power of God's Spirit.

Herod's face turned red, then purple. Furious beyond imagining, at first he was incapable of speech. Herodias could be heard gasping with rage. Before Herod could regain his breath, one of his top advisors whispered something in his ear. Nodding curtly, Herod swung on his heel and he and his entourage headed right back to Jerusalem.

Later, after the crowds around Yochanan had dispersed and there was no chance for a riot, Herod sent several guards and had the prophet bound and arrested for his remarks.

Hip throbbing, I propped up several pillows and lay back on them in a sitting position, knees bent for relief. The faint glimmerings of anxiety reached its icy fingers toward me. Remembering the Prophet Yochanan in the dungeon robbed me of any fragile claim to peace of mind I may have had. What was it Yeshua had preached today? *Repent, for the Kingdom of Heaven is near!* We at the palace were so very, very far from the Kingdom of Heaven.

The door to the room opened and I saw the silhouette of a man cross the room. Kuza. My husband. A fine man. I thought, as I often did, that I was very fortunate to be his wife.

Slight, of medium build, balding, brown eyes haggard from the demands of his job, Kuza was the type of man who was liked by most everyone due to the irresistible combination of unassuming competence with a non-threatening demeanor. In a world where all involved jostled and pushed for position and power, he seemed content to merely excel in the same position, year after year.

I almost hadn't married him. At sixteen years old, several suitors vied for my hand, and Kuza seemed one of the least exciting. Even his position at the palace—he was a clerk at the time—failed to thrill me as he neglected to make capital of the glamour, not realizing at the time how interested I would have been. I had pretty much decided that I wanted the boisterous Shimshon, since I was dazzled by his flashing white teeth and curly black hair. But Abba and Ema took me aside one day.

My father cleared his throat. "Yohie, *beeti*, you're a marriageable young lady now, no longer a child," he began.

"And we need to talk about who you're going to marry," finished my mother, interrupting him.

Raising his shaggy eyebrows at her, my father persevered. "We think that Kuza will make a good husband for you."

"Kuza!" I laughed. "Oh, no! It's Shimshon I love."

Abba and Ema didn't look surprised. "We don't think Shimshon will make you happy," Ema pointed out.

"Of course he will," I replied, with all the careless confidence of the young. "Why wouldn't he?"

"He needs a lot of attention," said my mother.

"He spends more time in front of the mirror than you do," grumbled my father.

"He keeps losing jobs," my mother reminded me.

"He has walked away from three possible betrothments that we know about," elucidated my father.

With these and many other arguments, they kept speaking to me day after day. And after a while, to my credit, I *did* notice flaws in Shimshon to which I had previously been blind. At the same time, Kuza looked more and more appealing.

It came about at this time that Herod the Great sickened and died. Treacherous and murderous, his passing caused no sorrow. Indeed, it was cause for rejoicing, or should have been. Evil to the end, he imprisoned the most illustrious men of Israel from every village and held them in the Hippodrome. His will ordered them killed at his death so that there would be mourning in Israel at the time of his passing since he knew that the Jews would otherwise hold a festival. Instead, after he died, his sister Salome and her husband, Alexas, freed these men and sent them home. There was no mourning in Israel.

Herod's kingdom was divided among his three sons. Archelaus inherited Judaea and Samaria. Philip received the northeast territories.

Herod Antipas succeeded him as tetrarch in Jerusalem, receiving the Galilean and Peraean portions of his father's kingdom.

The new administration of Herod Antipas entirely revamped the palace staff, and, as a result, Kuza was promoted to the post of undersecretary of finance. This new position came with a small suite of rooms on the lower level of the palace, as well as a substantial pay increase. Nothing appealed to my girlish fancy more than the idea of being in the center of all that was luxurious and powerful in Jerusalem.

The extra hours Kuza worked during this time also made him less available to court me. I was less and less able to take him for granted since he just didn't have the time to pander to my whims. This, combined with the allure of the proximity of royalty, succeeded in greatly elevating his desirability.

And for some reason he looked better. I didn't find him attractive when we first met, but as I grew to love and appreciate him, he got more and more appealing. Kuza has a nice face that is pleasing to the eye yet doesn't draw undue attention. Perhaps this is another reason he has lasted so long with Herod.

So we were married in the spring of my seventeenth year. I wore orange blossoms in my hair and a long sheer veil inherited from my grandmother trailed on the floor behind me. All of our friends and family stood in attendance, and one would have been hard-pressed to find a more perfect day. As the prophet Jeremiah stated, *Yet again will be heard in the cities of Judah and the streets of Jerusalem the sounds of joy and gladness, the voice of the bridegroom and bride.* That day, when Kuza lifted my veil and looked into my exultant eyes, and beheld the rosy bloom of youth on my cheek and the lush curls of my shining black hair, his eyes grew wet and he was overcome by happiness. I looked up at him through dark eyelashes, made even darker from kohl, and saw boundless vistas of realized dreams, a golden aura stretching far into the future.

And where is that elusive gleaming future now, I thought bitterly, turning restlessly on my side. The bed creaked as Kuza, now undressed, settled himself into bed next to me.

"Still awake, Yohi?" he asked.

"Yes, my love." I reached my hand out in the dark and he took it and grasped it. We lay silently for several moments, holding hands.

Then he spoke: "There's something I neglected to tell you earlier."

"What?"

"You know that it's Herod's birthday next week? Well, he's throwing a huge banquet and I'm expected to be there. It's mostly men, though, so you're off the hook."

Another banquet! These affairs came along far too frequently for my taste. They tended to be elaborate, never-ending drunken bashes, with enough food to feed half of Jerusalem stuffed down the palates of men who sought to imitate Rome with their unlimited appetites. As Herod's finance minister, Kuza was expected to be at these things, working the crowd, politically available. He treaded cautiousl,y though, as restraint was thrown to the wind once the drinking really got going. These were violent times we lived in, and volatile, angry men needed very little encouragement to blow up. I already knew that I would spend the night pacing our apartment until he returned safely.

"Oh, Kuza." I sighed. "I suppose there's no way out?"

I felt him shake his head in the dark. "None. But don't worry. I'll be fine. I'll just slip out at the first opportunity." He yawned. I wanted to keep talking but he needed to rest.

"*Lilah tov.*"

"*Lilah tov,*" he responded, voice fading as sleep overcame him.

All throughout the week that followed, I thought about Yeshua, and the words he had spoken at the Temple courts. Whether I was directing my servants in their daily duties, or shopping, or walking through Jerusalem, or sitting and reading, or lying in bed, I would see his face before me. The parable of the farmer scattering seed came back to my mind, and a longing I could not identify rose up in me, desiring to be the good soil. *My life has not been very fruitful thus far,* I reflected wryly, sitting in my rooms one bright afternoon, a book opened but unread on my lap.

Twenty-seven years had come and gone since the day Kuza had taken me for his wife. We greatly desired to have a family, only to bear dead baby after dead baby. Finally, one child lived, a girl. Small, sickly, fragile, but so beautiful that my heart would ache just looking at her. She was the light of our life for years, until...resolutely, I pushed those memories away. I could not yet face them.

One by one, those I loved dearly on this earth passed away or vanished, leaving me desolate. Mother, father, brother, child. When my dear father died, I inherited a substantial fortune. It seemed that the spice business was highly lucrative, indeed. I also discovered that my father had taken his extra profits and had quietly bought several houses in Jerusalem and the outlying areas, which he rented at a considerable profit. I suddenly owned half a dozen homes. Somehow, the thought of all that real estate comforted me in a way that money did not.

By this time (I was in my mid-thirties), palace life had lost all its charm so I suggested to Kuza that we move to the nicest one of these homes. The dear man would have done so, but Herod, in a fit of ill humor, said *no*.

"What does he mean, *no*?" I stormed aloud to Kuza, in the sanctity of our own apartment. "We're not his prisoners! Why can't we live in our own home?" And I kicked the leg of a chair, frustrated and angry.

Kuza attempted to calm me down. "He's the tetrarch, Yohana," he patiently explained, as if to a small child. "In effect, we *are* his prisoners. Being so close to the throne has many benefits but brings danger with it. You know that. Herod wants me available day and night. If I'm living outside the bounds of the palace, I'm not so accessible. And besides," he added with an inscrutable look, "it appears that I have become invaluable."

And so we stayed at the palace. At the beginning, it was exciting. I felt as if I were in the center of the universe. Why would anyone ever want to live anywhere else? I knew since birth that Jerusalem was a special city, one that Adonai claimed for his very own. Always I had great pride in being a daughter of Jerusalem. But to live in the palace itself! It seemed to me that life revolved around us, and that not even faraway Rome, where the Emperor lived, could be so significant. On those occasions when we traveled to Caesarea for the sea, or to Jericho for the winter palace, or to Masada to escape the cold winter rains, I looked with pity and disdain on the ignorant masses who lived out their lives away from the shadow of the palace. As the years passed, however, life in a small town away from the prying eyes and power struggles of the court seemed more and more attractive.

Herod himself grew more and more outrageous as he aged. In the beginning, he was a welcome relief from his crazy father, Herod the Great, who ruthlessly murdered his own wives and children. It was said about Herod the Great that it was safer to be his pig than his son. (He kept the kosher food laws and so didn't kill pigs.) Herod's oldest son, Antipater, poisoned his father's mind against Herod's two sons by Mariamne: Alexander and Aristobulus. Herod accomplished Antipater's goals and put his two sons to death for allegedly plotting against him. Three years later, Antipater himself came under suspicion and was executed within days of Herod's own death. We Jews really did not want to claim Antipas as one of ours. This son of Malthace grew increasingly like his father over time.

Herod Antipas at this time was married to a princess of Nabataea, the desert land south and east of the river Jordan, and south of the Dead Sea. Kuza and I always liked Mahalat.

The capitol of Nabataea, Petra, stuns the imagination I am told, having never been there myself. It is an impregnable city, surrounded by high cliffs and pierced by narrow ravines. Houses and tombs alike are carved into the rose red rock of the cliffs. Mahalat's great, great grandfather had opened trade routes through his land from south Arabia and the Persian Gulf, through Petra and into Gaza. Spices, silks and other luxuries from India and China were all taxed by Aretas I as they passed through his region.

Only six years before I was born, the trade routes were redirected across the Red Sea to Egypt. This was the start of the decline of Nabataea. My father was hit hard by this change, thus his investment in real estate. He adjusted to the new routes and recovered his spice markets relatively quickly, however: Abba always rebounded well.

Mahalat was a sweet little thing, very shy. She had inherited the long nose and sculpted lips of her father, though she was very slightly built. She tried to put away the gods of her childhood and worship Adonai but Herod didn't set the best example. She never quite understood Judaism. Regrettably, she failed to conceive a child. Though fond of her at first, Herod grew more and more dissatisfied with her tentative ways. Those of us who knew all the parties were not surprised when Herod divorced her and took up with his brother Philip's wife, that awful woman, Herodias.

The first time I laid eyes on her, I knew she was nothing but trouble. It was twelve years ago, just after her marriage to Philip, and the two of them came with much pomp and circumstance to Jerusalem to visit Herod. Although only seventeen, she exhibited all the wiles and cunning of a woman years older. Mahalat tried to be kind to her, but it was like a mouse placating a cobra. Herodias had no use for Herod's quiet desert wife and could barely bring herself to be civil to her hostess. Alas, even then, Herodias' beauty was legendary. I found her overt sexuality distasteful. Philip and Herod did not share my opinion.

Herodias wore her long, thick, black hair swept up and pulled back, little tendrils of curls framing her face in the Roman fashion. Flawless, olive-toned skin set off her full, pouty lips, which she colored a deep red. Thick lashes fringed dark, almost black, almond-shaped eyes, eyes which always seemed to be looking down that long, thin nose of hers. Her dresses were cut provocatively low and tight so no one would miss either

14

her full breasts or her slender waist. A certain indescribable allure wafted from her almost like perfume so that men fell all over themselves attempting to get closer to her. Even my Kuza, generally immune to women like this, came back from an encounter with Herodias distracted and glassy eyed. ("Snap out of it," I hissed at him. He did. Eventually.)

She had sauntered through the palace halls between the two brothers, both her natural uncles. Philip, so besotted with his new bride that he failed to notice anything else, and Herod Antipas, energized and alive under her purposeful attention, shedding years the way a snake sheds skin. Mercifully, their visit came to a close without anything obviously awful happening. We heard months later that Philip and Herodias had given birth to a daughter.

If Herodias was trouble at seventeen, as a woman of almost thirty, she caused havoc, exploiting her beauty and sexual powers. She apparently determined that Philip was going nowhere fast and that Herod would make a much better match. Gossip at the palace had it that Herodias drove Herod wild with lust and then refused to sleep with him until he divorced Mahalat and married her. So he did.

Life at the palace, never stable under the best of circumstances, became increasingly erratic. Herodias systematically and in cold blood set out to get rid of all who were glaringly loyal to Herod's first (and true, according to Jewish law) wife. She made it known early on that she was queen and we were the trembling subjects. I had to force my eyes down when she was near, fearing that if she looked closely at me she would see the smoldering hatred that threatened to engulf me. Fortunately, older women held little appeal for Herodias: often as not I was invisible.

This divorce infuriated Mahalat's father. As Herod was the more powerful king, there was currently nothing Aretas could do but bide his time. Which he did. For years. But all that comes much later.

One who hadn't escaped the new queen's notice was Yochanan the Immerser. Not merely content with destroying the man's life and health by imprisoning him, she had been overheard saying on countless occasions that she wanted him dead. As long as he lived, so did his rebuke of her behavior. Oddly enough, it was Herod himself who refused to have the *tzadik* executed. Kuza told me that Herod liked to send for Yochanan and listen to him speak. Yochanan talked about the coming Messiah and the need to repent while there was still time. Dirty and unkempt from his time in prison, eyes glowing with an intensity and passion foreign to the bored tetrarch, Yochanan both fascinated and frightened Herod. He knew Yochanan to be a holy man, one sent by God. Yet he failed to understand the limits to his own royal power, his own sin and the need for repentance. He felt that if he repented, that would diminish his royal power.

So it happened that on the evening of Herod's birthday celebration all of these events conspired together in a dreadful fashion. Kuza went, as planned, while I stayed back in our apartments, anxious and distracted. Rachel brought me my supper on a tray, and I picked at the food, unable to eat. At bedtime, I was wide awake so I had candles lit and sat in one of the chairs in our living room, brooding. Again and again I saw before me the face of the man called Yeshua. I felt such longing within myself to seek him out yet I was afraid, afraid! Me, who had some sort of wasting disease in my hip! Who knew how much longer I had to live, yet here I was, afraid! It was ridiculous.

I had heard that Yeshua went back up to the Galil, in the north. Who knew when he would return to Jerusalem? If I wanted to see him, I would have to travel. Was it worth it? Could he, would he, heal me?

I was so lost in thought that I didn't hear Kuza approach until he flung open the door and staggered into the apartment, his face ashen.

"Kuza," I cried, rising from my chair and rushing over to him. "What has happened?"

By way of response, Kuza sank into the chair I had just vacated and covered his face with his hands. Muffled and wavering, his voice floated out through his fingers. "I have just witnessed the most horrific display of idiocy ever imagined," he shuddered.

I went on my knees before him and held him until his face grew less pale and he was able to speak. I waited silently. Finally, he told this story:

"At first, Herod's banquet was no different from any other. I sat with several men who work with me (and here he named several names that I recognized) and we ate and drank to the health of the king with much abandon. At one point in the evening, that young daughter of Herodias, what's her name, ("Salome," I supplied. "Philip's daughter"). Yes, she comes in covered with gauzy veils and accompanied by erotic desert music and proceeds to dance and strip before all of us...but particularly before Herod."

"What?" I sputtered, shocked. "Why, the child can't be more than twelve! What was her mother thinking?"

"Wait," said Kuza, lifting his red-rimmed eyes to mine. "That's only the beginning. Anyway, this child, almost a woman but not quite, sways and dips and swirls much too seductively for someone her age, looking uncannily like her mother, only very, very young. None of us knew how to respond since she *is* Herod's stepdaughter. But we looked over at him and he was clapping wildly, red-faced and sweating from all the wine he had drunk, cheering this child on. So the men who were unsure followed his lead and pretty soon the whole place was stomping and applauding and carrying on as she lost veil after veil.

"When the child finally finished her dance, she stood expectantly before Herod, staring up at him with what I swear are her mother's eyes. It was obvious that she expected something from him."

"So what did he do?" I asked.

"The fool acted rashly. He says, 'Ask me for anything you want, and I'll give it to you.' Then he follows this statement up with an even more ridiculous one. He promises her with an oath, 'Whatever you ask I will give you, up to half my kingdom.' "

"I can't believe he said that," I moan. "So what happened next?"

"This is when it became evident that Herodias had engineered this whole debacle. The girl runs outside the banquet hall to her mother and in no time returns to the king with her request." Kuza fell silent.

"Yes?" I prompted him. "Which was?"

"The little wench asked for the head of Yochanan the Immerser on a platter. Right now."

"Oh Kuza, she didn't," I gasp, though even as I say this I realize that Herodias has come up with a diabolically clever scheme. "Can Herod tell the child 'no' or is he going through with this?"

"Went through with it, Yohana," revealed Kuza, sadly.

"What do you mean, 'went through with it'?"

"Just what I said. You know how Herod despises looking bad? Well, heaven forbid that he go back on his drunken word to Herodias' brat. So even though he was shocked by her request and looked like death warmed over, still he immediately sent for his executioner."

"Oh, my heavens," I slowly breathed out, greatly troubled by what Kuza was telling me. "What was he thinking? Yochanan is a great prophet revered by the people. How could he do such a foul deed?"

"How indeed?" muttered Kuza, mournfully.

"Did the little snit actually get Yochanan's head?"

"Yes," said Kuza. "We all sat in stunned silence after Herod sent for the executioner. Every last one of us was suddenly stone-cold sober. About half an hour later, he returns with the prophet's head on a platter, dripping with the blood of that innocent and holy man."

"What did Herod do?" I shuddered.

"He presented the gruesome thing to the girl, who turned a pale shade of green. But, true daughter of Herodias that she is, she accepted it and brought it to her mother, who had entered the banquet hall. Herodias embraced the platter, a smug, twisted smile of triumph on her painted lips."

I sat back, aghast by what I had just heard. "This Herod is no better than his father, is he?"

"Maybe worse, dear Yohie." Kuza rose unsteadily from his chair. "I need to sleep," he announced.

"Come," I said, taking his arm. "Let's both go in to bed. We can discuss this more in the morning." Leaning heavily on me, the agility in his step changed in an instant to the slow ponderous motions of an old man, Kuza allowed me to steer him to the bed. Both of us fell into deep, troubled sleep.

❧ ❧

The next morning, over a breakfast of fruit and cheese brought to us by Rachel, who quickly absented herself, we spoke more on what had occurred.

"Do you think," asked Kuza, absently biting into a grape and spitting out the seeds, "that the Lord God is angry about what happened to Yochanan last night?"

"I don't know. I guess so," I responded, startled. If the truth be known, though I called myself a Jew and celebrated all the Feasts and went to the Temple to offer prayers and for ritual immersion, I gave precious little thought to God Himself. Speaking of His awareness of earthly events was a new topic for me. It had never occurred to me that Kuza reflected on these things. "What do *you* think?" I countered.

"I've been convinced for quite some time that Yochanan was a real prophet of God. We haven't seen a real prophet in hundreds of years. I believe the last one was Malachi."

"When was that?"

"About 450 years ago. Here. In Jerusalem. He rebuked the people, especially the leaders, for all the things we're still doing today."

"Like what?"

"Well, like offering crippled and blind animals for sacrifices. And for, as he put it, breaking faith with the wife of one's youth. Malachi let us know that Adonai hates divorce in no uncertain terms. Herodias would not have been happy with him, either." Kuza pushed his plate away with a gesture of irritation. He glanced out the window then back over at me.

"You know what else Malachi said, Yohie?"

"No, what?" I asked, fascinated by Kuza's knowledge of the prophets, of whom I knew little.

"He spoke about the coming of the prophet Elijah before the great and dreadful day of the Lord. He said that Elijah would turn the hearts of the fathers to their children, and the hearts of the children to their fathers, or else the Lord would come and strike the land with a curse. Now Elijah had been dead almost 450 years when Malachi received this prophecy so it makes sense that he was speaking of someone coming in the spirit of Elijah, not Elijah himself. Do you know what I think?"

"Tell me," I said.

"I think that Yochanan is he of whom Malachi spoke. I also think that Yochanan was the rightful high priest, and not that upstart who bought his office off the Romans."

"That's amazing, Kuza," I exclaimed. "Why do you think that?"

"I have heard that both of Yochanan's parents were Levites descended from Aharon. I know that his father was a priest who ministered in the Holy of Holies. I have no proof, of course," he admitted. "But the facts are common knowledge among the people."

"But, Kuza," I cried. "If what you say really is true, then Herod is guilty of a greater sin than we even first supposed!"

"We're all guilty, Yohana," allowed my husband, wearily, the weight of the world on his slumped shoulders. "I see only one way out."

"Yes...?"

"Malachi also says that his messenger, who possibly was Yochanan, will prepare the way before the Lord. You know who Yochanan was involved with, don't you, the one whom he spoke about?"

"No, who?" I asked, completely mystified. "Who did he speak of?"

"The man from the Galil you saw at the Temple. Yeshua, of Natzeret."

TWO

It took two weeks, but in the end I had worked out a way to travel north for an extended stay in the new city of Tiberias, on the western shore of Yam Galil. Just three years prior, Herod Antipas founded this place and named it for the Roman Emperor. A little south of the city are some wonderful medicinal hot springs. Ostensibly, I would be heading to Tiberias for my hip. In reality, I would be seeking out the man Yeshua. I had found out that his ministry centered around the Capernaum/Beit Tzaidah area at the north end of the Sea.

After the beheading of Yochanan, Kuza grew more and more solemn. He secured a copy of the Hebrew Scriptures and started a most diligent study. I had never known him to show more than a cursory interest in the things of Adonai. I was awed and just a bit threatened by this new Kuza. Although I myself sought a healing from the Prophet, I chose not to contemplate what this meant to my view of God. He remained vague and shadowy on the outskirts of my consciousness; existing to be sure, but up in heaven and without much interest in the life of a mere mortal named Yohana.

As Kuza proceeded with his study of God's Word, particularly the prophets, he became excited about the possibility of my really being healed. I hadn't realized until now the extent to which Kuza had resigned himself to my possible death. The palace physicians diagnosed me with a tumor in the hip bone and prepared various and sundry herbal broths and hot packs as remedies. None of them helped. I focused on the worsening pain and crippling effect of the tumor. Kuza rightfully foresaw a malignancy that would eventually eat through my body until it killed me.

Now he saw a glimmer of hope that I would remain alive and be with him all his days. Gratified by his deep love, I also experienced a frightful shaking over my current condition. Although I knew intellectually that I could die, I hadn't yet really believed in my heart that it could happen.

This man Yeshua, whom some called "Lord," rose up before me as my only hope.

Much to my relief, Kuza was able to procure for my traveling comfort a lightweight chariot, such as the Romans used. The trip should only take 3-4 days with one of these things. He was sending Rachel with me, and one of his most trusted male slaves, a powerfully built albeit gentle Nubian named Adaba. "Knowing that Adaba is standing behind you flexing his muscles will bring me peace of mind," he gravely informed me, though his eyes were laughing.

"I'll be fine," I said, not quite as fiercely independent as usual. When the time came to go, I clung to Kuza, a catch in my throat. "I love you," I told him.

"I love you, too," he said hoarsely, kissing away the tear that had spilled out onto my cheek. "Come home to me well, okay?"

"Yes, I will. As soon as possible."

We stood together as my luggage was loaded into the chariot, then Rachel touched me on the elbow. "Can I help you into the chariot, my lady?"

"Please." Waving at Kuza, bright-eyed and determined, I stepped up into the chariot, followed by Rachel. Adaba sat in front with the driver, a paid fellow from the city streets of Jerusalem. A smile, a wave. and we were off, bumping down the stone-paved streets, on our way to rough country roads. With God's grace and a good bit of luck we would find a decent inn in which to spend the night

❧ ❧

Exactly one week later, I stood on the balcony of my rented villa in Tiberias, leaning on the railing and looking out at the glassy blue lake, angry and frustrated.

We had been here for three days and I had yet to discover any information on the whereabouts of the Prophet. Adaba had faithfully combed the countryside for me, asking all around, and the best intelligence he could glean was that the Prophet tended to be unpredictable. No one had seen him since he first came back from Jerusalem.

Years of living in luxury had made me impatient and short-tempered when I couldn't immediately have what I wanted. Now I fumed at the delay. I had been very good-tempered during the miserable ride to this heaven-forsaken outpost miles from the City, even though the long, bumpy ride caused me excruciating pain. I knew it would all be worth it as soon as I could find the Prophet. It had never occurred to me that he would not only be unavailable, but that no one would know where he was! Annoyed, I swung around to re-enter my bedroom, only to find myself face-to-face with Rachel.

She, of course, took one look at my frowning face and immediately knew my mood. Years of attending to me had enabled her to calm me down in a way rivaled only by Kuza. Gentle, patient, soothing, she put on a cheerful smile and laid a hand on my arm.

"Why don't we go to the hot springs today, my lady? They may help to relax you."

"Hot springs! You know I never put any credence in the recuperative powers of those things!" Still upset, I was about to complain even more but the sight of Rachel, so trusting, so sweet, shamed me and I bit my tongue. "All right, Rachel." I sighed, calming down. "You're right." I pretended not to see the smile that touched her lips. "Pack us a light lunch and have Adaba bring the chariot around. We'll leave in one hour."

"Very good, my lady," agreed Rachel, turning and leaving the room. In a moment I could hear her light but firm footsteps bounding down the stairs. *Ah, to move with the grace of a doe*, I thought wistfully.

Soon all was ready and Rachel helped me down the stairs and into the summer glare. The streets of the city were all but deserted during this hottest part of the day. Slowly, we drove away from the Inn and headed toward the plains south of the lake.

As we left the city proper, I noticed a most attractive young woman sitting by herself—with her head partially uncovered—on a stone bench under the shade of a stately old oak tree.

"Who can that woman be?" I asked Rachel.

Rachel's normally kind mouth tightened at the corners. "I do not think she is a nice woman, my lady," answered Rachel, a bit haughtily, I thought.

"Do you know anything about her?" I doggedly pursued.

Rachel frowned. "I have heard that she is from Magdala, and that her husband threw her out."

Curiously, I glanced back again at the woman under the oak tree. At precisely that moment she looked up and our eyes met. Even at this distance I could see that her eyes were exceptionally beautiful. But she looked quite sad. I tilted my head in a quasi greeting and then turned back in my seat, leaving the mysterious woman from Magdala behind.

After about an hour, we arrived at the hot springs. A bathhouse had been erected into which the warm waters flowed. Adaba stayed with the chariot while Rachel helped me over to one of the private rooms in the women's section, where I changed into a white linen robe suitable for walking down to the water. Very few people were about. The air was hot, dry, and very still. In the far distance I saw the shimmering blue of the Sea of Galil. Occasional breezes rustled the leaves of poplar trees scattered around the bathhouse, providing meager and sporadic shade. Rachel helped me to the water. I untied my robe and handed it to her, entering the water naked. It felt good. I walked in until I was waist deep and then sat down on one of the logs especially placed for the bathers. The water rose to my chin.

"How are you, my lady?"

"Good, Rachel, good." Closing my eyes, I let the warm waters drift over my body. The sun beat down on my head. Hot, too hot. Impulsively, I leaned back in the water until my hair was completely drenched *Oh, how refreshing.* Idly, I let my thoughts wander. Inside my eyelids, glowing from the brightness, I again saw the face of the woman on the stone bench. *Curious, that she should be in Tiberias,* I thought. Because Herod had foolishly built part of the city over a graveyard, Jews tended to stay away. It had basically become a Gentile outpost. And this woman was Jewish: I could tell by her choice of clothing. Of course, so was I. But I moved in and out of Roman circles so frequently that my caution around unclean things had diminished significantly.

A faint splashing caught my attention and I languidly opened my eyes to see who was there. A rather large woman, thoroughly undressed, was confidently plowing through the water. *Shalom, shalom,* she called out heartily, catching sight of my bobbing head. A jovial and open smile lit up her broad features. *Oh, no,* I groaned inwardly. *Here's a talker for sure.*

And she was. Immediately, she plopped herself down next to me with a happy exhaling of breath and proceeded to address me as if I were her long-lost cousin. I forced a smile, praying that she would quickly tire of me and sit quietly but such was not to be. So I nodded, making all the appropriate conversational sounds as I attempted to let her words wash over me like the small waves of the water. Suddenly the name *Yeshua* leapt out at me from the midst of her thousands of words like a bright, shining star.

"What did you say?" I interrupted, abruptly.

The woman (*did she say her name was Marta?*) peered at me. "Do you mean about Yeshua?" she asked innocently.

"Yes. What do you know about him?"

She smiled widely, revealing a gap between her front teeth. "Ah," she exclaimed. "I saw him cast a demon out of my friend's son. A troubled boy who repeatedly tried to throw himself into the fire. My friend brought the boy to Yeshua and the Rabbi commanded the demon to leave."

"Really?" I said, fascinated. Maybe this garrulous woman wasn't such a pest after all. "When was this?"

"The beginning of the barley harvest. Three months ago."

"Where?"

"The town where the Rabbi lives. Capernaum."

As I marveled at this unexpected piece of information, Marta began speaking of the incident with the boy, gratified to have an alert audience. "The boy," she said, "writhed and panted on the ground like a wild beast. The Rabbi took one look and before he said anything, the boy shrieked in a harsh voice unlike his own, 'I know who you are, Yeshua of Natzeret, you're the holy one of God!' 'Quiet!' the Rabbi commanded it. 'Now come out of him!' "

Out of the corner of my eye, I could see Rachel waiting for me by the water's edge. Waiting and listening.

"Yes," I said encouragingly, when Marta paused for breath, or effect.

"Well," she said dramatically, "the boy screamed and screamed." Every time she said the word *screamed* she smacked her fist against the water. I jumped as the water sprayed in my direction.

"When he stopped yelling," she continued, "he lay on the ground, eyes open and staring. Slowly he sat up and looked around. When he saw his mother, a sweet smile lit up his face and he held out his arms to her. The dear woman clasped him to her bosom, overjoyed at receiving her son back in his right mind."

"How has her son been since then?" I asked.

Marta blinked. "Why normal, of course."

Telling the tale of the demon-possessed boy appeared to have tired her out. The next several minutes were characterized by a calm silence, occasionally punctuated by the rippling of the water and the calls of the birds overhead in the bright sky.

"Where is this Yeshua now?" I cautiously asked, after a while.

Marta looked at me shrewdly. "Have you ever seen the Rabbi?"

"Once," I admitted. "And I was quite impressed."

"You should be," she admonished me...too familiarly I thought. "He's a man of God. A true prophet. Maybe *the* Prophet." She wagged her finger at me. "I don't know where he is now but he's in and out of Capernaum a lot. You have a better chance of finding him there than just about anywhere, I'd say."

Suddenly I had a headache. This afternoon sun was too strong. What had I been thinking, coming to the springs at midday? "Thank you so much for your company," I said cordially, albeit formally. "Please enjoy the rest of your day."

"God be with you," replied the woman, settling herself into the water such that only the top of her double chin could be seen.

I sloshed through the water to the edge of the spring and emerged, dripping wet. Rachel came right over to me and wrapped a robe around my body. "Are you going back in, my lady?"

"No, I've had it for the day. Let's go home," I told her. I headed over to the bathhouse to change when I suddenly gave a short gasp of pain. My hip, which I had expected to feel better after soaking in the hot springs, instead felt much, much worse! The heat of the water had apparently done something such that my joint froze. I couldn't walk.

"My lady! What's the matter?" worried Rachel.

Grimacing, I shook my head. "My leg doesn't appear to be moving," I grunted through pursed lips.

"Shall I get Adaba to carry you?" beseeched Rachel.

"No, no, I'll be fine. Just let me lean on you." Grabbing her arm, I attempted to pull myself along. It was no use. The pain flared up higher than I could stand. "Wait, wait," I said. "Just stand here a minute."

"I really think I should get Adaba....," pleaded Rachel, when my friend from the springs emerged from the water in all her naked splendor. Donning her robe, she came right over to us.

"You don't look good," she said. "Can I help?"

"I doubt it," I answered, curtly. Then, a little kinder, I added. "I have a problem with my hip and the hot water apparently made it worse, not better."

"Go to the Rabbi," urged Marta. "He heals."

"Can he heal me?"

"He can heal anyone. Why not you? Go," she said, extending her arm and pointing north. "Go to Capernaum. Seek him. I understand that those who seek him with all their heart find him."

I nodded. "Thank you." I stood there another few minutes, then gingerly tried to walk again. This time my hip had unstiffened to the point where I could hobble along with Rachel's help.

"Shalom," called Marta. "I will remember your need when I pray."

"Pray I can find the Rabbi then," I responded.

"All who seek him find him," she uttered, solemnly, mysteriously.

Then she turned and re-entered the hot spring. Rachel and I made our way to the bathhouse and from there to the chariot.

As we drove back to the villa, I kept hearing Marta's words reverberating in my head: *all who seek him find him. Please, please,* I prayed. *Let me find him.*

❧

I had forgotten all about the woman from Magdala. As we rolled into Tiberias and past the stone bench, empty now and forlorn in the late afternoon sun, I remembered her. *Hmm,* I thought to myself, *I wonder what happened to that woman?*

After we returned, I dismissed Rachel and took a short nap. I arose in the early evening, dressed and called for Rachel. She helped me downstairs into the small, enclosed courtyard in the center of the villa. The heat of the day had passed, and the first colors of sunset filled the nighttime sky. Comfortable with just a light shawl, I sat down at the carved wooden table and breathed deeply of the intoxicating fragrances that permeated the evening. Always, the flowers and fruit trees send their scent when the sun goes down. The stillness of the evening, the exotic location, the newness of the villa, the perfume filling my nostrils, the first stars, hard and bright as diamonds, emerging in the sky: all these things conspired to fill me with a longing I couldn't identify. I knew I wanted healing, that was sure. But what after? My old life at the palace, no matter how healthy I was, no longer interested me. In fact, it downright depressed me. Apart from Kuza, my life seemed so *empty.* And even Kuza...much as I loved him, he was my husband, not me. I couldn't live my life through him.

Sighing, I took a bite of the food Rachel had placed in front of me. While I was napping, Rachel had gone to the *shuk* in the center of town and purchased fish, which she then broiled over an open fire with garlic and the juice of lemons. *Ahhh, that tasted delicious.* What a treat to eat fresh fish. In Jerusalem, the only way we could get it was salted or dried. I slowly ate my fish, savoring every bite, distractedly contemplating my life's meaning, when a hesitant knock at the gate of the courtyard startled me.

"Who's there?" I commanded, realizing that both Rachel and Adaba were inside and I was alone out here.

"You don't know my name, Madam," came the low, melodic voice on the other side of the gate. "But I am the woman you saw in town today."

The woman I saw in town today? The Magdalit? What was she doing here? The proper thing for me to do would have been to call for my servants, but I made an impulsive decision that would have implications beyond anything I could imagine.

"You can enter," I said.

A rattling reached my ears, then after a moment: "I cannot open the gate from this side, Madam. Will you help?"

I rose out of my chair and limped over to the gate. Prying open the unfamiliar lock, I swung open the door and found myself face-to-face with the woman from the stone bench.

Unlike this afternoon, she was swathed head-to-toe in veils. All I could see of her was her oval face, pale in the starlight, and the glow of her spectacular eyes.

"Come in." I stood to the side so that she could enter. Nervously, she slid past me, glancing fearfully over her shoulder as she did so.

"Are you being followed?" I asked.

"I...I think so. Yes. Some men back there." She pointed vaguely in the direction of the market area. "I believe I lost them on the last street." She spoke quickly, tension evident in her soft voice. "Oh!" she exclaimed, clasping her hand to her mouth when she noticed my half-eaten meal on the table. "I'm so sorry. I've interrupted your dinner."

I looked at the Magdalit critically. My guess was that she hadn't eaten in quite some time. "Would you care to sit down and join me?"

Immediately I noticed those exquisite eyes light up. "I don't want to impose," she said politely, though her eyes strayed longingly to the food.

"My dear child, if you don't want to impose you should have thought of that before you came banging on my door." I stopped when I saw the stricken look on her face. I put my hand on her arm. "Don't worry," I said in a lighter tone. "I'm glad you're here. Now sit down and I'll get you some dinner."

Obediently, she sank down into one of the chairs that surrounded the table. I called for Rachel, who almost fainted dead away upon seeing my unexpected dinner companion! But I'll say this for Rachel: she has enough sense to keep her peace. She merely assumed a most disapproving demeanor and asked how she could serve me.

"Rachel, this lady has stumbled into our courtyard and is my guest for the evening. Please bring her food and drink. And some bread and oil," I added as Rachel stiffly set her shoulders and walked back inside.

I sat down across the table from my guest, keeping my silence. It wasn't until she had begun eating, with the controlled but focused

27

motions of a well-bred person who was truly starved, that I started questioning her. "Tell me your name, please."

"It's Miryam," she said, covering her mouth with her hand in order to keep chewing. Hastily, she poured more of the watered-down wine from the decanter on the table into her cup and drank deeply.

"Mine is Yohana," I informed her.

"Yes, I know."

I raised my eyebrows. "How did you know?"

"Oh, from the gossip in the marketplace. New people always attract attention."

Hmmm, I thought to myself. *I suppose a crippled wealthy woman, an attractive servant girl, and a Nubian slave larger than most walls would get some notice.* I smiled. Aloud I said, "And why were you interested in me?"

Miryam stopped chewing and cast her eyes down. She shook her head sadly. "I have nowhere to go," she confessed in a soft, anguished voice. "When I saw you today I felt as if you would be kind to me. I took a chance..."

"Well, you were right, weren't you?"

She nodded.

"Am I to assume that you need a place to sleep tonight, as well?"

"Oh, yes, Madam! I would be ever so grateful!"

"May I ask as to why you do not have a place to sleep?"

"It's an ugly story, Madam," she said in low tones, so low that I had to strain to hear her, though she sat not more than one meter from me.

I sat back in my chair and pulled my shawl more tightly around my chest. "Do you mind so very much telling me? We have all night."

Miryam turned her face to the side, as if contemplating something at the edge of the courtyard. The flickering flames from the candles that burned on the table lit up her profile. Her beauty astounded me. *Not even Herodias in all her gaudy splendor can equal this woman,* I marveled. I waited patiently, aware of the internal struggle within the woman I had come to think of as the Magdalit. Finally, she looked back at me, her eyes steady on my face.

"Yes," she said. "I will trust you."

"Thank you."

Miryam took one last bite of fish, followed by a gulp of wine, then delicately wiped her mouth with the cut square of linen provided by Rachel. "I had a wonderful life until I turned twelve," she said. "I grew up just north of here, on the sea, in Magdala. My father was a fisherman and I am the only girl in a large family of boys." She grew silent, dabbing at

28

her eyes.

"What happened when you were twelve," I prodded.

"Two things. The first was that I developed into a woman, and the second was that my father and two oldest brothers were lost at sea in a storm and we never saw them again."

"Oh, how dreadful!" I exclaimed.

"Yes," she affirmed. "My poor mother nearly lost her head from grief. She had me and my two younger brothers to feed but was so overcome that she could barely make it out of bed. At first, neighbors and friends helped us out, but we quickly became burdensome. So it came about that various men began to notice my new grown-up body and one in particular approached my mother for my hand in marriage."

"What was he like?" I asked, fascinated.

"Loathsome. Slimy, repulsive, serpentine but very, very rich. I begged my mother to say no, but she no longer cared about anything. Nahash (for that was his name) offered my mother enough shekels to take care of her and my two surviving brothers for several years to come. She grabbed the offer."

"Was he much older than you?" I wondered.

"Twenty years. Still a young man but already filled with all sorts of perversions from years of indolent living. Growing up I had heard all sorts of rumors about him, never dreaming that one day I would be at his mercy."

"You poor girl."

Miryam's eyes filled with tears. "Yes, I was at his mercy. He delighted in my beauty but for his own evil purposes. He forced me to get drunk again and again until I started to crave wine. He defiled the marriage bed with other men and women both, looking with lust on all of them. He spilled his seed on the ground when he lay with me so that a baby could not come along to interfere with his pleasure. I tried to escape once but he beat me so badly that I never dared to try again." She looked down at her hands, which were tightly clenched in her lap. "Eventually, I gave myself over to these things and became as despicable as he.

"But always within me remained a belief in the Holy God. Even when all seemed darkest and without hope I knew, *knew*, that God saw me and longed to have mercy on my soul.

"One day a miracle happened. Nahash threw one of his classic orgies and drank so much that he never woke up the next morning. He was dead and I was free! Not only free, but rich. Or so I thought until I found out just how much money he had burned though.

"It didn't take long for another man to ask me to marry him. For I was quite beautiful, you see, and still rather young. Eagerly, I accepted. This man, I knew, was a good and kind man. I was honored to become his wife."

"It sounds like life turned about for you, no?"

Wordlessly, she shook her head *no*, brushing away a few tears. When she regained control of her voice, she said, "No, because Nahash had ruined me. The drinking, the perversity, the indulgence into wickedness—even though it began against my will, eventually it became *me*. Unclean spirits entered into me. I no longer had control of my actions. Sin dominated me. I, I was not able to stay faithful to my new husband. I felt driven, *compelled* to cheat on him. He forgave me several times. Last week he threw me out and told me never to return." Here Miryam's voice broke and she buried her head in her hands, sobbing quietly.

Oh my, I thought as I studied my grief-stricken guest from my place across the table. *What kind of hornet's nest have I gotten entangled with here?* It occurred to me that I should call for Adaba and have Miryam escorted out so that no trouble would come to me, but my heart quailed even as I contemplated this. No, I was already involved. I would see this through.

"Miryam," I called softly. The Magdalit lifted tear-streaked eyes to me. Even thus, she was astonishingly beautiful. "Have you heard of Yeshua the Prophet?"

"Yes, I have heard tales."

"Are you aware that he expels unclean spirits?"

"Yes," she said tentatively. "I have indeed heard that report. But how can I go near a holy man, a *tzadik,* like this rabbi? He will be disgusted with one such as me." These words brought on a fresh torrent of tears.

"I don't think so," I said slowly. "This man is different from the Prushim and Torah teachers. I don't believe he will reject you if you go seeking God's mercy. I am in pursuit of him myself," I confided. "I am seeking him out in hopes that he will heal me." A crazy idea presented itself full-blown in my head. I tried to shake it, but it lodged itself even deeper into my brain. "All right," I surrendered, half-aloud. Miryam looked at me quizzically. "You can come with me," I suggested. "We'll seek the Prophet together."

"Really?" she exclaimed, eyes wide, not unlike a small child in her pleased astonishment.

"Yes, really," I replied. "Tomorrow we'll ride up to Capernaum and make inquiries. It'll only be a matter of time before we find him." Abruptly, I stood up. "It's getting cold, and it's late. Come into the villa and get some rest. We have a lot to do in the morning."

Miryam grasped my hand and kissed it. "Oh, thank you, Madam. Thank you! You are a gift from God Almighty! A priceless treasure! A blessing I don't deserve. Thank you!"

"Come, come," I said, embarrassed at this show of emotion. "Save your gratitude for the Prophet. I am merely a seeker, like yourself."

"Oh no, Madam," objected Miryam, though she dropped my hand and took a step back. "You are one on whom the Lord God has His hand. I will always be grateful."

Despite myself, I smiled, trusting that the darkness of the night concealed my face. I forced myself to sound no nonsense. "Well, come along then." Raising my voice, I then called, "Rachel!" And we went in for the night.

∾∾

Capernaum was nicer than I had expected. Not that I expected much, mind you. A small fishing village on the shores of the Lake, a market place, several streets of nondescript houses were what I envisioned. And basically that's what I found. Except that the *character* of the place surprised me, drew me in, enchanted me.

So idyllic. So unspoiled. So peaceful. So *protected*. A special place, tucked far away from the tumult and danger of Jerusalem. I breathed deeply of the fresh, sea air, basked in the warm but not too hot sunshine, feasted my eyes on the shimmering water, relaxed in the mild breezes. Already I felt better.

My companion, on the other hand, grew more and more nervous as the day progressed. She hid under what must have been suffocating hot veils, averting her eyes no matter how far off any passing stranger happened to be.

And she fidgeted nonstop.

"You must stop that," I finally said, as we sat on a wooden bench overlooking the sea, her foot keeping a constant *tap tap tap*. Adaba and Rachel had gone to the market for both food and information and had left us here. After eating, we planned to rent a couple of vacant rooms in the local inn for however long it took to locate the man Yeshua.

"Sorry," she apologized, stilling her foot. In a few moments I heard the fingers, *tap tap tap*. I put my hand over hers.

"Calm down, Miryam. It's all going to work."

"How can you be so sure? My life depends on the Rabbi helping me!"

"So does mine," I replied quietly. "So does mine."

Just then Rachel and Adaba pulled up in the chariot. Rachel disembarked and came over to us. In her arms was a loaf of bread, a small cheese and several dates which she had tied up in a piece of cloth. She looked happy.

"Good news, my lady," she said by way of greeting to me. She started to smile at the Magdalit and then remembered to be disapproving. She turned back to me. Miryam gave no notice; she was used to this type of rejection from other women. "Word in the market is that Yeshua and his talmidim went by boat to the other side of the Lake but should be back any day."

Rachel stopped talking while she handed me the food. I took a hunk of bread and some dates and put the rest on the bench between myself and Miryam. "Eat," I commanded her, not unkindly.

Obediently, she chewed on a date, her eyes brightening. From the nourishment or the news, I could not tell.

"That's wonderful, Rachel. After we eat, we'll see if we can find space at the inn and then..." I paused to chew some bread.

"And then what?" prompted Miryam.

"And then we wait here until we see Yeshua."

❦❧

Our luck held. Not only were we able to secure two rooms for ourselves (myself and Rachel in one, Miryam in the other, and Adaba in the stable with the horses) *but only two days later* Yeshua returned to Capernaum.

It was Adaba who learned from one of the stable hands that the Rabbi had come back. He sent word to Rachel, who then excitedly ran to me, filled with her good tidings. I was just finishing a late breakfast in bed when she burst in.

"My lady! Adaba has found out that the Prophet is down by the lakeside teaching. Let me help you dress and we can go right over!"

Startled, I put down the piece of bread I had been holding. Odd, but now that my goal was within sight I felt suddenly timid. What if this man prayed for me and nothing happened? Where could I go from here? Doubt and fear gripped my heart. My throat went dry.

Rachel looked at me curiously. "My lady, did you hear what I said? Are you all right?"

"I don't know, Rachel. Do you think this is such a good idea?"

"Do I think...?" Rachel's eyes grew very wide. "Isn't this why we left

Jerusalem? Of course it's a good idea!" She came over to the bed where I reclined and knelt down next to me, taking one of my hands in hers. "Remember the man with the withered arm, my lady? Both of us saw it with our own eyes! He was healed! Why should not you be healed as well?"

Why not indeed? *Because you're a selfish, indolent, impatient woman,* whispered a voice in my head. *You don't deserve to be healed.* A lump rose in my throat. Inexplicably, I was filled with dread at the thought of encountering Yeshua. What if he laughed at me? Ignored me? Declared me "unhealable"?

"My lady?" said Rachel, squeezing my hand and staring at me, worry evident on her caring face. "Come get dressed. Now is the opportunity we have been waiting for." Mechanically, I obeyed, allowing her to bring me clothes and arrange my hair, though my stomach surged with anxiety.

Unbeknownst to me, in the next room, Miryam of Magdala suffered similarly. My sins were known only to me and those who knew me best, but Miryam's sins were notorious. She felt utterly unclean and unworthy to go before one anointed of God. It wouldn't be unusual for a righteous man to spit in her face. Would Yeshua be different? Suddenly, she was not so sure. I discovered later that it took all of her strength and resolve of will to leave her room and come with us to seek Yeshua down by the lake.

All the way there, in contrast to the fleecy clouds sailing across the sapphire sky, dark shadows flitted across my mind's eye, hissing arrows of fear and doubt. They would have succeeded in turning me back had it not been for an image I had of a sorrowful Kuza weeping at my funeral. This mental picture gave me the fortitude I needed to move forward. It was more important to me to not disappoint my husband than it was to be safe from possible rejection and failure. Besides, what would happen to the Magdalit if I abandoned her? Left on her own, would she find the courage to approach such a holy man?

I'm not sure to this day what enabled Miryam to reach Yeshua. Most likely, it was the Spirit of God propelling her forward. It no doubt helped that I had a hand on her arm, Rachel walked beside her and Adaba, like a great stone wall, hedged us in from behind. She would have had to push us aside were she to make a run for it.

As we neared the shore, we could see a man standing high on a natural rocky embankment. He was surrounded by a multitude of people. We could see that he was teaching, but we were still too far off to hear him. Coming closer, working our way through the crowd, we soon settled in a spot not too far away. Adaba provided a stool for me to sit on.

The whispering of the waves lapping against the sand, the birds calling out to one another as they circled overhead, the murmuring that always comes with a large group of people, no matter how quiet they're attempting to be—all this I found distracting at first. But soon it faded into the background as I drank deeply into my very spirit the words that poured forth from the Prophet's mouth. His words were words of life, better than the finest meat and wine. Gold and silver were as dust compared to the wisdom that rolled off this man's tongue. I sat enthralled.

"Do not store up for yourselves treasures on earth, where moth and rust destroy, and where thieves break in and steal," the man said, his voice loud and clear. Amazingly, all of us made out his words with no difficulty. "But store up for yourselves treasures in heaven where moth and rust do not destroy and where thieves do not break in and steal. For where your treasure is, there your heart will be also.

"The eye is the lamp of the body. If your eyes are good, your whole body will be full of light. But if your eyes are bad, your whole body will be full of darkness. If then the light within you is darkness, how great is that darkness!" It seemed to me that he looked carefully at me as he said this, though of course I was only one of hundreds who were there that day. Even so, I felt my cheeks grow hot and averted my gaze. He continued.

"No one can serve two masters. Either he will hate the one and love the other, or he will be devoted to the one and despise the other. You cannot serve both God and money."

Ah, how true that is, I thought to myself. *I do not know God at all. But I do know money.* There were other things that Yeshua taught that day as well, but none stood out in my mind as much as his admonition against greed and the love of wealth. I had felt for some time that my riches should serve some purpose other than my own well-being, but what that purpose was, I did not know.

All too soon, Yeshua finished speaking and people surged up to him, asking for the help they desperately needed. I looked over at Miryam. She was trembling. "Come," I said. "Let's seek the Rabbi."

Wordlessly, like an obedient child, she nodded, following me as I got into one of the lines leading to Yeshua. Rachel and Adaba stood in line with us as well. Adaba, taking very seriously his commission from Kuza about protecting me, made certain that no one got close enough to bump into me. If a hapless soul did mistakenly get too near, Adaba glowered so menacingly (in direct opposition to his true gentle self) that whoever it was would promptly step away. Rachel stayed to my right, holding a fan made from bird feathers in the air over my head so as to shield me from the sun.

Miryam drooped along on my left, seemingly losing strength and vitality with each passing moment. She grew so dispirited that I stopped worrying about whether or not I would be healed and instead concentrated on her. "Are you all right?" I spoke into her ear.

She started at my voice. "Oh, Madam," she answered, anguish and panic marring her very features such that she looked almost unrecognizable. "If you only knew how these unclean spirits pull at me! They whisper to me, *GO, GO, the Rabbi is too holy to look on the likes of you.* It's all I can do to resist them." And she gazed at me, vulnerable and hurting, like a child seeking its mother.

I felt a rush of warmth toward this poor, unfortunate woman, battered about by life's cruelties and exhausted by her struggles to be free. "Hold my hand, Miryam," I told her. "We'll resist them together."

Gratefully, she slipped her small, delicate hand in mine and we waited for our turn with the Rabbi.

It appeared that the Rabbi had several men channeling the people into different lines. As I waited and observed, I noticed that some of the lines went faster than others. Obviously, we were prayed for by some other method than our place in line.

I noticed with great satisfaction that my line moved along quite quickly; not that it was tedious to wait. Oh, no. On the contrary, I had never been so fascinated. One after another, people left the presence of Yeshua crying with gratitude and joy. At one point, I saw Yeshua stick his fingers into the eyes of a blind man and, to my great astonishment, heard the man cry out, "Lord, I can see again! Thank you, thank you!" And he knelt at the Rabbi's feet and wept the tears of one beyond overjoyed.

Now I confess that hearing the Rabbi referred to as "Lord" alarmed me. I believed him to be a great prophet of God but to call any man "Lord"? I did not know what to think, so I pushed the whole issue aside for the moment by deciding that most of these people were ignorant and easily swayed, anyway.

Just then, one of Yeshua's talmidim, a tall, handsome, slender fellow with a close-cropped black beard and luminous brown eyes, approached us. I opened my mouth to tell him who I was and what I wanted, but before I could say even one word he turned to Miryam and said, "Daughter, the Rabbi has asked for you." My natural inclination at this point was to pull back and not interfere, but Miryam still held my hand, and indeed held it so tightly as to render me her prisoner. I followed her over to the Rabbi. Rachel and Adaba stayed right next to me. If he noticed (and how could he not?), Yeshua's talmid said nothing.

We came before the Rabbi. Silently, he placed his hand on our clasped ones, separating them. The warmth of his touch sent a surge of lightning through me. Dazed, I took a step backwards. Miryam immediately fell to the ground, head bent, hands and knees in the dust. "I am so unworthy," she moaned.

Then a very bizarre thing happened. She lifted her head, a look of utter, despicable lasciviousness on her face, and in a voice completely unlike her own soft one, growled impudently, "She's mine! She invited me in and I have every right to stay."

Yeshua seemed unperturbed by this. Instead, he knelt down and looked Miryam full in the face. She hissed and backed away from him. He held her wrists so she could not escape and, in a deep and resonant voice, said, "Do you want to be free?"

I held my breath as I watched. Miryam turned her head from side to side, a great inner battle raging within her. For several seconds she attempted to speak, only to choke on the words. Yeshua scrutinized her closely and with deep compassion. I could tell that he wanted her to win against these demons who held her captive. He would not help her, though. This needed to be her decision.

Finally, she regained control of her features and blinked at him. "Yes," she whispered. "I repent! Forgive me my sins. Set me free from these foul spirits!"

Solemnly, but with great pleasure, Yeshua released her wrists and stood up. In a loud voice he charged, "Come out of her this instant, you evil spirits!"

Miryam screamed. And screamed. High-pitched, piercing, seemingly never ending. Then she threw up. Foul, disgusting vomit.

"How many of you are there?" asked Yeshua, unperturbed.

"Seven," it replied, using Miryam's voice.

"Tell me your names."

"Lust," shrieked one.

"Adultery," moaned another.

"Deviancy," muttered a third.

"Lasciviousness," spoke yet a fourth.

"Perversity," drooled the fifth.

"Foul language," boomed the sixth.

"Hatred," spat the seventh.

"Go to the darkness reserved for such as you and never return!" Yeshua commanded, all power and authority resonating from him.

The force with which they left flung Miryam facedown on the

ground.

Yeshua placed a hand on her shoulder. "I say to you, arise. Your tormentors have left."

Slowly she lifted a tear-stained face to him. "How can I ever thank you?" she asked, rising to a sitting position.

"Miryam." Tenderly he touched a lock of hair that framed her face. "Now is your opportunity to live a pure life. Flee from sin and follow God."

"I would follow you," she murmured, gazing at him in reverent awe.

"God will make that clear to you," he replied enigmatically. Nodding at his talmid, the one who brought us to him, he then turned aside to me. Out of the corner of my eye, I saw the talmid approach Miryam, helping her up.

Now that my turn had come, my heart pounded furiously. Dimly, I was aware of the swelling of the crowds behind us, the lake in front. Yeshua reached his hand out to me. "And you, wife of Kuza, how do you want me to pray for you?"

"How did you know my name?" I wondered.

"Daughter," he spoke paternally, though he was many years my junior. "I have known you always. I saw you when you were sitting in Herod's palace, calling out to God for your hip to be healed."

"Then," I said, my voice trembling, "then you know how to pray for me."

"Tell me yourself," he urged.

"I want to be healed and healthy," I stated, feeling my eyes fill up with tears.

"Ah," he said, and he smiled. It was a smile unlike any I had ever seen. It was a smile that said, *I know you, I love you, I desire great things for you. But you must seek them yourself.*

"I can heal you," he stated. "But one day you will sicken again. And one day you will die."

"What is this you are telling me?" I asked, deeply perturbed.

"It is your sins that need to be forgiven, dear lady, more than your hip needs to be healed. Tell me, Yohana, wife of Kuza. Are there sins in your life holding you back from God? Is it the things of God you desire?" He looked deeply into my eyes and I, helpless to turn from his penetrating gaze, suddenly saw myself as he did. I saw my haughtiness, my impatience, my demanding demeanor, my complaining, my murmuring, my snobbishness. I saw the countless petty and nasty things I had done to other people while simultaneously bemoaning their actions against me. I saw many other things as well; things which went far back into my past, things I had forgotten but which now came to mind with startling clarity. I saw myself reaching out to God in His heaven with my arm outstretched, but getting further and further away, my sin pushing me out of the presence of such a pure and holy majesty.

"How can I be cleansed?" I cried.

Yeshua looked into my eyes, and the love I saw reflected there was unfathomable. "Dear lady, the Son of Man has all authority on earth to forgive sin."

"I do not understand," I said in a low voice. "Only God can forgive sin."

"Do you not know then who I AM?" he stated, using God's Name.

I stared at him, lost in awe, completely confused. "I can't reconcile..." The sheer electric presence of this man had me completely unnerved. All my social veneer dissipated and dropped from me as ripe figs fall from a tree. "You can't be, are you, how could you be...?"

"I say to you, your sins are forgiven. But so that you know who it is to whom you speak—"

And he placed his hand on my hip. The surge of warmth that came from his hand shocked me and I, like Miryam before me, fell to the ground.

Yeshua knelt down, saying, "I command you, be healed!"

Instantly, the pain left me. Amazed, I tentatively moved my leg in a way that normally would have caused agony. Nothing. "This is stunning," I whispered.

Yeshua looked at me and his eyes were laughing. "It's the power of God," he told me. He looked at me closely. "Seek God. There is a place for you in the Kingdom of Heaven."

I longed to speak with him further, but he had turned to minister to the person behind me. Yeshua's talmid ("My name is Yochanan," he informed me politely) encouraged me to rejoin my friends.

"They're over there," he said, pointing down toward the shore of the lake.

"Can I speak more with the Rabbi?" I asked Yochanan.

"Probably not today." He hesitated, seeing the longing on my face. "Look, you may find us here in the morning. Early. But we're never sure with the Rabbi. Plans change." Abruptly he left me as he was needed elsewhere.

Elated, I walked, then ran (*I ran!*) to where Miryam, Rachel, and Adaba waited. When Rachel saw me, she raced toward me, laughing and crying. "My lady, what wondrous thing has happened to you today?" she cried when she met up with me.

"I'm healed, Rachel. Really healed. Watch me run. No pain." Filled with mirth, I spun around and around, like a small child at play.

Rachel wiped tears from her eyes with the edge of her sleeve. "I am so pleased, my lady. I love you so," she said in a choked voice.

"I love you too, Rachel," I said, seeing with new eyes this special woman who had put up with my imperious ways and still could love me.

Adaba bowed graciously. "I am most gratified to behold your good health," he told me in his courtly manner.

Miryam as well came forward, discreetly, behind Rachel and Adaba, not wishing to intrude on our time but still eager to be a part of things.

"I have not known you long, Madam Yohana, but I am very glad that the Lord has healed you."

I turned my full attention to Miryam, noticing that her whole countenance had changed. Gone was the fearful, hunted expression. In its place radiated a confident peace. "You look like a new person," I marveled. The suffocating veils had dropped away—in more ways than one!

"I am a different person," she affirmed, a lovely smile lighting up her face.

"So what are you going to do now?" I asked her.

She glanced over in the direction of Yeshua and his talmidim, still praying over people, before answering. "What I would like to do is follow Yeshua to the ends of the earth. But what I am going to do is to return to my husband and tell him that I am cleansed. It's up to him as to what happens next."

I nodded. I, too, wanted nothing more than to follow after this man who claimed to be one with God. It seemed to me, newly healed as I was, that he shone with the light of heaven and that apart from him things faded into insignificance. Jerusalem, Herod's Palace, even, God forgive me! the Great Temple, all lost their luster in comparison with this man who was so without pretense yet wielded such extraordinary power.

Yet Kuza beckoned me as well. My husband, my sweet, kind husband, who, filled with faith, had sent me off hoping that God would touch me. He needed to know about the miracle that had been wrought. He needed to know that his trust had not been in vain. Together, he and I, we needed to discover who this Yeshua really was. Then we would decide what path to follow.

"I, too, plan to return to my husband," I told Miryam. "Perhaps we could travel with you to Magdala? I will wait and make sure that your husband welcomes you home."

Miryam's eyes filled with tears and she flung her arms around my neck. "Oh," she sobbed. "You are an angel sent to me from God above!" Tenderly, I hugged her back.

Rachel interrupted us, having overheard the whole conversation. "Does that mean that we are to leave in the morning, my lady?"

"Not first thing, Rachel. I desire to speak with the Rabbi again, if possible. I intend to come down to the lake at sunrise tomorrow and look for him."

If Rachel thought this a bad idea, she restrained from letting me know. Instead, she mildly suggested that we go back to the inn and have something to eat, as it was getting late.

I looked up at the sky. She was right; it *was* getting late. Already, the sun sank low in the sky to the west of us, tinging the horizon with streaks of red and purple. We had spent the whole day here! And eaten nothing! How unlike me to have not felt hunger pangs, or noticed the discomfort of a day spent outdoors under the hot, summer sun.

"You're right, let's go." Taking one last look at the place where Yeshua had healed me, I observed with a sinking stomach that he and his talmidim had left the spot. People still milled about, but apparently the Rabbi's work was done for the day. Despite my joy at being healed, it disturbed me to no longer see the Rabbi. His presence gave me the kind of secure reassurance I had not experienced since the long ago days when, as a very small child, my mother cuddled and held me.

With one last, lingering look at the place where both my hip became whole and Miryam was set free of her seven demons, I followed Adaba, Rachel, and Miryam back to the chariot, and then to the inn.

෫෪෫

The next morning, while it was still dark, we returned to the lake to look for Yeshua. The place was busier than I expected, with dozens of fishermen returning to shore hauling their catches. I scanned the coastline, straining my eyes in the gray of predawn, looking for him. Nothing.

"Do you see him?" I asked Miryam. She, too, anxiously sought another chance to encounter the Rabbi.

Miryam peered up and down the shore. At one point, she spotted a group of several men, and she raised her arm excitedly, saying, "I think they're over there," only to realize that she was mistaken. "No, that's not him." Disappointed, she lowered her arm.

For the next hour, we examined every fishing boat as it came into dock, as well as every person who came near or got into a boat. Nothing.

Finally, Rachel came over to us. "My lady, it's getting late. We really should start our journey. Already, the sun has risen."

I had been so preoccupied searching for Yeshua that I failed to notice the sky. Now I looked and saw that the last vestiges of the sunrise had evaporated into mist over the surface of the water and that indeed day had sprung upon us. "All right," I said. "God willing, we will meet him again, though it doesn't look like today is the day."

"Oh, Madam Yohana," said Miryam reassuringly, though she too suffered from disappointment. "I *know* that we will see him again! I am confident of it." She smiled, a glorious smile. Freedom encircled Miryam like a radiant halo of gold. Her joy was contagious. I felt my spirits lift; and, indeed, why shouldn't I be just as joyful? I had experienced a miraculous healing! But my very being ached to behold the Rabbi again.

The three of us ladies entered the chariot. Adaba drove (the fellow from Jerusalem whom we hired for the trip to Tiberias had left when we first arrived in the north, but Adaba, clever man that he was, had studied his driving carefully and now exceeded the previous man's skill) and we all relaxed. I immediately noticed how much better I felt. No longer did every bump and jolt (and there were plenty of those) disturb me. Instead, I felt exhilarated by the rush of air against my cheek. First cool, then increasingly warm as the morning progressed. Once we left the vicinity of Capernaum, we only caught glimpses of the lake on our left as we progressed down a winding, dirt, stone-cluttered road that alternatively hugged the lake and skirted clumps of trees.

By the end of the morning, we were just outside Magdala. Miryam became tense, and thoughtful. "Are you frightened?" I asked, clasping her hand reassuringly. Even Rachel drew nearer to Miryam, won over by the Magdalit's self-effacing ways.

"I am fine. Just a little nervous about seeing my husband again." Pensively, she rested her chin on her fist and stared out at the passing scenery. "He would be completely justified if he refused to see me, you know. I destroyed his life."

"Adaba," I called out. "Please stop the chariot." Both women looked at me questioningly. "We need to eat and compose ourselves before we reach Magdala," I explained. Then, to Adaba, "Just pull into the shade of those trees over there."

In a few moments, we were settled under a spreading oak, eating our packed lunch of bread, cheese, and cold fish. (Every meal at the lake included fish, I had come to notice.) A partial skin of watered-down wine quenched our thirst. I sat cross-legged on the ground, amazed that my body could contort in this direction so effortlessly, so painlessly.

"Miryam," I said.

She paused midbite, looking at me with those incredible eyes. "Mmmm."

"Before you see your husband, we need to pray together." Haltingly, I attempted to communicate my intentions as this was new to me. "I, well, I have never really sought Adonai except through giving money at the Temple, that sort of thing. But now I have this overwhelming feeling that we should just talk to Him and He will bend His ear down from heaven and hear us."

She swallowed her food and nodded slowly up and down. "Can you pray and I'll agree with what you say?"

"Well, we can start off that way. Let's see what happens."

"*B'seder*," she agreed.

I shut my eyes. "Lord of heaven and earth," I began. "Miryam and I come before You in thankfulness that You have healed and delivered us from the things that held us both captive. In gratitude we bless Your holy name.

"We long to be in the Kingdom of Heaven of which Your prophet, Yeshua of Natzeret, speaks. We ask that You would grant us favor and show us what we are to do. But now, Adonai, we ask that You would calm Miryam's heart and take away her fear as she prepares to encounter her husband. We ask that You would place forgiveness in his heart for her and that their marriage may be restored." I paused, uncertain as to what to say next.

Miryam took over. "Oh Lord," she prayed, her voice low and husky. "I love you so very much. Thank You for giving me back my life. Thank You for cleansing me of all that filth. Keep me holy before You. Show me if I should seek out Yeshua. Show me by my husband's response today what You would have me to do next." A smile of pure joy lit up her features. She reached out and took my hand. "Thank You for sending Your angel, Yohana, to me. Thank You that You never leave nor forsake us though we roll in the mud the pigs lie in. I will love You all my days. Amen."

"Amen," I said. I heard Rachel, standing behind us, also say *amen.* "Okay," I announced, standing up, brushing the crumbs from my lap. "I think we're ready to enter Magdala now. Agreed?"

"Yes," confirmed Miryam, eyes shining.

We had already passed through Magdala on our way to Capernaum. That time, the Magdalit had hidden herself in a corner of the chariot, under her veils, away from any prying eyes that could potentially recognize her. Today was different. She sat straight and tall, glowing with the confidence that came from knowing God had done a new thing in her life.

Always as we drove through a town or village, we attracted attention. Chariots were rare in Israel, except among the higher-level Roman officials. I could see by people's expressions that they were wondering what important personage I could possibly be to be driving around in transportation like this. Today, the stares went from me to Miryam and the shock of recognition instantly transforming many faces would have been comical if the outcome were not so serious for our dear girl.

Miryam herself behaved like a queen. She smiled kindly at whoever looked at her (and that was everyone) but did not allow herself to be jolted by their reactions, good or bad. She only spoke to give directions to Adaba. "Turn here, right there, watch out for the donkey, he always lies in the street. Left ahead. This is the house."

"Whoa," called Adaba, reining in the horses.

We all turned and stared at the abode before us. Nondescript, simple, relatively cared for, nothing unusual. Not the place I would have associated with one as exotic as Miryam. "This is your house?" I asked her, eyebrows raised.

"Was," she corrected, her impeccable poise fading somewhat.

"What does your husband do?" I asked, curiously.

"He's a fisherman," came the answer.

A fisherman. Of course. Not much else to do in these little towns that hug the coast of the lake. "Will he be home now?"

"He works nights. He's probably sleeping." Miryam continued to sit in the chariot, lines creasing her forehead as she looked at the house where she had lived until a very short time ago.

"Do you want me to go with you?" I asked her.

She hesitated, then shook her head. "No," she said softly. "It was my own sin that got me into this mess. I had better go alone." She carefully stepped out of the chariot and slowly walked to the front door. We sat, parked on the street, and watched as she stood there, fist raised in the air.

Then we saw her knock.

By now the neighborhood children had noticed us and we were surrounded by a crowd of boys and girls. Adaba had his hands full attempting to keep dirty little hands off the sides of the chariot and away from the horses' faces. Grunting, he climbed down from the driver's perch and stood tall, with arms folded against his chest. This caused all but the most brazen of the youth to back off.

I heard a click and saw the door to Miryam's house open. A man stood there, too far away for me to discern his features, but I could tell that he was tall, much taller than I had envisioned. A muffled conversation reached my ears. They were still standing in the doorway, which didn't seem good to me. After several minutes the man turned and went back into the house, slamming the door behind him. Miryam hurried over to the chariot, eyes teary, mouth trembling. Quickly, she climbed back in.

"Look, it's the whore," shouted one of the children, a boy of about twelve years. His companion, another boy, only younger, poked him in the ribs, frowning.

A sweet-faced girl started crying. "Don't say that about Miss Miryam," she yelled at the boy. Looking up at us, she called out, "Shalom, Miss Miryam. I've missed you. Don't listen to Ben." But Miryam already had her face in her hands, shutting herself off to the commotion that surrounded her.

Adaba scattered the children, pulled himself back into the driver's seat, and prodded the horses forward. "Let's go," he commanded them. Obediently, they trotted off.

As we left the group of children behind, some taunting, some waving, only I noticed the face at the window of what used to be Miryam's house. Her husband. Watching us go.

$$\mathcal{L}\mathcal{P}$$

It took us two hours to reach the villa in Tiberias. Half of that time, I had my arm around Miryam as she sobbed. Finally, she reached a point where she raised her head, wiped her eyes, blew her nose, and was ready to talk.

"I can't blame him for not wanting me anymore," she allowed. "I sinned against him in the most grievous way imaginable. I broke his heart, crushed it under my feet. He doesn't believe that I've changed. And why should he? I've done nothing to prove to him that it would be any different. As it is, I've made a spectacle of both of us in this town. He can barely hold his head up in public anymore. I've ruined him." She stared glumly ahead of her, unaware of the passing landscape.

"All that's true," I agreed. "But the fact remains that you *have* changed. Would Yeshua have set you free of those seven demons only to have your life destroyed anyway? Something wonderful is going to happen with the rest of our lives, Miryam. I just know it."

"You think so?" she asked, looking at me hopefully.

Actually, that had never even occurred to me until those words unexpectedly popped out of my mouth. Now I felt committed to them as a course of action. "Of course," I reassured her, trying to sound confident. "What we have to do now is decide what's next."

"Well, I have one less option," she said gloomily.

"Miryam, Miryam, you're too pessimistic," I chided her cheerfully. "What we'll do first is go back to the villa, have a nice supper, a good night's sleep, and then you'll come with me back to Jerusalem."

"To Jerusalem?" she repeated, incredulous. "What will I do there?"

"I'm not sure yet. Kuza, my husband, will help us determine what's next."

"Oh, Madam Yohana," protested Miryam. "I know that you wish to be kind, but I have a bad reputation. I do not want to do anything that will cause you difficulty. You're better off leaving me in Tiberias." She bowed her head.

"To do what?" I asked crisply. "To roam the streets looking for food? No, Miryam, I believe that we've been put together for a reason, and I will not be frightened into abandoning you. Besides," I added, more gently. "I've grown quite fond of you."

"Oh, Madam!" Miryam threw her arms around me and hugged me tightly. Embarrassed, I extricated myself as soon as was seemly.

"So will you come with me to Jerusalem?" I asked Miryam again.

"Yes," came the reply. "I would be most honored to."

THREE

One week later, Miryam and I were dining privately with Kuza at the palace. We had arrived the day before, early in the evening. Adaba had gone to the stables with the horses while Rachel, Miryam, and I immediately set out for my apartment. Miryam was in awe of everything she saw. Never had she encountered such grandeur. My eyes, grown dull over the years to the opulent surroundings, saw things afresh through her eyes. After the modest fishing villages I had just seen, this *was* quite extraordinary. Huge hallways with marble floors, decorated at intervals with brilliantly colorful mosaic pictures. Tall, graceful pillars, each one a carved work of art, held up the ceiling above our heads. Servants everywhere, dressed better than most free men, scurried around importantly. An extravagant abundance of fruit trees from the gardens roundabout swept their perfume in with the gentle, warm breezes. As we walked through the vast halls, nodding and smiling to those we encountered (I eventually decided it would be best for Miryam to pose as a maidservant), I suddenly caught sight of my husband approaching us from the opposite direction. As usual, he was preoccupied with his own thoughts and hadn't yet observed us.

"Kuza," I shouted, filled with tenderness at the oh so lovely vision of him. I then did something I hadn't done in many years. I picked up my skirts and *ran* to him. Gracefully, fleet of foot, pain-free, fast. Startled, he peered through the darkening evening shadows (servants were just beginning to light the evening lamps) at this crazy woman leaping toward him.

"Yohana?" he said. Then, "*Yohana!*"

He strode to meet me, catching me in his arms and hugging me, holding me close to him. "I've missed you," he murmured into my hair. Then, holding me at arms' length and looking into my eyes, he asked, "Are you...?"

"Yes," I assured him, eyes sparkling like a young girl. "I am healed. No more pain. No more limping. It's simply amazing."

"Simply amazing," he repeated slowly, incredulously. Then, "Come to our rooms. Have you eaten?"

"We're famished."

"Good. We'll eat and you can tell me about everything that's happened. Ah, there's Rachel. Shalom, my girl."

"Shalom, sir," she said, bowing respectfully.

He noticed Miryam, standing awkwardly next to Rachel. "And who is this?" he asked, pleasantly, quizzically.

"My new maidservant, Miryam. I found her in Tiberias," I answered, a little loud, a little artificially.

Kuza looked at me oddly. *Why do you need another maidservant?* said the frown between his eyes. But aloud he merely said, "Welcome to Jerusalem, Miryam. We're glad to have you here."

"Thank you, sir," she whispered, bowing as she had seen Rachel do.

It wasn't until we were safely in our apartment, away from any prying ears, that I was able to fill Kuza in on who Miryam was and some of what had happened on my trip to the lake. He, understandably, was stunned at what he heard. But overriding all of his apprehensions and concerns was his insurmountable joy of finding me healed and restored.

"It's a miracle from God," he repeated over and over again.

As I looked with great love on the face of my husband, it struck me how blessed I was compared to Miryam. What she would have given to have had her husband greet her with even a fraction of the tenderness with which Kuza greeted me! I knew that none of this had escaped her notice. Glancing in her direction, though, I ascertained no envy in her eyes. She rejoiced with me. A truer friend after such a short time then most of the "friends" I had known for decades! This was a revelation.

That first night of being reunited with Kuza always stands out in my mind as a jumble of emotions, impressions. The flickering candlelight on his thrilled face, the delectable odor from the garlic-encrusted roasted lamb on my plate, the beautiful eyes of the Magdalit, filled with wonder and respect, the luxury of home, my comfortable bed heaped with silken pillows.

Rachel helped settle Miryam into a section of her room and then Kuza and I retired for the night. The biggest delight of all awaited me: I could love my husband freely, without pain.

The next night the three of us dined together again. We discussed all that had transpired, but mostly we talked about Yeshua.

Kuza was full of questions. After we had satisfied his desire to know everything about Yeshua that we could recount, he asked us the most difficult question of all. "Is he the Messiah?"

"How can any man claim to be God!" I cried.

"But how can any man heal and cast out demons as this man did?" countered Miryam.

"What did he say about himself?" demanded Kuza. "Did he call himself God?"

"Not to me," said Miryam. "At least, not directly."

"He did to me," I told them, remembering the time of my healing. "He said the Son of Man has power to forgive sins. He called himself I AM. He proved it by touching my hip and rebuking the disease. I...I haven't thought about it too much yet because it's so preposterous. To call oneself God!" I looked beseechingly at Kuza. "What do you think?"

"While you were gone I did a lot of reading in the books of the Prophets," he began. He pushed back his plate and stood up, pacing as he spoke.

"Did you know," he said, "that seven hundred years ago the prophet Micah spoke of one coming from Beit Lechem who would be ruler over Israel, whose origins were from of ancient times? I understand that this Yeshua is of the tribe of Judah and that he was born in Beit Lechem."

"That doesn't necessarily mean anything...," I began.

Kuza cut me off. "That's only one prophecy. There are hundreds! The more I find out about Yeshua ben Yosef, the more he fits the profile of these messianic prophecies."

Miryam and I looked at each other. She raised her eyebrows in an "I told you so" look. I shrugged. Kuza noticed my skepticism.

"Let me tell you the most astonishing thing I read," he told us. "The prophet Daniel speaks of a period of time from the issuing of the decree to restore and rebuild Jerusalem after it was destroyed by the Babylonians until the coming of the Anointed One, or the Messiah. He says that there will be sixty-nine sevens, or 483 years."

"How long has it been since the decree was issued?" I asked.

"Four hundred and eighty-one years," he replied, sitting back and watching our amazed expressions.

"So let me get this straight," I said, my voice rising. "You're saying that Daniel predicted the Messiah would come *now*?"

"That's right."

"But, but," I sputtered. "Don't all the Torah teachers and religious leaders *know* this? Why aren't they acknowledging Yeshua, if this is true?"

Kuza laughed but his eyes were sad. "My dear Yohana. Have you really lived so close to the seat of power all these years and not learned that most men will do anything to keep their influence? Once you've tasted power, it's very, very difficult to relinquish it."

"He's right," observed Miryam.

We both turned to look at her. Kuza regarded her kindly. "Tell us your opinion, Miryam. Who do *you* think Yeshua is?"

Miryam hesitated. She had gotten used to me up north in her home territory, but here at the palace with Kuza I believe she was entirely overwhelmed. We must have seemed like royalty to her. I could tell she was reluctant to look Kuza in the eye. But he was such a kind soul, and so father-like, that she took the chance. Now she twisted the linen square used for wiping her mouth into little shapes before answering. We waited.

"I'm not well versed in Scripture like you, sir," she said finally to Kuza. "Nor am I quick of wit like you, madam." She turned to me. "But I believe that if God Himself were to come down from heaven He could not be any different than this man. It's not only that he heals and casts out demons," she went on intently, "but he *loves* us, despite our sin, with understanding and compassion. He expects us to strive for holiness, but he forgives what has come before. I don't know of another religious leader who would have treated me with the respect he did. Most of them would have been heaving stones at me..."

"Boulders," I interjected, wryly.

"Yes," she said, acknowledging my interruption. She continued. "At the same time, he does not condone sin. It was very clear to me that though we were forgiven, we were not given permission to go bathing in the same mud pit with the pigs as before."

"Very well said," approved Kuza.

"Thank you, sir," answered Miryam. In her passion to speak of Yeshua, her cheeks grew flushed and her large, expressive eyes softened. I thought her a very beautiful woman, but had no jealous or competitive feelings toward her. Instead, I felt protective of her, motherly. I glanced over at Kuza. Hopefully, he felt fatherly. Now he spoke.

"Then, Miryam, it would be fair for me to put the question before you: do you believe that Yeshua ben Yosef is the Messiah, the Anointed

One of God?"

This time there was no hesitation. She nodded vigorously. "Yes, I do."

"You realize that this is a dangerous belief to hold, don't you?"

Miryam turned her fathomless dark eyes to Kuza. "All I know, sir, is that I was lost, and now am found. I was a prisoner in the blackest pit of a dungeon, and now am set free to walk in the light. I was in abject misery and despair, and now hope fills my heart like the fragrance of roses. I have decided that I will follow this man to the ends of the earth. He is the image of the living God."

After this speech, we all three sat in silence for a while. I pondered what Miryam had said. I hadn't appreciated the extent of her devotion to Yeshua. Of course, she had nothing to lose whereas I....I let that thought hang in the middle of my mind.

"How about you, Kuza," I asked my husband. "Do you think he's the Messiah?"

Kuza ran his fingers through his hair and folded his hands behind his neck. "I think there's an extraordinary possibility. I want to meet him for myself. This puts me in a very tricky spot with Herod, though. He doesn't make room on the throne for another king." He walked over to me and put his hands lightly on my shoulders. "And you, dear Yohie, you've been healed. Tell us what you believe."

I shook my head. "I can't say yet. I'm uncertain."

That night I had a dream. In my dream I saw a bright light off in the horizon. I myself stood in swirling gray mists and was shaking with cold and hunger. I knew that the light contained all that was good in life: warmth, food, love, companionship, my loved ones who had died. I could just make out the edge of a broad green field awash in wild flowers. The distant music of a mountain brook reached my ears. The luscious smells of lemons, oranges, figs, pomegranates, and berries wafted toward me. I grew even colder and hungrier. I struggled to get closer to the light, but the mists weighed me down despite their gossamer appearance.

I made slow, painful progress. Soon, the light, which had been so far off, loomed just ahead. Joyfully, with the last vestiges of my might, I lunged forward, only to find that I had thrown myself against a door! A transparent door, but a barricade nonetheless! As I touched this defense to the light, it suddenly transformed before my very eyes into Yeshua! I couldn't get past him!

As I struggled back to consciousness, I heard repeated over and over in my brain, *I am the gate. No man gets to the Father but through me.* Pulse racing, I awoke.

❧❧❧

I couldn't talk about my dream yet, not even to Kuza. All day long it haunted me. Even though I had an abundance of material possessions in this life, something within me thirsted to enter the beautiful land which I had so tantalizingly glimpsed in my dream. All my heart's desires were there. It was clear to me that the land represented heaven. But Yeshua as the door? Was this a sign from heaven? A warning? A direction? How did I go *through* him?

About four o'clock that afternoon it hit me. Of course! *Belief* was the key to opening the door! Belief that Yeshua was, who? The Anointed One? God Himself? Suddenly, a desperate longing to know flooded my soul.

I did something I hadn't done in many, many years. I knelt down on the tiled floor and cried out to God. Not with the rote prayers I had chanted listlessly at the Temple but with the passion of a heart bursting to comprehend. *Who are you, God? Are You hiding in the heavens far above our heads or are You manifested in the body of a carpenter's son? If Yeshua is really the Messiah, then I can face Herod or anyone else. But if he's not, stop me now!*

It was then that I felt the most incredible wave of love wash right over me! Exquisite, powerful, all-encompassing—it pushed me further to the ground. I lay facedown on the floor, the coolness of the tiles seeping through the thin linen of my dress. How long I stayed like that, I do not know. I do know that when I arose, I had an assurance in the inner core of my being that God had answered my prayer. Suddenly, my future was crystal clear. I knew what I had to do next.

❧❧❧

"Are you serious?" Kuza asked me, frowning. "You want to what?"

Patiently, I explained for the third time, my newfound serenity wearing a little thin. "I want to follow after Yeshua, go where he goes, that sort of thing. I'd like to help fund the ministry out of the monies my father left me." I sat very still, waiting for Kuza to process what I had said.

"This is just preposterous," he exclaimed, agitated. "Do you realize the *danger* to which you'd be subjecting yourself? Running around with a group of unwashed fishermen and their families...?"

"I thought you believed the Rabbi is the Anointed One," I protested.

"I don't know what I believe." Kuza started pacing back and forth like a caged beast. Whenever he was in turmoil, he grew restless. Such was the case now.

"But you said—"

"Never mind what I said. Examining the Scriptures and running off wildly, putting one's life in jeopardy, are two entirely different things."

"I'm not running off wildly!" I argued, sidestepping the second issue. "Did you hear me when I told you about my dream and what happened when I prayed to God today?"

"I listened very closely," he assured me, his demeanor serious. "I always listen when you speak."

"I love you, Kuza."

"I love you too. I just received you back from the dead. Don't grab your shovel and start digging."

Despite myself, I laughed. "Oh, Kuza, don't be ridiculous! I have no intention of getting healed only to throw my life away! It's life I'm seeking after. *Real* life. Not this fake existence we slough through here at the palace."

"Thank you," he commented, drily.

"Oh, I don't mean *you're* fake!" I hastily reassured him. "You're the bright shining jewel of my life. You're my prince!"

Slightly mollified, he stopped pacing. "Give me time to think about this, Yohana. I can't have an immediate answer for you."

"*B'seder*. Take as much time as you need, my love."

❧ ❧

The week that followed proved to be the nicest week in recent memory. Taking Adaba, Rachel, and Miryam with me ("Make sure that girl covers her face," warned Kuza. "She's the sort who could cause a riot"), I proceeded to give Miryam a tour of Jerusalem. We visited both the Jerusalem of my childhood as well as the current sites bound to interest any tourist.

I awoke on the morning following my conversation with Kuza longing to see my childhood home. After my mother had passed away, fifteen years ago, the place had been sold. In the beginning, I had gone back several times, just to stand on the road outside and gaze at it. But the last time I had been there, a dog, barking furiously, lunged at me. The animal's owner grabbed him before he hurt me (*"Kelev!"* came the angry shout) but that incident succeeded in making me feel unwelcome. I never went back. That is, until now.

"You grew up here." It was a statement, not a question. I could hear the longing in Miryam's voice as she surveyed my childhood home.

I had to admit, the years had not detracted any from the beauty of the house, or, for that matter, the neighborhood. If anything, with the trees and bushes much larger than when I was small, the whole area exhibited a lushness that served as a soothing balm to tired eyes.

A soft breeze rustled the leaves on the trees, cooling us. Although only nine o'clock in the morning, already we could feel the heat. Within the week, the Jewish Feast of Trumpets, known since the Babylonian Captivity as *Rosh Hashanah*, would be upon us. Then, the Day of Atonement, followed by the Festival of *Sukkot*, or Booths, would fill Jerusalem to overflowing with thousands upon thousands of pilgrims coming to the Temple. This week was our last opportunity for at least a month to be able to get around Jerusalem with any semblance of sanity.

I watched Miryam looking at the house. "Look," I said. "I hope it's not going to upset you to see this."

"Oh, no," she assured me. "It's just that I hadn't realized people could grow up under such idyllic circumstances. You were so fortunate."

"You never understand at the time, though," I reflected aloud, remembering my youth. "When one is a child, one doesn't often repeat *how lucky I am*! No, it's only later, through the experienced eyes of an adult, that we can begin to grasp what it was that we held to so loosely."

"What about your family now?" inquired Miryam. "Where are they?"

"Dead," I replied shortly. "Just one older brother." Abruptly, I changed the topic. "Enough of the house. There's a spectacular view of Jerusalem in the hills above us where I used to play as a child. It's not to be missed."

"Lead on."

I took Miryam (and Rachel and Adaba) up through winding paths behind my old neighborhood and up into the hills surrounding Jerusalem on the west side of the City. These were paths my brother and I used to scamper up, but now I felt my breath coming laboriously. Miryam, however, breathed easily.

"I must be getting old," I muttered aloud.

"Too many chariot rides, madam," giggled Miryam.

I shot her a dark look. She didn't notice, however, because Rachel, who was about twenty paces ahead of us on the path, stopped suddenly and pointed at the valley below our feet. "Look!" she exclaimed.

We both turned and peered toward the City, gasping with pleasure as we did so. Shining in the bright light, with the sun reflecting off its countless limestone buildings, gleamed the most spectacular city in the world. Radiating brilliance over on the east side, like the largest jewel in a monarch's crown, stood the Temple. Flashes of gold dazzled our eyes as the sun bounced off roofs and pillars. Flanking the Temple like smaller jewels, burning with a magnificence of their own, rested Herod's palace, another that had been his father's palace, and the elaborate domicile of the chief priest. Ringing the City were several pools, among them the Sheep Pool and the Pool of Siloam, their waters a refreshing blue. The towers of Phasael, Hippicus, and Mariamne stood sentry below us, in the west, while to the east and the south both the Kidron and Hinnom Valleys cut deep slashes like wounds in the earth.

"There's nothing like it in the world, is there?" reflected Adaba, coming up behind us and uncharacteristically speaking without being spoken to first. His deep, resonant voice with its foreign accent pleased my ear, so I encouraged him to continue.

"Well," he said, suddenly shy now that all three of us women gave him our full attention. "Well," he said, again. Then, in a burst of emotion, "I grew up in a land with spectacular vistas spreading out in all directions as far as the eagle could fly. Ice cold streams poured down the sides of lofty mountains, flowing through deep and tremendous ravines carved by the waters since the beginning of time. Snow crowned the highest of these mountains even in the midst of a dry and scorching summer. Green fields of fertile abundance mantled the valleys, spread like the fingers of God between the summits. Our mighty river, the Setit, ran north and west out of our country until it joined its brother, the powerful Nile. When I was captured and sold as a slave, taken far from my native land, I wept for many days." He paused while I looked down at my feet, a little unsettled by this unexpected glimpse into Adaba's soul.

"But," he said, his voice growing stronger, emotion making it vibrate. "I have come to love this city," he gestured over Jerusalem, encompassing the whole vista with a mighty thrust of his powerful arms. "I love it with a love not borne of my own making. In the mountains, when I ran wild and free, I believed that I was in God's country. It is here that I know I am in the outer courts of His Temple." Adaba's deep brown eyes grew misty and his ebony skin pulled taut over his high cheekbones. Unexpectedly, he sank down on one knee and directed his speech to me alone. "My lady, if the master gives you permission to follow after the Rabbi, take me with you! I see in him the same spirit that envelops this amazing city."

Before I had a chance to respond, Miryam threw herself on her knees next to Adaba. "Yes," she cried. "Take me with you as well! Every day my heart longs more and more to see the Rabbi! I would go and drink in the sweetness of his presence."

As if this were not enough to overwhelm me, Rachel joined in. Rachel, calm, obedient, organized Rachel. I didn't recognize her voice, trembling with passion, urgent, intense.

"And me, my lady. I have come to believe that my life, that all our lives, are tied up with this man and that all time spent away is wasted time. Bring me with you as well. I will serve you with all of my heart. Just let me be near him."

To say that this outpouring of pent-up emotion amazed me would be an understatement. Truly, I was in awe.

"Well," I said, trying to keep my tone light so I would not burst into tears. "It looks like everything is dependent on Kuza and what he decides. Pray that he agrees."

"My lady," said Rachel, hesitantly. "Could we, all of us, pray together?"

"Um, all right. Would you lead us?"

Rachel rose to the task. "Lord God," she prayed, looking out in the direction of the Temple. "Please tell Master Kuza to let us seek after Your Messiah. Amen."

"Amen," we all said, with varying degrees of firmness.

Life at the palace had not stood still while I was up north. Kuza told me that since the execution of Yochanan the Immerser, Herod had exhibited violent fits of temper interspersed with the most docile and benevolent of moods. One of the long-time palace employees, a chef by the name of Shammah, allegedly made a joking comment about poisoning the king's soup. This reached Herod's ears, and though the violently trembling Shammah voraciously denied ever saying any such thing, it was too late. An enraged Herod had Shammah brutally tortured and killed. Kuza was quite upset over the whole matter. "He's left behind a lovely wife and four young children," he sadly narrated.

"Why would he ever take such a chance then?" I asked.

"My understanding is that he said nothing about Herod, but that he *did* make a flip and disparaging remark about Herodias one evening when she sent meal after meal back into the kitchen with complaints."

"*Another* 'evil Herodias story'? They're piling up faster than Roman soldiers at a riot," I exclaimed.

"Shhh," cautioned Kuza, though we were alone in a locked apartment, speaking softly. "I don't want to sound overly fearful, my dear, but you need to watch *every word* that comes out of your mouth. As you can tell by what happened to poor Shammah, it is only too easy to experience dire consequences for the least little thing."

"I really don't want to live like this anymore, Kuza." I thought of Yeshua, unafraid of any man, eager to serve God alone. And I thought of Yochanan the Immerser, likewise not afraid and how he died at the hand of Herod. "Have you decided yet about my seeking after the Rabbi?"

"No," said Kuza. "Though it's been on my mind continually." He saw my look of disappointment and came over to me, tenderly framing my face in his hands. "Don't you see, Yohana," he said, looking into my eyes, "that, if anything, this Yeshua is even more radical than Yochanan the Immerser? Don't you know that if Herod will kill someone for a thoughtless remark concerning his wife that he will grow truly vile if he perceives those closest to him, like you and I, as following after another king? Don't you see how threatening someone like Yeshua is to Herod?"

"There's no one like Yeshua," I whispered.

Kuza nodded. "No, there's not. And when Herod sees that the heart devotion he could never command is available for the asking to a common laborer from the Galil, he will foam at the mouth."

"Perhaps he will see that Yeshua is the Messiah, and not a man to compete with?" I asked hopefully.

Kuza took his hands off my face and took a step backward, still meeting my eyes. "You have more faith than I," he said.

"What is faith? All I know is that I was in pain and now I'm not; I limped and now I walk straight and tall; I was dying and now I live. Is it faith to see the obvious?"

"It depends on what the obvious is, I suppose. Is it obvious that Yeshua is the Messiah?"

"You asked me that question several days ago and I didn't have an answer. Now I believe I can say to you with conviction that yes, to me at least it is obvious that he is the Messiah."

"It will be dangerous, dear Yohie. To follow him we will put our lives in great peril."

We? "We, Kuza? You'll come with me?" Eagerly, hopefully.

Slowly, regretfully, he shook his head. "I think it would be most unwise if I were to vacate my post. We stand a chance of escaping Herod's wrath if you go and I cover for you but not if we both leave."

"*B'seder.*" I sighed, knowing all along there was no real possibility of him coming with me but greatly desiring it all the same. "Are you really in agreement with my going?"

"Of course not. I want you by my side, not gallivanting around the countryside exposing yourself to all sorts of dangers. You're my wife."

"Oh, Kuza." I put my arms around his waist and buried my face in his shoulder.

"But," he continued, absently stroking my back with his hand, "I think this thing is bigger than us. You'll always regret it if you pass up this chance to sit at the Rabbi's feet."

"So, I can go...?" I asked again, my voice muffled.

"Tell you what. The Feast of Trumpets is almost upon us. It's my guess that once Jerusalem is overflowing with people, Yeshua will show up at the Temple. It seems to me that he wouldn't want to miss the chance to reach so many at one time. I want to meet him for myself before you go anywhere. If I hear that he's in the City, I will make it my first priority to see him. If, after meeting him, I still believe that it's possible that he really is the Messiah, then I will, with great reluctance and trepidation, let you go. Fair?"

"Fair," I agreed, looking up at him. We gazed into each other's eyes for several moments, not saying anything. Then Kuza kissed me, slow and long, like when we first were married. "Are you trying to get me to change my mind?" I asked him, once I had caught my breath.

"Is it working?"

"No, but I think we have some time before Rachel brings us our dinner."

"Yohana! I'm shocked," grinned Kuza as he led me by the hand into our bedroom.

✥✥✥

Kuza was right (which didn't surprise me. He usually is). Yeshua *did* enter Jerusalem during the Feast of Trumpets. He came with his twelve talmidim, and several other followers as well. He taught daily in the Court of the Gentiles at the Temple.

As soon as we realized that there was a possibility of his being near, Miryam, Rachel, Adaba and myself made daily pilgrimages to the Temple beginning a few days before the Feast. Ostensibly, I went to contribute money to the Temple treasury, but in reality I was looking and listening for any sign or word of the Rabbi.

On the second day, Rachel overheard two men, members of the religious ruling class, the Prushim, talking:

"...and everywhere he goes the crowds go wild...."

"...healing on Shabbat...."

"...will cause trouble for us with the Romans...."

"...understand that he's staying in Beit Anya and should be here anytime...."

She repeated this conversation to me, excited about the news of Yeshua's closeness but somewhat disturbed by the hostile tone of the men. "What do you think it all means, my lady?" she asked me, her voice troubled.

Hmm. I've never been overly fond of the religious leaders. To me, they always seemed like a bunch of outrageous hypocrites. They play up to the Roman rulers, Pilate and his crowd, but at the same time hold them in bitter contempt because they're Gentiles. The Prushim make a big show of following God. They sweep along the streets with their long *tallitot,* trailing their *tzit tzit,* pulling at their beards in supplication to God while meanwhile shaking off the beggars and children who lift emaciated hands to them, pleading for alms. Most of these men treat women with absolute contempt and I, on more than one occasion, had been ignored and frozen out of conversations like I didn't exist. This happened to *me,* a wealthy woman with an influential husband, so I can only imagine how most women would fare with these fellows!

I hadn't given it much thought before now but it made perfect sense that these men would be absolutely green with envy over Yeshua's success. They spent their lives pushing religion with the dismal results that our levitical system grew more corrupt by the year. Instead of being overcome by awe and reverence for one of these men, the "common man" saw them as stern taskmasters to be avoided at all costs.

Of course these men decried the likes of a poor carpenter's son attracting a huge following. Yeshua was everything they weren't: humble, honest, powerful, loving, forgiving, but mostly, *effective!*

Now Rachel waited for me to respond, concern filling those big, brown eyes of hers. "Well, Rachel," I said. "Success always breeds jealousy."

"Do you think they will harm him?" she asked, hand clutching her throat.

I laughed. "If he really is the Anointed One of God, do you think anyone could touch him?"

Dutifully, she shook her head *no* but still seemed agitated.

The next day, the four of us again left the palace and headed east over to the Temple grounds. Miryam had absolutely fallen in love with the Temple. "It is so fantastic," she gushed. "I never imagined anything so spectacular could exist." As Kuza had directed, she covered herself with a veil so as not to draw undue attention.

This morning, however, was a fine, cool, morning; a relief after so many hot days in a row. As we approached the Temple Mount, the crowds intensifying around us despite such an early hour, we heard snippets of conversations that confirmed for us that Yeshua was indeed teaching today in the outer courts! In her excitement at seeing the Rabbi and being near her beloved Temple, Miryam started running ahead of us, joy in her steps. Her veil slipped off her face and hair, falling in the dirt at her sandaled feet.

"Miryam!" I called out sharply. "Your veil!"

But it was too late. A group of about five or six men, between us and Miryam, had also noticed. One of them picked up the veil while another whistled menacingly when he glimpsed Miryam's lovely face. A third grabbed her by the arm, speaking softly to her.

I could see from this distance that Miryam's face, high with color just moments before, had gone a deathly white. She stood very still, as if paralyzed. "Adaba, help her!" I demanded shrilly. He was already three steps ahead of me.

Needless to say, even with six men together, once Adaba came to the rescue they backed off pretty quickly. But the incident sobered us all. Miryam wrapped her now disheveled veil tightly around her face so that even her eyes barely showed. Rachel and I walked on one side of her, Adaba on another. The men were not far behind us. Every so often, one of them shouted something lewd in our direction. Adaba swung around angrily once or twice and that momentarily settled them down. But not for long.

"My lady, do I have your permission to beat their heads together until the melon seeds run all over the road," he asked me, leaning in my direction, his eyes glittering dangerously.

I laughed nervously. "Of course not, dear Adaba. Master Kuza would be charged for cleaning up the city."

He didn't smile but set his lips in a firm line, staring straight ahead, posture very erect. Miryam herself cowered, head down, trying to look as inconspicuous as possible. To my surprise, Rachel had her arm around Miryam and was treating her very tenderly. *When did they become so friendly?* fleetingly jumped across my brain. *And Adaba, look how protective he is of her!* Really, all three of us had come to love the Magdalit in a very short time.

Within a few more minutes, we were so close to the Temple, and so many people pushed and milled about us that the troublesome men soon were lost to sight. All around us I could see Jews and converts to Judaism from literally all the nations of the world. God-fearers from Partha, Mede, Elam, Mesopotamia, Cappadocia, Pontus, Asia, Phrygia, Pamphylia, Egypt, Libya, Rome, and, of course, all over Israel. All descending on Jerusalem so that they could offer sacrifices in the Temple in accordance with the word of Moshe as given in Torah.

And in the Temple courts Yeshua: teaching, preaching, healing, casting out demons. Available. Near. Electrifying. *Yeshua.*

Not all the people were interested in him. In fact, a great many passed him by, treating him as one more curiosity in this frantic, pulsating, cosmopolitan city. But the ones who were intrigued pressed in closely.

We fought our way through the multitude, jostled and hemmed in on all sides but still making progress. When we were a short distance from him, a familiar face spotted us.

I saw him first, his brown eyes lighting up in pleased recognition when they met mine. *Yochanan! It was the talmid who helped when Yeshua prayed for Miryam and me.* He beckoned toward me. *Come,* he mouthed, hands cupped in front of his face, voice carried away on a sea of noise.

"Oh, look," I said to my companions but they had by now seen him as well and were pushing toward him.

Yochanan fought against the surging crowd and when he reached us, grasped my hand firmly. "Come, follow me. It's wild here today."

Wordlessly, we trailed after him. First me, then Miryam, Rachel and, finally, Adaba. Astonishingly, a path opened up before Yochanan and we glided through, as if pulled by an unseen hand.

In a corner of the Court of the Gentiles, against a back wall, stood Yeshua. From what I understood later, he had already spent some time this morning teaching and praying for people and now was taking a short break in preparation for a second teaching.

When we arrived, he was engaged in a heavy discussion with three of his talmidim. The four men stood in a tight circle, and I could see Yeshua's hands gesturing as he spoke, everything about him screaming *life! life!* Never had I seen a man so alive yet simultaneously devoid of the frenzy that tended to characterize the highly energetic.

The man receiving the brunt of the gesturing was heavier than the others, broad in the shoulders with powerful, muscular legs. His short, curly brown hair and beard framed a face devoid of any guile. *Simple, honest, kind* were words I would use to describe my impression. I was to learn that the name of this talmid was Shimon Kefa.

The other two were also unknown to me. Out of the corner of his eye, Yeshua spotted Yochanan, broke off talking with the other men, and turned to greet him. When he saw us, he smiled.

"Ah," he exclaimed. "You've returned." He said it so naturally, so spontaneously, as if Jerusalem were *his* city and the Temple *his* home. As if he weren't a Galilean, weren't from the poor working class. As if I, a born and bred Jerusalemite, were newly come to this place.

But...he was right. It *was* I who had returned. To him. To God.

I felt undone by his presence. I sank down before him, my face to the ground. "I am your maidservant," I whispered.

"As am I," murmured a soft voice to my right.

The owner of the voice was the Magdalit! She had crept forward and thrown herself onto Yeshua's feet and was hugging him around the ankles.

Frankly, even though I was being extremely emotional for *me*, I still felt that I was within the bounds of propriety. Miryam's behavior, on the other hand, seemed really way too much. I started to rise so I could pull her back at the same time Shimon Kefa purposefully strode over to do, I assume, the same thing. Yeshua stopped Shimon.

"No," he said, his hand up in the air, his back to Shimon, not even bothering to turn around. "Do not rebuke her. She is expressing her love and thankfulness. It is a good thing."

Shimon obeyed but continued to watch Miryam very carefully. I slowly got to my feet. Miryam let go of Yeshua and sat back on her heels.

"Yes," she said, her voice quavering. "I *do* love you. Please. Please let me follow after you. I will do anything—clean, cook—just let me be near you."

Yeshua's response surprised me (although by this time I should have been used to the fact that he often did the unexpected). Instead of answering Miryam directly, he turned to me. "Yohana, *eshet* Kuza, what have you to say to this?"

61

"Well, Rabbi." An uncharacteristic shyness overtook me. I did my best to shake it off. "We (and I motioned with my hand in a way that included Miryam, Rachel, and Adaba) came to find you so we could offer our services. I have some money that I wish to use to help with your expenses and we all want to be available in any way we can." I kept my eyes on his face, memorizing every feature in case he said *no*.

But he didn't. He clapped his hands together such that the noise startled me. "It's a beautiful offer," he approved, looking on me with the delight a father would show to his young daughter. "But," he proceeded, before any words could rush out of my mouth, "I need your husband to come and see me and give his approval before all of you can come. Understood?"

"Oh, yes," I practically sang out, so excited over this amazing conversation. "He would like nothing more than to meet you."

Yeshua touched my shoulder lightly, made eye contact with Rachel and Adaba, in turn, and then allowed himself to be led off by Shimon and the other two talmidim so that he could begin teaching the now huge and restless crowd.

The four of us sat on the ground where we had stood, bright-eyed over the sweet future that loomed in front of us.

Several hours later, when Yeshua had finished teaching, I expected to speak with him again and work something out so he could meet with Kuza. So it was with a disappointed heart that I saw him leave the Temple area, escorted by his talmidim, with nary a backward glance.

I hadn't noticed, however, that one of his men stayed behind. As I stood up, shaking out the folds of my garment and stretching my stiff legs, he came and bowed before me.

"Madam," he said quietly, a Galilean accent evident in his speech.

"Yes?" I answered, noticing that he looked like a shorter, thinner version of the talmid, Shimon.

"The Master wants me to tell you that he will meet with your husband tonight at sundown under the great olive tree in *Gat Shmanim*."

"Oh, thank you," I said eagerly. He turned to go. "Wait! What is your name?" I called after him.

"Andrew. Of Beit Tzaidah."

When we returned to the palace, I immediately went in search of Kuza.

I hurried across the marble floored courtyard that linked the wing with our apartment (and others) to the wing that housed many of the administrative offices. It was in close proximity to the throne room so I held my breath, praying I would not run into Herod or, even worse, Herodias.

My good fortune held. I swept into Kuza's office, past a bored-looking guard who nodded at me. Kuza himself looked up, startled, from the eternal paperwork to which he seemingly dedicated his life.

"Yohana," he murmured, his kind eyes smiling. "You look like you're bursting with excitement."

"I am." I closed the office door and sat in one of the chairs across the desk from Kuza. I lowered my voice confidentially. "Guess what?"

"You've seen Yeshua."

"How did you know?"

"How did I know? You've been stalking the Temple grounds for days! It doesn't take a—"

"*B'seder, b'seder*," I cut him off, waving my hand. "Listen to this. He *remembered* me and seemed to anticipate my request about joining the ministry. He did say that he needed your approval. He wants to meet with you at sundown tonight, on the Mount of Olives."

"He wants to meet me?" Stunned pleasure changed Kuza's normally inscrutable expression to one wreathed in smiles.

"Can you do it?"

He shuffled some parchment scrolls on his desk. "I'm going to need to juggle some things around, but thankfully I don't have a meeting with Herod tonight. Where on the Mount of Olives?"

"A small garden at the base called Gat Shmanim. Under the large olive tree. Do you know the place?"

"Yes, I do. Funny he should suggest there." Kuza got a faraway look in his eyes.

I looked at him curiously. "Why? What's the significance?"

"Probably just a coincidence. But before I ever met you, I used to go there to be alone and talk to God."

This piece of news truly surprised me. "You, dear Kuza? You used to talk to God as a young man? What did you say?"

"I said..." Kuza's voice faltered as he struggled with an unnamed emotion. "I wanted to know," he began again, "if He was real. I used to wait for Him to reveal Himself to me right there, under the olive tree." He stared at a point behind my head. "But He never did."

"Until now," I remonstrated softly.

"Until now," he agreed, meeting my eyes.

In years to come, Kuza never could talk about what happened that night between himself and Yeshua without great emotion. And, as excessive emotion was not a quality either one of us cared to exhibit in alarming quantities, he tended to hold it in his heart.

Even with me, his beloved, the one person with whom he could confide in without reservation, he still revealed precious little. The most I was able to get out of him was his complete and unequivocal conversion to the position that Yeshua ben Yosef was indeed the Messiah of Israel. As a result, my husband became my greatest ally in helping me to liquidate several of my properties so I could contribute my riches to Yeshua's ministry.

As Herod's finance minister, Kuza was, without doubt, the most competent financial person in the kingdom. Instead of putting his superior knowledge exclusively to use for Herod, he now dedicated part of that talent toward managing my money in such a way that it would bring the greatest blessing to the Rabbi. He arranged several things in regard to this with Yeshua during that first meeting, along with working out my part in the ministry.

Yeshua told Kuza that already several women traveled with him and his twelve talmidim, using their own resources. He mentioned someone whom I had yet to meet, by the name of Shoshana. Also among them were some of the wives and a few mothers.

The women didn't go *everywhere* the men went, but were still very involved. They stayed together as a group, sleeping in separate quarters. Sometimes we stayed in homes, or public inns. Other times we would assemble a makeshift tent camp. I was to be among them, as well as the Magdalit.

Much of the money necessary for food (I would come to be amazed at just how much thirteen hungry men and those who traveled with them could eat), lodging, support of the families of the talmidim, taxes for the Romans, came from these women. We also routinely gave large amounts of money to the poor. It was the first time in my life that I saw grinding poverty close up. The poor looked very different eye-to-eye than from the height of a chariot seat.

Kuza had also arranged for Rachel and Adaba to accompany us. He told me that Yeshua assured him I would be safe without them but that it was the hunger in their hearts for God that motivated the Rabbi to include them in the Company.

I was instructed to keep my personal belongings down to one change of clothes and necessary toiletries. "We do a lot of walking from village to village," explained Andrew to Kuza. "Traveling as light as possible enables us to move quickly when the Spirit of God tells us to."

The Company of Believers (as I came to think of them—*us!*) was in Jerusalem until the end of the Festival of *Sukkot.* Already I was able to be of use as this was a time when Jews from all over the known world flooded into the City, resulting in outrageously high rents. The expense of lodging and food during a holiday season cut deeply into the ministry purse. I gave substantially and so derived a great sense of satisfaction from the benefit and pleasure it brought to these men and women of God.

I myself still lived at the palace during this time. As yet Herod didn't know of Kuza's and my involvement with the Rabbi, but it was obviously only a matter of time. This troubled me and hung over my head like a dark cloud, but Kuza remained unperturbed.

"The Rabbi urged me not to worry about Herod, Yohie. He encouraged me to obey my earthly master with the same fear, trembling, and single-heartedness with which I obey God. I admit I was surprised at first, because I naturally thought that Yeshua would tell me to get out from under Herod's thumb."

"Especially considering what he did to Yochanan the Immerser," I reminded him, frowning.

"Yes. But I notice that Yeshua doesn't think the way we do. Many of the principles of the Kingdom of Heaven, which he preaches, are counterintuitive."

"You mean..."

"I mean that many of the things God wants us to do are contrary to human nature. Like, for example, if I were to have told you six months ago that you would not only *not* be resentful at providing food and housing to a bunch of uneducated Galileans you don't know, but that you would instead be downright fulfilled, you never would have believed me.

"Also," he continued, before I could agree or disagree. "If I told you to forgive Herodias for every offense you hold against her, and to love her with the love of God, what would you say?"

My answer sprang out of my mouth without thinking. "She doesn't deserve to be forgiven!"

"Yes, but neither do you, according to Yeshua."

I turned hurt eyes to him. "What do you mean, neither do I?"

"I mean," he explained patiently, "that, according to the Prophet Isaiah, all have sinned and fallen short of the glory of God. All. That includes you. And me."

"So what hope do we have?"

"Our hope lies where it always did: in God's mercy. Yeshua is pointing the way into the Kingdom of Heaven. *You're* the one who had the dream. Not me. You were privileged to receive the vision that Yeshua is the door to God."

I wrinkled my brow. "Are you trying to tell me that I should make Herodias my closest friend?"

"I'm telling you no such thing," admonished Kuza cheerfully. "I *am* telling you that you can't hold bitterness and hatred in your heart against her."

"Even though she was responsible for having Yochanan murdered."

"That's for God to sort out; not you."

Frustrated, I stared at Kuza. "This is really hard," I muttered.

He laughed. "It's not such an easy thing you want to do, following after Yeshua. His interpretation of Torah makes what we're used to look like a walk in the desert at sundown in the spring."

"Oh." I sighed. "That sounds nice. When can we go?"

"How about this spring if we both still have our heads attached to our bodies?"

"Kuza, that really is *not* funny," I scolded him.

He came over and wrapped his arms around me and nuzzled his face against my hair. "You're right, I'm sorry. It wasn't." But he didn't retract his statement. We both fell silent.

‿১৯১‿

The Day of Atonement, or *Yom Kippur*, occurred ten days after the Feast of Trumpets. While the Feast of Trumpets, punctuated by the blast of the shofar, called people to repentance, the Day of Atonement allowed a covering for the sins of the people. The high priest made atonement for the community with the blood of goats. The Law of Moshe made it clear that we were to deny ourselves on this day and that if we did not, we were to be cut off from the people of Israel. This "denying oneself" meant a twenty-four-hour fast from food and drink as well as from sexual activity.

In the past I had always endured this day, suffering silently until it was over. But today, as I joined Kuza and thousands of others at the

Temple to partake in the animal sacrifice, I beheld it differently. Today I finally understood that I *did* need an atonement for my sins. I saw that my sins were real and that they separated me from God. I saw that without a covering I was cut off from Adonai. I realized that God was waiting for me to repent.

I watched as the current high priest, Caiaphas, dressed in the sacred linen tunic with a linen sash around him and a linen turban on his head, presented two goats before the Lord at the entrance to the Holy of Holies. He cast lots for the two goats—one for the Lord and the other for the *azazel*, the scapegoat. Caiaphas then brought the goat whose lot fell to the Lord and sacrificed it for a sin offering. This was the lot held in his right hand, which was considered to be a good omen. The other goat was to be sent alive into the desert as a scapegoat.

I have to admit I don't like Caiaphas. Never did. But today in the full splendor of his holy office (no matter how he actually finagled it) he was awe-inspiring. Tall and thin, with a regal face, shrewd, penetrating eyes and high forehead, he presented the picture of the ultimate high priest. I, of course, was privy to all sorts of gossip at the palace and knew him to be a greedy, manipulative cold-hearted, ambitious snake. He obsequiously pandered to Pilate and the Roman rulers but cut dead any of his own people who got in his way.

Now, however, all that faded as he performed the ancient ceremony from the Day of Atonement as handed down from the original high priest, Aharon, brother of Moshe. Caiaphas next slaughtered the bull intended as a sin offering for himself and his household. Ironically, I thought to myself that the huge animal strapped to the altar was still not big enough to cover Caiaphas' sin. After Caiaphas slit its throat, he took a censer full of burning coals from the altar before the Lord and two handfuls of finely ground fragrant incense and put them behind the curtain of the Most Holy Place. He put the incense on the fire before the Lord as the smoke of the incense is supposed to conceal the atonement cover above the Testimony, so that the high priest will not die. Then he took some of the blood of the bull whose throat he had just slit and sprinkled it seven times with his finger on the front of the atonement cover.

Next he sprinkled the blood from the goat on and in front of the atonement cover for the uncleanness and rebellion of the House of Israel, whatever their sins have been. He likewise sprinkled some of the blood from the bull and the goat on the horns of the altar. Afterward, he brought forward the live goat. He lay both of his hands on its head and confessed over it all the wickedness and rebellion of the Israelites and put them on the goat's head. He then called forward a man who had been appointed for the task of sending the goat away into the desert. The goat would carry on itself all of our sins to a solitary place.

Afterward, Kuza and I went to an obligatory breaking of the fast with Herod and several hundred other people in the large banquet hall at the palace. The solemn, introspective mood that had so characterized my day shattered in the midst of the free flowing wine and revelry that always accompanied any of Herod's gatherings. I longed to be with Yeshua and his company but Kuza insisted that it was necessary for us to make an appearance here. "Don't look for trouble," he warned. "Believe me, it will find you soon enough."

I did allow Miryam, Rachel, and Adaba to join Yeshua for his break the fast. Now I endured the event I had to attend, anticipating at least being able to hear later from the Magdalit all about her time.

While sitting at our table, picking listlessly at a piece of raisin-sauce-drenched lamb on my gold embossed plate, I reflected that I should make an effort to *love* these people. It was just so hard to get through to them on a spiritual level. Plus, let's face it, I was plain *scared* to open myself up to attack by speaking of Yeshua.

I guess that I could at least speak of some of the things I've learned from him, I thought to myself. *Even if I don't actually talk about him.*

I looked around the table. Everyone, it seemed, was absorbed in a conversation with someone or other. Kuza, on my right, spoke soothingly in low tones to the man on *his* right, a florid-faced, sweating envoy from some outpost in the Roman Empire called Syracuse. This man kept drinking wine and complaining of the awful heat he had to endure in Israel. Kuza was very valuable to Herod, not only in financial matters, but also in pacifying diplomats like our *shvitzing* friend here.

On my left sat a woman whom I could only describe as a Herodias wannabe. She had the same coloring, the same style dress, the same method of applying—or overapplying—make-up. Even her perfume smelled suspiciously familiar. But where Herodias exuded all the confidence of the original, this woman appeared to me to be desperate, distraught.

As I studied her, my mind began to run in its usual circles. I felt myself to be superior to this poor, grasping creature and dismissed her as not worth my while. As I bit into a large, luscious date, the words of the prophet Isaiah came unbidden into my mind: *all of us have become like one who is unclean, and all our righteous acts are like filthy rags; we all shrivel up like a leaf, and like the wind our sins sweep us away.*

Chastened, cognizant that I was no better than she, I decided that I would take advantage of the next break in the conversation to attempt to get to know her. So, with a nervous stomach, I listened as she spoke to the man next to her, punctuating her high-speed conversation with laughter too loud, too frenzied.

Soon the man turned to his neighbor on the other side and she fell momentarily silent, gulping impatiently at her wine.

I took a deep breath. "Shalom," I said brightly. "My name is Yohana."

The woman gave me a blank stare.

I tried again. "I'm Yohana," I repeated. "Kuza's wife."

A flicker of recognition passed over the woman's features as she looked over at Kuza, still deep in conversation with the Syracusan. "I am Elana," she pronounced in heavily accented Hebrew.

"Is he your husband?" I asked, motioning toward the heavy fellow from Syracuse.

Pause. A look of distaste. "Yes," she admitted.

"When did you get to Jerusalem?"

"One week ago." Elana picked up a small, ivory-handled fan and languidly waved it in front of her face. "Is hot here, no?" she stated, rather than asked.

"I'm used to it. I've always lived here."

Elana nodded vaguely, her eyes scanning the crowded banquet hall, her interest in me quickly ebbing. I realized that if I were to have any influence with her it was now or never.

"So," I said, plunging in, "do you worship God in Syracuse?"

Startled, she turned back to look at me again. *At least I've gotten her attention*, I thought grimly to myself. *Help me, Lord.*

She pursed her lips. I noticed there was a crimson stain on one of her front teeth. "We worship many gods in Syracuse," she allowed.

"Is there one in particular you like?"

"I go to the Temple of Artemis. Great is her name." She blew a kiss at the ceiling superstitiously.

"I worship Adonai," I told her.

"Oh?" she said, bored. "The God of the Hebrews?"

How did this woman ever marry a diplomat? And why did Herod let these pagans dine with us?

"Yes. The God whose Day of Atonement it is today. Did you go to the Temple?"

"No. We stayed in our room." I could tell that I had definitely lost her by now. Elana carefully avoided looking at me, probably wishing I would go away. Well, could I? I found her so unappealing, yet, at the same time, compassion for her rose up in me like a small flame. Persistently, I pressed on, very aware that though my words offended her, yet, they were the staff of life to a dying world.

"Since you didn't go to the Temple, let me explain what happened today. Atonement is what happens when God forgives us for our sin. It's impossible to be in God's presence without a covering. The innocent blood of the sacrificed animal is that covering for us. However, we need to make atonement year after year."

Elana narrowed her eyes at me. "Oh, yes. Artemis expects gifts from us. I bring her gold and silver."

"But that doesn't take away your sin," I explained gently.

"What sin?"

I took a chance. "For instance, sleeping with a man not your husband. That's a sin." I could tell I had guessed correctly by the way she flinched and glanced surreptitiously at her husband. "Also, speaking badly of other people. That's sin, too."

"So what? Artemis doesn't condemn us for these things."

"Yes, but does she have any power? Adonai made the earth, the sea, and everything in them. He has the power to redeem your life from the pit and bring you up into a good place." I was speaking fast and forced myself to slow down so that she could follow my Hebrew. "Now, in Israel, a man has come from Adonai who can do great and amazing miracles. He tells us that if we repent of our sin and return to Adonai—the one true God—He will welcome us as a father welcomes a long-lost son. He wants to draw all men to himself so as to save them and bring them into Heaven."

I had her attention. She really looked at me. I saw the real Elana behind the painted facade. Her dark eyes reflected sadness and pain. "Who is this man, and what is his name?"

"His name is Yeshua ben Yosef, of Natzeret. He is a prophet. He healed me of a wasting disease in my hip." Suddenly I became aware that the conversations around us had fallen silent and people were staring. I stopped talking, self-conscious and apprehensive.

Kuza stood up, taking charge of the situation. "Nice to have met you all, but it's getting late. Come along, Yohana." He held the back of my chair as I hastily gathered my few personal items and stood up along with him.

"Shalom, Elana." I smiled at my seating companion. She smiled back at me, her countenance changed, a new look in her eyes. A contemplative look.

"Good-bye," she said. Then, she took my hand and pressed it. "I will remember what you said."

Our eyes met, then Kuza pulled at me and I hurried after him, out of the banquet hall and into one of the many hallways that connected different parts of the palace. He was walking very fast and it took me a few moments to catch up to him.

"Kuza, wait!" He slowed his steps until I had gotten just behind him and then he speeded up again.

"What is wrong with you?" I hissed at his back.

He swung around. "I'll tell you what's wrong with me!" He lowered his voice to a hoarse whisper. "I can't believe that you were telling the Gentiles from Sicily about Yeshua! Taking a chance like that! For what? For the goyim!" Exasperated, he grabbed my arm and marched me along with him to our apartment.

I kept silent until we entered our private living quarters and then I charged him. "Do you think that Yeshua came to reconcile only the Jews back to God?"

"Don't you?"

"No! Look at Adaba. He's not a Jew, but his heart is on fire to follow the Rabbi. How is this woman any different?"

Kuza opened his mouth, only to shut it again without saying anything. "Well, maybe Adaba has been converted in his heart to Judaism," he finally said.

"Oh, Kuza." I laughed. "That's terribly lame and you know it." A thought occurred to me. "Aren't *you* the one who has been reading the Book of Isaiah? Doesn't he say that the Messiah will be a light for the Gentiles? To bring salvation to the ends of the earth?"

Kuza stared at me. "How did *you* know that?" he wondered, amazed.

"I don't know." I grinned. "It just popped into my head."

After that, my husband, a little grumpy, retreated to his study. When I poked my head in later to say good night, I noticed that his scroll of Isaiah was out on his desk and he was examining it by candlelight, frowning slightly.

"*Lilah tov,* dear Kuza." I blew him a kiss.

He didn't look up. I heard something that sounded like a cross between a 'night and a grunt. Humming ever so slightly to myself, I went to our bedroom.

Five days after Yom Kippur is the Feast of Sukkot. This seven-day festival is one of the three great feasts in which Adonai commands His people to come to Jerusalem. The other two are Pesach and Shavuot.

During Sukkot, we Israelites build booths reminiscent of the temporary structures we dwelt in during our forty-year sojourn in the desert fifteen hundred years ago. For seven days we live in these dwellings. The booths are built of tree boughs and palm branches, and decorated with all manner of fruits, flowers, and vegetables. Truly, some of them are works of art! It is a season of great joy and gladness of heart. Young men and maidens dance, and shake tambourines, shouting their praises before the Lord. It is not uncommon for weddings to burst forth soon after Sukkot.

Since I already live in Jerusalem, my booth was always set up in the exposed outer courtyard of the palace, nestled against an inner wall. Typically, I would be back and forth between the sukkah and my apartment all day long; eating and sleeping in the sukkah but generally doing my daily living as normal.

Many others who lived and worked at the palace also had their sukkot in the same courtyard. The air throbbed with a festive beat and everyone, or so it seemed, greeted life with greater enthusiasm. Then, of course, the week ended and we scurried back to our individual holes.

This year, I approached Sukkot with a very different attitude. For seven days I was to dwell in a temporary structure that was nevertheless attached to my old, comfortable life. At the end of this time, though, I was to bid Kuza and all that was familiar *shalom* in order to follow Yeshua from village to village and from town to town. It would be untruthful for me to say that I did not have a certain amount of anxiety over the future. That which is safe and familiar, though it becomes boring and sometimes despised, yet, when daring adventure beckons, takes on a golden aura of *home*. Now I wandered through my apartment, trailing my hand lightly over the many artifacts that filled the place, flicking a mote of dust from the spout of a pottery vase, polishing with the edge of my sleeve the heavy gold cosmetics jar Kuza had presented me with on my 30th birthday.

Miryam, Rachel, and Adaba were staying exclusively, by this time, with Yeshua's Company. I understand that Miryam sat at the Rabbi's feet, starry-eyed, until someone (usually Shimon) pulled her away, while Rachel and Adaba had made themselves indispensable with their superior servant skills. Kuza and I had agreed that it was best for me not to be too obviously involved before I actually left, so as not to invite potential difficulties.

On the last and greatest day of the Feast, known as *Hoshannah Rabbah*, I woke up early and went with the rest of the crowds down to the Temple. This was the morning when the annual water pouring ceremony was held, and I tried never to miss it as it so intrigued me. As did all the other worshipers around me, I carried in my right hand the *lulav*, which is a myrtle and willow branch tied together with a palm branch between them. This was in fulfillment of the command in Torah that tells us to take these things and rejoice before the Lord. In my left hand, I cradled the *etrog*, a variety of citrus, which represented the fruit from the same verse of Scripture. Some call it a paradise apple; fruit of the forbidden tree in the Garden of Eden.

Some of the festive multitude remained in the Temple to attend the morning sacrifice. Others went in procession to a place called Emmaus where they cut down willow branches, with which, amid the blasts of the priests' trumpets, they adorned the altar, forming a leafy canopy around it. But it was with the third group that I went.

We followed a priest who held a golden pitcher. We walked down to the Fountain Gate over to the Pool of Siloam, the overflow of which feeds a lower pool, in the southeastern corner of the City. Originally, this pool was made by King Hezekiah seven hundred years ago in order to divert a besieging army away from the spring of Gihon yet bring its waters inside the city wall. Now we watched as the priest filled his golden pitcher from its waters. We then proceeded back to the Temple, timing it so we arrived just as they were laying the pieces of the sacrifice on the Altar of Burnt Offering, toward the close of the ordinary morning sacrifice service.

The priest with the pitcher was now joined by another priest who carried the wine for the drink offering. Together, they ascended to the altar and poured both the water and the wine into two silver funnel openings, which led down into the base of the altar. This was symbolic of God pouring out His blessings of salvation and prosperity on His people.

Many decades ago, a high priest by the name of Alexander Jannaeus had poured the water not in the funnel but on the ground, to prove some obscure theological point. In the riot that ensued, he himself was nearly murdered and six thousand people were killed in the Temple. Needless to say, the priests are now very careful to pour the water *only* into the silver funnel.

It was during this part of the service that I thought I caught a glimpse of Yeshua in the crowd, head thrown back, dancing with abandon. But I couldn't be sure. The crowd teemed with people dancing, singing, shouting with great shouts of joyfulness. Even I was able to join in the dancing!

Next, to the accompaniment of the flute, this whole great assembly chanted, with responses, the great Hallel. This is the portion of Psalms 113-118. As the Levites responsible for the singing intoned the first line of each psalm, we would repeat it; while to each of the other lines we shouted *hallelu Yah.*

At the close of the Hallel, in Psalm 118, we not only repeated the first line, *O give thanks to the Lord,* but we also repeated *O now work salvation, Yahweh.* Never before had I sung with such fervor, such assurance! Never before had I really believed that it was not only possible but imminent that Adonai would work salvation and dwell among us! I felt faint with emotion, delirious with the knowledge that God's Messiah had healed me, that my life was forever and irrevocably changed.

All together, we proceeded out of the Temple, shaking off the leaves on our willow branches and beating our palm branches to pieces. That afternoon we dismantled our booths. The Feast was ended.

FOUR

Once Sukkot ended, events moved so quickly that, in retrospect, it all seemed a blur. Barely had we taken apart our sukkah and brought the last of our belongings back into our apartment when I found myself bidding farewell to my husband.

A more bittersweet leave-taking could not easily be discovered; for though I was achieving my heart's desire in being allowed to join Yeshua's Company, taking leave of the fair sight of my beloved's face caused me much grief. Kuza kissed me tenderly, encouraging me in my mission, reiterating that what lay before me was the chance of a lifetime. It was only much later that I learned from others how subdued and disheartened he was for days after my departure.

I have to admit that, prior to going, I had only a vague, shadowy picture in my mind as to what my place would be like in Yeshua's Company. I assumed that Rachel and Adaba would continue to serve me (seeing how they belonged to me!). I thought that when the crowds gathered, I could be used to pray for some of the women who sought out the Rabbi. Over all this existed a rosy hue tinged with gold.

Reality came with a jolt. I discovered that Yeshua set no store by the wealthy and prominent in his midst. He expected those who were *greater* to serve. He frequently chided us when he saw that we were grasping for position. "You know," he would say, coming upon us suddenly, always knowing when a word or touch from him was needed to calm ruffled tempers. "It's the rulers of the Gentiles who lord it over people. But *you*," and he would pause, regarding us with love and approval such that even the densest among us squirmed under the conviction of sin, "Not so with you. Instead, whoever wants to become great among you must be your servant, and whoever wants to be first must be slave of all. For even the Son of Man did not come to be served, but to serve, and to give his life as a ransom for many."

This reference Yeshua made about giving his life as a ransom seemed to me so odd that I didn't even puzzle about it. Rather, I was much more focused on the part about the greatest among us being a servant of all. This statement was completely the opposite from the philosophy at the palace. Kuza would fit this into the counterintuitive category. How I missed him!

I hadn't realized the amount of work expected of me. I had assumed that Rachel and Adaba would carry at least some of my load. But no. Adaba had proved so invaluable to Yeshua's talmid Thomas that I almost never saw him. When he wasn't helping Thomas transport baggage and provisions he made an excellent bodyguard. If I did happen to catch sight of him, he would flash me a blinding white, toothy smile, obviously happier than ever before.

Rachel I saw much more frequently. But instead of her assisting me, often I would be placed under *her* supervision. Once my initial resentment subsided, I saw the wisdom in this. Rachel excelled in those areas where I had little skill.

And what was I called to do? Cook, mostly, and clean. Pack up belongings. Help where needed. Listen. Learn.

To be in such close proximity to Yeshua was awesome. At times I felt I was living in the very courts of heaven. At other times, though, all my worst qualities sprang up, bigger than ever. Sometimes I thought walking barefoot over hot coals would be minor if it meant following Yeshua. On other days, I fretted and complained about aching feet, poor sleeping conditions, too many bugs. Some days I loved everyone we met and could understand Yeshua's constant love for them—and me. Other days, everyone got on my nerves and I was irritable and annoyed. I noticed everybody's flaws.

Most of the time, I gamely poured myself into the work, whatever it was. Even the dull routine chores were fun with some of the women I had met. I was fascinated by many of them, particularly Shoshana.

She was a woman like me in many ways. Fortyish, attractive, wealthy, she followed Yeshua with deep love and respect sparked by her healing from an eye disease that had been steadily progressing to blindness. Now she could see perfectly and her heart overflowed with love for the Rabbi.

Shoshana came from the hill country of Ephraim, not far from Ramah, which was renowned as the birthplace of the ancient judges Devorah and Shmuel. Her husband, deceased for five years, had owned several olive groves. She was mother to two living children, both married and settled with families of their own. Several men had asked for her hand in marriage, attracted to both her and her substantial fortune. But she never felt right in her spirit about any of them and so had resisted remarriage. Then, three years ago, her sight began to fail her. A blind wife, though rich, is still not as appealing as a seeing one. The suitors slowly disappeared, leaving her alone in a world increasingly gray and shadowy.

"And then I heard about the Rabbi," she said, face radiant as she spoke of him. "When he came to my town, I sent my servant to invite him to stay at my home as my honored guest—guests plural, that is, since he travels with such a large group." Much laughter accompanied this remark; by now we had all witnessed first-hand the surprised look on the face of a prospective host upon seeing just how many people traveled with Yeshua.

"He accepted," she continued. "And I prepared the finest banquet my household had seen since before my husband, Shaul, passed away. I so hoped that I might regain my sight, but at the same time, I was a little frightened...."

"In case he failed to heal you and your hope was killed," I interjected.

She shot me a sidelong glance. "Yes, exactly. So I waited until the evening was over, the dinner cleaned up and the guests trundling off to bed. I gathered my courage and approached Shimon Kefa.

" 'May I ask the Rabbi for prayer?' I cautiously inquired. He furrowed his brow in that way he has and started to put me off.

" 'It's late,' he said. 'The Rabbi has been up since before sunrise. Possibly in the morning...'

"Just then Yeshua looked up at us from across the room. 'Don't stop her, Shimon,' he warned. 'Can't you see that her heart is breaking?' Then he walked over to me and his eyes were so full of love that I almost drowned in them. 'Ask me for that which you most want, my dear daughter Shoshana.'

"Well, the words *please restore my sight* trembled on the tip of my tongue. But it was not those that emerged from my mouth! No. The words which came out were *please, Lord, forgive me*.

" 'You have spoken well,' said Yeshua. 'Your sins are forgiven.' Then he gently spit on each of his thumbs and placed them directly on my eyes. He prayed softly, musically, in a language unknown to my ear, a language I now know he shares with the angels. After a time he stopped and spoke once more in our tongue, his thumbs still on my eyes. 'You have chosen the best thing and God would reward you for your pure heart. In the name of God the Father, I command the foul spirit of disease to leave these eyes and for Shoshana to once more experience the excellent sight of her youth.' Then he clapped his hands loudly—I jumped at the sound—and raised his hands in the air toward heaven. I blinked three times, I distinctly remember that, and then realized that *everything* was startlingly vivid.

" 'Oh, my,' I gasped, shocked by this astonishing miracle. Yeshua peered at me intently, his face glowing. I fell to my knees and grasped his hand, kissing it while my tears fell. Yeshua placed his hand on my head and stroked my hair.

" 'You called me 'Lord,' and rightly so,' he said, his hand still on my head. 'Know that the Son of Man has come to bring light to a dark and dying world.' We stayed like that for some time, though I sensed that Shimon Kefa waited protectively nearby, ready to spring if Yeshua needed him. Then Yeshua withdrew his hand and I rose, trembling, before him.

" 'It is late, and you are my guest. I will not detain you any longer. I would just have you know that all I have is yours.'

"A smile touched his lips. 'We'll speak more of this in the morning,' he said, and he took his leave."

There was silence for a few moments as each of us in the group surrounding Shoshana recalled her own specific encounter with the Rabbi.

"So," I said, breaking the silence. "How are your children doing with all this?"

Shoshana shook her head sadly, a cloud passing over her face. "They're simply furious," she said, as her shoulders drooped.

"Is it the money?"

"No, not really. *Their* portion of the inheritance is set apart. I won't—can't—touch that." She stared off into the distant horizon. "I think that it's the sheer unconventionality of their dignified, sedate mother suddenly touring the country with all sorts of people whom they consider to be disreputable."

"What about your sight being restored? Are they amazed by that?" I persisted.

"You know it's funny," Shoshana reflected, after a while. "But I've come to notice that healing is much more dramatic when it's personal. My sight is so much more important to *me* than it is to even those who love me most."

"*I* love you, Shoshie," I proclaimed impulsively, draping my arm around her shoulders.

Her face lit up. "I love you too, Yohana. What a blessing to have you with us!"

Just then we felt a presence across the center of the circle in which we were sitting. I looked up and was glad to see Yeshua standing there, listening. He seemed very pleased. He praised us then with words I will treasure in my heart for the rest of my life:

"The love you have for one another is the greatest witness of all. More than healings, more than deliverance from demons, more than words, it is this love that will show everyone you are indeed my *talmidot*." Then, "Watch yourselves, for the Enemy would seek to ruin that love. Always forgive, always trust, always hope, always endure. Nothing can come against love." He prayed over us, his hands strong on our backs, his breath warm on our upturned faces.

Such moments carried me through the lack of sleep, the hard beds, the poor food, the weariness of constant travel, the road grime and, mostly, the ache in my heart from missing Kuza.

Everywhere we traveled, Yeshua would speak in the local synagogue on Shabbat. I became accustomed to sitting on a hard wooden bench, on the women's side, while the Master taught from Torah with an authority completely inconsistent with his humble beginnings.

I grew to cherish Shabbat in a way I never had previously. Kuza and I had been sloppy in our observance of the commandment to rest on the Sabbath, but not Yeshua! He obeyed scrupulously. I learned to not do commerce, to not light a fire (we made good and certain that the ones from the sixth day were banked!), to not carry a load, to not cook.

However, we *did* worship at the various synagogues, we *did* take a break from our normal routines to spend time with one another, we *did* sit around and argue the meaning of the Scriptures. We *did* the things of God. If a person needed healing, Yeshua healed him.

I also came to know Yeshua's twelve talmidim, some better than others. I was especially drawn to Shimon Kefa and his brother, Andrew. These two men, along with another pair of brothers, Ya'akov and Yochanan ben Zavdai, were partners in a fishing business. They came from Beit Tzaidah, on the western side of Lake Kinneret, but were currently living in Capernaum.

Andrew impressed me as a sweet, studious young man. No matter how busy, he always had time to lend a helping hand. He treated the women with the greatest respect, and often sat with us and gave us the latest news. His brother, Shimon, was younger but physically larger. Shimon loved to joke and play, but I learned not to be fooled by his merry heart. He was as serious and passionate about following God as anyone, maybe more so.

I asked the brothers how they had met Yeshua and they shared the following tale: "Several of us," narrated Andrew, "were thirsting after true knowledge of God. We were fed up with the religious leaders and Torah teachers. They are such hypocrites! We didn't know where to turn. One day, I heard people talking about Yochanan. He was immersing on the east side of the Jordan River, all the way south in Beit Anyah. So I told my fishing partners that I wanted to meet this man. They were very kind and said, *go ahead*. After I got down to Beit Anyah, saw Yochanan, and heard him preach, I knew that I had found the real thing. So I stayed with him and became one of his talmidim. I sent word back that I had found a true man of God, a prophet. Shimon came to see who Yochanan was, as well as two of our friends, Philip and Nathaniel.

"Just before I reached Beit Anyah, Yeshua had come to Yochanan for *mikveh*. He then went into the desert to fast and pray. He returned to town just after Shimon joined us, and one day I was standing with Yochanan and another fellow when Yeshua passed by. Yochanan said, 'Look! God's lamb!' Immediately, this other fellow and I followed after Yeshua. When Yeshua noticed us, he said 'What are you looking for?' and all we could think to say was, 'Rabbi! Where are you staying?'

"He told us, 'Come and see.' So we followed him and stayed the rest of the day. It was amazing. We spent hours asking Yeshua questions and hearing answers the likes of which we had never gotten from any Torah teacher. Scripture opened up before our eyes like the water of the lake before the stern of a boat. Right after we left Yeshua, I looked for my brother and told him, 'We've found the Messiah!'

"I knew," Andrew said, "Just how hungry Shimon was for God. There was no way I could keep this from him!"

At this point in the story Shimon cuts in and says, "When Andrew told me about the Rabbi, I immediately demanded to be taken to him." So Andrew, praying that Yeshua would still be in town, took his brother to him. To his relief, Yeshua was there, and even seemed as if he were expecting them.

When he saw him, Yeshua, smiling, laid his hand on the top of Shimon's head and declared, "You are Shimon Bar Yochanan; you will be known as Kefa." (Or rock).

"I was ready to follow him anywhere," grins Shimon.

It was the next day that Yeshua found Philip, and said, "Follow me!" Much as Andrew had sought out Shimon, Philip went to tell his good friend Nathaniel that he had found the one Moshe wrote about in the

Torah. "It's Yeshua ben Yosef from Natzeret!"

"Natzeret?" scoffed Nathaniel. "Can anything good come from there?"

"Come and see," Philip said to him.

Nathaniel did go and see, and Yeshua anticipated him as well. "Here's a true son of Israel—nothing false in him," said Yeshua. And, "Before Philip called you, when you were under the fig tree, I saw you."

Nathaniel was overwhelmed by the Lord's intimate knowledge of his spiritual struggle. "Rabbi, You are the Son of God! You are the King of Israel!"

Yeshua crossed his arms in front of his chest and laughed deeply. "You believe just because I said I saw you under the fig tree?" He turned his intense gaze to Philip as well. "I tell you (all of you) that you will see greater things than that! You will see heaven opened and the angels of God going up and coming down on the Son of Man!"

"Did he mean like the Patriarch Ya'akov's ladder in his dream?" I asked Andrew. "Is he comparing himself to that ladder?"

"Seems like it, doesn't it," concurred Andrew.

"Then Yeshua is saying that he is the bridge between heaven and earth," I realized, trying to work this out in my own mind.

We pondered the possibilities for a while, until Andrew had to leave. He told me he would fill me in later on what had happened next. What I did know was that two days later, Yeshua left Beit Anyah for Kana in the Galil. There he went to a wedding and took the brothers with him. This was the first of Yeshua's miracles. He changed water into wine after the wine ran out!

"That was also where we met his mother and brothers for the first time," shared Shimon.

"What are they like?" I asked.

"His mother couldn't be nicer," said Shimon, studiously avoiding the question of the brothers.

I changed the topic. "How did your wife feel when you became a talmid of Yeshua?" I asked Shimon, knowing how hard it must have been for a young wife with three small children to see her husband disappear for long periods of time in order to follow a *tzadik*.

"She wasn't so thrilled at first," he confessed, looking pained. "But a few days after the wedding in Kana, her mother grew terribly ill with a high fever. Yeshua visited our house and saw this poor woman wasting away, her face flushed, lips dry and cracked. He sat down at her bedside and prayed over her, touching her hand. Right away, the fever left her and she got out of bed, insisting on serving us. My wife cried with relief. That night, she told me that she understood my desire to follow after Yeshua and would do whatever she could to help me."

"What a remarkable woman," I commented, impressed. "What's her name?"

"Chana," he said softly.

"Chana," I repeated. "A beautiful name. Has she come with you on your travels?"

He shook his head. "She's very responsible, very organized. Chana believes that to leave the children would be wrong and to bring them even worse. When they're older, she says. That's when she's promised to come with me." He looked so utterly young and hopeful that my heart wrung with pity. I was about to offer words of comfort when he said, "We're in Capernaum a good deal so I get to check on them."

In addition to these six men were six others: Matthew, also known as Levi, who was one of the despised tax collectors for the Romans before Yeshua changed his life; Thomas; Ya'akov Ben Chalfai; the talmid we referred to as the other Shimon (the Zealot); Yehuda ben Ya'akov; and another Yehuda, this one from K'riot.

Yehuda from K'riot handled the money. He was arguably the most handsome of all the talmidim, but I found him offensive. He went out of his way to be charming to me and Shoshana. At first, I really enjoyed the attention but then I noticed that he wasn't nearly so attentive to Rachel and some of the other, poorer, women.

I also noticed over time that Yeshua treated Shimon, Andrew, Yochanan, and Ya'akov with greater intimacy than the other men. He would always invite them to go places with him. This puzzled me until I realized that these four were the ones who were always available. Many of the others were only sporadically available. Yeshua didn't argue with people when they gave him excuses as to why they couldn't do something (*my father is sick! My oxen died! I just got married!*) but he tended not to approach them as quickly the next time. I determined in my heart to never disappoint him.

Another person whom I would grow to greatly love and admire was the Rabbi's mother, Miryam. I hadn't been with the Company very long, maybe a month, when one day Yeshua spoke to a particularly large crowd. It was one of those fine days in late fall, before the winter rains set in. We'd been invited to a large, borrowed house. At the front of the interior courtyard, the crowd overflowing into the street, Yeshua spoke about what he called the "Kingdom of Heaven." He again used the story of the farmer sowing his seed. Now he unfolded this image to us, showing how we could be that good soil. "Don't light a lamp only to hide it," he admonished. "Let all see your light so that everyone sees how much your Father in heaven loves you." He warned us to take him seriously; those who understood would be given more; but those who took it lightly would lose even the little they had.

As the people mulled over these difficult statements, Yochanan approached Yeshua. He began to whisper to him, but Yeshua would have none of it. "Speak to me plainly. Nothing is hidden," he told Yochanan.

Yochanan stood awkwardly, shrugged, and said in a voice that carried, "Your mother and brothers are standing outside and want to see you."

At this, men and women alike strained their necks in an attempt to see Yeshua's family. I, too, felt my interest quicken. I expected him to excuse himself and hurry after Yochanan. But that's not what he did.

"My mother and brothers are those who hear God's message and act on it," he said deliberately, eyes scanning the crowd. He then proceeded to continue teaching.

Yochanan looked a bit nonplused. Exiting the room, he caught sight of me and beckoned. Intrigued, I got up and followed him.

"What is it?" I asked, hurrying to keep up with his long strides.

"Come," he said. "I need your help." As I scampered after him, flattening my body to contort through the throng of people, he spoke in low tones over his shoulder. "I'm going to sit with the Lord's family until he's free to see them. I think his mother will find you engaging."

Engaging? Me? "Of course, I'm glad to help."

As we emerged into sunlight, I noticed, as I did more and more these days, the increasing numbers of people who came to hear Yeshua. Both men and women were squatting on the lawn and sitting in the road, barely able to hear his voice but refusing to leave. They were desperate for a touch from the Rabbi; all of them yearning for something and looking to him to fulfill it.

Yochanan walked down to the edge of the lawn, and off to the side. I saw a small group of people, standing in a huddle, waiting.

They don't look too happy, I observed. There was a woman and four men. The woman must have been a few years older than me, late forties, brown hair streaked with gray, partially hidden under a head scarf. Her face was kindly, and I could tell that she smiled often, but not now: conflicting emotions flitted across her face and she seemed tense. Her dress was common and it was apparent that this was someone who had worked hard all her life.

She was surrounded by tall, muscular, young men. They did not seem as kindly, and all were frowning. Yochanan and I reached the edge of the group in time for me to hear one of the men explode with, "This has gone on far too long! We need to take him home already! If only Abba were here!"

To which another of the men, motioning toward Yochanan, cautioned, "Quiet down, Shimon! Look, that fellow's back."

The one called Shimon looked up and saw Yochanan. The scowl rolled off his face like a log down a hill. He came toward us. "So, can we see him already?"

"He's teaching right now," said Yochanan, a pleasant smile plastered on his face. "The Lord will be with you when he's done for the day."

I could see that the words *the Lord* infuriated the men. They started murmuring to each other and clenching their fists. The woman who was with them exhaled her breath in a loud *sshhh*. She asked Yochanan, "When do you think that will be?"

"It's hard to say," he began, shrugging apologetically. He pointed to me. "This is Yohana. She and I are available to take you around, answer any questions, help you out, while you're waiting."

"That's very kind of you," said the woman. She turned to me and smiled. "My name is Miryam."

"You're Yeshua's mother," I said, somewhat stupidly.

"Yes," she confirmed, obviously used to the attention her position as the Rabbi's mother afforded her, though not entirely comfortable with it.

Meanwhile, Yochanan had the harder job as Yeshua's brothers ranged from impatient to downright hostile.

It was clear that they wanted to storm the house and drag Yeshua out. Only the presence of their mother kept them in check.

"I apologize for the behavior of my sons," she told Yochanan. "Since the passing away of my beloved husband, they all feel responsible for the maintenance of the family." Then she introduced each one, in turn:

"This is Shimon (which we knew)." He glowered. "This is Yaakov." He gave us a tight-lipped smile. "Yehudah." A curt nod. "And Yosef." A grunt, which I chose to think of as "shalom."

"Why have you come for your son?" I asked Miryam.

"We're concerned," she said. "We've heard..." She hesitated. "Things."

"What kind of 'things'?" Yochanan queried.

Before Miryam could answer, Shimon spoke up. "Things like you calling him *Lord.*" He shook his head angrily. "No man is Lord but Adonai alone. He can get himself killed if he persists in speaking like this."

Yochanan and I exchanged glances. "Do you have any idea who your brother is?" I asked Shimon. Unfortunately, I felt myself slip back into my privileged, authoritative palace personality and Shimon bristled.

"I grew up with him," he said. "How long have *you* known him?"

"I don't think the issue here is how long we've known him." Yochanan stepped in. "I think it's more *what have we seen him do that makes us believe in him.*" He looked around at the faces of Yeshua's brothers. "I've seen your brother do things that are far beyond the capability of any mortal man. So has Yohana. In fact, she was healed of a crippling disease not very long ago."

"That's right," I said.

"And," Yochanan continued, "we constantly see him pray over people who are healed of blindness, deafness, paralysis, and many other diseases. Do not our Scriptures say only the Messiah will do such things? We see him command demons to leave people, and they do. We hear him teach in ways that show an authority and understanding of the Holy Scriptures that is unlike any other rabbi. He is God's anointed. Don't mock him."

At this two of the brothers looked away, while two still seemed hostile. Miryam kept silent.

"Look at all these people," gestured Yochanan, indicating with a sweep of his arm the crowd around them. "They come from far away, with little provision, sleep on hard ground, all so they can have a touch from Yeshua. Are they all wrong?"

"We're not here to fight with you," said the brother named Yaakov. In appearance, he favored Yeshua more than the other three. I suspected that he was the next in age after the Rabbi. "We love our brother. This is getting out of control: we're worried about him."

Yochanan softened. "I love him too." The two men considered each other. I knew that above all else Yochanan treasured his relationship with Yeshua. The two men had a meeting of the minds and heart and understood each other in a special way. Not even Yochanan's brother Yaakov (a different Yaakov) understood the Rabbi so well. Sometimes the other talmidim seemed a bit jealous, but as Yeshua exposed any sin that tried to gain a toehold in the camp, the jealousy tended to be short-lived. Now I wondered if Yeshua's brothers envied us, those with whom he chose to spend his time.

In the end, the family had no choice but to wait for as long as it took.

When Yeshua did take a break from ministering to people, he came over to greet them. He kissed his mother on the cheek, obviously pleased to see her. She, for her part, hugged him briefly but fiercely before allowing her sons access to him.

The brothers tried to be commandeering with Yeshua but he was very comfortable being the older brother. He explained that though things seemed out of control to them, in reality they were very much in God's hands. He spoke to them of teaching, healing, and the call of God on his life. They could not win. Their words fell to the ground, fluttering down like dead leaves in winter. Finally, they left, without him. Miryam left with them, torn by the family schism and saddened, her lips forming the word *shalom*.

Yeshua had stood firm but was saddened by this visit. He went off by himself to pray when darkness fell, and we did not see him again until the following morning. When he returned, he spoke forth David's words from Psalm 69:

> *"May those who hope in you*
> *not be disgraced because of me,*
> *O Lord, the Lord Almighty;*
> *may those who seek you*
> *not be put to shame because of me,*
> *O God of Israel.*
> *For I endure scorn for your sake,*
> *and shame covers my face.*
> *I am a stranger to my brothers,*
> *an alien to my own mother's sons;*
> *for zeal for your house consumes me*
> *and the insults of those who insult*
> *you fall on me."*

After this, we spent two more weeks in the vicinity of the lake. One day, Yeshua and the twelve talmidim got in a boat and sailed to the other side of the lake, to the region of the Gerasenes, across from the Galil. We women and some of the other men in the camp (like Adaba) stayed behind. Apparently, on the way there, the Rabbi fell asleep in the boat. A little while later, a squall came down on the lake, so that the boat was being swamped and they were in great danger. Huge waves, seemingly from nowhere, pounded the boat, threatening to overturn it. Rain pelted down in great sheets while the wind blew so hard that even the words that came from one's mouth were instantly swept away across the menacing, dark waters.

I heard this story from Shimon Kefa upon their return to the camp. He said they all panicked, and in the chaos of the moment it took a few minutes before Andrew found the Rabbi and awakened him.

"We screamed, 'Master, Master, we're going to drown!' " narrated Shimon in his wonderful storyteller's voice. "Of course, we could barely be heard over the roar of the wind."

Shoshana sat on one side of me, the Magdalit on the other, with Rachel next to her. We had all taken a break from the morning's chores and had rushed over to hear about the men's trip as soon as they returned.

"What happened next?" breathed Rachel.

Shimon shook his head, and his eyes sparkled. "The master got up and rebuked the wind and the raging waters." A broad smile lit up Shimon's familiar features as he recounted the story. "He stood there and spoke to the elements as if they were merely unruly children. Absolutely incredible. Almost immediately, the storm subsided and all was calm, as if there had never been a storm at all."

"Of course the wind and water obey him!" cried the Magdalit. "He is the Holy One of God!"

Shimon shot her a glance. "You are right," he admitted. "The Master even said to us, 'Where is your faith?'

"But that's not all," continued Shimon, full of news and unable to conceal his wild excitement over the last few days. "Then we sailed to the region of the Gerasenes and were immediately accosted by a crazy man as soon as we stepped on shore. This fellow was na..." He stopped suddenly when he remembered that his audience was comprised of women. "Uh, that is, he was without proper garments," he said instead, red-faced.

Just then Shimon's brother, Andrew, came over to us. "Getting into trouble, are you?" he teased Shimon.

Shimon took a playful jab at him. "Sit down," he commanded. "I'm telling the ladies about our time away."

Andrew sat beside his brother while Shimon proceeded with his story.

"Anyway, this fellow had been living in the tombs on the outside of town, completely demon-possessed. No one wanted anything to do with him. He had been chained up day and night and kept under guard, but had broken his chains with superhuman strength and been driven by his demons into total isolation.

"It was like he was waiting for us. As soon as he saw us he cried out. He fell at the feet of the Master, shouting at the top of his voice, 'What do you want with me, Yeshua, Son of the Most High God? I beg you, don't torture me!'

"And we could see it on his face—it was torture for the demons to be in the Master's presence! Then Yeshua asked those demons, 'What is your name?'

"A voice said their name was Legion, because there were so many of them. They kept pleading with Yeshua not to send them into the Abyss."

"Oh, that poor man!" sympathized the Magdalit, tears of compassion welling up in her beautiful eyes. Rachel took her hand and stroked it softly.

"Yes, yes," I said impatiently. "Then what?"

"Then," began Shimon but Andrew cut him off.

"Then," said Andrew, "these demons were so desperate not to be sent into the Abyss that they pleaded with Yeshua to be allowed to enter a herd of pigs on the hillside. He permitted this, and the next thing we knew the entire herd of pigs thundered down this really steep bank." He started laughing at the memory of it and while he was in this condition his brother took over the story.

"We couldn't believe it," Shimon recalled. "All those pigs *threw* themselves into the lake."

"What happened to them?" gasped the Magdalit.

"Why, they were all drowned, of course," answered Shimon, matter-of-factly.

Andrew wiped his eyes. He had recovered from his bout of mirth. "The pig herders were not amused by this, let me tell you. They ran right to the town and spread around what had happened. Before we knew it, all these people showed up."

"Were they angry?" I asked.

"Well, before they even had a chance to be anything, they saw the demon-possessed man sitting at Yeshua's feet, dressed and in his right mind. That terrified them more than the pig incident."

"Weren't they glad to see him set free?" wondered Rachel.

"You would think they would be, wouldn't you, Miss Rachel," said Shimon, turning and smiling at her. "But they weren't. They were afraid of the power that was stronger than the demons. And they were afraid of financial ruin. After all, a large herd of pigs was dead."

What Shimon just said bothered me. "Wait a minute," I exclaimed. "We all agree that Yeshua is the Messiah, right?"

Right, everyone nodded.

"Well, then the Messiah has to be without sin, or so I'm told. Wasn't it a sin to destroy those pigs?"

Andrew and Shimon looked at each other. "Pigs are unclean animals," began Shimon. "No one should be eating them."

"But the people of the Gerasenes are Gentiles," I reminded him. "What difference does it make what they eat?"

"I guess it makes plenty of difference," said Andrew. "Maybe even the Gentiles are held to a certain standard. Yeshua wouldn't have sinned by allowing those demons access to the pigs. I think that Gentiles are expected to understand the difference between what is clean and what is unclean." He furrowed his brow. "But you've brought up an interesting question, Yohana. I'll ask the Master about this and tell you what he says."

"Okay, thanks," I replied, gratified that I was being taken seriously. Kuza would approve.

"But what about the poor man?" asked Miryam, always aware of the suffering of others, even after the rest of us had moved on to theological considerations.

"Oh," said Shimon, lifting his eyebrows. "I felt bad about that. You see, the people urged us to leave and he desperately wanted to come with us. He didn't want to leave Yeshua's side for an instant. Yeshua said no, though. He told this fellow to return home and tell how much God had done for him."

"And he agreed?" I wanted to know.

"He had no choice," said Andrew. "But, yes, I think he did. He wanted to do whatever Yeshua said. The change in him was really just amazing."

"Yeshua was right in not letting him come, even though it was a hard decision," affirmed Shimon. "Those people were so frightened of us that I don't know if they would have heard anything we had to say. This man is one of their own, and I think he'll be able to convince them of God's mercy and love very effectively."

Then the two men stood up. "Time to get going," announced Shimon, cheerfully. "We've given you all our news." They walked away, engrossed in conversation with each other.

We watched them. "It must be difficult for them to be away from their wives and children so much," remarked Shoshana.

"Why don't they join us?" asked Rachel.

"And what would we do with all the children?" I asked her.

"We'll put them to work," she answered.

"No," chimed in Shoshana. "They'll put *us* to work!" Laughing, our hearts light, filled with anticipation over the future, we returned to our day.

⚚⚛

Later that night, Yeshua found me as I was making a valiant effort to scrub the cooking pots. Sometimes we were invited to dinner but more often we fended for ourselves. I had grown to appreciate the hard work that went into preparing and cleaning up the meals that once appeared as if by magic on my table.

I was intent on what I was doing and didn't hear him come up behind me. When I turned around to grab another pot and saw him standing there, watching me, I gasped. "Lord! How long have you been here?"

"Just a minute." He regarded me critically. "You're getting good at this, aren't you?" He indicated the newly washed pots.

I felt my face redden. "Uh, I'm trying."

"Well, you're more than trying. You're succeeding." Yeshua sat down on the ground and invited me to join him. "Andrew spoke to me about your concern regarding the destruction of those pigs across the lake." Those warm brown eyes studied me.

"I wasn't accusing you of anything," I said hurriedly. "I just didn't understand."

"Don't apologize, Yohana. I want my disciples to think. You shouldn't blindly follow me. If I am who I say I am, then no question will be a difficulty. Right?"

"Right," I said, relieved.

"So," he said, sitting forward, chin in his hand. "Allowing those demons to drown the pigs wasn't a sin. Do you know why?"

"Why?" I breathed, happy just to be near him; to be treated to this unexpected time alone with the Lord.

"Because pigs are not food. They're scavengers. Those pigs were expressly being raised to be butchered for food. My Father set up guidelines as to what is food and what isn't."

"Even for the Gentiles?"

"Let me ask you a question, Yohana. Is God the God of the Jews or of the Gentiles, too?"

This seemed like such an easy question, but I realized I did not know the answer. The Gentiles were such pagans in my eyes. I thought about all their gods. I thought about their lewd and wicked practices. I thought about their foreign ways. Did God love them, too? Meanwhile, I was conscious of Yeshua's eyes upon my face, waiting.

"What about the woman from Syracuse at the Break the Fast?" he prompted softly. "She's a Gentile, yet God wanted her to know the truth, didn't he?"

"Lord, you know about her?" I don't know why I was amazed, but I was.

"I've come to the lost sheep of the House of Israel, but those in the nations who seek me with a broken and contrite heart will also receive salvation. I will turn away no one. My Father said of me that 'it is too small a thing for you to be my servant, to restore the tribes of Jacob and bring back those of Israel I have kept. I will also make you a light for the Gentiles, that you may bring my salvation to the ends of the earth.' "

"I've lived among the Romans at the palace, Sir. I've seen what they can do."

Yeshua put his hand on mine. "They're living in darkness. Can't you see that they're prisoners of their own sin?" His voice grew in passion and strength. "But so are the Jews. Human nature is consistent. All have sinned and fallen short of the glory of God."

"Then what hope is there, Sir?" I asked, alarmed.

"There's hope in me, Yohana. I am the door to the Father." He looked at me intently and I suddenly remembered my dream. He still held my hand. Now he squeezed it lightly. "Tell me, Yohana. Who do you think I am?"

I started to speak but was overwhelmed. The words caught in my throat. I breathed deeply and tried to talk through the storm of emotions which gathered within my breast. "You're my healer," I whispered. "You're my rabbi. You're my leader. You're my Lord." As I spoke, conviction grew and the words started to fly forth from my mouth. "You're the Messiah, the Son of the Living God."

"And how do you know that?"

"Well, there are the works that only the Messiah will do—and you have done them all! The blind see, the lame walk, but there's even more to it, isn't there?"

He nodded.

"It's as if the very truth of it is caught up in my spirit. And every day I spend with you convinces me more and more that you are not the same as the rest of us. And I mean that in a good way."

He laughed. "I understand." His eyes took hold of mine as he changed the topic. "Is there something you would like to ask me?"

"Ask you? Like what?"

"I know you have questions about events that took place long ago. I know you wonder about...Hana."

Hana! The very mention of her name shocked and jolted me. Instinctively, I tried to snatch my hand away from his but he held it fast.

"I don't understand," I mumbled. "How do you know about *her*?"

"I was with the Father in the beginning," he said. "Don't you realize that I know all things?"

"Then you know that I can't speak of her," I said stiffly, tears gathering underneath my eyelids.

"It's time, Yohana. It's time to give me the grief and the pain. It's too heavy a burden for you to bear anymore. You've carried it long enough." Yeshua looked at me intently. "You've carried it for ten years."

Ten years! Had it been that long already? Ten years since my precious little girl breathed her last. Ten years since Kuza and I buried her small body and a part of my heart with her, cold, dead, untouched. Now Yeshua was forcing me to expose that cold heart to the warmth of his love. I felt it begin to thaw with exquisite pain. "I don't know if I can do this," I confessed miserably. "I'm angry."

"Why are you angry, Yohana?"

"Because, because she was the only one, and God took her from me as well." The tears started to flow down my cheeks. Yeshua put his arms around me and held me close.

"It wasn't the Father who took Hana from you," he murmured soothingly into my hair. "There's sin in the world. When Adam and Eve ate the forbidden fruit in the garden, death entered the world. Not only death, but all the things leading up to it: pain, pestilence, sickness, grief. God mourned with you."

"Then why didn't He keep her alive?" I sobbed. "He has the power."

Yeshua sighed. "God is not a master puppeteer, constantly interfering with the affairs of man. It's true that he has brought people back from the edge of death, but that's the exception. Sin is powerful. Death is an enemy. The Son of Man has been sent into the world to conquer sin and death."

I raised my head. "Does that mean death will be no more?"

"Eventually. Not yet. Not until the one destined for the lake of fire has been completely subdued. That time is still to come. Meanwhile you must trust that God holds your life in the palm of His hand. You must

92

persevere." And he continued to hold me tightly.

As the Lord held me, and my sobs quieted, I could feel the pain and anger loose their claws from my heart. In their place burned love. Love is painful, too, I realized. Love leaves one naked, exposed, alive, and vulnerable.

The love with which Yeshua held me was totally protective and sheltering. I had no embarrassment over being in his arms. Instead, I felt like a small child cradled by her father. Deep waves of security and contentment washed over me. I soaked in the glory of his presence.

Soon I felt rather than heard the movement of his chest as he prayed to his father. The words, not Hebrew, were unrecognizable to me. I knew it was the language of angels that he spoke. As he prayed, he held me with one arm and with the other placed his hand on my head. I thought I could feel oil dripping down my face, but when I checked later, it was dry.

Later, much later, Yeshua kissed my forehead and said good night. As I cleaned up the last of the pots, drained but glowing, it occurred to me that he hadn't mentioned my brother Yishai. But of course he knew that I was not yet ready.

⤜⤛

The next day, the sun had barely risen in the east when the first wave of men, women and children descended on our camp. They were looking for Yeshua, looking for healing, looking for a touch, a word, a glance.

Yeshua, as was his custom, had risen while it was still dark and had gone off into the nearby hills to pray. When he returned, he immediately began to minister to those who sought him.

"I would that he at least eat something first," protested Miryam, alarmed that Yeshua had plunged right into his day without food.

"He'll be fine. Don't worry about it," I reassured her, though secretly I was fighting with being overwhelmed by seeing so many people this early. I felt I needed a little time to run through my usual morning agenda. I hadn't even had time to splash water on my face! But Yeshua felt no such restriction.

As the Lord prayed for those with various diseases, a man came rushing into the camp, surrounded by a small group of men. He was distraught, fatigued, weary from travel. On his head he wore the traditional covering of a synagogue ruler. I recognized Ya'ir, from Capernaum.

When he saw Yeshua, he gave a loud cry and fell down at Yeshua's feet, bowing his head into the dust.

"Please," he cried, looking up at the Lord with desperation in his eyes. "Please come to my house. My little girl is," he choked on the last word, "dying."

A collective gasp went up from the crowd around him. Ya'ir was well known in the local lake area. He and his beautiful wife, Sarah, had three sons, all older, but only one daughter. She was a delightful girl of only twelve years old, and both Ya'ir and Sarah doted on her. Always this child danced about, joyful and full of life, and so the news that she lay on her deathbed shocked many.

Yeshua and Ya'ir knew each other, and Yeshua immediately ceased ministering to the crowd around him and prepared to accompany Ya'ir back to his home. Capernaum was nearby; a five-mile walk from our campsite. The entire camp set out with Yeshua. "Pack some day provisions," yelled Shoshana, as we scrambled to ready ourselves for the walk. Hurriedly, I put a skin of water, some dates, almonds, and a hunk of barley bread into a bag. I strapped on my sandals, grabbed my walking stick, and rushed to catch up to the Lord.

Everywhere today there were people. More and more of them seemed to materialize out of nowhere. I noticed that Shimon, Andrew, Ya'akov, and Yochanan had formed a protective barrier around Yeshua as he walked, so that he would not get crushed by the hordes who kept throwing themselves at him.

The day was hot and the walk swift and uncomfortable. At one point, I had to break into a run to pull even with the Lord.

It was then that I saw her. A woman, probably no older than thirty-five, but as thin and wasted-looking as a seventy-year-old. She kept darting around the group directly behind Yeshua, one hand gripping her stomach, the other extended, a frightened yet determined look on her face.

She concerned me. I watched her carefully, working my way through the crowd so I could get closer to her. Once, I was within two people but was unable to get past them. I happened to look down and noticed what looked suspiciously like a few tiny drops of blood on the ground, mingling with the dust and the sparse vegetation.

Is she bleeding...? I thought to myself, horrified at the possibility. Torah clearly states that women who have a bloody discharge of any kind are considered unclean and that anyone who touches them will be considered unclean. *I hope she's not thinking about touching a tzadik, a holy man, like Yeshua,* I thought grimly.

I pushed my way through the crowd harder. Some people glared at me, but I ignored them. Just as I got within an arm's length of the woman, she succeeded in maneuvering herself directly behind Yeshua. I screamed out, "Watch it, Lord!" at precisely the same moment she reached down and touched the edge of his *tzit tzit*, the ritual fringes that hang off the edge of his cloak.

Abruptly, Yeshua stopped walking and stood still. "Who touched me?" he demanded.

He could not have heard me over the noise of the crowd. When the woman touched his garment, there was no way he could have felt it in the crush of people. We were all dumbfounded that he could single out one touch.

Everyone denied it, and Shimon even said, "Master, the people are crowding and pressing against you."

But Yeshua looked around. "Someone touched me; I know that power has gone out from me." His gaze rested on the face of the woman behind him, who stood trembling with fear. She had taken a great chance as she could easily be stoned to death for hiding her uncleanness. I saw that she realized she could not hope to remain anonymous, so she fell on her knees at Yeshua's feet and haltingly told him that it was indeed she who had reached out and touched his *tzit tzit*.

"Please forgive me, Sir," she cried. "I've had bleeding for twelve years and gone from doctor to doctor. They took all my money and my hope was almost gone when I heard about you. I knew you could heal me but how could I ask? But," she added, awe coming over her face, "I can tell that I've been delivered from that which made me an outcast!"

While this exchange was going on, Ya'ir stood impatiently, shifting his weight from foot to foot, restless for the Rabbi to stop talking and keep walking to his house. Yeshua, however, would not be rushed. He spoke kindly to the woman, encouraging her to tell more of her story, nodding in sympathy as she confided in him (and to the rest of us) details of the years of suffering she had endured. She gazed up at him adoringly. I recognized the signs: he had made another disciple.

Finally, the Lord brought his time with this woman to a close. He placed his hand on her head and blessed her, saying, "Daughter, your faith has healed you. Go in peace."

I could see Ya'ir's relief that they were done and could keep walking. But hardly had Yeshua finished speaking when a man came running toward us from the direction of Capernaum. When Ya'ir saw this fellow, his face turned a deathly white. "Why are you here, Sheva?" he croaked, his voice uneven. "What's going on?"

"I came to tell you," the man called Sheva panted, worn out from running. "Your daughter is dead. Don't bother the Rabbi any more."

A loud moan went up from the crowd and Ya'ir, blanching, seemed to crumble. But Yeshua grasped him by the elbow. Speaking urgently to Ya'ir, he said loud enough for us all to hear, "Don't be afraid; just believe, and she will be healed."

Ya'ir started to say, "But," when Yeshua stopped him. "No, man, don't go there. *Just believe.*"

A very subdued group of people followed Yeshua and Ya'ir to Capernaum. Upon arriving, they quickly made their way through the streets to the beautiful, spacious villa where Ya'ir lived.

Ya'ir's wife, Sarah, saw us coming and ran out of the house, eyes red from weeping. She threw herself at her husband, sobbing loudly. "You took too long." She wept brokenly. "Our child, our beloved daughter..." Numbly, she allowed the rest of the sentence to lapse.

Ya'ir put his arms around her. "Shh, shh," he comforted her. "Don't despair. The Rabbi says to believe and she will be healed."

Sarah lifted her tear-streaked face to Yeshua, and hope mingled with despair passed over her face. *Could it be?*

"Come," said Yeshua. He summoned Shimon, Yochanan, and Ya'akov and told them to accompany him into the house, along with the child's parents. He refused to let any of the rest of us follow.

Meanwhile, the crowd was wailing and mourning for the dead girl.

"Stop it," Yeshua shouted, annoyed by the commotion. "I tell you, she is not dead but asleep."

What happened next infuriated me. *The crowd laughed at Yeshua!* The same people who had been so desperate for a touch from him that they raided our camp at sunrise now jeered and mocked. Across the heads of a half-dozen people, my eyes met Shoshana's and I could tell she felt the same as me. I pushed my way over to her.

"Can you believe these people?" I fumed, once I was next to her.

"Yes," she said sadly. "I can."

Then the two of us held hands and prayed for the Lord to bring forth a powerful miracle this day in the Name of Adonai.

Later, Shimon and Yochanan told us that when they entered the house, cool, dark, and quiet in sharp contrast to the tumult outside, Sarah had silently led them to the bedroom where the dead girl lay. Her long, dark curls fanned out on the clean, white pillow, her small face thin and serene. Her young body, usually so active, now lay still and becalmed, like a boat caught out on the lake on a day with no wind.

In great surprise, the talmidim witnessed Yeshua take her hand in his, since the Torah of Moshe commands us not to touch any dead thing, lest we be unclean till evening. He sat next to her for some time, softly praying. Then, still holding onto her hand, in a loud, strong voice he spoke to her, saying, "Little girl, get up!"

With utter amazement, Ya'ir, Sarah, Shimon, Yochanan, and Ya'akov watched as the child's long dark eyelashes fluttered, and her eyes opened! Next, she pushed aside the bed covers and climbed out of the bed, blinking. Sarah and Ya'ir astonished, rushed to embrace their daughter.

"How can we ever thank you," they cried out to Yeshua, the child clasped in their arms.

"First, give her something to eat," he told them. Then he added something puzzling. "Don't tell anyone what happened."

❧ ❧

"Why not tell people?" I asked Shimon, when he related this story to me.

He frowned, scratching the back of his head. "None of us were sure. But," he added, in a moment of uncompromising honesty, "no one wanted to ask him!"

"Well," reflected Yochanan, "I think Yeshua probably doesn't want to draw undue attention to himself."

"Draw undue attention to himself!" I sputtered. "What about those huge crowds that follow him?"

"There may be a line between drawing undue attention and *really* drawing undue attention," commented Yochanan, wryly.

We all sat quietly then. I thought about Herod, and the palace, and the greedy Romans, and the high priests. I thought about political intrigue, and how powerful men desired to crush anyone who presented a threat to their control. I had become so immersed in the world of ministry that I had forgotten these things. Now a cold hand of fear touched its icy fingers to my heart.

"Do you believe there's any danger to Yeshua?" I asked the men.

"I don't see how there can be," pondered Shimon. "After all, he's the Messiah, isn't he?"

FIVE

The cold rains of winter were upon us. Yeshua called all of us together, and outlined his plans for the coming months.

He told us women that we were to return to our homes until spring. He would send word when we were to resume our time with the ministry. He entrusted the Magdalit to my care.

The twelve talmidim were being raised to the next level of ministry. Instead of all of us together, with Yeshua in our midst, they were to be sent, in pairs, out on their own. "I give you power and authority to drive out demons and to cure diseases, to preach the kingdom of God and to heal the sick," he told them.

"Take nothing for the journey—no staff, no bag, no bread, no money, no extra tunic. Whatever house you enter, stay there until you leave that town. If people do not welcome you, shake the dust off your feet when you leave their town, as a testimony against them."

The talmidim were elated by the trust Yeshua showed them. Eager to set out for the surrounding villages, they were gone within the space of two days. Several other people left and the camp had that breaking apart feeling. Yeshua himself planned to return to Capernaum. He resolved to spend intensive time in prayer; plus he had some family issues to attend to.

By the fourth day, Adaba, Rachel, Miryam, and myself had packed up several donkeys and were heading up to Jerusalem. The days of traveling in a lightweight chariot were a distant memory. Now I considered myself fortunate to be able to ride on an animal and not have to walk.

Although I looked forward with great anticipation to seeing Kuza, I was decidedly unsettled at leaving Yeshua. His presence brought such peace! Such security! I found that when I was near him, I had strength for anything. Now, as every jolting step of my donkey brought me further from him and closer to Jerusalem, I continually found that my mind strayed to worries and fears about my re-entry into palace life. I had no idea what, if anything, Herod had known of my departure.

The trip was a dreary one. Thankfully, we did not encounter either bandits or Roman soldiers. Wrapped in cloaks against the winds and rains, we endured the long journey. It occurred to me once or twice that six months ago this kind of grueling excursion would have killed me, but not now. My healing, followed by months of simple food and hard work, had transformed my flabby, luxury-fed body into a lean, hard one.

In fact, all of us, even Adaba, who had already seemed to be the picture of physical fitness, were much stronger than ever before. If only I could push away my anxiety about the palace!

My reunion with Kuza was deeply satisfying, if not a little subdued. He seemed older than I remembered, fine lines around his eyes and more gray in his hair. I could tell that he was worried, concerned about the direction Yeshua's ministry was taking, concerned about the constantly shifting power base at the palace, concerned about us.

I spent hours and hours relaying to Kuza everything I could remember that had happened since I had last seen him. Fascinated, he rarely interrupted, except for occasional clarification on some point or other. When I told him about the young daughter of the synagogue ruler being raised from the dead, and how Yeshua had cautioned the parents not to say anything, Kuza grew agitated.

"What is it?" I asked, ever sensitive to his moods.

He shook his head. "Why doesn't Yeshua want his most amazing miracles known?"

"Well," I ventured, "Yochanan believes that there's such a thing as drawing too much attention to oneself."

"Yes, I understand," said Kuza. "But if he's the Messiah, the coming King, he should want to galvanize the people. Heaven knows we desperately need to replace this corrupt government. Why isn't he proclaiming himself king and driving Herod and the Romans out?"

"What's wrong, Kuza?" I queried, putting my arms around him.

"It's getting worse and worse every day, Yohana," he said bleakly, his voice hoarse. "The fantastic sums of money being spent on sheer nonsense while all over this country men and women are struggling to survive after paying huge taxes to Rome. I swear, Herod gets crazier every day."

"Don't swear," I admonished him.

"What?"

"Yeshua says not to swear," I patiently explained. "He says let your yes be yes and your no be no. He says that we don't have the power to turn even one hair white."

Kuza stared at me. "Thank you, my dear wife, for that teaching," he said, a slight edge to his voice.

"I'm being annoying, aren't I?"

"I'm happy to have you home," he said, by way of not answering.

"Has my absence been noticed?" I asked, changing the topic.

"You're really more noticeable than you think," he answered. "Of course it's been noticed!"

"What have you said?"

Kuza grimaced. "At first, nothing. I avoided the questions. Then I found myself, contrary to all good judgment, telling the truth."

My eyes widened in surprise. "You told the truth?" I repeated incredulously.

"Don't be so shocked," he chided me. "It's not the first time."

I laughed. "Oh, I know that, my love. But what have people said? And what, exactly, did *you* say?"

"I kept remembering Yeshua cautioning me against fear. That, and the fact that my relief and pleasure at your extraordinary healing bubbled up in me daily. I started talking about it to those who asked about you. I started talking about where you were...about *Yeshua*."

"And how was it received?"

"There was a definite mix of reactions. Some people grew highly agitated and didn't want to hear any more. A few were just the opposite; they came to me repeatedly with more questions. And one or two already knew about Yeshua but had been secretive."

"Who already knew?" I asked, curiously.

Kuza looked at me. "Remember that pleasant young man from the Sanhedrin we met a few years back at the Feast of Sukkot? Nakdimon?"

"*Him!*" I squeaked, astonishment elevating my voice an octave. "*He knows the Lord?*"

"He was desperately grateful to have someone to talk with," reflected Kuza. "Apparently, he had met with Yeshua surreptitiously some time back. He had heard that Yeshua came as a teacher from God. He believed that no one could do the miracles which Yeshua did if God was not with him. Yeshua spoke with him extensively about being 'born again.' "

"Yes," I said. "I've heard him use that expression."

"Nakdimon was profoundly affected by the concept of being born from water and the Spirit. He told me that Yeshua said to him that God so loved the world that He gave His only and unique Son, so that everyone who trusts in him may have eternal life, instead of being utterly destroyed. He realized that Yeshua was referring to himself as God's Son." Kuza paused, then added. "Nakdimon believes that the Sanhedrin will put Yeshua to death for such statements."

"Even if they're true?" I objected, angrily.

"Even if they're true," confirmed Kuza, with a sad smile.

"But they can't, since he's the Messiah," I announced triumphantly. "He'll destroy all his enemies."

"Will he?" murmured Kuza.

"What do you mean, 'will he?' " I demanded.

"He's not acting like a messiah who will conquer and rule his kingdom. What you told me about the synagogue ruler's daughter, and how when she was raised from the dead he didn't want it known—these are not the actions of a man who intends to take Jerusalem by storm and plant himself on the throne."

"What are they the actions of then?" I asked with trepidation.

Kuza bit his bottom lip and stared thoughtfully at me. He drew in his breath, started to speak, then stopped. I waited as he paced nervously back and forth. Finally he said, in a voice so quiet that I had to strain to hear him, "These are the actions of a man who knows he's going to die."

ⅆⅆ

As it turned out, Yeshua had become very well known. All of Jerusalem buzzed with rumors of this mysterious prophet who performed miracles unheard of since the days of Elijah the Prophet. Different people came forth with different theories as to who he was. Some claimed that the Yochanan whom Herod had murdered had been raised from the dead. Others believed that Elijah himself had appeared. Still others hypothesized that one of the prophets of long ago had come back to life.

Herod himself grew interested, and indeed, was not a little perplexed. "I had Yochanan beheaded," he confessed. "So who is this about whom I keep hearing such things?"

Herod greatly desired to see Yeshua, and it came to his attention that I had traveled this past fall with Yeshua's Company. He told Kuza that he wished to speak with me, and set a time for Kuza to bring me into his presence the next morning.

When Kuza returned to our apartment that afternoon, burdened and tense, he held me to himself for a long time before he told me all this.

"Well, we knew it was only a matter of time," I said, trying to keep my voice light despite the sudden wrenching in my gut. "Will you be with me?"

He nodded.

"Obviously, we need to pray. I'll call Miryam, Rachel, and Adaba to join us. Can you stay, or do you need to get back to work?"

"I have some time, not a lot," said Kuza.

Quickly, I summoned my three companions and filled them in on the latest news. The five of us clasped hands and stood in a circle. We began to pray, calling out to God the Father for favor and deliverance from Herod. After several minutes, Miryam, her eyes still closed, spoke up. "We need to fast," she proclaimed.

"Fast?" I repeated.

"Yes," she said, "Like Queen Esther."

Now five hundred years before, during the Babylonian Captivity, Queen Esther had called a three-day fast for herself, her maids, and the Jews of Susa in order to prepare the way for Esther to approach the King, her husband, about the diabolical plot of wicked Haman. He wanted to annihilate all the Jews in the entire Persian Kingdom. I, however, was scheduled to see Herod in less than twenty-four hours.

"I'm seeing the king tomorrow morning. It won't be a three-day fast," I informed Miryam.

"It may be before we're through," she predicted. "I really feel that we should devote ourselves to prayer and not eat until we have an assurance that your interview with Herod went well." She looked around the circle at our faces. "What do you all think?"

We all nodded.

"Sounds good," agreed Kuza. "Look, it's getting late and I need to get back to work. I'll see you all later." He hurried out of the apartment.

After he left, an idea occurred to me. I turned to the Magdalit. "Wait a minute, Miryam. Didn't Yeshua tell Yochanan the Immerser's talmidim that his talmidim *didn't* fast because the bridegroom was still with them? And that when the bridegroom was gone there would be plenty of time to fast? So do you think we should fast?"

"My lady," she answered me, tears in her eyes. "With all due respect, look around. He's not here."

I couldn't argue with her logic. However, I did have an assurance that the Lord would send for us by spring. *If* I emerged unscathed from my interview with the king. I sighed. I certainly did not feel like Queen Esther. Maybe on my wedding day I felt as beautiful as the legendary monarch but definitely not in my mid forties. I sighed again. It was also going to take the favor of God for me to fast for an indefinite period. I tend to be thin (some, rather harshly, would even dare to call me bony!) and fasting for even the one day at Yom Kippur stretched me. I had one thing in my favor, though. My stomach hurt at the thought of seeing Herod.

I spent most of the rest of that day and night on my knees before God. Never have I invested so much sweat and tears into a supplication before Him. Even when disease ravaged my body, I had not the motivation to pray that I did now. My husband and friends joined me in prayer, and the linking of our hearts was sweet indeed.

Adaba asked if he should try to find Yeshua and let him know what was happening. After briefly thinking it over, Kuza told him no. "There's no time," he explained. "It would take you at least three days to find him, and that's too long. Stay here with us. Pray and fast. God will hear us."

Reluctantly, Adaba obeyed. I could tell that he longed to find the Lord. I had to trust that God heard my prayers. It was so easy to have faith when Yeshua was right there.Now God was pushing me to trust Him even when I looked around and couldn't physically see the Lord.

All too soon, it was time to go in to see Herod. Kuza had already left for his office but came back to escort me into the throne room. We said little to one another on that long walk through the familiar pillared, marbled halls. It was only when we reached the massive double doors that led into the throne room that Kuza reached out and grasped my hands.

"It's up to God," he said, simply.

"Yes," I said. And pushed open the door.

All I could remember afterwards was the buzzing in my head and my shaking knees. Kuza assured me that I answered quite coherently and even looked Herod in the eye. The king was actually quite pleasant, for him. He greeted me amiably and bid Kuza and me to sit down. Then he pushed himself off his throne and came over to us, his long, regal robes swirling about his legs. He sat close to me, very close, and peered into my face. I was faintly repulsed by the cruel lines around his mouth, and his overly pampered and perfumed hair and skin. I kept my face as neutral as possible, desperate not to betray my emotions.

I vaguely recall a series of questions about Yeshua, and I tried to answer them in as honest a fashion as I could, while not giving away any information that could bring harm to either Yeshua or anyone in his camp.

It soon became apparent that Herod's greatest concern was whether Yeshua was Yochanan the Immerser come back from the grave. I did my best to assure him that they were two very different men. I admit that I was not so brave as Yochanan, and did not attempt to rebuke Herod for his actions in murdering Yochanan; nor did I call him to repentance.

I also spoke carefully when it came to telling Herod that I believed Yeshua was a prophet, sent from God to call men to repentance that they might enter the Kingdom of Heaven. I tried not to in any way suggest competition between Herod's earthly kingship and Yeshua's heavenly one, though I had no idea what the future held. I attempted to communicate Yeshua's respect for authority and the fact that he did not seek to capitalize on his popularity with the common people. I also tried to tone down that popularity, so as not to enrage Herod.

When Herod asked if I intended to leave Jerusalem to follow Yeshua in the coming days and months, I swallowed hard, my mouth dry, and said as nonchalantly as possible (though my heart pounded in my chest so hard I feared that the guards on either side of the throne room could hear it), "If it meets with your approval, O most worthy king."

Herod drummed his fingers thoughtfully and grunted something incoherent. Then he wanted to know if I could arrange a meeting between himself and Yeshua.

I started to panic, but I felt Kuza's steady gaze upon my face and it calmed me. "I'll try," I heard myself say. "I haven't seen him in some time and don't expect to before spring, but when I do, I'll let him know of your desires." I held my breath and prayed, aware that Herod had sent men to torture chambers for failing to meet his demands immediately, no matter how unreasonable.

Mercifully, my answer seemed to satisfy him. He gave me a half-hearted attempt at a smile and waved us up. "You may go," he allowed. "Kuza, I'll see you later." He turned his back on us and languidly settled himself back on his throne, waiting for his next appointment.

Kuza and I bowed and backed out of the throne room. Once outside, I knew better than to try to speak so I kept silent as we walked back to our apartment.

"I'll just walk you home," said Kuza, both to me and for the benefit of anyone listening to us. "And then I'll be at the office. There's a finance meeting this afternoon."

"Very well," I responded, automatically.

When we reached our apartment, and were safely inside, I was immediately caught up in an embrace from both Rachel and the Magdalit. I sank against them heavily, my face drained of color.

"Is she all right, sir?" the concerned women enquired of Kuza.

"Yes, everything is fine," he assured them, half-walking, half-carrying me to the nearest chair.

Rachel ran and poured wine into a goblet and brought it to me, beseeching me, "My lady, please drink. It will revive you."

But I refused. "No, no, the fast...," I protested, weakly. "It's too soon to break the fast."

It was obvious that both women desperately wanted to find out what had happened but hesitated to push too soon. Kuza took pity on them.

"Do you want to know how things went?" he asked innocently.

Miryam's eyes flashed while Rachel murmured a demure, "As it pleases you, sir." But they both looked up.

"All in all, better than could be expected," began Kuza.

I rallied. "Do you really think so?"

"Definitely. The king was actually quite mild, I thought. The real test will be if he thinks about this too much and calls you back in the next few days."

"Then we need to keep fasting," put in Rachel, quickly.

"Yes," consented Kuza. "Also, he asked Yohana to arrange a meeting for himself with Yeshua. If, or when, that doesn't come to pass I'm not sure what Herod will do."

"There's only one way to find out about that," I stated, rousing myself.

"What," they all asked.

"Ask Yeshua."

❦

As it turned out, I saw Yeshua much sooner than I expected. Two weeks later was the Feast of Dedication, or, as it is popularly known, *Hanukkah*.

I quite enjoy Hanukkah. About 190 years ago, the Syrian Greek forces of Antiochus Epiphanes invaded Israel. Not content with merely draining us financially, they also attempted to destroy Judaism. In an effort to make everyone uniformly Greek, Antiochus built a gymnasium in Jerusalem. He banned the study of Torah, the keeping of Shabbat, and *brit-milah* (circumcision). He also offered sacrifices to idols and defiled the Temple with foul and unclean practices. Most people bowed down to his dictates but those who would not were tortured and killed.

One of the most diabolical methods of subduing people was to nail mothers to a stake with their dead babies tied around their necks. The decaying bodies of the little ones hastened the vicious death by crucifixion. The Romans still kill people today by crucifying them. It is a horrible way to die.

In a series of miraculous events, we, the Israelites, led by Yehuda the Macabee, drove the Syrians out of our land and regained the Temple. Levites flocked to Jerusalem to begin the arduous task of cleansing God's house. A legend has been handed down through the generations that only a one day's supply of holy olive oil needed for lighting the *ner tamid* could be found. It would take eight days to acquire more. But, impatient for the sacrifices of the Temple to begin, the priest lit the menorah anyway. The oil which they had for one day lasted eight! I have also heard that the Festival of Sukkot, banned for several years, was now celebrated by all the people during these eight days.

Every year, in the winter month of Kislev, we light candles for eight days in commemoration of the rededication of the Temple back to Adonai. It is a festival of lights, a beautiful, glowing reminder during the dark, cold winter that miracles *do* happen, and that victory *is* obtainable. It never ceases to amaze me that Pilate and the rest of the Roman conquerors allow us to celebrate Hanukkah. Makes me wonder if they fully understand our hope to rid the land of such as them.

This year, I went with Kuza to the Temple for a candlelight ceremony at dusk. Wrapped snugly in a warm, fur-lined cloak, my head covered, I eagerly anticipated the beauty of the coming liturgy.

Most everyone there was bundled up. Earlier in the day cold rains had descended. Though the sun came out about an hour or so before it was due to set, puddles uncharacteristically dotted the ground and the chill set one's teeth to chattering.

Still, it was exhilarating to be in the midst of such a great company of revelers. Friends and families greeted one another in a burst of holiday good will. Rivalries and concerns over the Romans were put aside as together we Jews celebrated the rededication of the Temple.

And the Temple itself! The Levites had outdone themselves in polishing, cleaning and enhancing the already spectacular brilliance of God's holy house. An enormous nine-branched menorah dominated a section of one wall in the Court of the Gentiles. The middle candle, known as the *shamash*, or servant, was used to light the other candles. Since it was the first night, only one candle would be lit. A big vat of olive oil fueled the candle. The resulting flame shot high up into the sky and could be seen at great distances.

As I joined with the assembly, transfixed by the reflective light, shadows everywhere dancing and leaping with the movement of the flame, I suddenly became aware of a man standing very still on the other side of Kuza. His face stayed hidden by the hood of his cloak but his stance...*oh my, it was the Lord!*

My first impulse was to scream and kiss his feet, but I quickly gained control of myself. Clearly Yeshua did not desire to be recognized, not with Herod desperate to corner him. And Herod had proven himself to be a menace where true prophets of God were concerned.

Instead, I poked Kuza in the ribs with my elbow. It took a couple of jabs but he got the message. Turning to me, brow furrowed, about to rebuke me for hitting him, he abruptly stopped when he saw the warning glance that flashed from my eyes. I ever so slightly tilted my head in the direction of Yeshua. Kuza slowly looked at the man next to him who pulled back his hood just enough to reveal his true identity.

He spoke to us softly, confidentially. "I know what you have been going through," he said, keeping his voice barely above a whisper. "And I tell you *do not fear.* Stay strong and believe. No harm will come to you." Then he said something that I will treasure for the rest of my life. "I am honored to call you my friends." He bowed his head and slipped away into the crowd.

Kuza and I gripped hands. When we looked at each other, I saw his eyes were moist, as were mine.

৵৶

At the palace, we continued to walk cautiously for the rest of that dreary winter. Herod only brought up Yeshua to me one more time and when I disavowed any knowledge of where he currently was, seemed to be satisfied. Grunting, he waved me away, seemingly forgetting about me.

Kuza, Rachel, Miryam, Abada, and myself all learned to spend more and more time in prayer. We derived great strength from Yeshua's directive not to fear. If I felt panic or anxiety coming on, I stopped as soon as I had the chance and prayed to God the Father, putting before Him the promise Yeshua himself had given me. Always, *always*, I experienced relief and quiet.

Two months after the end of Hanukkah, at the *rosh chosesh*, new moon, at the start of the month of Adar, I received the signal that it was time to rejoin Yeshua and the talmidim. This time Kuza agonized greatly over whether or not to accompany me. Finally, after much prayer and deliberation, he came to the conclusion that he was supposed to remain where he was. Both of us clung to the promise of Yeshua's protection. It was not an easy parting.

I found subtle changes upon my reunion with the Company. The hierarchy surrounding the twelve talmidim had crystallized. Where once all had easy access to the Master, now only Shimon Kefa, Andrew, Yochanan, and Ya'akov did. The others needed to go through these four men in order to see Yeshua.

I noticed that Yeshua's relationship with Yochanan ben Zavdai had altered the most. An intimacy, a bonding of hearts, drew the two men together. A friend closer than a brother were words that could be used for them. Yochanan sat at Yeshua's feet and thirstily drank in all that the Master taught. He reminded me of the Magdalit in this regard. I tended to be more like Shimon Kefa. I think we both loved the Lord as much as Yochanan and Miryam, yet we had trouble slowing down and just soaking in the Lord's presence. We did it...but not to the extent we had the opportunity. Of course I regret that now.

Yehuda from K'riot seemed even less agreeable than before. He was not around as often as he should have been, which tended to annoy the other talmidim. I have to admit that I felt a sense of relief over his many absences.

Another change in the Company was the addition of Yeshua's mother, Miryam. I had met her briefly but now relished the possibility of befriending her. An opportunity came soon. A gentle, unassuming woman only a few years older than myself but without having lived my life of luxury, she nevertheless exuded an aura of dignity. She had a humble yet commanding presence. Obviously used to hard work, to which her calloused hands testified, she didn't take advantage of her status as the Rabbi's mother to avoid the more menial tasks. On the contrary, she was at all times a model for us by her selfless and cheerful behavior.

I stood in awe of her at first, and hesitated to get to know her as I didn't want it to look as if I were attempting to ingratiate myself. Shoshana soon disavowed me of that notion.

"Miryam is a truly astonishing woman. You really should get to know her," she told me one day as we were packing up belongings for a trek to yet another town bordering the lake.

"I don't know," I said, in what I hoped conveyed a humble tone. "I don't want to seem grasping."

108

Shoshana stared at me, incredulity stamped on her noble brow. "Tell me you're joking," she exclaimed. "For you to miss an opportunity to get to know Miryam because you're afraid of how it would make you *look* is just the silliest thing I think I've ever heard."

"I just don't want to seem like I'm chasing after her because she's Yeshua's mother."

"Give her more credit than that. She knows that you wouldn't be here if you didn't love and believe in her son. To her, that's plenty."

I took Shoshana's advice. Interestingly enough, the very next day I found myself side by side with Miryam, washing clothes at the lake while the men went into town to let people know that Yeshua would be teaching in the afternoon.

"Shalom," I greeted her, dipping a shirt into the cold water, dabbing some lye on a stain and trying not to wince as the caustic soap bit into my hands. The winter at the palace had softened my callouses.

In reply, Miryam looked at my tender, red hands. "Here, let me help you," she generously offered, as she took the shirt from me and plunged it into the lake.

"I need a few more weeks to get accustomed to this life again," I apologetically told her, relieved to have her take over and also excited at my first real conversation with this most interesting woman.

Miryam laughed. "I was five years old when I started helping my mother do the wash. Tell me about yourself, Yohana. I know so little."

Tell about me? I thought to myself. *I want to hear about you.* Obediently, I filled her in with some sketchy details about my early life and then told her of Kuza and life at the palace. Her eyes grew moist as I recounted the murder of Yochanan.

"His mother, Elisheva, is my cousin," she told me. "It saddened me greatly to hear of his death."

"How is she?"

"She's no longer alive. She was much older than me and passed on a few years ago." Miryam paused in her scrubbing and gazed out over the lake. "I still miss her."

"Were you very close?" I asked, enjoying my time with Miryam, eager to keep her talking.

"She was the person I hurried to see when I discovered that I was with child. With Yeshua."

My heart beat faster as Miryam made allusion to the birth of Yeshua. Rumors circulated to the effect that his was no ordinary birth and that it was a fulfillment of prophecy by Isaiah that a virgin would bear the

Messiah. At that time, Miryam's story was not widely known. "I would very much like to hear about that time in your life," I ventured with what I hoped was the right blend of deference and interest.

"Do you have some time?" she asked, wringing out *was that her third? fourth?* shirt and placing it smoothly onto the dry sand. When I happily nodded in the affirmative, she reached into the basket and pulled out several squares of cut linen that we used for towels, shook some lye on them, handed a few to me, and together we thrust them into the water. As she and I worked, she spoke, her soft voice soothing in the warm, morning sun.

"When I was a young girl, fourteen years of age, I became betrothed to a carpenter from my hometown. He was about ten years older than I, handsome and kind. His name was Yosef ben Ya'akov. I couldn't wait to marry him." Miryam stopped agitating the towels and paused, hands in the water, a smile lighting up her face as she recalled her beloved as a young man.

"I was a serious and devout girl, always eager to obey Adonai. Within a few weeks of becoming engaged to Yosef, I had a most spectacular experience."

"What?" I asked, enthralled.

"I saw a *malach,* an angel. He appeared to me early one morning during my prayers. He said his name was Gavriel and that God was with me."

"Oh my," I said, shielding my eyes with one wet hand so that I could look at Miryam more closely. "What did he look like?"

"Huge and powerful. Dazzlingly white. I can't really describe him because words are so inadequate. I instinctively knew that he meant me no harm but still I was terrified by his glowing appearance. Gavriel told me not to be afraid and informed me that I would become pregnant, give birth to a son whom I would name Yeshua, and that this child would inherit the throne of King David and rule forever."

"Stunning," I exclaimed, awed.

Miryam looked at me and nodded. "Especially for a fourteen-year-old."

"What did you possibly say to such amazing words?"

"The only thing that came to mind was that I was a virgin so this was impossible!" She laughed at the memory. "The angel responded by informing me that the *Ruach HaKodesh,* or Holy Spirit, would come upon me and the holy child born to me would be called the Son of God. He further let me know that my cousin Elisheva was to have a baby boy as well in the next three months."

"What did you do? Did you tell your parents?"

Miryam shook her head. "I was so overwhelmed by the experience and so unsure as to people's reactions that I immediately left for Elisheva's house, knowing that she more than anyone would understand what had happened to me. By the time I reached her home in the hill country of Judah, I was already with child."

"Did she understand?"

"More than I could even hope. Before she even said shalom, she said, 'Blessed are you among women! And how blessed is the child in your womb! But who am I that the mother of my Lord should come to me?' She said other things as well, which confirmed for me that my experience with the Angel Gavriel was very, very real."

"Did you stay with her until you had the baby?"

"No, only three months until little Yochanan was born. After his *brit milah*, I returned to Natzeret. It was time to tell Yosef about my pregnancy. My time with Elisheva had served to strengthen and encourage me so that I could face him without fear."

She grew silent and I reflected on her words. How frightening it must have been for the young Miryam! For a betrothed girl to present herself with child to her intended would have given him the right to have her stoned to death for betrayal. Miryam needed to trust that God would take care of her. Obviously, she was a woman of remarkable character and resilience.

"How did Yosef respond?" I asked, eager to hear more of her fascinating story.

She smiled wryly, tucking a stray lock of hair back inside her head covering. "He was outraged. But even worse than that, he was very, very, hurt. I tried to tell him what had happened, but he pushed my words away. The pain inside of him was terrible to behold. He told me he loved me and was sick that I had been with another man. And then he cried."

"Oh, Miryam!" I, too, wanted to cry for the Yosef of years past. "Did you explain that you were still a virgin?"

"I tried, but it sounded ridiculous to him. Who had ever heard of such a thing? A virgin with child? Impossible! I had no choice but to watch him walk away from me, shoulders bent, head down. I went home and got on my knees and prayed to God for hours, begging Him to make it all right."

"What happened then?"

"I found out later that Yosef loved me so much that he intended to break the engagement quietly so as not to hold me up to public ridicule, or worse, stoning. But that night, the same night I cried out to Adonai, Yosef fell into a fitful and uneasy sleep and an angel of God appeared to him in a dream and said, 'Yosef, son of David, do not be afraid to take Miryam home with you as your wife; for what has been conceived in her is from the *Ruach HaKodesh*. She will give birth to a son, and you are to name him Yeshua because he will save his people from their sins.' "

"Absolutely spectacular," I breathed.

Miryam stood up and spread the now clean towels on the sand to dry next to the shirts. "Yes, it was," she agreed, her eyes brightening at the recollection. "I've always known God's love and protection, Yohana. All my life He has been training me to trust Him implicitly."

I sat back on the warm sand, wriggling my toes contentedly. "Tell me more," I implored, ready to listen all day. But Miryam politely declined.

"That's enough for now," she said, with such a charming smile that I couldn't be disappointed. "It's time to get back to the others." She glanced at the clothes drying on the ground. "We should be able to come back for these in less than an hour."

Stretching, elated over my burgeoning friendship with Miryam, I grabbed the basket and followed her back to the camp.

⚘⚘

"You were right," I crowed to Shoshana later that day, when we were washing the evening dishes together.

"About what?"

"Miryam, Yeshua's mother. I really like her. I can't wait to get to know her better."

"That's wonderful, Yohie," Shoshana dutifully replied in a tired voice.

For the first time that evening I noticed that my usually joyful friend was silent, almost gloomy. I put down my wet dish.

"Tell me," I insisted. "What's troubling you?"

Shoshana's expressive eyes filled with tears. "It's my children," she confessed. "They're so angry, so—" she groped for the right word—"hostile. When I left to come back here, they threatened me. Told me that if I kept following after Yeshua and continued to call him 'Lord' that they would tell the Temple authorities and have me thrown out of the synagogue." She slumped down on the ground and cradled her head in her arms. "I can't believe it," she cried, her voice muffled. "My babies to whom I gave birth and nursed!" She started to sob.

"Oh, Shoshie!" Lowering myself to the ground next to her, silently praising God for healing my hip such that I *could* bend in this direction, I put my arms around her and held her while she cried. I didn't know what to say, so I silently prayed for God to comfort her, and allowed her to give vent to her emotions.

After a while her sobs abated. She rested her head on my shoulder, occasionally sniffling. "*B'seder.* I'm okay now. I love it here. I love Miryam, I love the other Miryam (she meant Yeshua's mother), I love *you,* I especially love Yeshua. But I also love my children and it's so hard to watch them cut themselves out of the most extraordinary opportunity of their lives." She pulled away from me, hugged her legs, and stared out across the camp. "Do you realize, Yohie," Shoshana said, still gazing at the vista before her, "that we're in daily contact with the *Messiah?* Does it never cease to astound you that the one whom the prophets longed to see *is actually here in our midst?* That's he's the true king of Israel, not that cruel man back in Jerusalem? That we can see him, touch him, laugh with him, eat with him? That he knows our names and loves us? Oh, that my children could see the salvation waiting right before their eyes!" She picked restlessly at a few straggly blades of grass next to her. "Instead, they're panicked over what the neighbors will say!"

"I know, Shosh, I know. I see them all the time at the palace. Men and women so caught up in gathering power or riches for themselves that they've forgotten that they can die any day. Forgotten, or never bothered to understand, that this life is temporal but eternity is forever. Forgotten that the gold and silver they accumulate will long outlast them, and it will not care who its next master may be. That's why Kuza and I are risking the wrath of Herod. We have finally realized that even if Herod were to kill us, he is powerless to touch our souls. But if we die, rich, fat, comfortable and full of years, but apart from the presence of God, what hope have we?"

"None," she answered, and then we both sat quietly together, drawing comfort from the presence of the other, lost in our own thoughts.

SIX

During the course of our travels throughout Israel, I got to meet some very interesting people. Three of my favorites were two sisters and a brother who shared a home outside of Jerusalem, in Beit Anya.

The brother, Elazar, owned several vineyards that he had inherited from his father. A tall, lean man in his early thirties, he was the sort of relaxed, affable person who naturally drew people to himself. I soon learned that his congenial smile hid a very sharp intellect. Knowledgeable in a myriad of subjects, Elazar was endlessly fascinating to converse with. Even better, his heart was pure and he sought after God. I noticed that Yeshua not only enjoyed spending time with Elazar but actively looked forward to it. The two men would walk off by themselves, deep in conversation, ambling through the neatly cultivated rows of grapevines. Every so often the sounds of laughter drifted toward the house, in which worked several of us women. We helped the two sisters prepare food for the copious amounts of us who descended on their kind hospitality.

The older of the two sisters, Marta, reminded me a bit of me. I liked her immediately! Her face wasn't classically beautiful, but very pleasing, with strong determined lines. She was tall, like her brother, and people often remarked on their similarity of look. However, where Elazar was casual, Marta tended to be driven. She had a gift for organization and liked everything just so. Their home, already elegant, gleamed under her watchful eye. The food she offered to us was likewise a high point in our generally monotonous diet. Succulent lamb braised with almonds and raisins, fattened calf gently cooked in a mint yogurt sauce, mouth-watering treats dripping with sticky honey, wine so red that it sparkled like rubies—these were but a few of the delights that came our way when we visited.

The younger sister, Miryam (another Miryam!), had more of Elazar's personality but not his looks. She was small and fragile-looking, with large doe-like eyes set in a heart-shaped face. Sleek hair, seemingly too heavy for her small frame, lay braided and coiled at the nape of her neck. She exhibited a mighty thirst for knowledge and knew more of Torah and the Scriptures than most women. Both sisters loved Yeshua, but Miryam particularly followed after him like a small lap dog in search of its master.

Their parents had been dead for several years, and Elazar, as the only brother and also the eldest, took care of his sisters. They, in turn, took care of him. I think this arrangement was entirely too congenial for all involved, because so far not one of the three appeared interested in marrying.

Yeshua's friendship with the family dated back several years to before his ministry started. Apparently he had met Elazar in Jerusalem one year during the Feast of Pesach. They had been next to one another in line with their unblemished lambs, waiting for their turn at the sacrificial altar. Elazar, always talkative and friendly, had summarily treated Yeshua as a long-lost brother, expounding on how he perceived the questionable way the high priest ran the sacrificial system at the Temple during Feasts. This was a topic near and dear to the Lord's heart, so the two men entered into a long and vigorous debate about the corruption that had a stranglehold on the people who came to worship Adonai.

By the time they slaughtered their lambs that day, Elazar and Yeshua realized that in each other they had found one of God's greatest gifts: a true friend. Once Yeshua's official ministry started, after his immersion by Yochanan, he was able to only sporadically see Elazar, and then usually with an enormous amount of people, but that was all right. Elazar and his sisters, more than just about anyone, understood who Yeshua really was and the necessity for him to work while it was still day.

That spring, on the way up to Jerusalem for the Feast of Unleavened Bread, or Pesach, we stayed with the three siblings just before we entered the City. It was a wonderful respite; all of us were weary after several weeks of ministering nonstop to hordes and hordes of people. I could really see a difference in the levels of Yeshua's popularity from just a few months prior. He had reached a point in his ministry where he had absolutely no time for himself unless he got up hours before dawn and hid himself so that he could speak with the Father. Forget about relaxation. So this time of being among old friends vastly appealed to him.

Several members of the Company had gone ahead to Jerusalem, including Rachel and Adaba. The only ones with Yeshua at the home of Elazar were Shimon, Andrew, Ya'akov, Yochanan, Philip, Nathaniel, the

Magdalit, Shoshana, myself, and a woman named Shlomit. She was the mother of Ya'akov and Yochanan, the sons of Zavdai, and had only recently joined us. Yeshua's mother, Miryam, had gone to Jerusalem with her other children. We would meet up with them there.

I didn't take to Shlomit as quickly as I had to Shoshana and both Miryams. Shlomit, the mother and wife of fishermen, did well enough financially within her own small circle in the little lakeside town of Beit Tzaidah to the point where she always felt "in charge." She reminded me of some of the high-born women at the palace who just knew they were superior to you. At first I found it amusing because the wife of a fisherman, even a prosperous one, couldn't hold a candle to even a *servant* of one of the ladies of the court. But soon it grew irritating, especially when one time she treated me as barely her equal.

(I think someone—possibly one of her sons—must have told her who I was because the next day she spoke to me quite deferentially.)

I'm almost certain that Shlomit did not initially join our Company in order to follow the Lord, but rather to keep an eye on her two sons. Word had it that their father, Zavdai, was none too pleased when his boys abruptly quit their fishing business in order to travel around the country with Yeshua. Zavdai lost not only his sons, but also Shimon and Andrew, his partners.

A short, plump woman with a round face, Shlomit appeared to notice everything and everyone. Her shrewd, brown eyes were ever watchful, ever alert. Within a week of being with us, though, I could tell she was softening. After a few times of witnessing Yeshua heal broken, hurting, dying, people, she was completely won over.

"I see now why my boys left their father sitting alone in his boat to come with you," she solicitously told Yeshua. He smiled broadly and, leaning over, kissed her on the cheek.

"Thank you, *Dodah*," he said affectionately, while she, bemused, reached her hand up and touched the now sacred spot on her face.

Lately she had become part of what I thought of as the 'inner circle.' We were the group with whom Yeshua spent the most time. At first I flattered myself with the conjecture that he liked us more, but soon I could see it was because we were most available. Shlomit suddenly seemed to always be around. Whatever the reason, it was glorious to not only be able to work with the Lord but also to be present when he privately spoke, laughed, relaxed. And nowhere did he relax as much as when he visited his dear friend Elazar.

After the early greetings and cries of *shalom, shalom*, Marta ushered us into the shady, tree-lined courtyard whereupon we had the road dust washed off our feet and then sat and drank sensational concoctions of crushed grapes cooled to perfection in a nearby brook. After a while, the women followed Marta into the cool recesses of her spacious, luxuriously furnished home in order to help with the numerous preparations necessary for the feeding of so many guests.

And it wasn't just feeding them. No. With Marta, every bite, every dish, had to excite the palate. She loved Yeshua, and strove to present before him a feast the likes of which even King Herod had not seen. But of course Marta knew that Yeshua rarely, if ever, traveled alone these days. So the many delicacies needed to be repeated over and over again so that all those who accompanied her treasured lord could also eat. In the past, she had attempted to make a platter of really special foods just for Yeshua, but he always shared it. So now she just treated everyone the way she would the Master.

This visit was no different. If anything, the menu planned proved even more elaborate than any heretofore. Amid much instruction, and with two kitchen maids to lend a hand, we all started peeling, cutting, dicing, basting, kneading, etc. etc. At first, between much good-natured joking, and catching Marta up on what had been happening with the ministry, all went well. But later on, Marta excused herself to bring more drinks out to the men. She chanced on a much more sober group than the one left behind in the kitchen. Out here, only Yeshua spoke, and he so earnestly and with such passion that Marta felt herself to be interrupting a sacred time. Hastily putting down the tray of drinks, she turned to go when she caught sight of her sister.

Sitting quietly at the Lord's feet, arms clasped around her knees, head leaning back, eyes closed, happy smile on her face, oblivious to all and any but what her precious Lord should say, this was Miryam. But Marta, taking the scene in, left angered.

When she re-entered the kitchen, no longer talkative, a frown on her normally pleasant features, we immediately knew something was wrong.

"Tell us," urged Shoshana. "What happened?"

Shaking her head, Marta refused to speak, then a few tears slid down her cheeks.

Shlomit laid an authoritative, motherly hand on Marta's arm. "Has it to do with the Lord?"

"It's my sister!" erupted Marta. "Here I am, slaving away so that everything can be perfect, and she's *doing nothing*! Sitting with the men, like a small girl. Treating me like the old mother. She knows that I can always be expected to take care of things so she doesn't even try! I'm so mad at her!" She burst into tears.

We all glanced at each other. The Magdalit raised her eyebrows at me. I shook my head in warning at her. *I know what you're thinking but don't say it,* I cautioned her with my eyes. It had, I knew, been only a supreme act of the will that forced the Magdalit herself to follow the women and not remain behind like Miryam.

Shoshana, always compassionate, took charge. "Sit down, Marta. You have been working hard, too hard, for hours. Let me get you a cold drink."

We fussed over Marta for a bit, and she bore with us stoically. Seemingly recovered, she led us in finishing the dinner preparations. When all that needed to be done was the setting up of the tables, she marched off to the courtyard, determined to enlist her sister's help for at least some work.

Entering the courtyard, she announced that dinner would be served momentarily. This news brought a welcome response from the men. Pleased by their enthusiasm, Marta then put her hand on Miryam's shoulder, and whispered loudly, "Come. It's time for you to help."

Miryam swatted her sister's hand away. "Not now, Marta," she protested, tilting her sweet face up to peer at her sister.

"Yes, now," commanded Marta, firmly, her face reddening as she became aware that Yeshua had stopped talking and was paying attention to this little scene.

But Miryam was not to be shaken from her spot. Rarely did she have the opportunity to be so close to Yeshua with so few people about. To her, it was like ripping a hole in the fabric that separated earth from heaven and getting to gaze in at the glory, wonder and majesty of God. She would work it out with Marta later, she decided.

Marta saw that Miryam would not be budged. Suddenly infuriated, she lost the already fragile grasp on her composure. Petitioning Yeshua, she cried, "Sir, don't you care that my sister has been leaving me to do all the work by myself?"

However, the Lord answered her, "Marta, Marta, you are fretting and worrying about so many things! But there is only one thing that is essential. Miryam has chosen the right thing, and it won't be taken away from her."

Pricked by the Lord's rebuke, all of Marta's anger and frustration deflated. She hung her head in shame. Yeshua came to her and cupped her distressed face in his hands. "The Father sees your good works," he assured her. "But the most important thing is relationship. I will not always be available to you the way I am today. Don't waste this time."

At the Lord's words, *I will not always be available to you the way I am today*, Shoshana and I glanced at each other in alarm. But Marta did not question Yeshua as to what he meant. Instead, she put her arms around his waist and leaned her face against his chest. He hugged her, whispering more words into her ear that were for her alone. After a few moments, she nodded and then slowly, obediently, walked over to her sister.

The two women conversed gravely together, their heads huddled close. Subsequently, the tinkling of laughter alerted the rest of us to their repaired relationship.

The dinner that followed was superb. Contrary to custom, after we woman helped serve, we sat down at the table and joined the men. The Lord sat at the head of the table with Elazar on his right and Yochanan on his left. I sat between Shoshana and Shlomit. Across from me dined Marta, a thoughtful smile on her face.

Never had I seen Yeshua so carefree, so light-hearted! Again and again, I looked up from conversations with my dinner partners towards bursts of loud laughter from the head of the table. At one point, Shimon Kefa told a story about one of his first fishing trips where he was in command and anything and everything which could go wrong, did. His engaging, expressive style of storytelling drew all of us in until the other conversations stopped and everyone listened exclusively to him.

When Shimon finished his tale, and the last ringing of laugher died away, the mood turned more serious. Elazar questioned Yeshua as to his reception by the religious leaders, particularly the mucky-mucks from the Prushim.

Sighing heavily, Yeshua raked his fingers through unruly brown hair. "They don't understand who I am and why I'm here. Most of them anyway. A few do."

"You mean like Nakdimon," I offered impulsively from my end of the table. It grew very quiet as everyone turned to stare at me. I felt my cheeks grow hot.

"Yes, Yohana," said Yeshua, solemnly. "Like Nakdimon. But," he went on, "even Nakdimon is unwilling to take a public stand for faith in me. And now I see traps set for me wherever I go."

"What kind of traps?" questioned Elazar.

"You name it. Traps about whether or not it's lawful to heal on Shabbat, traps about paying taxes, traps about *n'tilat yadayim* (ritual hand washing), traps...."

Elazar interrupted. "What happened with *n'tilat yadayim*?"

"Last month, a group of Prushim and Torah teachers from Jerusalem had gathered around me and saw that some of my talmidim (here Shimon politely coughed) neglected to observe the elaborate ritual of hand washing before they ate."

"Oh, oh. That must have set their teeth on edge," chuckled Elazar.

"They went wild," put in Philip. "Those guys wash *everything*. Cups, pitchers, kettles..."

"Yes," said Yeshua. "They've taken the holy word of God in Torah and added onto it in order to make the traditions of the elders. Then *that* becomes more important than the living, breathing, actual word of God.

"So they got aggressive with me. 'Why don't your talmidim live according to the *tradition of the elders* instead of eating their food with unclean hands?' they asked me."

"What did you say?" asked Elazar.

"He let them have it," remembered Shimon, gleefully.

Yeshua stared balefully at him. "Everything I said, Kefa," he patiently but sternly explained to the suddenly squirming talmid, "was to open their eyes and bring them closer to the Kingdom of Heaven." He turned his gaze back to Elazar. "I quoted the portion of Isaiah in which he prophesied:

> " '*These people honor me with their lips,*
> *but their hearts are far from me.*
> *They worship me in vain;*
> *their teachings are but rules taught by men.*' "

When Yeshua quoted Scripture, his voice, already melodic, deepened in pitch such that we all sat mesmerized. He spoke the words not as one who learned them by rote, but rather as one whose very being was intertwined in the ancient poetry.

Yeshua then went on to say he had recited for his detractors a list of laws that they avoided doing but instead, out of hypocrisy, had built up hedges of traditions so their consciences would be assuaged.

"And with the ritual hand washing," he explained, answering Elazar's question, "I made it quite clear that any dirt left on a person's hands did not make him unclean when he ate. Rather, I told them that it is the things which come out of a person which make him unclean."

"Such as...?" prompted Philip.

"We went over this, Philip," sighed the Lord. He turned to his talmidim. "Who remembers what I said?"

Nathaniel raised his hand. "Tell us," acknowledged Yeshua.

"Out of a person's heart come forth wicked thoughts, sexual immorality, theft, murder, adultery, slander, arrogance, foolishness. All these wicked things come from within, and they make a person unclean," recited Nathaniel. He shot Philip a look of triumph.

"Excellent," approved Yeshua. "But watch the arrogance." Nathaniel's face fell as Philip, vindicated, laughed.

We went on to speak of many other things that night. Indeed, it was well past midnight when the last of us straggled off to bed. Miryam had set the tone for the evening by refusing to move from her position at Yeshua's feet. All of us were reluctant to leave the Master. The fellowship tasted so sweet, the air so peaceful. Had we known then what was coming, I doubt if any of us would ever had left that safe haven! Alas, all too soon our idyllic visit ended and we continued on to Jerusalem, for the Feast of Unleavened Bread.

∾∾∾

Jerusalem is wall-to-wall people at Pesach. The normal population of the city swells from 300,000 to almost three million people. For these to partake of the sacrificed lamb commanded by God in Torah, over one-quarter million lambs are slain.

On the fourteenth day of the month of Nisan, early in the afternoon, the lambs are sacrificed. Long lines form before a multitude of priests, who blow a threefold blast from their silver trumpets when the lambs are slain. The person offering the lamb for their group (no less than ten, no more than twenty persons) slaughters the animal himself. Lines of priests catch the blood in alternating silver and gold bowls. They then pass the bowls from priest to priest until, finally, the bowls culminate in the hands of the priest at the altar who flings the bloody contents at its base. While this is happening, constant praise to God ascends to heaven in the chanting of the *hallel*, Psalms 113-118. Undulating choruses of *hallelujah* sweep through the scene.

Shimon Kefa, Thomas, and Yeshua's brother Ya'akov, slaughtered paschal lambs for our group. Several wives and children had joined their husbands for the Feast so we had about sixty people with us. Yeshua picked a camp spot for us outside the city walls, as he aspired to a certain level of anonymity.

Kuza and I had decided that it was prudent for me to not return home, lest Herod take notice. He slipped away from the palace, intending to be with me for as much of the Feast as possible. I was quite gratified by Yeshua's response upon encountering Kuza: he kissed him on both cheeks and looked on him with much affection. I could see that Kuza also was deeply moved.

That night, we sat around a blazing fire, roasting lamb which we then ate with matzah and bitter herbs. Earlier that day, I had helped make the *matzot* by mixing flour and water, kneading it and then rolling it very flat. We baked it quickly over the fire. I loved the crispy yet somewhat soft texture of the bread. It was a once-a-year treat. After a week, though, my bowels reminded me of why it was called the bread of affliction!

Yeshua led our seder. Leaning contentedly against Kuza in the flickering light of the fire, I listened as the Lord shared the Passover story, recounting the well-known tale of Yosef and how he was sold into slavery by his jealous brothers. Yeshua described Yosef's meteoric rise to prime minister of Egypt after God used him to correctly interpret Pharaoh's dreams. He spoke of our father Ya'akov moving his family to the land of Goshen, and how, many years later, after the Israelites had multiplied exceedingly, the new Pharaoh enslaved them in a cruel and terrible bondage.

I had heard the Passover story so many times in my life that I had grown somewhat immune to it. But now as I listened to Yeshua speak of the awful backbreaking slavery of those long ago days, his voice filled with compassion as he described the great cities, pyramids, palaces, and the brutal methods used to build them, I saw that era with new eyes.

The rest of the company and I sat enthralled when Yeshua spoke of Moshe. Not just the baby Moshe rescued by Pharaoh's daughter but the young prince Moshe determined to rescue his fellow Israelites by his own strength and cunning. Later, we saw the chastened and humbled Moshe monotonously leading sheep to pasture in the desert, day after day, year after year. We felt his surprise upon seeing a bush that burned yet was not consumed; we experienced his awe when the Lord God spoke to him. We understood his reluctance to return to Egypt, and the courage it took to obey God. We felt his fear when his shepherd's staff turned into a deadly snake, and his shock when his hand turned leprous and then healthy as he put it inside and out of his cloak. We understood his trepidation when he and his brother Aharon entered Pharaoh's palace and demanded that the Israelites be allowed to leave Egypt and go worship the Lord in the desert;

and his anguish when Pharaoh's response was to increase the burden on the Israelite slaves so that the people were worse off than before. All of these things Yeshua described as if he had been there himself. No longer a rote exercise in commemoration, the Passover story sprang to life.

At the beginning of the narrative, we all stood and chanted the blessing over the first of the traditional four cups of wine. *"Baruch Atah Adonai Eloheinu Melech haolam, boray pree hagofen.* Blessed are You, O Lord, Our God, King of the Universe, who creates the fruit of the vine." Together we drained that first cup, the Cup of Sanctification, the cup which signifies that God has set us apart.

The second cup, the Cup of Deliverance, came close on the heels of the first cup. "Let us remember that God rescued us from being slaves," said Yeshua as he raised his cup of wine high in the air. "Let us also remember that He can rescue us from the slavery of sin." He then led us in the chanting of the blessing for the second time that evening, and we drank again.

When it was time for the third cup, the Cup of Redemption, the saving of our souls, Yeshua spoke about the blood of the innocent lamb that was painted with a hyssop brush onto the doorposts of the homes of the Israelites during their last night in Egypt. The Angel of Death, when he passed over the land of Egypt, would not enter those homes that were protected by the blood of the lamb. "What happened to those Israelite families who neglected to paint their doorways with the blood of the sacrificial lamb?" he asked us.

"They lost the protection of God," offered Andrew.

Yeshua nodded at him. "That's right. It's only through the covering of the blood slain for us that we have atonement for sin. Remember, the life is in the blood." Then he poured wine into the third cup, and, with us all, chanted the blessing, and we drank.

The fourth and final cup, the Cup of Completion, signaled an end to the seder. It came after Yeshua told of the ten plagues, and the miraculous departure of the Children of Israel from Egypt. He spoke of the 600,000 men, plus women and children, who left in haste in the middle of the night, with their belongings, livestock, and the plunder they had requested from their Egyptian neighbors. He spoke of the fear, trepidation, excitement, bewilderment as a nation of slaves followed after Moshe and Aharon. He spoke of the Lord leading Israel in a pillar of cloud by day and a pillar of fire by night. He spoke of their terror as Pharaoh's army pursued them, with all the spears, swords, chariots, and horses of a mighty military power while they (the Israelites) had nothing—nothing that is, except the Lord Himself. He spoke of that long and terrible night when the pillar of cloud separated the two armies so that darkness came to one side but light to the other. He spoke of how in faith Moshe stretched out his hand over the sea and how all that night the Lord drove the sea back with a strong east wind and turned it into dry land. He spoke of a nation of terrified slaves who had no choice but to walk through the sea as on dry ground, with a wall of water on their left and on their right. He spoke of God's mighty deliverance, of how the Egyptian army set out after the Israelites only to be drowned in the furious waters that flowed back to their rightful place.

Kuza and I sat enraptured, as did the others. It seemed to us as if we had never heard our own history before, so vivid did it become in Yeshua's telling. Our hearts burned within us and we wondered, *Could he, was it possible, was he there?* But we didn't dare ask.

That night marked the end of any time of intimacy with Yeshua. By morning, word had somehow gotten out that he was here and after that he was continually mobbed. From dawn until well after dark, he spent each day teaching, praying, healing. It seemed to me that all three million people passed before my eyes that Passover, one at a time.

Like everyone else, we ate the bread of affliction that week. Yeast, representative of sin, was strictly forbidden. I prayed that God the Father would enable me to rid my life of sin with the same diligence with which I was ridding my life of yeast.

With the end of Passover, I pleaded with Kuza to leave the palace for good and come with us back north to the Galil. To my great delight, he agreed. Imagine my surprise then when Yeshua himself contradicted our plans.

"No," he said to Kuza when he learned of our intentions. "It's not yet the time for you to vacate your post." He laid his hand on Kuza's shoulder and stared intently into my husband's now pale face. "Trust me, there is nothing I would like better than to have one such as yourself among my followers. But you will do our cause more good by staying where you are and speaking out the Word of God to those who have ears to hear. Trust me. No harm will befall you." He kissed us both, and turned to other matters, leaving us to work out our conflicting emotions. It was a hard parting.

Our ministry exploded. There's no other way to describe it. We went from ministering to crowds of hundreds to crowds of thousands. The pace grew unbearably hectic. If it weren't for the deep conviction each of us had that we were following the King of Israel come to reclaim his rightful throne, none of us would have been able to endure.

One time in particular stands out in my memory. We had gone to Beit Tzaidah for a few days of rest and restoration. The crowds, however, learned of this plan and followed us. Though the rest of us were inwardly wincing with frustration, Yeshua welcomed them and spoke about the kingdom of God. He healed those who needed healing. Hour after hour after hour he prayed for one person after another. Finally, late in the afternoon, the talmidim came to him and strongly advised him to send the crowd away.

"Send them to the surrounding villages and countryside so that they can find food and lodging, seeing as we are in a remote place here," said Thomas, who acted as spokesman.

But Yeshua challenged us. "You give them something to eat," he replied, arms folded, gaze level.

Everyone looked at each other in consternation. *Give them something to eat? There must be as many as five thousand men here, plus women and children! How can we possibly give them anything to eat? We have barely enough for ourselves!*

"We have only five loaves of bread and two fish," ventured Andrew, "unless,"—and here he gulped nervously— "unless you want us to go and *buy* food for all this crowd." (He was willing to spend the money if that's what Yeshua commanded, but it would completely wipe us out financially.)

To our relief, Yeshua didn't agree to this plan. Instead, he told the talmidim, "Have the people sit down in groups of about fifty each."

Mystified, we (I say *we* but really the men passed out the food) did so, and everybody sat down. Needless to say, this took a while but eventually the multitude followed the plan.

Yeshua then took the five loaves and two fish and, looking up to heaven, he said the *b'rakhah*, the blessing, and broke the bread and fish. Then he gave the pieces to the talmidim for them to serve the people. The most amazing thing happened: as Shimon, Andrew, Yochanan, and the rest handed out fish and bread, it multiplied! No matter how much and how often they reached their hands into the baskets to pull out food, more appeared! So much so that, when it was all done, everyone there had eaten to his heart's content and *still* there were twelve basketfuls of broken pieces that we picked up.

After these events, Yeshua spoke privately to us. "You are amazed at the miracle with the food. I tell you that if you are willing to feed people spiritually, there will always be enough to supply your needs. The time is coming, when the Son of Man must suffer many things and be rejected by the elders, chief priests and Torah teachers, and he must be killed and on the third day be raised to life."

We didn't understand what he meant. All of us expected him to announce his kingship and take Jerusalem by storm. Getting rid of the Romans, overthrowing the corrupt reign of the high priesthood, these were the things we expected Yeshua to do. No one said to him, "What are you talking about?" It just wasn't done. So we talked amongst ourselves and decided that he was spiritualizing truths that were as yet too difficult for us to fathom.

Yeshua then said to all of us, "If anyone would come after me, he must deny himself and take up his cross daily and follow me."

Isn't that what we were doing? Hadn't we left all to follow him around the country?

"For whoever wants to save his life will lose it, but whoever loses his life for me will save it."

Lose his life? We were safe with Yeshua, weren't we? Hadn't he told Kuza not to be afraid, that no harm would come to him?

"What good is it for a man to gain the whole world, and yet lose or forfeit his very self? If anyone is ashamed of me and my words, the Son of Man will be ashamed of him when he comes in his glory and in the glory of the Father and of the holy angels. I tell you the truth, some who are standing here will not taste death before they see the kingdom of God."

Ashamed of him? How could we ever be ashamed of him! We loved him so!

These words were unsettling. Our preconceived notions about who we were and who Yeshua was and who we were in relation to him all started to shift. Some of us grew uneasy.

It was about this time that our giving to the poor increased dramatically. I have to say that since leaving Jerusalem I had been shocked by the degree of poverty we had encountered. Always, in the City, poor people abounded, but over the years they had gotten somewhat invisible to me. Now my eyes were opened and I saw them everywhere: pockmarked, oozing sores, tattered clothing, missing limbs, crumbling, brown teeth, bloated bellies, greasy hair. The list goes on.

I had never seen anyone as generous as Yeshua when it came to giving to the needy. He didn't flinch from those who smelled, or seemed repulsive to me. No, he gathered them in his arms and loved them.

Yehuda of K'riot acted as our treasurer and, as successive encounters with the poverty stricken significantly reduced our collective purse, he grew increasingly sullen.

Eight days after the miracle of the bread and fish, Yeshua handpicked Shimon (whom he also called 'Kefa"), and the two sons of Zavdai and took them with him up onto a mountain to pray. While they were away, groups of people began flowing into the camp, looking for a touch from God.

Now Yeshua had trained all of us to pray over people for healing and deliverance. We had seen some spectacular results and, frankly, some of us were feeling relatively confident about the power of God made manifest. So when hundreds of people along with several Torah teachers poured into the camp, we were certain that we could carry on without Yeshua.

The first hour wasn't bad. A young, husky fellow complained of a headache that had lasted for days. Andrew placed his hands on the man's head and prayed to God the Father. Not exactly immediately, but soon enough, the man reluctantly agreed that he was better. Meanwhile, Philip and Nathaniel prayed together over a woman with a fever.

"I'm healed," she announced, satisfied, and walked away. Philip and Nathaniel looked at each other, relieved.

I did notice that without Yeshua there, the talmidim had less expectation that prayers would be answered. They seemed almost surprised when someone declared himself healed.

Shoshana, myself ,and the rest of the women supported the men. In the cases of women needing prayer, we either helped or took over completely.

As all this was occurring, a man arrived, holding a young boy by the hand. Hollow-eyed and slightly desperate in appearance, the man kept a strong grip on the child at his side.

The child himself behaved in a very unusual manner. He rolled his eyes, periodically emitting low, moaning sounds. Saliva dripped down his chin. Features contorted, he seemed more like a wounded animal than a human being. Instinctively, the crowd parted on either side of this pair, unwilling to get too close. The man pulled the boy right up to the front of the crowd, to the talmidim.

From where I stood, I could see Thomas and Andrew glance nervously at each other. They clearly did not feel comfortable with the situation in the making.

"Help me! Can you help me?" entreated the man immediately upon reaching someone whom he perceived to be in charge.

"What can we do for you?" asked Andrew, using a tone and an expression learned from watching the Rabbi.

"It's my son!" answered the man, indicating the bizarre child at his side. "He's demon-possessed. Please help us!" And he thrust the boy forward so that the child came right under Andrew's nose.

"Describe for us what the demon does," commanded Thomas.

"It seizes him, lets out a shriek, and throws him into convulsions. He foams at the mouth, and recovers with greater and greater difficulty." The father of the boy looked frantically from Thomas to Andrew and back to Thomas again. Hope and despair struggled against each other in his eyes. Briefly, hope prevailed. "Can you deliver him?"

Without answering, Thomas placed his hand on the boy's head and began praying. Andrew joined him. After several minutes, Thomas commanded the demon to leave.

Everything was quiet. Thomas smiled and the father looked hopeful. Suddenly, the boy let loose a long, loud, raucous laugh, wildly inappropriate for one so young. Startled, everyone, *everyone,* took a step backward and I distinctly remember gasping. Then a horrible, unearthly shriek came from deep within the boy and left through his mouth, echoing and reverberating for what seemed to be an endless time. He fell to the ground, shaking and rocking back and forth. His eyes rolled up in his head such that all that was visible were the whites and, precisely as the father had said, foam poured from his mouth. The father, more practiced in this than the rest of us, quickly grasped his son's chin and inserted a thick wad of what looked to be cloth in the boy's mouth. I later found out that this was intended to keep him from swallowing his own tongue.

Philip, Nathaniel and the other Shimon came running over in an attempt to help. Soon every single talmid plus we women stood in a circle around the boy, praying and attempting to cast out the demon like we had seen Yeshua do so many times. And we had done as well. Only this time it wasn't working. And the longer the demon stayed, the less faith and confidence we all had.

Finally Andrew said to the father, "Look, I'm sorry to disappoint you, but we're not having much success here. Maybe you can come back another time." And he smiled apologetically.

"What do you mean you can't help me?" wailed the father, his eyes dark with pain. "I've traveled so far. And for what?" Moaning, he sobbed loudly.

Others in the crowd picked up on the man's distress. "How come you can't do what the Rabbi does? Aren't you his talmidim?" sneered one fellow.

Murmuring spread like wildfire. What moments before had been grateful people looking for healing from God abruptly turned into angry people looking for someone to blame. I felt nervous before such erratic behavior. *Oh Lord*, I prayed. *Please send Yeshua back now!*

Andrew, Philip and Nathaniel conferred with one another in whispers. "Stop your muttering," threatened an untidy, sullen-looking man, shaking a cane for emphasis. "We want Yeshua!"

"We want Yeshua! We want Yeshua!" One by one, the cry reverberated throughout the crowd. The tempo picked up so that the words had a rhythmic beat, a menacing beat. Yehuda from K'riot strode over to Andrew, Philip, and Nathaniel. I saw by his excited hand gestures that he was suggesting something. Andrew shook his head dubiously but Yehuda pressed closer, more persuasively. Finally, with the other talmidim still looking unsure, Yehuda addressed the mob.

"Friends," he boomed. "Listen to me." Slowly, the noise, punctuated by various *shhhs,* settled down.

"If it is Yeshua you want, then you only have to go toward that mountain back there," he said, pointing to the towering shape several miles in front of him, its dusky blue peak visible in the late morning sky. "That's where he went and that's where he'll be returning from."

As if they were one man, hundreds of heads turned in the direction Yehuda indicated. Quiet reigned briefly. A lone voice from the middle of the crowd called out, "That's a good idea."

"It is, isn't it?" responded his friend. And on and on until finally the whole lot of them, with the man and his demon-possessed son in their midst, set out for the mountain.

Yehuda watched them leave, arms crossed against his chest, a satisfied smirk on his handsome face. "Well that worked, didn't it?" he boasted.

"Only if you call shouting out the Master's whereabouts to the whole world *working*," retorted Andrew, eyes glowering.

"Oh, come on," countered Yehuda. "He's due back any time now. I doubt they'll even get all the way to the mountain before running into him."

Thomas looked concerned. "I think several of us should go with the crowd and tell Yeshua what happened here," he volunteered.

"I'll go," offered Shoshana, before I had a chance to open my mouth.

"No," said Andrew. "Too dangerous. This group is unpredictable.

The women stay here."

Shoshana sighed, but nodded obediently.

"I'll stay with them to protect them," decided Yehuda.

"How generous," commented Thomas dryly.

In the end, all of the men went except Yehuda, the other Shimon, and the other Yehuda. They walked for at least two hours heading for the hill country.

When Yeshua, Shimon, Ya'akov, and Yochanan emerged from the hill country, who should meet them but the talmidim and a huge crowd! Andrew, Thomas, and Philip ran right over to them and breathlessly explained what had happened earlier that day back at the camp.

As this was going on, the man with the demon-possessed son suddenly yelled from the middle of the crowd, "Rabbi! Look at my son, I beg you, because he's my only child! What happens is this," he said, immediately launching into his story before anyone could stop him. "A spirit seizes him, and suddenly it lets out a shriek and throws him into convulsions with foaming at the mouth; and only with difficulty will it leave him! I asked your talmidim to drive the spirit out, but they couldn't." He and several others pointed accusing fingers at Andrew and Thomas, who drew back in alarm.

Yeshua's eyes darkened as he perceived the angry mood of the crowd. Placing his hand on Andrew's back, he faced the crowd. "Perverted people, without any trust! How long do I have to be with you and put up with you? Bring your son here."

It was rare to see the Lord incensed with the common people. With the religious leaders, yes, but rarely with the *am ha'aretz*. Each of the talmidim felt vast relief that the Master had returned and taken charge.

Meanwhile, the father pushed his way through the crowd with his son, but even in that short time, the demon dashed the boy to the ground and threw him into a fit. But Yeshua rebuked the unclean spirit, healed the boy, and gave him back to his father.

The change in the mood of the crowd was stunning. Struck with amazement at the greatness of God, men and women who just moments earlier had snarled vindictively now fell to their knees, praising God. While this was going on, Yeshua gathered around himself his talmidim and spoke with them urgently, in low tones.

"Listen very carefully to what I'm going to say. The Son of Man is about to be betrayed into the hands of men."

What? Does he mean this crowd, now gentle as a newborn lamb? What does he mean, betrayed into the hands of men?

The talmidim didn't understand what he meant and they were afraid to ask him. The only ones who didn't seem afraid were the three who had emerged from the hill country with Yeshua. They seemed like they were in their own world. Pensive, contemplative, glowing. Yeshua himself also seemed taller, brighter. Shimon, Yochanan, and Ya'akov followed behind him, all (especially Shimon) uncharacteristically quiet. Later on, when they arrived back at the camp, the difference was still noticeable. I asked Shimon what had happened and he opened his mouth, then closed it again and shook his head.

"I can't say, Yohana. Not yet." He looked at me and his eyes blazed. "I will tell you this one thing. Follow him anywhere no matter what. You'll not ever regret it." Then he left and went off by himself.

SEVEN

Through that summer and into the fall, Yeshua taught and healed and delivered and healed and delivered and taught. Often he spoke in parables that we barely understood. Frequently, he illustrated his points by using stories about kings, farmers, vineyards, weddings, fig trees, harvest time, and many other examples to which his listeners could relate.

During this time, my relationship with Yeshua's mother deepened. Soon enough, it reached the place where I felt free to refer to her as my "friend." At first, I was excited about the connection because she had such an exalted status as the Lord's mother, but, as time went by, I loved her more and more for the incredible woman God had made her to be. Soon I ceased to think of her altogether as "the Lord's mother" and only considered her in terms of herself.

Shoshana grew closer to Miryam as well. Every so often, the two of us would encourage Miryam to share stories from Yeshua's childhood. Not often, for mixed with Miryam's godly humility was a desire not to overstep what her son may or may not want her to say. But occasionally she shared about the past.

Like the time she told us about their flight to Egypt when Yeshua was two years old.

The three of us were resting after a particularly brutal day of ministering. I had long lost track of how many healings we had seen. Yeshua himself seemed ready to drop with fatigue by the time the last person was ministered to. I noticed that the power of God would surge through his body, leaving him limp and exhausted. After only a few hours' sleep though, Yeshua roused himself before dawn and headed into the hills to pray. He always came back restored and revitalized.

Anyway, Miryam, Shoshana, and myself were lying on three pallets in the same goat hair tent. All of us were completely and totally drained, yet wound up from the excitement of the day. As we lay there in the dark, speaking quietly to each other, Miryam casually remarked, "I don't remember being this tired since that time my husband woke me up in the middle of the night and we fled with our baby to Egypt."

"*WHAT?*" Shoshana and I shrieked simultaneously.

"You don't know that story?" asked Miryam, innocently. I imagined a small smile playing about her lips.

"No, tell us!" we cried.

"Okay, where should I begin?" she said aloud.

"As far back as possible," I suggested hopefully.

"Do you know about the three sages from the East who came to see us after the birth of Yeshua?"

"I vaguely recall...," I began while Shoshana quickly said, "No."

"Ah. Well." Miryam hesitated a moment before she said in her soft voice, "Do you want to hear the whole story or should I tell it from the three sages?"

"The whole story!" cried Shoshana and I together, then we giggled over how we kept saying things at the same time.

Miryam laughed with us. "*B'seder,*" she agreed. "Here's the whole story." She settled herself into a more comfortable position, then began. "Back in the days of Herod the Great, when I was expecting my first child, Caesar Augustus issued a decree that a census be taken of the entire Roman world. Everyone had to go to his own town to register."

"Oh, I remember this!" I interrupted. "I was twelve. My father had just returned from a long trip away and had to leave again almost immediately to register us. I remember being really angry about how idiotic the whole thing was."

"Yes," concurred Miryam. "If losing your father for an additional however long bothered you, then you can imagine how I felt...fifteen years old and almost nine months pregnant. I was not happy."

"Where did you go?" asked Shoshana.

"We went from Natzeret all the way to Judea, to the town of Beit Lechem, because Yosef, my husband, belonged to the house and line of David."

House of David! Royalty! I whistled softly. Later I'd learn that Miryam also was of the royal line; a distant cousin of her husband, Yosef.

"Stop," said Miryam, embarrassed.

"Why didn't Yosef leave you at home," asked Shoshana, curiously.

Miryam sighed. "Even though Yosef had that incredible encounter with the angel Gavriel and believed that I had not been disloyal to him, there were still plenty of people in our town who gossiped about me. Still do," she added sadly. "But my Yosef, such a good man, worried about me. He was afraid to leave me alone. Also, he had been thinking about making a fresh start in another place and this seemed like a good opportunity to him. So he loaded all of our worldly possessions and me onto our poor donkey and off we went."

"How big was the donkey?" I asked.

"We didn't have many things." Miryam patted me on the hand. "It would be different if you and Kuza took this journey, dear Yohie. You would have needed an elephant!"

"Maybe a herd of elephants," put in Shoshana.

When our laughter died down, Miryam continued her story. "By the time we got down to Beit Lechem, the Feast of Sukkot was about to begin. We were only five miles away from Jerusalem so there were people *everywhere*, heading to the Feast."

"Tell me about it," I grumbled, ever the irritated Jerusalemite.

Miryam ignored my comment, intent on her story. "Yosef looked all over for a place to stay. The main inn was bursting with people, and the innkeeper refused to let us take up even a corner of a room. By now we were both hungry, and tired, and dirty, from traveling. All I wanted was to wash my feet, eat something, and go to sleep. *That's* when my first labor pains came."

"Oh, you poor dear. I wish I had been there to help you," clucked Shoshana. "Whatever did you do?"

"I wish you had been there too, Shoshie," murmured Miryam, the anxiety, pain and, ultimately, wonder of that long ago night flooding back into her mind. "My strong, handsome Yosef, so good at making furniture, wasn't such a wonderful midwife. He started banging on doors of houses, begging for help. "My wife is having a baby, we have nowhere to stay. Help! Help!" One family, God bless them, already had about twenty people staying in a small home but told us we could spend the night in their stable. By then we were so exhausted it looked like a palace to us.

"The wife was very, very kind. She brought us food and went and got her sister, who was a midwife. That very evening, I gave birth to Yeshua."

Her soft voice grew even softer. "Such a beautiful baby! So calm, so intelligent. So much love in his sweet little eyes. I fell in love with him right away." Her voice trailed off and she blew her nose. Then, "So I wrapped him in some cloths that I had felt prompted to bring with me and the fellow who owned the stable cleaned out the manger so we could put the baby in there."

"You put your new baby in a manger?" I asked, horrified.

"It wasn't so bad," protested Miryam. Her voice sounded faraway in the pitch black even though she was inches from me. "Most of the time I held him and nursed him."

We all fell silent as the image of a nursing baby brought back memories for each of us. For Miryam, the baby Yeshua, now a grown man come to an incredible destiny, released from her protective arms. For Shoshana, her children back when they loved her unconditionally. For me, the sheer joy of Hana after so many dead babies, her tiny rosebud mouth opening for milk. I braced myself for the onslaught of grief that always hit me when I thought of her but this time it didn't come. I had found...peace! *Oh my, could it be?* I thought back to the conversation I had with Yeshua about my daughter and realized that I had been healed of the terrible sorrow. I now had hope that one day Kuza and I would be reunited with our child—with *all* our children—in heaven. I breathed deeply.

"Miryam?"

"Yes, Yohana?"

"You have an amazing son."

More silence. Then, "He is. It's hard for me to even remember when I used to teach him. Now he teaches me. He's so far beyond me. He's—" she hesitated, then spoke more firmly—"he's being taught by his Father, now."

"Amen," said Shoshana, her voice fading..

"Amen," I added, as well. I propped myself up on one elbow. Both of the other women were breathing more regularly. I sensed sleepiness descending on us. "Is it too late for you to tell us about the sages? We never got to that."

"I think so," replied Miryam, drowsily. "Tomorrow, okay?"

"Okay," I replied, sliding into delicious sleep myself.

It was several days before the three of us had another opportunity to talk. Yeshua had given the order that we were to pack everything up and travel around the Galil. The journey would take a while because we were to walk and would be stopping in villages along the way. As usual, everywhere we went, we attracted large crowds.

That first day we headed out, however, was a little calmer than the ones that were to follow. All of us in the Company walked in small groups:

two there, four here, three there, etc. Yeshua led the way with several of his talmidim around him. We women tended more toward the rear of the group (except for the Magdalit, who was *always* in the vicinity of her Lord!).

It so happened that Shoshana, Miryam, and myself were together. I immediately seized on this opportunity to plead with her for more of her story. Shoshana chimed in with me.

Good-naturedly, Miryam consented. "Where was I?"

I wiped my brow. "You had just given birth to Yeshua," I prompted.

It was a hot, still day. Though the sun had risen only two hours ago, already I was perspiring. I covered my head with a white linen scarf, leaving an overhang so my face would be in shade. Still, the glare hurt my eyes. Typically, on a day like today I would shelter myself from the blazing sun in the cool marble palace, delicately eating fruit and resting. Only in early evening would I venture out—once the day cooled off.

But at the palace, I reminded myself, I wouldn't be able to walk with Miryam and hear her fascinating stories. This is definitely better, I decided, my attitude improved.

"So," Miryam was saying, "I believed everything that the angel had said to me, but it was so fantastic that I kept it to myself, only occasionally speaking to Yosef about it. Imagine my astonishment when several shepherds showed up at the stable the next day, asking to see our baby.

" 'Our baby? How did you know to find us? Who *are* you, anyway?' Yosef asked them, stunned to see these weather-beaten strangers crowding into our temporary shelter.

" 'We're shepherds,' patiently explained the tallest of the men, brandishing his long, curved shepherd's crook as proof. 'Last night, we were out in the fields nearby, minding our own business, tending to our flocks when suddenly an angel of the Lord appeared to us, and the glory of the Lord shone around us.'

" 'We were terrified,' put in the youngest, a boy of about fifteen.

" 'Well, yes,' admitted the first man. 'But the angel told us not to be afraid; that he brings us good news of great joy for all the people. He told us that today in the town of David a Savior has been born; the Messiah.'

"Yosef and I looked at each other in amazement. *Another angel!* These men couldn't have known that we ourselves had also been visited by angels only months before. We knew how convincing and awe-inspiring were these messengers from God.

" 'And where did the angel tell you to find this Messiah,' I asked carefully, my voice shaking.

"The first man spoke again. 'He said that a sign to us would be finding a baby wrapped in cloths and lying in a manger,' he answered, his eyes riveted to my new infant son, now sleeping peacefully in the manger.

" 'And then,' put in a third man excitedly, 'A great company of angels appeared with this angel, praising God and saying,

'*Glory to God in the highest,*
and on earth peace to men on
whom his favor rests.'

" 'It was absolutely the most unbelievable thing we have ever seen in our lives,' he added...somewhat unnecessarily, I thought.

" 'So,' continued the first man, 'after the angels left and went back into heaven, we said to one another, 'Let's go to Beit Lechem and see this thing that has happened, which the Lord has told us about.'

" 'And here you are,' observed Yosef, his voice filled with awe."

Miryam stopped talking and took a long drink from her water skin. It really was a hot day. Shoshana and I likewise took out our water skins, gulping thirstily.

Just then Rachel and Shlomit approached us. "We heard you telling stories," said Shlomit to all of us, but particularly to Miryam. "Mind if we walk along and listen?"

"Of course not. Please join us," Miryam warmly welcomed the two women. I smiled at Rachel, who smiled back at me. She who had always been sweet and beautiful had blossomed into a deep woman of God.

Miryam picked up her story where she had stopped. "The shepherds left us and spread the word about Yeshua such that we became something of a local curiosity." She laughed. "Yosef and I took advantage of all the goodwill coming our way and established ourselves in Beit Lechem, instead of returning to the Galil. We found a wonderful little home, with a workshop attached, which we rented, and Yosef began plying his trade as a carpenter. For several months it was an idyllic lifestyle."

"Uh oh. What happened after several months?" Shlomit queried.

"Well, first a good thing and then a very bad thing. One day, when Yeshua was just taking his first baby steps, three men came to our door. I had never seen anyone like these men! Sages they were, from far away to the east. Wealthy, well-traveled, older men with many servants and a caravan that stretched down the dusty street, well past our humble home. These were not the type of people Yosef and I *ever* came in contact with! They entered our home and, immediately upon seeing Yeshua (who was standing up and balancing himself by holding onto the edge of a table Yosef made), they threw themselves prostrate on the floor and started to worship him."

"Were you shocked?" I asked.

"Just a little," responded Miryam, dryly. "I was really shocked when they presented us with the most extraordinary gifts."

"What kind of gifts?" Shlomit wanted to know.

"Costly incense, myrrh, and gold."

"Gold!" we all gasped.

"Do you still have it?" wondered Shlomit.

"Do I still have it? Heavens no. We sold everything when Yeshua was a small child so that we could finance our journey to Egypt."

"Egypt! Why did you ever go to Egypt?" I asked.

"Ah," answered Miryam, pursing her lips and shaking her head. "That's the sad part of the story. It turned out that the sages had followed ancient prophecy from Daniel and were aware that the coming of the Messiah had to be at that time. They determined through a combination of several things, including astronomy, that a certain star signified the Messiah and so they followed it all the way from the Babylon area to Jerusalem. Once in Jerusalem, they searched throughout the City, asking people, 'Where is the one who has been born king of the Jews? We saw his star in the east and have come to worship him.' "

"That would have been during the reign of Herod the Great, wouldn't it?" I observed.

Miryam nodded.

"I think I know what's coming," I said. "But I never realized the connection before."

"Yes," said Miryam. "Then you know that Herod was extremely disturbed at the mention of *another* king and summoned the chief priests and Torah teachers for an explanation of where the Messiah was to be born. He was told that the prophet Micah proclaimed,

'But you, Beit Lechem, in the land of Judah,
are by no means least among the rulers of Judah;
for out of you will come a ruler
who will be the shepherd of my people Israel.'

"Only concerned with his own power, Herod secretly sent for the Magi and asked them for the exact time the star had appeared. He then sent them to Beit Lechem to find Yeshua, adding craftily that they should report back to him." Miryam stopped to take another drink of water and also dabbed some on her neck. What a scorcher of a day!

"God protected us. The men were warned in a dream not to return to Herod so they left for their country through a different route. When Herod realized he had been tricked, he sent soldiers into Beit Lechem and they put to death all the baby boys two years old and under." She shuddered, her eyes filling up with tears. "Such a vile, despicable thing to do! All these years, my heart has ached for those grieving mothers."

"You would think the sages would have had enough sense to avoid Herod in the first place," I stated angrily.

"Oh, I don't think they could help it," protested Rachel, an odd look in her eyes. "Jerusalem was the only place it made sense to go to, and they asked around before they encountered Herod. You know how it is, Madam, when important foreigners come into the City, everyone at the palace immediately knows what's going on. Once Herod summoned them, they *had* to go to him. And then they were stuck."

"Hmm," I said, grudgingly, not entirely convinced that the men couldn't have used more foresight.

"Anyway," put in Shoshana, turning towards Miryam. "You never told us—how did you escape?"

"Oh," she said. "Well, that very night the Magi left, Yosef had a dream in which an angel of the Lord appeared to him. He told Yosef to get right up and take me and Yeshua to Egypt because Herod is going to search for the child to kill him. And of course," she added, "Yosef was no stranger to God using dreams to tell him things so he immediately woke up, woke me up, and we packed."

"How long did it take until you left?" I asked, thinking that for me and Kuza, it would take at least a week to gather the most basic of our goods.

"Two hours," she answered. "And that included food provisions and nursing a sleepy baby. Which is why I told you the other night that I was never so tired as I was that night. By now we had been able to purchase a second donkey so we loaded those poor animals up as much as we could. I tied Yeshua in a shawl around my neck and Yosef and I each rode an animal. We were on the road heading out of town before sunrise."

We were silent for a while, then Rachel quoted in a still, small voice,

"A voice is heard in Ramah,
weeping and great mourning,
Rachel weeping for her children

and refusing to be comforted,
because they are no more."

"Why, that's beautiful, Rachel," I told her, surprised at the poetic words. "Did you make it up?"

"It's from the Prophet Jeremiah," answered Miryam, before Rachel could speak.

"Yes," confirmed Rachel.

"So," asked Shlomit, eyeing Rachel shrewdly. "Why does a young girl like you know that passage of Jeremiah by heart?"

Rachel colored. She was not used to being the center of attention.

"You don't have to...," I started to say, but Miryam held up her hand. "Let her talk."

Rachel gulped. "It's just that, it's because," she began. Breathing deeply, she started again. "It's because the older brother I never knew was one of those babies killed in Beit Lechem."

WHAT? Shocked, we all stopped walking and stared at her. Suddenly, Rachel burst into tears. Miryam went to her and held her tightly, much as a mother would hold a young child. The rest of us gathered around Rachel, petting her hair, stroking her back, speaking soothing words. After a while, she regained her composure and pulled back from Miryam's embrace, wiping her nose. Slowly we started walking again, Yeshua and the talmidim by now only small dots on the distant horizon.

I wanted to speak with Rachel, to discover more about her family, but she and Miryam were walking alone, locked in a special conversation for just the two of them. Wisely, the rest of us left her alone, understanding the miracle of healing that God had worked out for them. For Miryam, a face had been put on the devastated families of long ago Beit Lechem, and she could mourn with those who mourn. For Rachel, understanding what had been at stake back then brought meaning to an awful family tragedy.

It was on this same trip around the Galil that I first experienced the indescribable joy of placing my hands on a desperately ill person and seeing her healed before my eyes. I had by now, of course, seen many, many healings, and had participated in several of them. But this was the first time that it was me praying alone for someone.

By the second day out, the crowds discovered us, and we could barely keep walking, such were the huge needs which, like a cloud, enveloped us. Yeshua, the talmidim, and the dozens of other men who had by now joined us were all busy laying hands on people and praying for them. The women plunged into the crowds as well, meeting demands everywhere. I was drawn to a determined-looking mother tightly holding by the hand what appeared to be a ten-year-old girl. You could tell that this had been a beautiful girl, but now hideous scar tissue slashed across her face in several spots. My heart hurt at the sight.

Speak to her, whispered the Spirit of God to my soul. Obediently, I placed my hand on the woman's shoulder. "I am with the Rabbi," I informed her. "I can help you."

Wordlessly, she and the girl followed me over to a more secluded spot. The woman regarded me with some ambivalence. "Can I see the Rabbi?" she pleaded. "We've come a long distance. My daughter..."

"Yes, I see," I said. "The Rabbi won't be able to see you today." I pointed to the left and all three of us turned our heads at once, seeing a flash of Yeshua's raised arms as he ministered in the midst of what looked to be several hundred people. Two sets of disappointed eyes swung back around to look at me. "But I'm one of his talmidim," I continued brightly, "And I can pray for you."

The mother stared at me for what seemed to be a long time. "*B'seder*," she finally said. She placed her arm around the girl at her side. "This is my daughter, Hadassah. A few months ago, she had a terrible accident and her face was splashed with burning oil." The mother's eyes filled with tears. "She is a brave girl and has handled the pain well, but how we long for her to be restored to her original beauty."

I nodded sympathetically. "How about you, Hadassah," I asked, turning to look directly at the girl. Her guileless brown eyes stared sadly back at me. "Is this what you want?"

Determinedly, she shook her head *yes*. Then she whispered something incoherent.

"What?" I asked, bending closer to her. "I'm sorry. I didn't hear you. Could you repeat that?"

The girl spoke in a tiny voice. "I said," she whispered slightly louder than before, "I want to get married and have babies. I want to be pretty."

The mother turned away, dabbing at her eyes with the edge of her sleeve.

"Hadassah, do you know that God loves you?"

She lifted her thin shoulders in a little shrug, a puzzled look on her face. I tried again. "Hadassah, I want you to know that the King of the Universe, Adonai, the Lord of all, the Great I AM, loves *you*, sweet Hadassah from..."

"Cana," supplied the mother.

"Cana," I finished.

"Then why did this awful thing happen to me?" asked the child, her scarred face a mockery of the beauty that lay underneath.

"God didn't cause the accident," I explained patiently. "Sin is in the world. Bad things happen. But we have a heavenly father to whom we can cry out to and to whom we can look for deliverance." I noticed some light coming into Hadassah's eyes.

"*B'seder*," she said. "Please pray for me."

I reached into the sash around my waist and pulled out a small ceramic vial of olive oil. Pouring some of it onto my fingers, I applied it to Hadassah's face, touching each of the areas that were scarred. Silently, I prayed, *Help me, Lord. Only You can heal this girl. I can't do anything.* Then I held her face between my hands and prayed aloud, "O Lord, we come before You today and lift up your daughter Hadassah to You. Lord, we know how much You love this little one, and our hearts are broken over the terrible accident that has brought her and her mother such pain and despair. We know, Lord, that You look on the heart, not the face, but we also know that You desire to give gifts to Your children. We pray now that You would take this scar tissue from Hadassah's face and replace it with fresh, new skin. We pray that Hadassah will be Your willing maidservant for the rest of her life, and everywhere she goes she will tell of Your goodness and love. Amen."

I kept my hands on her face and my eyes closed for several more minutes. An unnatural warmth, not associated with the heat of the day, worked its way down my arms, into my hands, and onto Hadassah's face. She kept very still as I held my hands thus. After a while, I noticed that the heat lessened, and then vanished altogether. I opened my eyes and removed my hands.

Was it my imagination, or did she look better? I couldn't tell. "Let's keep praying," I told the girl and her mother. "God is here and is powerful. Don't give up."

Three times I laid hands on Hadassah and prayed for her healing, each time thanking God for His love and mercy. After the third time, I had a sense of peace. I opened my eyes and I don't know who screamed louder, me or the mother! *Hadassah's face was absolutely clear! The scar tissue was entirely gone!*

"What? What?" cried the girl, tentatively putting her hands to her face. We watched, transfixed, as she moved her fingers gently in a circular motion, and rejoiced as realization dawned in her bright eyes that she was feeling smooth skin, not gritty pocks. "I'm healed," she said, slowly at first, then faster and louder. "I'm healed! I'm healed!" Jumping up and down, clutching at her mother, then me, soon all three of us were crying with joy and amazement.

"Come, Hadassah," I said, taking her hands when we had calmed down a bit. "Let's pray and thank God for this wonderful miracle He has wrought." Hadassah, her mother and I held hands then, each of us shouting our praises to the Maker of all that is.

Soon they left, heading back to their home far to the north, happy beyond happy, newly aware of the love their heavenly Father sought to shower on their heads; and others took their place in the prayer lines.

Later, much later, I heard many reports from the others about the grace that God poured out as we prayed for people.

"You see," exclaimed Yeshua that night when we were settled into our camp and the crowds had finally dispersed. He walked around, seemingly inexhaustible, while the rest of us were either lying prone or slumped in a sitting position. "You see how you are able to do the things you see me do! If you are called to be my talmidim, you will do all I do, and more."

And more! Already, we had witnessed him raise a girl from the dead and here he said we would do even more than he did! Hearing this, heaped onto the successes of the day, we felt invincible. We felt like a mighty army out to conquer, out to establish the Kingdom of Heaven within our midst. Why, soon we would be powerful enough to route the miserable Romans. The current governor of Israel, a man called Pilate, had caused no end of disturbance at Herod's palace by his many acts of brutality against the Jews. To crush such a foreigner and rid our nation of him and his cohorts caused sweat to break out on my brow in frenzied anticipation.

This man, Pilate, had recently stolen money from the Temple treasury in order to build an aqueduct. Tens of thousands of my fellow Jews—many from the Galil—came to Jerusalem to protest this action. This was during a festival and the City was, as usual, packed. Pilate disguised his troops and sent them out among the protesters, who they then slaughtered mercilessly. Herod was outraged that Pilate did this. Never very fond of Pilate before, he now violently despised him....

More and more, as the crowds followed after us, so did groups of the religious authorities. Often they mocked Yeshua, and attempted to ensnare him into a punishable offense by the testimony of his own lips. They often asked questions that had no answer. Always, he eluded them, but the interchanges made me wary. I noticed how they took notes on all he did.

It was about this time that Yeshua addressed the people who came after him and were looking for *things*. He referred back to the times when he had blessed the bread and fish and it had multiplied. Bluntly, he told them that *he* was the bread of life; living bread that had come down from heaven. *My own flesh is this bread*, he announced in a strong, unwavering voice. *And I will give it for the life of the world.*

I cannot begin to describe the tumult that came at the heels of this statement. *Eat his flesh? Is he really telling us to eat his flesh? This can't be kosher! He must be mad*, the religious leaders shouted.

But this wasn't all. While teaching at a synagogue in Capernaum, Yeshua next said something even more outrageous. Not only did he say we must eat his flesh, but that unless we eat his flesh *and* drink his blood, we will not have life in ourselves. "Whoever eats my flesh and drinks my blood has eternal life—that is, I will raise him up on the Last Day. For my flesh is true food and my blood is true drink." He went on to say that he lives through the Father, and we need to live through him: the living bread sent down from heaven. We were all appalled and not a little shaken. Even Miryam, Yeshua's mother, seemed shocked.

Many of our numbers deserted us at this point. Grumbling could be heard reverberating throughout the camp. *This is a hard word. Who can listen to it?* We all had to wrestle within ourselves as to whether we truly believed with all our heart and soul that Yeshua was the promised Messiah. Or not.

The Master wasn't happy about the murmuring. He plainly confronted us about our lack of trust. He spoke of branches broken off from the olive tree of life because of unbelief. Shaking his head, he seemed terribly saddened. We weren't used to seeing him like this and it greatly disturbed us.

The Magdalit crept over to him and kissed the *tzit tzit* on his robe. "I love you, Lord," she cried. "I'll always love you!"

He stroked the top of her head fondly. "Tell me," he asked the talmidim, hands held out from each side of his body, more vulnerable than I had ever seen him. "Tell me, are you leaving as well?"

Several of the men moved to speak but Shimon Kefa responded more quickly than the others. Falling to his knees in front of the Master, tears in his eyes, he called out, "Lord, to whom would we go? You have the word of eternal life. We have trusted, and we know that you are the Holy One of God."

A smile touched Yeshua's lips; the pain in his eyes diminished.

Look how important they are to him, flitted across my mind, as I studied the scene before me. The Magdalit sat back on her heels, watching intently as well.

"Didn't I choose you, the Twelve?" he exclaimed. "Yet"—and his eyes filled with pain—one of you is an adversary."

An adversary? Who? Who could he mean? The men looked fearfully at one another. *Could it possibly be me?* each man thought, tormented by the idea.

❦

Very soon after this event, we resumed our traveling. Because of the hostilities exhibited by the religious leaders, Yeshua determined not to enter the region of Judah to the south. However, it was time for the Fall Feasts so we really needed to head up to Jerusalem.

It was at this same time that Yeshua's brothers reappeared, ostensibly to visit their mother, but I think they really wanted to see what was going on. Right away, they started harassing the Master.

Shimon. Yaakov. Yehuda. Yosef. I remembered them from the previous year. Little about them had changed, whereas I felt myself to be a different person entirely. It seemed eons ago that I had first encountered them. I wondered at Yeshua's patience.

"Why don't you go to Judah?" taunted Shimon.

"Let your talmidim see the miracles you do!" enjoined Yaakov. Didn't he understand we had already seen more miracles than the world could hold?

"Don't do your acts in secret!" commanded Yehuda.

"If you're doing these things, show yourself to the world!" pressured Yosef.

"Look," Yeshua said. "It's all right for you to go any time you want to. The world doesn't hate you the way it hates me. I—"

"And why does it hate you?" Shimon cut him off. I winced at the lack of respect.

"Because I keep telling it how wicked it is," responded Yeshua, staring at his brother.

Shimon lowered his head.

"Go on," Yeshua spoke to his brothers. "Go up to Sukkot without me. I'm not going now because it's not yet the right time."

Displeased, they left. Once they were gone, Yeshua also sent the rest of us up to Jerusalem. Much to our disappointment, he himself remained behind, keeping only Shimon, Ya'akov, and Yochanan with him.

Reluctantly, not happy at being parted from the Master, we left. Within a few days we reached Jerusalem, in time for the Feast of Trumpets. This time there was to be no camping out: the Company scattered into various homes and inns made available to us. Andrew took me aside and let me know that the Master told him that he thought it best for me to avoid the palace altogether this time.

"But my husband," I protested, though pleased that Yeshua had thought enough about me to give specific instruction.

"Your husband will know where to find you," Andrew promised me.

And he did. Somehow he received word. The first night I spent in the second floor bedroom of a rented home on the west side of the City, I had Kuza as my companion.

How good it was to see him! So long it had been: the longest we had ever been separated. I worried when I saw him, he looked so pale and thin.

"Is it Herod?" I asked, tenderly stroking his beloved face, once we were alone on our bed.

Kuza grasped my hand and kissed it. His eyes met mine, and I noticed the dark shadows underneath. He spoke quickly, softly. "Time is running out. I am determined to leave the instant I perceive that God has released me from my duties at the palace."

"Do you think that may be now?"

He shook his head. "Not yet. But soon."

"Don't be so gloomy, dear Kuza. A little more of this and Yeshua will announce his kingship and Herod will be history!"

Kuza examined me critically. "Do you really believe that?"

"I thought we agreed that Yeshua is the Messiah!" I cried, upset at his skepticism.

"We do," he replied. "That's not what I'm questioning."

"Then what are you questioning?" I probed.

He lay on the bed next to me, hands behind his head, looking up at the ceiling. He coughed slightly. "I'm not so sure that Yeshua will claim his rightful authority."

"What? Of course he will!"

146

"Why?" Kuza demanded, turning on his side so that he could look into my eyes. "Why do you think that? Did he specifically *say* that's what he plans to do?"

I started to speak, then stopped. Now that Kuza mentioned it, *no*, Yeshua hadn't said that at all. We just all assumed it, from Yeshua's right-hand man, Yochanan, to the person who joined the Company last. In fact, the things that Yeshua did say were downright troubling. But no one spoke about that.

"I, I guess you're right. He hasn't said what he plans to do." I hesitated. Something pricked at the edges of my memory.

"What?" asked Kuza.

"I don't know," I answered, pulling the light blanket tighter around me. *What luxury to be in a bed like this, next to my husband!* "I just remembered something Yeshua said, months ago, that no one understood."

"Tell me," insisted Kuza.

"Well, he said something to the effect that the Son of Man, meaning himself of course, would be delivered into the hands of wicked men. That he would suffer, die, and be raised to life on the third day." I stared at Kuza apprehensively. I had almost forgotten that Yeshua told us these things, so great was my excitement over the miracles in which I had played a role.

"Didn't anyone question him as to what he meant by these fantastic statements?"

"No." I shook my head. "Unless some of the talmidim did in private, and I just don't know about it."

For the first time, Kuza smiled. "You miss very little, my dear wife. I'd be surprised if there's more to the story than what you know."

"What do you mean?" I sputtered, disingenuously. Kuza ignored me. Already he was processing what I had said. I could almost see his brain working behind his forehead. I knew to keep quiet when he was thinking like this.

After a while, he reached out a hand and absently massaged my neck. "Can you think of anything else he may have said along these lines?"

Hmm. I searched my memory. Everything Yeshua had said that made little or no sense, I took out of my head and placed before Kuza. Sleepily, I watched him as he lay on his back, next to me, thinking.

Just as I was drifting off to sleep, he spoke. I opened one eye.

"The only thing that makes any sense to me," he reflected, "is if he were to be killed, come back to life like that little girl, and then take over the kingdom after that."

"Killed! Really killed?!" His words startled me out of my drowsiness. "But he's the Messiah! How can he be killed?"

"I don't know, Yohie. I'm just trying to figure out the possibilities from what you've told me. The Master wouldn't say these things if they meant nothing."

No, he wouldn't. Every word that dropped from his sweet lips had significance.

"Ah, well," Kuza said as he wrapped his arms around me and snuggled close for the night. "I'll ask the Master when I see him." Happy to be together, tired out from the day, we both fell asleep.

EIGHT

I was careful while in Jerusalem to veil my face, lest anyone from the palace recognize me. The last thing I wanted was for any remembrance of me to cross Herod's mind. So it was that when I returned with the festive throng from the Temple back out into the City on the Day of Atonement that I saw my brother Aharon before he saw me.

"Look!" I exclaimed, grasping Shoshana's arm (for we were together).

"What?" she asked, looking around.

"That man. Over there," I said quickly. "The one with the light blue border design on his sleeves and hem. He's my brother."

"Your brother? How wonderful! Should we catch up to him?"

I hesitated. I wasn't sure how Aharon would react to this new, changed Yohana. I couldn't necessarily count on him to be secretive about seeing me. On the other hand, he *was* family. And—the idea suddenly occurred to me—he needed to know about Yeshua. He needed an opportunity to encounter the Kingdom of Heaven. My decision made, I turned to Shoshana. "Yes, let's hurry."

Pushing our way through the crowd, hungry and irritable from the long day of fasting, we walked rapidly in pursuit of Aharon. Unwilling to yell out his name so as not to draw undue attention to ourselves, we nevertheless began to despair when he wove his way through the crowd, getting further and further out of our reach. I really wanted to overtake him before he arrived at his house so that I wouldn't have to have my first conversation with him in the midst of his family and possibly many friends. I wanted to meet up with him alone. Now he was so far ahead of us that I could barely see him. In a few moments he would be out of sight entirely.

"Oh, Shoshie!" I wailed, frustrated. "We're losing him."

Shoshana got a determined look. "How much do you want to see him, Yohie?"

"I think it's important," was my response.

She grabbed my hand. "Stay with me," she ordered. Then she snaked her way through the groups of men and women as if she were a six-year-old street urchin and not a respectable grandmother. Giddy with the pace, I followed her, allowing myself to be pulled along at a truly breathtaking speed. Soon, very soon, we reached the point where we were directly behind Aharon. Out of breath, I spoke his name as loud as I dared without yelling.

Startled, he spun around, eyes scanning the crowd for the caller of his name. He completely ignored Shoshana and myself, obviously assuming that two women alone he didn't recognize had no way of knowing him.

"Aharon," I called again, this time lowering my veil so that my features became visible.

His eyes widened in surprise. "Yohana? Is that you?"

"Yes." I bowed in greeting as the teeming masses of humanity swirled around us on all sides.

Despite the fact that we lived in the same city, I hadn't seen my brother in over two years. Now he seemed genuinely bewildered at my appearance.

I hadn't realized quite how much I had changed until I saw myself through Aharon's eyes. The last time he saw me I had been dressed in the latest styles, hair arranged perfectly, expression haughty. And, oh yes, I limped. But now! Now I dressed in common clothes, my hair hidden. I suspected that my countenance had changed radically (though I had no idea just *how* radically). I walked freely, without pain.

"You're better." It was a statement; some surprise, arched eyebrows.

"Yes."

We threaded our way through the crowd over to the side of the street and took refuge in an alley way between two buildings. I could tell that Aharon was perplexed.

"This is Shoshana," I said to my brother. Gravely, politely, he acknowledged the introduction. Shoshana murmured something in return.

"What's going on with you?" asked Aharon. "I've heard rumors...." He let the rest of the sentence hang in the air, his hands raised palms up in the air.

"Have you heard of the Rabbi Yeshua from Natzeret?" I asked him bluntly.

"Who hasn't? This name is everywhere." His eyes narrowed as he looked at me closer. "Why?"

"I've been traveling around the country with him and his talmidim for about a year."

"You must be crazy." Aharon spoke quietly so as not to be overheard, but each of his words were distinct.

"I'm not crazy." Irrationally, tears sprang to my eyes at his rebuke. I suddenly felt like a little girl. "He's an amazing man, Aharon. He speaks of love, and power and the coming Kingdom of Heaven. He performs many miracles. He healed my diseased hip. You noticed how much better I walk."

"That's right," spoke up Shoshana, for the first time. We both looked at her. "He healed my eyes," she told Aharon. "I was blind."

Aharon stared at her for a moment, mouth pursed, arms folded. Obviously he had no desire to be rude to this woman whose acquaintance he had just made, but it was clear he believed not a word.

Relentlessly, I continued on. "He's the Messiah, Aharon. He really and truly is." I placed my hand on his arm. "You need to come and listen to him speak. You'll be amazed."

Although agitated, my brother attempted to speak calmly. "Are you aware of what's been happening in this City? Do you know that Herod *and* the religious authorities are out to get him? Do you realize the kind of trouble you can get in by associating with this fellow?"

I wanted to tell him about all the wonderful things Yeshua had done and his transforming power in my life, but the words stuck in my throat. My tongue felt heavy and leaden; I was unable to speak further. This was not to be the time.

"*B'seder*," I said. I stood on my tiptoes and kissed him on the cheek. "Give my love to your wife and the children." Shoshana and I slipped back into the crowd, leaving Aharon standing in the alcove with a concerned expression.

❧❦

Later, I berated myself for allowing rejection to get a grip on me so easily. I thought of myself as equal to any situation, but found that my brother's displeasure intimidated me. I was aggravated that telling him about Yeshua hadn't gone well.

I shouldn't have rushed off. I should have stayed and talked to him more, even if he seemed less than thrilled. Oh well. At the very least Aharon would pay closer attention now when he heard Yeshua's name. And one day soon Yeshua was coming to take over in Jerusalem as the true king. Herod would be judged, Pilate and the rest of the nasty Romans vanquished, and a new kingdom of righteousness established. Wine and oil would drip down from the hills as all people everywhere streamed to the Temple of the one true God. Our hearts will rejoice and we will flourish like the grass. Even brother and sister will learn to live in love and mutual harmony. Oh that the day would hurry and be here!

⊷⊶

Sukkot came and still there was no sign of Yeshua. "Did he say he was coming?" asked Kuza, anxious to see the Master, yet at the same time concerned because of local politics.

I pursed my lips, trying to remember. "I think what he said was he wasn't coming to Jerusalem now because it wasn't yet his time. I took that to mean that he would be here later than the rest of us. I don't think he meant that he wasn't coming *at all*. How could he not come to the Feast?"

"I don't know," said Kuza. "But everyone is talking about him."

It was true. At the festival, everywhere we went, we heard whisperings about the "prophet from the Galil." Some people said, "He's a good man," but others said, "No, he is deceiving the masses." No one would speak openly of him for fear of the religious leaders.

We disciples of Yeshua were widely dispersed throughout the City, only occasionally coming into contact with one another. So it was that no three of us were together when Yeshua finally did show up.

Four days into the festival, Yeshua suddenly appeared in the Temple courts and began to teach. Shoshana found out first and immediately came to get Kuza and me. "Hurry up," she said by way of greeting, as she entered the makeshift sukkah that leaned against our rented home. "The Master is here! He's in the Court of the Gentiles."

Posthaste, I stuffed some food provisions and a cloak for evening into a bag and we followed her over to the Temple.

When we arrived, we were just in time to overhear one of the Torah teachers exclaim loudly, "How does this man know so much without having studied?"

Somehow in the huge, jostling crowd of people, Yeshua knew of this comment. "My teaching is not my own; it comes from the One who sent me," he boomed out by way of reply.

Oh, there he was, there he was! It seemed so long since I had the privilege of gazing at his beloved face, though in actuality it had been maybe three weeks.

Surrounded on three sides by Shimon, Ya'akov and Yochanan, the Lord went on to explain that the person who desires to do the will of God will understand that he is from God. Murmuring from the Torah teachers accompanied this instruction.

Yeshua chose not to ignore the whispered comments. Aggressively, he confronted the religious leaders. "Didn't Moshe give you the Torah? Yet not one of you obeys the Torah!"

Beside me, I heard Kuza's hasty intake of breath. Yeshua had thrown down a challenge that demanded an answer. What would come of this? I saw Shimon glance nervously to his right, and left.

"Why are you trying to kill me?" demanded Yeshua, hands in the air, reaching toward heaven. The place grew deathly quiet. Yeshua scanned the crowd, looking into each face. Most turned away. "Why are you trying to kill me?" he repeated.

"You have a demon!" someone screamed. "Who's out to kill you?"

"It's because I heal on Shabbat!" said Yeshua, continuing to look into each man's face, one by one. He pointed a finger in the air. "You will do a boy's *brit milah* on Shabbat so that you follow the Torah of Moshe. I, however, make the whole body well! So why are you angry with me? Stop judging according to the surface appearance and judge the right way!"

Behind us, I heard someone mutter, "Isn't this the man they're out to kill? Yet here he is, speaking openly and they don't do anything. Maybe the authorities think he's the Messiah."

"Surely not," replied another man. "We know where this man comes from but when the Messiah comes, no one will know where he comes from."

"Beit Lechem," I murmured to Kuza. "The Galil."

"Shh," he admonished, listening to the men speak.

Yeshua proceeded to teach, crying out, "Indeed you do know me! And you know where I'm from! And I have not come on my own! The One who sent me is real. But Him you don't know! I do know Him, because I am with Him, and He sent me!" Yeshua stood in the front of the crowd, seemingly towering over everyone, though in reality he was not exceptionally tall.

"Oh no," Kuza said, aware that Yeshua had just challenged the religious authorities by implying that they did not know God. "Now they're going to go berserk."

Kuza was right. Almost as if planned in advance, several of the leading members of the religious ruling party, the *Prushim*, swiftly moved forward simultaneously toward Yeshua. It was clear that they intended him harm.

"Oh no! Watch out, Lord, watch out!" I screamed uselessly.

"Stay here," ordered Kuza, as he pushed his way forward.

Oddly enough, none of the Prushim were able to reach Yeshua. He, plus Shimon, Yochanan, and Ya'akov with him, seemed to vanish. They were gone!

Puzzled, but relieved, Kuza came back over to me. "Well," he said, scratching his head. "It appears that the Master has everything under control." Then he grinned like a young boy.

Shaken but happy, I slipped my arm through his. "Let's go home."

"Good idea. This crowd could turn in any direction," observed my husband. His eyes alertly scanned the area as he spoke. "I want to get you out of here before anything violent happens."

Violent? I pulled my veil closer down over my face, tucking a stray lock of hair behind one ear.

So we left, struggling against the teeming crowd, heading for the street. While walking, we overheard many variations of the same theme: words that filled us with hope and elation.

When the Messiah comes, will he do more miracles than this man has done?

Though we had some interaction with a few of the talmidim over the next few days, Kuza and I did not directly encounter Yeshua again until Hoshannah Rabbah, the last day of the Feast.

Still living together in our rented home (actually in the sukkah *attached* to our rented home), we set out early that morning for the traditional water pouring ceremony at the Temple. Holding our lulavs in our right hands and our etrogs in our left, we followed the priest with the golden pitcher to the Pool of Siloam and back to the Temple. During the very solemn part of the ceremony, where the priest with the water pitcher and a second priest carrying the bowl of wine ascend the altar and pour out their symbolic offerings of salvation and prosperity, an amazing and completely unexpected thing happened. A man in the midst of the assembly stood and cried out in a loud voice,

"If anyone is thirsty, let him keep coming to me and drinking! Whoever puts his trust in me, as the Scripture says, rivers of living water will flow from his inmost being!"

Oh my goodness! It is Yeshua!

The crowd was electrified by his words. Nothing like this had ever happened before. From my vantage point, I could see the high priest turn purple with rage. He and several of his fellow priests conferred hurriedly. Meanwhile, all the people around me realized it was Yeshua and began talking about him.

"This is the Messiah," emphatically declared one woman to her neighbor.

"Surely this man is 'the prophet,' " boldly stated a fellow behind Kuza to whoever would listen. Murmurs of approval greeted these statements.

Others differed. "How can this be the Messiah?" argued an elderly gentleman whose long gray beard all but hid his face. "Doesn't the *Tanakh* say that the Messiah is of the seed of our revered King David, and from the town of Beit Lechem? Isn't this man from the Galil?"

When I heard that I wanted to shout, *he is from Beit Lechem! He is from the line of David! His mother told me!* But Kuza and I held our peace, listening to the many comments all around us and praying silently for God's protection over Yeshua.

Then I noticed that the high priest had called over the Temple guards. After several minutes of impassioned instruction, they headed off in the direction of Yeshua.

"Oh, no, Kuza, look!" I pointed to the guards who were already almost at where the Master stood. My heart pounded and my throat felt dry. "What's going to happen, Kuza? Are they going to hurt him?"

"I don't know, Yohie. Just keep praying."

Eyes wide open, praying under our breath, we watched in fear as the guards reached Yeshua. Behind him, Shimon, Ya'akov, and Yochanan stood, faces pale, slightly hunched. *They must be terrified,* I thought. *I know I would be.*

Time seemed to stand still while the guards spoke with Yeshua. No one laid a hand on him; indeed, they seemed quite deferential. I could see the Master talking but had no idea what was being said. After a while, the guards turned away and went back over to the high priest. Yeshua, also, turned and left the Temple grounds, followed by the three talmidim.

"Praise God," breathed Kuza.

"Amen to that," I fervently echoed.

The guards said something to the high priest and the Prushim. A short exchange followed and then the ceremony continued. It was, to say the least, very anti-climactic.

Later, I found out from Nakdimon what had happened. Apparently, the high priest was completely incensed when the guards, whom he had sent to arrest Yeshua, returned empty-handed. "Why didn't you bring him in?" he raged.

One of the guards shrugged and avoided looking the high priest in the face. "No one ever spoke the way this man speaks," he mumbled, deathly afraid of the seething leader before him.

Carefully restraining himself before the crowd, which was widely sympathetic to Yeshua, the high priest coldly retorted, "You mean you've been taken in as well? Has any of the authorities trusted him? Or any of the Prushim? No! True, the common rabble do, but they know nothing about the Torah. They are under a curse!"

Later, after the ceremony ended, the religious authorities held a brief meeting. They discussed arresting Yeshua when the people weren't around to start a riot in his favor. Bravely, Nakdimon said to his colleagues, "Our Torah doesn't condemn a man, does it, until after hearing from him and finding out what he's doing?"

When Nakdimon repeated this portion of the story, he smiled ruefully. "I thought they were going to stone *me* right on the spot. Everyone turned angrily on me and yelled, 'You aren't from the Galil too, are you? Study the Tanakh, and see for yourself that no prophet comes from the Galil!' Then the meeting adjourned and we all went to our own homes."

About the time that Nakdimon's meeting ended, Kuza and I, not knowing where to find Yeshua, went back to our rented home. In silence, we helped the servant girl dismantle the sukkah. Later, she brought us a simple supper of fruit, cheese and wine. After she departed, we spoke of the day's events.

"You know," I said, biting into a piece of apple on which I had carefully stacked several slices of cheese, "it's amazing to me the way Yeshua keeps walking out of the traps that are set for him. It really does seem that he's immune to danger."

Kuza looked at me thoughtfully, sipping his cup of wine. "If that's the case, then why has he mentioned his own death? How can we reconcile these two things?"

I shrugged. "You had mentioned that maybe he would die and be resurrected like the synagogue ruler's daughter. If that happens, then perhaps he will have total control over when and where. What do you think?"

Kuza toyed with several grapes. He concentrated on building a little grape pyramid before answering me. Used to his thoughtfulness, I waited patiently. "You know," he said, "our understanding of the Messiah from

Scripture is very limited. The Master is not who we expected, is he?" His brown eyes looked up and held my gaze.

"No, you're right. He's nothing like I would have imagined the Messiah to be. But once you see the miracles! And the man himself!" I leaned forward excitedly. "When he spoke about rivers of living water, well, really and truly this is a perfect description of the transformation of my soul since meeting him. Except for you, dear Kuza," I laid my hand on his affectionately, "I was dry and dull, lifeless and parched, like the Negev. But now!" I smiled broadly and my eyes glistened. "Now I feel like a well-watered garden. Now I could be the maiden in King Solomon's poem who's strengthened with raisins, refreshed with apples." My voice broke as a sob caught in my throat. "To sit here and discuss his death! Never!" I fell silent.

We each sat then, lost in our separate thoughts. Slowly, the rays of the setting sun filtered the light in abrupt and shifting patterns over the room in which we rested. Soon it would be dark. Kuza stood, and offered me his hand. "Come, Yohana. Let's go to bed. Tomorrow I must return to the palace."

Rising, I took his extended hand, and, shivering a little in the chill of twilight, followed my husband to the bedroom.

&cy&co

To my great relief, Herod seemingly forgot about my very existence. He never mentioned me to Kuza, nor did anyone else in the palace. The whole thing was so bizarre that I knew it must be the hand of God.

Both Kuza and Yeshua agreed that I, along with Rachel, Adaba, and the Magdalit, should stay with Yeshua throughout the fall and winter. "Use however much money you need," advised Kuza. "Just make sure all of you stay in a decent house somewhere. Give the Lord whatever he needs." He kissed me several times, tenderly caressing my face. "Every time you leave gets harder," he murmured, pulling me close.

"When can you leave the palace for good?" I pleaded. "When can you come with me?"

"I don't know. Not yet." Kuza continued to hold me tightly. "Yeshua has told me that he will let me know as soon as my time with Herod is over. I have to trust him."

Yes, Kuza was right. We had to trust him. But to separate was hard, so hard! To be without my husband meant that I myself was incomplete. And yet....And yet to be near the Lord! What an immense privilege! To me, he represented the fullness of life. He *was* God himself in fleshly form in our midst. Never before in human history had a people been so blessed that they could fellowship with their God. Not since the Garden of Eden, when Adam and Eve communed with the Lord God in the coolness of the day, among the lushness of the fragrant vegetation, had mere human beings gazed on the face of their Lord.

I couldn't get enough of him. I followed after him, longing for time spent near. When he spoke to me, I treasured every word, mulling it over in my mind again and again. When he praised me, I knew true joy. Occasionally, when he had to admonish me, sorrow weighed down my very soul, only to find relief through instant and bitter repentance. And I was not alone in this. Oh no. We *all* loved him passionately. He was more than friend, more than father, or brother, or son. He was king, lord, messiah. He was...the reason for life.

As I look back over that final time with the Lord before returning to Jerusalem in the spring, so many images, so many impressions, press into my mind. The very morning after Yeshua cried out at the Feast of Sukkot, he immediately came back into the Temple courts to teach. As the people who really wanted to hear what he had to say gathered around him, the religious authorities had their lackeys set another trap. A group of men, maybe six or seven, paraded into the area directly in front of Yeshua. They were pulling someone along who was hidden in the midst of their circle. When they reached the Lord, and let go of their human burden, we were all shocked to see a woman, long dark hair unbound, hastily dressed, anguished and sobbing. The Master stood there, looking at them, shaking his head ever so slightly, not saying anything.

The burliest and most brusque of the men spoke, a smile of fake piety plastered to his heavy features. "Rabbi," he said, with a pretense of respect. "This woman was caught in the very act of committing adultery. Now in our Torah, Moshe commanded that such a woman be stoned to death. What do you say about it?"

They wanted the Lord to deny the Torah, and so invalidate himself. But Yeshua knew what they were up to. So instead of answering them, he dropped down onto his heels and began tracing his finger in the dust.

The men were visibly annoyed. *What is he doing? Why won't he answer us?* they murmured one to another.

I stepped closer, peering at the ground. It looked like he was writing words! Yes, there they were: *adultery, lying, theft, murder, covetousness, greed, fornication*, and so on.

"Well," glared another of the men, this one tall and thin with bad teeth. "Should we stone her?"

"Answer us, Rabbi," threatened a third, taking a large, smooth stone out of the folds of his garment and ominously tossing it in the air.

One after another, they berated him with questions, pushing him to pass judgment. The woman, meanwhile, moaned softly, with the look of a terrified, trapped animal.

Finally, Yeshua straightened up and spoke to them for the first time since they had shown up. Eyes dark, he said, "The one of you who is without sin, let him be the first to throw a stone at her." Then he bent down and continued writing in the dust.

"All right," taunted the man who had been tossing his stone in the air, but then he looked down at the ground. Next to the word *fornication*, Yeshua was writing the name *Amnon*. Blanching, the man met Yeshua's eyes, then dropped his stone and turned away, his sneering attitude suddenly gone. The next man saw his name written next to the word *greed*, and his friend beside him paled when his name appeared in the dust beside *adultery*. One by one, they silently turned away and left.

While this was going on, I have to admit that my feelings toward the woman were critical and condescending. Not one to be drawn toward adultery, I have little tolerance for those who do. My love and acceptance of the Magdalit does not express my normative reaction. I believe that God gave me a supernatural love for Miryam such that I instantly forgave her everything.

But this woman, she was not the Magdalit. And I had no supernatural love for her. As these thoughts passed through my mind, and as the last man departed, I saw Yeshua write again in the dust. The word was *critical*. He looked up and his eyes met mine. Shame and recognition hit me. He moved to put what I am convinced was my name next to that ugly word when he paused and looked at me again. Tears gathered in my eyes, and I silently mouthed the words, *forgive me*. His face broke into a smile, the first since the men had appeared. What beauty illuminated his face when he smiled! *Fair as the moon, bright as the sun.*

Yeshua stood up again, turning his attention to the cowering female before him. "Where are they?" he gently asked her. "Has no one condemned you?"

Though trembling with fear, a flicker of hope crossed her red and blotchy tear-stained face. "No one, sir," she whispered, bowing down at his feet.

Infinitely compassionate, Yeshua spoke to her again. "Neither do I condemn you."

The woman lifted her head and her eyes opened wide. "Oh, thank you, thank you sir," she babbled, overcome with her miraculous pardon from certain death. "I..."

But Yeshua held up his hand, stopping her flow of words. "Now go," he commanded her. Then, more sternly. "And don't sin anymore."

"Yes, sir, yes, sir, I mean, no, I won't," she promised, gazing at him with the lovesick eyes that betrayed a future *talmidah*. Then, perhaps realizing how disgraceful she looked, with her loose hair and inadequate clothing, she spun on her heel and dashed out of the temple grounds.

∾∾

Another incident that made quite an impression on me occurred just days later, before we had left the Jerusalem area to itinerant preach. Just south of the city, on the road that eventually led to Beit Lechem, we encountered a fellow whom Yeshua healed. Now this was not in itself at all unusual, but I remember the man and the event clearly for two reasons. One, because the man was one of those rare individuals who immediately grasped who Yeshua was and would not be the least bit cowed into compromising this understanding; and two, because the day was a Shabbat.

We were walking down a long, dusty road in the early afternoon. Any day now, the first of the fall rains were due but so far nothing had fallen, so it remained extremely dry. Other than the relentless blue of the sky, the only colors noticeable in the surrounding landscape were brown, beige, tan. Since the day was Shabbat, no one was out working. Everyone was in their home resting. Well, almost everyone.

Far up, on the right hand side of the road, sat a man. As we drew nearer, it became evident that this fellow was blind, both from his clothing and also from the erect way he held his head, sensing our advancing presence with his ears, not his eyes. As he was the only relief in the monotony of a dreary vista, we all noticed him. Plus, it seemed odd that he was sitting on the side of the road during Shabbat, as this was not a day for begging.

"Rabbi," asked the talmid named Shimon, also known as the Zealot. "Who sinned, this man or his parents, to cause him to be born blind? Is this the outworking of the sins of the parents being visited on the children to the third and fourth generations, as Torah states?" Shimon, a short, muscular man with a broad nose and high cheekbones, tended to be less talkative than some of the other talmidim; so it was interesting for me to hear what was on his mind.

Yeshua stopped in the middle of the road, allowing all of us to catch up before answering. Sensing a teaching moment, I pushed closer in, as well. When he saw that we were all paying attention, he said to Shimon (and the rest of us): "His blindness is due neither to his sin nor to that of his parents; it happened so that God's power might be seen at work in him." The Master also strongly encouraged us to continue doing the Father's work. That said, he led the way over to the blind man.

"Shalom," called out Yeshua when he was across from the man. "Why are you out here in the middle of the day on Shabbat?"

The man's face twitched. He jumped to his feet. To my surprise, I observed that he was a much younger man than I had anticipated; probably in his twenties. "Who is it speaking?" he asked carefully.

"My name is Yeshua ben Yosef. I am traveling with my talmidim and helpers."

"*Baruch ha Shem!*" cried the man. "I heard you were coming this way and I have been out here waiting for you." His sightless eyes looked right at us, his head held at an alert angle.

"And why were you waiting for me?" prompted the Lord.

"I heard that you are a healer," the man answered eagerly. Hope radiated off him. "I heard that you open the eyes of the blind."

"You heard correctly." Thus saying, Yeshua stooped down onto the ground, spat, made a compound of mud with his saliva and proceeded to apply this mud to the blind man's eyes. We all watched intently. You could see the mixture of breathless excitement and desperate hope on the man's face. Slowly, very slowly, he turned his head, looking this way and that after Yeshua had applied the mud.

"Lord," the man said in a small voice. "I don't see anything."

"Go, wash off in the Pool of Shiloach," commanded Yeshua, sending the man back to the very place where he had just recently called all people to himself. (We probably weren't more than a mile from the pool at the time.) To the man's credit, he didn't argue or falter. Instead, with hope rebounding, he grasped his walking cane tightly in his right hand and immediately set off in the proper direction, leaving us gazing after him. Once the blind man was out of sight, we continued on our way.

The next two weeks were spent teaching and preaching in the many small villages that clustered around the outskirts of Jerusalem. Toward the end of the second week, one of the local men, a fellow named Yossi, sought the Master.

I wasn't too thrilled with Yossi. He was just a little *too* respectful and helpful, if that makes any sense. If a difficulty existed which one needed to be chagrined by, there he stood, clucking his tongue. I gritted my teeth and merely endured him when he was around.

"Rabbi," he said solicitously when he had access to the Lord, "have you heard what happened to the blind man whose eyes you healed?"

Yochanan and Shimon exchanged glances. Shimon raised his eyebrows. *Which blind man?* they seemed to be saying to one another. *There's been more than one, you know.*

"A couple of Shabbats ago," Yossi added.

"Tell me," prodded Yeshua. Several of the talmidim stood around, listening as well.

Pleased that he had an expectant audience, Yossi importantly dragged out his story. "Well," he began slowly, eyes bright as he looked around at us all, "apparently he regained his eyesight as soon as he washed in the Pool, just like you told him to, Sir." This last comment was directed entirely to the Master, who sat, leaning back against a tree, arms crossed against his chest. "When he returned to his home, the neighbors argued about whether or not it was really he, since he could now see and no longer spent the days begging for alms.

"Some people said, yes that's him, while others said, no, it merely looks like him." Yossi paused to discreetly spit in the dust behind him. We waited. He continued. "So they asked him, and the man confirmed that it was, indeed, he. Then they wanted to know how his eyes were opened. He told them it was you, Sir, and he told them what you told him to do and how he obeyed. Then they wanted to know where you were, but he said he didn't know."

"Very true," commented Yeshua.

"Yes, Sir," said Yossi. "Next, he was taken to the religious authorities, who argued about you, Sir. They were annoyed that you healed the man on Shabbat."

Yeshua didn't seem at all surprised. "What did the blind man say to the Prushim?"

Yossi scrunched up his face, remembering. "Oh, yes! He told them that you're a prophet."

"And how did they respond to that?"

"Not well." Yossi grinned. "They summoned the man's parents, and asked them how it was that their son could now see. The parents were

162

afraid, and told the Prushim that this was between the Prushim and their son; he was old enough to give testimony so don't involve them. The religious authorities called the man back for a second time, interrogating him. When they pushed at him, he told them that they don't listen, and wondered aloud if perhaps they wanted to become your talmidim, as well."

"Oh, oh," laughed Shimon Kefa, thoroughly caught up in the tale of the blind man. "What did they do when he said *that*?"

Yossi looked over at Shimon. "They snarled that *he* might be Yeshua's talmid, but *they* are talmidim of Moshe. Then they implied that, begging your pardon, Sir (to Yeshua), you weren't from God."

"It's okay, I've heard worse," acknowledged Yeshua, shrugging.

"Yes, but wait, Sir," said Yossi. "The blind, well I mean, the *formerly* blind man, didn't let them get away with any of it. No, Sir! He told them straight out that God doesn't listen to sinners, but to those who fear Him and do His will. If it were true that you, Sir, weren't from God, why then, you couldn't do a thing, much less open the eyes of the blind!"

Yeshua nodded approvingly. "And the man...?"

"Threw him out, Sir," came the prompt response. "Called him a bastard and threw him out of the synagogue."

Not good, I thought, appalled at the lack of wisdom and respect shown by the Prushim. The Lord thanked Yossi for his superior storytelling abilities, causing Yossi, already flush with success, to grin some more.

Not much later, Yeshua and Yochanan left with Yossi in search of the formerly blind man. It wasn't very hard to find him. Seated cross-legged under a shady tree not too far from the place where we had first encountered him, his chin propped up on his fist, he stared dreamily into the distance. He hardly stirred when the men approached, only looking at them when they stopped right next to him.

"Here he is, Sir," announced Yossi, the proud tracker.

The formerly blind man blinked, drawing back warily. "What is it?" he asked with some trepidation, rising to his feet.

Yeshua got right to the point. "Do you trust in the Son of Man?"

When the formerly blind man heard Yeshua's voice, a huge smile came over his sunbaked features. "Sir," he answered, not taking his eyes from Yeshua's face. "Tell me who he is, so that I can trust in him."

Yeshua answered him by saying, "You have seen him. In fact, he's the one speaking with you now."

"Oh, Lord!" exclaimed the man, immediately getting to his knees before Yeshua. "Lord, I trust!"

Yeshua grasped both of the man's hands. "I know you do," he said, warmly. "Persevere in your trust. I will be with you always. Now go! Return to your parents, and your home. Tell them what God has done for you. Glorify God! And do not fear."

He said many other things to the man as well, before sending him off.

❧ ❧

It was about this time that I started getting these nagging reminders of my brother Yishai everywhere I went. A certain smell in the air would take me back to an event in my childhood in which he figured prominently; or I would catch sight of a familiar face in a crowd and my heart would momentarily stop until I realized it only *looked* like him; or (and this was the worst) the Lord would be having one of those fantastic intimate times with us and he would reiterate the need for us to forgive *all* those who have sinned against us, no matter what, and I would freeze, thinking of Yishai.

For years now, I had considered Yishai as good as dead; and quite possibly he was. I mourned for him as one mourns for a loved one who no longer walks this green and vibrant earth. But when last I saw Yishai, he was very much alive. Let me explain.

When Kuza and I first married, we often had the pleasure of visits from my brother. At the time, he, along with Aharon, were assisting my father with his spice business. Like all businesses, this one had busy times and lulls. During the lulls, Yishai would come almost daily to our apartment at the palace, lie on our couch, eat enormous handfuls of almonds and raisins, and talk incessantly. We both adored him. His easygoing, cheerful demeanor contrasted greatly with the intense, frantic pace of the palace, and helped us to relax and recover our sense of humor.

Women also adored Yishai. His dark, curly hair, neatly trimmed beard, strong, handsome features, and sparkling eyes won them over completely. They liked him and he liked them. So we should have seen it coming.

One day, while visiting us at the palace, Yishai and I were on our way to Kuza's office when Yishai spotted the daughter of a traveling dignitary heading in our direction. A young girl, probably not more than sixteen, she trailed through the elaborate pillared hallway several paces behind her parents, gazing in awe with big, curious eyes at the artistry etched throughout this massive facility I so affectionately referred to as "home." A Roman girl, she had apparently just taken the leap into adulthood, as

164

evidenced by her glossy, upswept hairstyle and clinging white gown. Friendly dark eyes lighted on our faces, and she smiled, displaying even white teeth. I nodded politely while Yishai elaborately bowed, causing the girl to blush prettily.

"An honor, miss," announced my brother grandly, staring at her boldly. "Allow me to introduce myself. I am Yishai ben Hezron, of the illustrious tribe of Judah. And this is my sister, Yohana." He indicated me with a back sweep of his hand, never taking his eyes from the girl's face. She in turn bowed to us both.

"I am a visitor to your great city, sir," she exclaimed, a little breathlessly. Nervously glancing at the quickly retreating backs of her parents, who were too engrossed in their own conversation to notice their daughter's absence, she seemed to make an internal decision to take her time. Turning her full attention back to us, she smiled at Yishai. "My name is Claudia. My parents and I are here from Rome."

"Will you be here long?" he murmured, taking a step closer to her.

"About a month," came the prompt reply. Then, "I had best catch up to my parents." Another warm smile directed to Yishai. "So nice to have made your acquaintance." And she was off.

"What was that all about?" I hissed at Yishai, when she was gone. "It's very inappropriate for you to flirt with a Roman girl like that."

"I wasn't flirting," he lied.

I was about to reply when I realized that the likelihood of their paths crossing again were virtually non-existent. Better not to make a fuss over the matter. Resolutely putting it from my mind, I neglected to even mention the encounter to Kuza.

But I was very, very, wrong. Yishai grew obsessed with the girl and sought her out. She, on her part, became entranced by the charming young Israelite and recklessly agreed to secretly meet him. I grew suspicious when Yishai came to the palace every day but spent most of his time restlessly wandering the grounds, careening from wildly energetic to withdrawn and moody. Gone was his relaxed, affable attitude. He turned into a stranger I did not recognize.

It was only when, toward the end of the month, I chanced to come into a room where he paced alone, that I understood what had occurred. His back to me, unaware of my entrance, I heard Yishai beseeching God to hear his prayers so that he and his "beloved Claudia could marry." I gasped with shock, Yishai swirled around on his heel, and the two of us stared at each other for what seemed an interminable period. My brother's eyes were ringed white with desperation, but hope lodged there as well.

I found my voice first. "Have you gone crazy?" I demanded. "The girl is not Jewish! Whatever have you been thinking?" I sat down hard on the nearest chair and stared up at Yishai with angry eyes.

He stood there, towering over me, clenching and unclenching his fists. "I can't help it, Yohie. I'm totally, utterly, absolutely in love with Claudia." His eyes took on a dreamlike expression. "She is the most beautiful woman who ever graced the earth. She is stunning. She is—"

"Enough!" I shouted, interrupting his litany of praises. "She is not for you, Yishai! She is the daughter of a dignitary from the court of the Emperor himself! Do you think they want her to marry a Jew from one of their conquered nations? And do you think Ema and Abba want you to marry our enemy? A pagan from that despicable country across the Sea?"

Yishai drew back from my tirade as if he had been stabbed with a spear. He pursed his lips together and shook his head *no*. Backing away from me, continuing to shake his head, he reached the door and slipped out quickly.

I got up and ran to the open doorway. My brother was running hard, fast. Already, he had become no more than a small figure in the distance. "Yishai!" I yelled as loudly as I could. He did not pause or turn back. Mindful of not making a scene, I let him go.

Though I did not know it then, that was the last I would see of my brother. In his desperation to have Claudia as his own, he did some incredibly reckless things. Finding, as I had predicted, both sets of parents against this union, he stole money from my father and convinced his lady love to flee the country with him. She, foolish girl, needed very little persuading, and the two lovers vanished in the night.

The resulting uproar at the palace when Claudia's parents discovered their daughter's absence almost sunk Kuza's career. For a few months, we were very scared, not sure if our necks were to compensate for the lack of Yishai's neck. Fortunately, the hysterical parents removed themselves back to Rome and the whole matter died down. But not for my family.

My parents were horrified by their son's actions. More than that, though, they were heartbroken. "Where did I go wrong?" wailed my mother, wringing her hands and sobbing.

My father aged visibly overnight; the lines around his eyes and mouth tighter, angrier. Not as vocal as my mother, still he gave vent now and again to his grief. "My son, why? Why?" He took less interest in his work and acted as though Yishai were dead and grieved accordingly.

Aharon grew exasperated with our parents. Finally he could take the heartache no more. "Forget it! Just forget about him!" he snapped harshly. "He's obviously forgotten about you."

Needless to say, this choice comment failed to alleviate my parents' pain, but it did serve to cause them to be less demonstrative.

Not long after these things occurred, my father died of a heart attack. I always believed that his sorrow over Yishai hastened his death. My mother didn't last long after her beloved husband passed. She grew weary, despondent. Aharon married, moved into his own home, and became more and more distant. In the space of two years, I went from being a newly married young woman whose parents and brothers added a richness to the fabric of my life to a married orphan with one brother as good as dead and the other elusive. Kuza became my whole life. And then I birthed dead baby after dead baby. It was an awful time.

For a while I hoped to hear a piece of gossip; or some tidbit from a traveling merchant which would give me a clue as to Yishai and Claudia's whereabouts. Though I had a great deal of anger against Yishai; still, I was curious as to what had happened to him. I never heard a word, however. He seemed to have fallen off the map. After a few years, I ceased to think about Yishai, locking him out of my mind and heart. All that remained was a dull ache.

Since Yeshua had touched my icy heart regarding my daughter, though, the layers of anger, unforgiveness and loss relating to *Yishai* were slowly being shed, exposing more and more of my true emotions. I was getting wise to this game. I could see that the Master expected me to forgive my brother.

One day, just before the Feast of Dedication, I sought an audience with Yeshua. He was relaxing in his room at the inn outside Jerusalem where several of us were staying.

"What's it about?" quizzed Shimon, reluctant to let anyone (even me!) disturb the Master when he had a moment to rest.

This was hard! Not only did I have to face things I'd rather ignore, but I had to push, persevering to do it! Gritting my teeth, I answered Shimon's question as best I could. "Uh, there's someone from my past who I think God wants me to forgive and I need to talk to the Lord about it."

Shimon looked unconvinced. "Of course God wants you to forgive people. Why can't you just pray and ask for His help?"

This was so maddening. "Because," I patiently explained, though my head was starting to pound behind my temples, "I need help. The Lord's help."

"Well, look, Yohana," Shimon began, extending one big meaty hand my way, palm up, "why don't you pray with me instead?" He cast a fleeting glance behind him at the closed door to the Lord's room. "I hate to bother him. He's so tired. He never stops."

I glared at him. *I don't want to pray with you. I want to pray with the Master*! I opened my mouth, only to close it again. Shimon was always so nice to me. It would be nasty to treat him as inconsequential.

Maybe I should trust him enough to tell him about Yishai. Besides, it was becoming more and more apparent that he was *not* about to let me have access to Yeshua.

"Well," I said slowly, "It *is* somewhat personal...."

"Oh, in that case," he said, his face brightening, "why don't you pray with one of the women, then? Like Shoshana, or Miryam?"

He looked so relieved that he might be off the hook with me that, despite myself, I had to laugh. "All right, Shimon. Don't worry about it. I won't bother the Rabbi. You *will* let him know that I came to see him, won't you?"

"Of course," he promised, his face a study in innocence. "Why wouldn't I?"

∝∽

Why wouldn't you indeed! I huffed to myself, as I hurried back to the room I currently shared with Shoshana and the Magdalit. When I arrived, they were both lying on their respective beds, resting.

"Where were you?" asked Shoshana, opening one sleepy eye

"I tried to see the Master, but Shimon wouldn't let me through."

"Good for him!" This from the Magdalit.

"I beg your pardon?" I remarked, a little disconcerted.

"The Master needs to be protected," remarked Miryam. "He never turns anyone away, but that doesn't mean that he doesn't need his rest just like us."

"*B'seder*!" I threw my hands in the air dramatically. "I give up!" I sat down heavily on my bed, bending down to untie my sandals.

"Are you all right, Yohie dear?" asked Shoshana, in a motherly tone. Her kindness disarmed me. "No!" I cried, and burst into tears.

Both Shoshana and Miryam practically flew off their beds, rushing over to comfort me. "Is it Kuza?" murmured Shoshana, holding me close.

I shook my head *no*, unable to speak.

"Is it one of us?" asked Miryam, worried.

Again, I gestured an emphatic *no*. My two friends looked at each other over the top of my head, perplexed. Finally, I drew a shaky breath as my sobs abated. "It's my brother," I managed to say, as I blew my nose.

Shoshana looked confused. "Your brother? You mean that fellow that we saw during Yom Kippur?"

"Aharon?" I raised my head and smiled weakly. "No, it's my other brother, Yishai."

"I've never heard you mention him," said Shoshana.

"That's because I haven't talked about him in years. It's been too...painful." I wiped my eyes and sat back on my bed, my two friends flanking me on either side. "It's been close to thirty years since I last saw him. He did something awful and I've held unforgiveness against him all this time. That's why I wanted to see the Master. To pray with him about all this."

Shoshana took my hand and held it firmly. "Why don't we pray together, the three of us? Is that okay with you?"

"Yes," I whispered, closing my eyes.

The Magdalit took my other hand, and Shoshana started praying. "Lord God Almighty, *Adonai Tsvaot*, we come to You because You and You alone can take our burdens from us. Our dear sister Yohana has a heavy millstone of unforgiveness hanging around her neck and she no longer wants to carry this thing. We come before You, pleading that You help her get rid of it."

"Oh Lord God," I cried, slipping to the floor so that I could kneel before Him. "I don't want to be bitter! I don't want to be poisoned by unforgiveness! I hold up before You both Yishai and Claudia. I forgive them now for their lying and treachery. I forgive Yishai for rejecting his family. I forgive him for hastening my parents' deaths. I forgive him for causing trouble for Kuza and me. Bless him, Lord. Bless and prosper him. Restore our relationship, if he is still alive." I stayed on my knees, silently praying. Suddenly, that heavy weight in the middle of my chest dissolved. I felt free!

"Oh my!" I exclaimed, looking around at my friends. "I feel better!"

"*Baruch HaShem!*" exalted Shoshana, kissing me on the cheek.

I turned to Miryam, but she was lying on the floor, stretched out full length. "Help me to forgive as well, Lord," she wept, her voice muffled against the floor. "Help me to forgive my husband for rejecting me. I give Dan to you...," her voice broke and she lay there, crying.

I sat on the floor next to her, stroking her back. Shoshana eased herself onto the ground as well and placed her hand on Miryam's head. "Shh, it's okay."

"Oh, oh," Miryam sobbed, her long, dark eyelashes wet with tears. "I'm sorry. I hadn't realized that I was so angry at Dan until we started praying just now. I thought that *he* had to forgive *me*. I didn't realize I needed to forgive him as well."

"Have you heard from him?" I asked, not having broached this topic for a while as it was so delicate.

She shook her head. "I haven't seen or spoken with him since that day we went to my house together." She paused. "I have heard that he lives alone. He hasn't divorced me."

Shoshana and I exchanged a meaningful look. "Well that means something, don't you think, Miryam? He must still love you."

She shrugged. "I don't know what to think. Whether or not I ever see him again, it's in God's hands."

"Do you want to pray and tell God that you've forgiven him?" This from Shoshana.

"Didn't I just do that?"

"I heard you ask God to *help* you forgive Dan. I didn't actually hear you say, *I forgive Dan.*"

"You're right. Let's pray again." Miryam sat up straight and tall, pulling her long, heavy hair back from her face and wound it into a bun, tying it tight with a long tress. "Dear Lord," she said softly. "Thank You for Your deliverance and forgiveness in my life. Thank You for the indescribable privilege of knowing Your Son. When You've forgiven me so much, how can I not forgive those who have sinned against me as well? So I forgive, I forgive...."

I patted her on the back. "Keep going," I whispered.

Taking a deep breath, Miryam continued. "I forgive Dan for any and all sins he has committed against me. I no longer hold anger or bitterness against him. I release him to You. Amen." She sat quite still, a small smile playing around the corners of her lips. "*Yofee.* That was good to do."

"Yeshua will be proud of us," noted Shoshana, looking pleased herself. "This is what he wants: for us to learn from his teachings and know how to approach our heavenly Father."

"Come on," I said, rolling onto my bed and snuggling into the pillow. "Let's follow his other example and get some rest."

Laughing, Miryam and Shoshana took my advice.

170

NINE

The Feast of Dedication, or *Hanukkah,* saw Yeshua and his talmidim (myself included) back in Jerusalem. Despite the increasing seriousness of the religious leaders' threats against him, the Master refused to be intimidated. Instead, he pushed to step up his teaching, preaching and praying.

During the Feast, Yeshua came daily to the Temple. One day, when we were walking in Solomon's Colonnade, a group of synagogue authorities surrounded us. They taunted the Master about his proneness for speaking in parables, saying, "Don't keep us in suspense any longer. Tell us plainly if you are the Messiah."

"Look," Yeshua said boldly, standing up to them and not shrinking back while Shimon Kefa looked as menacing as his kind face allowed, "I have told you but you don't believe. If you can't believe the miracles, then it's because you're not my sheep." He gestured to his talmidim. "These are my sheep. They listen to me; I know them and they follow me. I give them eternal life and they shall never perish. No one can snatch them out of my hand or my Father's hand." Then Yeshua made a statement that dispelled any remaining doubt as to Who he believed himself to be. He raised his hands in the air and proclaimed fervently and passionately, "I and the Father are one."

Furious, seething with hatred over what they perceived as blasphemy, the men who had come to confront Yeshua now grabbed stones with which to kill him. Faces contorted by rage, they moved menacingly toward him.

"Come on, Master, let's go," urged Shimon, one voice among many ready to flee.

But Yeshua stood his ground. Unafraid, he spoke ironically to the religious leaders. "I have shown you many great miracles from the Father.

For which of these do you stone me?"

Pausing in their violence, one of the men replied, "We're not stoning you for any of these, but for blasphemy, because you, a mere man, claim to be God."

"The miracles speak for themselves," answered Yeshua calmly, purposely ignoring Shimon and Yochanan who were desperately gesturing for him to get away. "You need to understand that the Father is in me and I am in the Father."

Thus said, he was now willing to leave the Temple area and escape his would-be assassins. Several of the men lunged at him in an attempt to grab and hold him so that they could kill him. They were unable to contain him, however: it was as if his very flesh repelled their touch. Confused, they sluggishly tried again, but he and the talmidim ran off.

After this latest flagrant attempt on his life, Yeshua decided to leave Jerusalem and head back across the Jordan River to the place where Yochanan the Immerser had immersed in the early days of Yeshua's ministry. We established a camp in the wilderness by the river, and scores of people came to us there. Yeshua performed many miracles, and great numbers of people put their trust in him. We stayed there the rest of the winter.

❧ ❧

One day a man ran into the camp. Breathless, he declared, "I have an urgent message for the Rabbi. Where is he?"

Shimon and Andrew went to meet him. "Tell us," they said. "We'll convey whatever you have to say to the Master."

But the man shook his head. "Only the Rabbi," he insisted. "Those were my orders."

"Orders?" wondered Shimon. "Orders from whom?"

"From the sisters in Beit Anya. The friends of the Rabbi," answered the messenger.

Shimon and Andrew looked at each other. "Come with us," said Andrew, and they took him in to see Yeshua.

"Rabbi!" exclaimed the messenger, when he saw Yeshua. "I have a message for you from the sisters in Beit Anya: Miryam and Marta."

"Let's have it, man," said the Lord, eyes alert.

"They want you to know that the one you love is sick," he cried urgently.

Yeshua closed his eyes. He said nothing.

The messenger grew impatient. "What shall I tell the sisters? Will you return with me?"

Yeshua's eyes flew open. "Tell them that this sickness will not end in death. Tell them that it is for the glory of God, so that God's Son may be glorified though it."

The messenger's face brightened. "So does that mean that you're coming to Beit Anya?"

"No, not now," said Yeshua, to the messenger's obvious disappointment.

"But the sisters...," sputtered the man. "They're expecting you! They were so sure that you were coming..." His voice trailed off.

"Now, now," cautioned Shimon, who had been present at this interchange. "Don't hassle the Rabbi. He knows what he's doing."

"Of course," the man quickly said. "I just know how much they were hoping to see him."

"It'll be all right," said the Lord. "Just give them my message. I say it again, this sickness will not end in death."

"*B'seder.* I will return then," said the man.

"Will you stay the night?" This from Andrew.

The messenger shook his head. "They were really frantic when I left. I don't want them to wait anymore than they must." He glanced at the sun, now directly overhead in the sky. "If I go now I should make it by dark. Some food and water is all I request."

"Most assuredly," consented Andrew. "Come with me."

"God be with you," called Yeshua. He had a thoughtful look on his face.

The messenger left. Word soon traveled throughout the camp about Elazar's sickness. *Why didn't he go?* most of us wondered. We all knew how much Yeshua loved Elazar. *Why didn't he go to his friend in what was obviously a time of great need?* I have to say, many of us were unsettled by Yeshua's behavior.

The next couple of days were business as usual, if that's what you can call the blind seeing, the lame walking, and the deaf hearing. Then suddenly Yeshua announced, "Let's go back to Judea."

"But Rabbi," protested the same talmid who had just assured someone else that the Lord knew what he was doing. "The religious leaders tried to stone you. Do you really think it's a good idea to go back there?"

"It's our friend Elazar," explained the Lord, his eyes tired in the glare of the desert sun. "He has fallen asleep, but I am going there to wake him up."

None of us understood what Yeshua meant by "falling asleep," so he had to be more blunt.

"He's dead. For your sake and the sake of your faith, it is best that we go now and not before. But go we must."

Many of the talmidim were exceedingly nervous to go back into the territory around Jerusalem after the violence we had escaped at Hanukkah. But what were we to do? We had vowed to follow the Master, and follow him we would. It was Thomas who summed it up best:

"Let us also go, that we may die with him."

❧

The journey there took time; more time than expected. Yeshua seemed particularly disinclined to rush, and spent what seemed like inordinate amounts of time with everyone and anyone who needed him. Which is why it took over three days for a one-day trek.

"The sisters must be beside themselves," I muttered to Shoshana as we waited around yet again for the Master.

"It seems more like it's *you* who's beside herself," observed my friend, eyeing me critically. "What's the matter, Yohana?"

"Nothing's the matter!" I fumed, agitated. "It's just that I know how close Elazar and his sisters are to Yeshua. It seems odd to me that he's being so, so..." I wanted to say the word *careless* but wisely refrained. "So *casual,*" I supplied instead.

"Do you really think he's not affected by the news about Elazar?"

"What do you mean?"

"I mean, look at him! He's not rushing to Beit Anya, I'll grant you that. But I can tell that he is preoccupied, even sad."

"All right," I conceded, somewhat ashamed. "But it looks to me like he is purposely *stalling.*"

"Well, maybe he is," retorted Shoshana. "And just maybe," she added mischievously, "he's smarter than you and knows what he's doing, even if you can't immediately see it."

That shut me up for a while. And twenty minutes later, when we stopped to pray for a leper who waited expectantly at the side of the road, I was able to add my heartfelt prayers to those of Yeshua's for the poor, diseased man, and not be annoyed that we were going to be even later.

On the morning of the fourth day we reached the village of Beit Anya. It was one of those spectacular days when the winter rains have stopped, it's still relatively cool, the sun is out, and all those brilliant red, yellow, blue, purple, pink, and white wild flowers cover the ground. Big, fleecy white clouds drifted in the blue sky, toward the western horizon. The crunch of the dirt and stones under our sandaled feet as we walked up the familiar road toward the village had a reassuring sound, as well.

Before we even got to the village, we met up with several of the friends and relatives who had come in from Jerusalem in order to offer their condolences to the sisters. We learned from them of Elazar's death. Needless to say, as soon as folks saw Yeshua, he was instantly in demand. Even the people who were hostile to him came right over (mostly to start arguments, but still, they wanted to talk). One of the men in the group ran up to the house to let the sisters know that Yeshua had come. So it was that we hadn't budged from this particular spot when Marta showed up.

My heart broke when I beheld her. Strong, determined Marta! Eyes red from weeping, shoulders bent forward with the weight of the world, her beloved brother, gone! Yeshua had been talking with one of the many friends who had lingered in the village since the burial, but as soon as he noticed Marta coming, he broke off the conversation and quickly ran over to her. She, for her part, ran right into his arms and sobbed for several minutes while he held her.

Finally, she looked up at him, her eyes wet with tears. "Lord, if you had been here, my brother would not have died." There was no accusation in her tone, only a terrible bereavement for what might have been. Still, she clung to hope stubbornly. "But I know that even now God will give you whatever you ask."

Yeshua looked at her, and his eyes reflected myriad points of light. "Your brother will rise again," he told her, addressing her heart's desire.

Murmurs of anticipation undulated through those of us standing there. I confess that we all pressed in, trying to overhear as much of their conversation as possible.

Marta looked confused. Hope and resignation struggled for dominance in her eyes. "I know he will rise again in the resurrection at the last day," she allowed, cautiously.

Yeshua stood up straighter, looking even more like a king than ever. "I AM the resurrection and the life," he proclaimed forcefully. "He who believes in me will live, even though he dies; and whoever lives and believes in me will never die." He caught Marta's trembling hand in his sun-bronzed one, hardened from years of work yet still graceful with long, flexible fingers. He looked deep into her eyes. "Do you believe this?"

The forbearance that had dulled Marta's eyes now gave way to glorious hope. Pain and suffering eased from her countenance as she got down on her knees before her Master. "Yes, Lord," she assured him, "I believe that you are the Messiah, the Son of God, who was to come into the world."

At this, several among the friends and relatives began grumbling. *What is she saying? Why, it's blasphemy! Shh, leave her alone, she's in enough distress!* And so on.

Marta rose from her knees, and I heard Yeshua say to her, "Go! Call your sister. I would speak to her as well." She bid him farewell, then, and without so much as a glance in the direction of any of the rest of us, returned quickly to her home.

Presently, in what seemed no time at all, Marta returned, her sister Miryam striding quickly alongside her. When Miryam saw Yeshua, she ran right over to him, ignored everyone around her, and fell to the ground at his feet. "Lord, if you had been here, my brother would not have died," she sobbed, uttering the same words as Marta had earlier.

Miryam's weeping caused a fresh outbreak of wailing and mourning amongst the friends and relatives who were crowding around Yeshua. Cries of "Elazar, Elazar" became distinguishable in the midst of the din. Many tore their clothes and sprinkled their heads with dust, as a sign of grief. All of us loved Elazar, so were caught up in the sadness of the occasion.

Yeshua himself appeared deeply moved in spirit and troubled. "Where have you laid him?" he asked of Miryam and those who attended to her.

"Come and see, Lord," came the response and the people who were there beckoned us to follow them as they led the way to the caves cut into the sides of the nearest hill.

Yeshua knew this path well, having trod it often in the past with Elazar on his happy visits to this most congenial of locations. Now his heart was heavy and his face sad. Tears flowed freely from his eyes only to be lost somewhere down his beard. Grief enveloped him like a cloud. Several cast curious glances in his direction. "See how he loved him!" exclaimed many.

But others cast aspersion on the Master. *Could not he who opened the eyes of the blind man have kept this man from dying?* And they used this opportunity to find fault with the Lord.

While these things were being said, we trudged up the hill and soon reached the caves. One had a stone rolled in front of it and I knew it to be the tomb of Elazar's parents. Another, next to it, which used to be empty,

176

now had a stone blocking the entrance as well. "This is he," pointed out Miryam, breaking into a fresh torrent of tears.

Yeshua stood still and looked at the tomb. Then he closed his eyes and prayed silently. We all watched him intently. When he opened his eyes he said to some of the men who had accompanied them, "Take away the stone."

Nobody obeyed. Rolling the stone away from a tomb! It seemed wrong.

Marta put into words what everyone had been thinking. "But, Lord," she protested, troubled. "By this time there is a bad odor, for he has been there four days."

Yeshua admonished us sharply. "Did I not tell you that if you believed, you would see the glory of God?"

We all looked at one another. Marta went over and spoke some words to the men Yeshua had just told to take away the stone. They argued with her, but she persevered. Backs erect, heads held at an "I'm unhappy with this" angle, six of the men went over to the stone.

"At three!" the biggest one yelled. "One, two, three!" Muscles straining, knees bent, they rocked that enormous stone back and forth until enough momentum was gained so that they were able to roll it out toward us. Then, avoiding looking inside the tomb lest they gaze upon a corpse, the men sauntered off to the sides of the crowd.

All this time, Yeshua had been standing in the same spot, praying. Now he looked up to heaven and said aloud, "Father, I thank You that You have heard me. I know that You always hear me, but I said this for the benefit of the people standing here, that they may believe that You sent me."

I waited breathlessly for what was next. I had an idea of what was to come. Could it be?

Yes! In a rich voice filled with power and authority, Yeshua called into the tomb. "Elazar, come out!"

All around me I heard people shrieking and screaming. Some even hit the ground in a dead faint. For emerging into the bright sunshine from out of the cold darkness of the tomb was the (formerly) dead man! His hands and feet were wrapped with strips of linen and a cloth was about his face. He moved stiffly, as though dazed.

Yeshua called to the same men who had just grudgingly moved the stone. "Take off the grave clothes and let him go," he instructed them. This time, they sprang into action immediately.

Miryam and Marta didn't know quite what to do. Oddly reluctant to touch their brother, whom they still thought of as dead, they instead clung to Yeshua in a state of shock. Finally, Yeshua had to walk them over to Elazar once the resurrected man was set free from his grave linens.

"Here is your brother," presented Yeshua. "He is a testimony to the glory and goodness of God the Father." He put his arm around the somewhat shaky man. When Marta and Miryam saw Yeshua do this, they felt free to touch Elazar as well. Shyly, each sister took one of his hands. Elazar, however, had eyes only for Yeshua. He stared at his friend as one mesmerized.

"You are my Lord and my God," he avowed, in tones ringing with awe and reverence. Then he was seized with a fit of trembling. Alarmed, the sisters held him, one on each side, like bookends.

"He's fine," Yeshua answered the unasked question. "Get him out of the sun and give him water and something to eat." Several people rushed to help, and they walked Elazar back to the house.

Every one of us there was, of course, utterly amazed over what had just happened. Yeshua spent the rest of the day telling now receptive hearts and minds about the Kingdom of Heaven, and the need for repentance and a turning from sin. He described God the Father to many who thought they understood God's character but had really barely touched the most minute aspect. Light fell on them, and they said one to another, *Can any man know God better than this man? Indeed, he is the promised Messiah of Israel!* But there were some there that day who loved darkness better than light and slunk stealthily away to the religious authorities in Jerusalem in an attempt to cause trouble for Yeshua.

Looking back now at all these events, I can say with some authority that the raising of Elazar from the dead was the high point of our time with Yeshua. We knew that we were in the company of the greatest man ever to walk the face of the earth. We knew that not even Moshe Rabbeinu had accomplished such great feats. We knew that only God alone could do what this man had done. We knew that this humble, sun-darkened, simply dressed carpenter from the Galil with his ready smile and burning eyes was the true king of Israel. We were ready to follow him anywhere, no matter what. We were fearless in the company of such a man. Herod had receded in my eyes like one who becomes a gnat, or an ant. He could do nothing.

We spent several days with Elazar, Marta, and Miryam. Hourly, Elazar gained strength and vitality. He refused to discuss with anyone other than Yeshua what he had seen while dead. Before Elazar's sickness and death, he and the Lord had seemed the closest of friends. Now they were more intimate than brothers. They shared something the rest of us had yet to understand. Elazar still had joy, but it was a more somber joy, a profound joy.

The sisters showed their pleasure in different ways. Marta hovered over her brother and the Master, offering them twelve different types of delicacies all day long. Miryam sat on the floor between the two men, leaning her head against her brother's knee, sneaking glances at his face every so often as if to reassure herself that he was really there. If either man got up and walked around, she would follow them with her eyes. And if they left her presence altogether, she would move restlessly about the house, eager for their return.

All in all, the time spent there was a glorious time, basking in the glow that shone from the glory and praise lavished on God through the testimony of His Son, Yeshua.

On our fourth day at Elazar's house, a visitor came to us by night. Nakdimon, a member of the Sanhedrin, or ruling council, but also a talmid of Yeshua, brought the Master alarming news. It seemed that some of those present at the resurrection of Elazar had reported what had happened to the Prushim, who in turn called a special meeting of the Sanhedrin.

Distraught, his face clouded with apprehension, Nakdimon closeted himself in with Yeshua, Elazar, and Yochanan for over an hour. When the men emerged, their faces were grave. Yochanan took one of Elazar's servants aside and instructed him in something. The man then proceeded to gather together all the members of Yeshua's company, including several of us who had already retired for the night.

When we were assembled in one place, the Master made an announcement. "It seems that our current high priest has inadvertently prophesied that it is better for one man to die than the whole nation to perish," he began a bit wryly. "That being the case, fear of the Romans is driving our leaders to seek my death."

"Should we arm ourselves then, Lord?" asked Shimon, fists clenched, eyes dark at the prospect of battle.

"No, Kefa!" rebuked the Master sharply. "This is not the time for swords and spears. My Kingdom is not of this world. I will not fight according to the world's standards."

Shimon looked away, accepting the reprove stoically, but I could see that his fists were still clenched.

"No," the Master said, softer this time. "I want everyone to gather together his possessions. Tomorrow morning we leave for a secluded place near the desert, west of here." Rather abruptly, Yeshua said good night and left for his sleeping quarters.

After he had gone, we each spoke to our neighbor, voicing our concerns, doubts, anxieties. *Why doesn't he claim his rightful kingdom?* could be heard, with many variations, again and again.

⁂

Indeed, the next morning, which came with all-too-sudden brilliance, witnessed the perpetuation of these same murmured concerns. I am ashamed to admit that I, too, participated in this second-guessing of the Lord.

"I really don't understand why we have to flee to some remote part of the desert," I grumbled to Shoshana as we hurried to keep up with the rest of the Company (we were in our customary position in the tail of the procession). "Why can't the Master call down angels from heaven and destroy the Romans? *Then* the religious authorities would have no choice but to recognize his deity and acknowledge him as king."

"Do you really think so?" asked Shoshana in the irritated voice one generally reserves for misbehaving small children and sullen servants. "What makes you think that *anything* will make them believe?"

I chose to ignore her offensive tone. "Don't *you* think that if something as spectacular as angels descending from heaven slaying our enemy happened, that they would notice?"

Shoshana stopped walking and faced me, hand on one hip, incredulity stamped all over her face. "Yohana, the Lord just *raised a man from the dead!* For almost three years now he's been performing miracle upon miracle. You and I can attest to amazing things in our own lives! Has this made any difference to the mindset of certain people? Any difference at all?"

"To some people, yes it has," I argued, unwilling to relinquish my position. "We've seen many people acknowledge Yeshua as Messiah."

"And how many of them are from the Sanhedrin," pressed Shoshana, her eyes narrowing. "Besides Nakdimon," she quickly added, just as I opened my mouth to speak.

"There are some others." I valiantly defended my weakened position. "What about that fellow Yosef of Ramataim? You know, the silver-haired handsome one?"

"Yes, yes, I know who you're talking about. Unfortunately, he's not acknowledged publicly that he believes in Yeshua. So I refuse to count him." Shoshana pursed her lips into a tight, thin line and kept walking, pulling her head scarf down over her forehead.

I ran to keep up with her. "You know, Shoshie, I think you're being unfair to Yosef. He loves the Lord, I know he does. I'm sure he's just biding his time, keeping an eye on what's happening behind closed doors, that sort of thing. Like the way Nakdimon was able to come and pass on information to us last night."

"Hmpf," was all she said in response.

She's really nudged, I thought to myself, as I silently walked alongside her. *But I guess she's right. If the Prushim can witness a man raised from the dead and still not believe, why then even if God Himself came down from heaven and spoke to them, they would come up with a reason as to why it wasn't really God...oh I guess that is what's happening now, isn't it?* Unexpectedly I laughed. Shoshana eyed me suspiciously. I flung my arm around her.

"Forgive me, Shoshie. You're right. *Nothing* will make people believe who have already made up their minds against something. Or maybe I should say, almost nothing."

Shoshana gave me a small smile. "I'm sorry too, Yohie. Sorry to be so irritable. No one would be happier than me if Yeshua were to set up his kingdom on earth now, this very day. But we believe that he's the Messiah, so we need to trust his decisions, and not second-guess him."

"All right," I agreed, chastened. "I will go joyfully to our desert hideout." I hoisted my bag into a more comfortable position on my back and settled in for the long day's walk.

❧

Soon enough we arrived in the village of Ephraim, a little place west of Jerusalem but still plenty far from the Great Sea. We were able to rent rooms in several houses, thereby accommodating our whole group.

Despite my initial reluctance to go to Ephraim, I ended up truly enjoying my time there. The village was clean and industrious; the people good-natured and trustworthy. They took us in and kept silent to outsiders so that we were not disturbed during our sojourn there.

After the tumultuous months of travel, ministering to crowds from dawn till dusk, some days so tired that one wondered how it was possible to do this again (but one did), the quiet pace of life in Ephraim was like a soothing dip in a hot spring. Not that we were idle. Oh no! Yeshua took this opportunity to teach us many things.

One thing we learned here was how to pray for extended periods of time. Of course, we had prayed before now, but it was rare for any of us other than the Lord himself to take several hours and sit before God. I had thought that waking up in the middle of the night and going off to pray until the sun rose was the kind of thing one expected from a prophet like Yeshua. I didn't think it was what I was expected to do. How wrong I was!

"Do what you see me doing," counseled the Lord. Again and again. "I do what I see the Father doing and you need to do what you see me doing. I and the Father are one. If you want to know the Father, you must emulate me." Patiently, day after day, he modeled for us the lifelong habits that would mold our spiritual disciplines as we approached a holy God.

"Know the Scriptures," he encouraged. Every evening, we gathered together and would take turns reciting Scripture from memory. Starting with *Beresheet* and going through the Prophets, the Lord tested and corrected us as we haltingly spoke forth the Word of God. Many times, we stopped to discuss the passages recited. In this way, we came to know and understand many of the messianic prophecies hidden throughout Scripture.

The Book of Isaiah particularly came alive. I'll never forget the reading of the fifty-third chapter. It was Yochanan's turn to recite, and he stood in the center of the courtyard in one of the rented houses, the glow of the setting sun bathing his face in soft orange light. The rest of us, including Yeshua, sat in a circle around him, some on chairs, some on the ground. I sat on a small stone bench next to Miryam, Yeshua's mother. She smiled as she looked at Yochanan.

"He's a good boy," she said approvingly. "You can see how he has taken the words of God and integrated them into his very soul."

I nodded. Some of us had been inclined to envy Yochanan for his extremely close relationship to Yeshua, but all of us, even Yehuda (who had been, in my opinion, excessively jealous) had to admit that here was a man who sought after God with every fiber of his being. He *got* it. He understood the Lord's heart.

Now he closed his large, brown eyes and recited from memory the first few verses of Isaiah 53:

"Who has believed our message
and to whom has the arm of the Lord been revealed?
He grew up before him like a tender shoot,
and like a root out of dry ground.

He had no beauty or majesty to attract us to him,
nothing in his appearance that we should desire him.
He was despised and rejected by men,
a man of sorrows and familiar with suffering.
Like one from whom men hide their faces
he was despised, and we esteemed him not."

Yochanan paused and, opening his eyes, looked directly at Yeshua. Slowly, the Lord nodded as if to say, *yes, it is as you think.*

Shimon Kefa, always quick to observe the interactions between those two, blurted out a startled, "Not you, Lord!"

"Shh," admonished Yeshua. "Listen to the word of God!"

As if on cue, Yochanan continued reciting,

"Surely he took up our infirmities
and carried our sorrows,
yet we considered him stricken by God,
smitten by him, and afflicted.
But he was pierced for our transgressions,
he was crushed for our iniquities,
the punishment that brought us
peace was upon him,
and by his wounds we are healed.
We all, like sheep have gone astray,
each of us has turned to his own way;
and the Lord has laid on him
the iniquity of us all."

Pierced? Crushed? Punishment? How did this apply to Yeshua? I grew pale at the thought. Beside me, Miryam gripped my hand, her fingers dry and cold.

"He was oppressed and afflicted,
yet he did not open his mouth;
he was led like a lamb to the slaughter,
and as a sheep before her shearers is silent,
so he did not open his mouth.
By oppression and judgment he was taken away.
And who can speak of his descendants?
For he was cut off from the land of the living;

for the transgression of my people he was stricken.
He was assigned a grave with the wicked,
and with the rich in his death,
though he had done no violence,
nor was any deceit in his mouth."

The poetic, haunting words of the prophet Isaiah rolled off Yochanan's tongue, hammering at the edges of our minds with a dreadful insistence. *Slaughter, grave, death?* That was all I heard.

Yochanan looked around the circle of faces. It had grown deathly quiet. No one uttered a sound; each one of us was grappling internally with the Scripture being read.

"Go on," spoke Yeshua. "Finish the chapter."

Eyes sad, Yochanan paused for a moment, then spoke,

"Yet it was the Lord's will to crush
him and cause him to suffer,
and though the Lord makes his life a guilt offering,
he will see his offspring and prolong his days,
and the will of the Lord will prosper in his hand.
After the suffering of his soul,
he will see the light of life and be satisfied;
by his knowledge my righteous servant will justify many,
and he will bear their iniquities.
Therefore I will give him a portion among the great,
and he will divide the spoils with the strong,
because he poured out his life unto death,
and was numbered with the transgressors.
For he bore the sin of many,
and made intercession for the transgressors."

When Yochanan finished, he went over to Yeshua and sat down next to him. Yeshua, however, didn't stay seated long. Rising up, he paced around the courtyard, speaking to us as he walked.

"You are waiting for a king and a messiah, and rightly so," he began, the last vestiges of the sunset touching his profile with an unearthly light. We stared at him, transfixed. When he had reached the end of the courtyard, he swung around. I blinked, and the flair of his robes and the authority with which he held his head made me see majestic white horses, glittering gem studded thrones, magnificent palaces heaped with

184

sparkling treasure. I blinked again, and there he was, simply dressed in his travel-worn brown tunic, the final glow of the sunset extinguished, his face hidden by the darkness. Two servants entered and lit the torches that ringed the perimeter of the courtyard.

Yeshua continued speaking, and his voice *was* the voice of a king: carefully measured words ringing with confidence and authority. "I've said it before and I will keep saying it: my kingdom is not of this world. I have come to establish a kingdom in the hearts of men; a kingdom of righteousness and truth. A kingdom that in its lowliness and humility will vanquish the strongest enemy.

"Do not be alarmed at the things which are to come. My Father holds me in the palm of His hand. Every thing I do, I do because it is His will. There is nothing, *nothing*," he repeated with added emphasis, "that I do apart from the Father. I and the Father are one."

Curiously, I looked around at the faces reflected in the glow of the lit torches. All listened intently to the Master. Miryam's face held a sadness that caused a surge of protective love to well up inside of me; Yochanan gazed at the Lord with serious understanding; Shimon looked somewhat perplexed; the Magdalit's face glowed with adoration; Shoshana looked pensive; Andrew appeared thoughtful; many of the others were variations on these same themes. Only Yehuda from K'riot differed in expression from all around him. His swarthy, handsome features had an angry look, eyes dark and brow furrowed. He sensed my eyes upon him and turned his head so that our gaze met. Methodically, he smoothed away the anger and replaced his expression with one of smooth tranquility. Disconcerted, I looked away.

After these things, Yeshua dismissed us and we went to our separate lodgings for the night. Miryam and I walked together, still hand in hand.

"Do you want to talk about it?" I asked her tenderly, oh so tenderly! It was dark and I couldn't see her face. We knew by heart every twist and turn in the rocky path that led to the house we shared with several of the other women. Carefully, so as not to trip on something unexpected, we felt our way there.

"There was a prophecy when Yeshua was born," she said haltingly, her voice low and strained. "Yosef and I went to the Temple to offer our sacrifice for the birth of our new infant son. We met a man there, a very devout *tzadik*. At the time, he looked as old as Methuselah to us, with a long white beard down to his waist. He came right up to us in the courts of the Temple and pulled Yeshua out of Yosef's arms."

"Did you try to stop him?" I asked, thinking how upset I would be if some stranger tried to lift my child out of my or Kuza's arms.

"Oddly enough, no," came Miryam's voice from the darkness. We reached the front door of our house and I followed her in. A few oil lamps were scattered about on some tables and so we were able to see now. I realized that I didn't want Miryam to get ready for bed and so lose the rest of this story.

"Come sit next to me," I urged, seating myself on a chair in the shared living quarters. Don't go to your room until you finish telling me what happened."

Miryam laughed gently. "I wouldn't do that to you, dear Yohie. Don't you think I know by now how much you enjoy my memories?"

"You're a wonderful woman, Miryam," I told her devotedly.

"I'm just like you, Yohie. I seek after God like everyone else. Don't make too much of me. Anyway," she said hastily, shutting down this subject, "To get back to my story, no, we weren't upset when Shimon (for that was his name) took the baby. One could tell how kind, how gentle, was this man. He held Yeshua and looked right into his little baby eyes, a tender smile on his lips. He praised God, saying that he could die in peace since now he had seen the one who would be a light for revelation to the Gentiles and would bring glory to the people of Israel.

"Yosef and I marveled at the precious words of this *tzadik*. After he gave the baby back, he placed one hand on Yosef's head and one hand on mine and prayed a blessing over us. It was prophetic." She stopped talking and grew pensive.

"What, Miryam? What did he say?"

She took a deep breath. "He said, 'This child is destined to cause the falling and rising of many in Israel, and to be a sign that will be spoken against, so that the thoughts of many hearts will be revealed.' " She grew silent.

"That's certainly true," I agreed. "Did he say anything else?"

"One thing." Her voice broke and she stifled a sob. "He told me that a sword will pierce my soul."

"Oh, Miryam!" I knelt down beside her and put my arm around her shoulders. Suddenly she began to cry.

"My heart aches, Yohie. It aches. I believe that the time for that prophecy to be fulfilled is upon us. I love him so much...." She dabbed at her eyes with the edge of her sleeve.

"Let me pray with you, Miryam," I begged. "Let's take this before God."

"Yes," she whispered, as we clasped hands.

"Oh Lord God, dear Adonai," I prayed. "Please be with Your servant Miryam. She believes that now is the time when a sword will pierce her soul, as was foretold over thirty years ago. Lord, You know how we love Your Son. You know that as much as any of us love him, it's Miryam who has the most intimate relationship with him. It's Miryam who has had the privilege of bearing him, nursing him, raising him. It's Miryam who has known for many years the astonishing things You have planned for her son and the great cost associated with these plans. Comfort her now, Lord. Comfort her and hold her in Your arms. Cover her in the shadow of the Almighty. Rebuke fear and dread from her heart. Speak life to her."

"And Lord," added Miryam. "Thank You for Yohana. Thank You for all these dear and wonderful people whom You've brought into my life. Thank You that they believe in Yeshua the way I believe in him. Forgive me for discouragement. Forgive me for fear. Banish these things from me and make me strong with Your strength so I can bear whatever I must bear." She grew silent and we sat in an attitude of prayer for several more minutes. A most amazing thing happened. A supernatural peace descended on us and filled our souls with oil-drenched healing. After a while, it receded and we released hands simultaneously.

"Thank you, Yohie," said Miryam. "*Lilah tov.*"

"*Lilah tov,*" I replied, and we went to our respective beds for the night.

Two weeks before the Feast of Passover, Yeshua announced that we were leaving Ephraim and would be heading to the home of Elazar in Beit Anya. We packed up, sad to leave our near-desert oasis but at the same time anticipatory about seeing Elazar and the sisters. Looming behind all this was the great city of Jerusalem and the threats on Yeshua's life which awaited us there.

When we arrived at Beit Anya, I was stunned to observe the difference in Elazar. He looked to be about as healthy a man as I'd ever seen: fit, glowing, bronzed from the sun. He went right to Yeshua and hugged him. Immediately the men spoke of the political climate and the dangers from the chief priests and Torah teachers.

"It's getting ugly," Elazar told Yeshua. "Not only do they want you dead but me as well." He chuckled wryly. "This may be an awfully short resurrection."

I noticed that Yeshua didn't smile. "We have the victory," he told his friend. "Remember that."

I was so happy to see Miryam and Marta; they had become family. Right away, Shoshana, Miryam, the Magdalit, Rachel, Shlomit, myself—we all took up our regular roles of helping out at the house. Soon all of us were crowded into the kitchen, putting together one of the many huge meals necessary for feeding everyone. Even Miryam, Marta's sister, stayed with us at first. After a few hours, she slipped off to be near Yeshua. This time, Marta, though she noticed, didn't seem upset.

The second night we were there, a dinner was given in honor of Yeshua. Supervised by Marta, we women served. All of the men reclined at the table: Yeshua, Elazar, the talmidim, and several of Elazar's trusted friends.

As usual, the meal was a spectacular event. Huge bowls of cut flowers graced the table, as well as smaller bowls of scented warm water useful for washing fingertips and mouths. The actual plates and utensils rivaled anything I had seen at the palace, glittering in the soft, golden glow of the many candles and oil lamps scattered throughout the large dining hall.

The crowning touch was, of course, the food. Platter after platter of savory and succulent meats and greens appeared, their pungent smells perfuming the air around us. All of us were busy bringing dishes out, gathering empty ones back, quickly washing them, attending to all the needs. Toward the end of the meal, we made up plates for ourselves and joined the men. It was then that Marta noticed that her sister had disappeared.

"Where's Miryam?" she asked, puzzled, eyes scanning the room.

Where was Miryam? No one knew, and just when Rachel pulled back her chair to go search for the missing girl, she suddenly showed up in the curved archway of the room.

Conversation died away when Miryam appeared, and all eyes were drawn to her. She hesitated briefly, obviously hiding something behind her back. Then she resolutely walked straight over to where Yeshua sat, an unspoken message between them.

Kneeling at his feet, she reached up and unpinned her long, dark hair. It tumbled down to her waist in a cascade of silky tresses. I heard someone behind me gasp. Then she brought out a bottle from behind her back and pulled out the stopper. *What is that?* I wondered.

Miryam poured the contents of the bottle over Yeshua's feet. A very familiar scent filled the air with its heavy perfume. I sniffed delicately. *Yes, it was nard!* Once Kuza had bought me a tiny bottle for a special occasion. I used it sparingly, reluctant to see the last drops gone. *Don't expect it too often,* he warned. *It costs a fortune.* That was ten years ago. I haven't had any since.

But the bottle Miryam had must have held at least half a liter! An immense amount. But all this went out of my head as I, along with everyone else in the room, watched what Miryam did next.

Once she had covered his feet with the nard, she gathered up her long hair, half in her left hand and half in her right, and proceeded to use it to work the perfume into Yeshua's skin. As she worked, she sang a sweet, sad song of worship and adoration. Tears ran down her face.

Yeshua watched her intently, a solemn smile on his lips. When she had wiped up the last of the nard, so that all the oil was either absorbed into his skin or her hair, she sat back on her heels. Yeshua then placed his hand on her head and prayed over her, blessing her. He released her then, and she withdrew to the back of the room, next to her sister, who slipped an arm around her waist.

We were all quiet, astonished with the incredible scene we had just witnessed when a jarring thing happened.

Yehuda from K'riot burst out an objection in an angry, strangled voice. "Why wasn't this perfume sold and the money given to the poor?" he sputtered, red in the face. "It was worth a year's wages!" (Yehuda acted as our treasurer...a fact that caused Kuza's face to go pale when he met him. Kuza recognized the type from being Herod's treasurer and was convinced Yehuda was dishonest. In fact, Kuza even went to Yeshua to protest this appointment, but Yeshua refused to remove Yehuda from his post. "Let him have an opportunity to decide for righteousness of his own free will," said the Lord cryptically.)

We were all shocked with Yehuda's behavior. Shimon started to respond, but Yeshua held his hand up and rebuked Yehuda. "Leave her alone," he warned. I glanced at Miryam when he said this. She was gazing at him with such love and devotion that I felt like an intruder. I looked away.

Meanwhile, Yeshua continued to chastise Yehuda. "It was intended that she should save this perfume for the day of my burial." He then made reference to Yehuda's supposedly pious objection. "You will always have the poor among you, but you will not always have me."

Yehuda glared at the Lord briefly before backing down and turning aside. As he strode toward the exit, Thomas grabbed his arm. I saw Yehuda shake him off angrily and disappear. Thomas followed him. The sound of yelling could be faintly heard.

Inside, though, the fragrance of the nard hung heavy. A few of us dared to say, *Lord, what do you mean, we won't always have you?* But the Lord swept these queries aside. Instead, he circled the room, praying over each of us.

It was an intensely personal time. We sat, stood, or reclined. Some lifted their voices in worship while others prayed, silently or aloud. I soon felt as if I were in an antechamber to heaven itself. I saw Yeshua approach his mother and gather her in his arms, holding her as if he were the parent and she the child. He spoke softly into her ear, one hand around her shoulders and with the other gesturing emphatically in the air. She nodded slowly at first, comprehension and resignation mixing with raw pain on her fine features. I looked away then; this also was too personal for me to witness.

Lying down on the floor, I stretched out on my back, drew my knees up, and prayed silently to God. I poured out before Him my love for Yeshua, for Kuza, for the different men and women I had gotten to know these last two years. I told Him of my concerns and fears regarding the future; and my deep desire to see a free Israel. I confessed to Him that I didn't always understand what Yeshua said, and that frankly some of what he said was so upsetting that I didn't *want* to understand it. All the while the scent of the nard permeated my nostrils and filled my head.

And then I knew: it wasn't about me at all. It was about *him*, about Yeshua. It was about *his* glory, *his* divinity, *his* majesty. Whether or not I lost those I loved, whether or not I lived to see another day, year, decade, didn't really matter. What mattered was that he came and dwelt among us and that we were privileged to know him. Whatever he did, however it ended up: I had no control. I was his, and that was never going to change.

Suddenly I felt a warm hand on my brow, and sparks of electricity penetrated my skull. "I am pleased to call you my friend." The resonant tones of Yeshua's voice as he knelt beside me thrilled me. I attempted to sit up but felt pinned to the ground by a supernatural force.

"I say to you, do not fear! Stay strong and don't lose heart, no matter what happens. There are many of my followers who will draw strength from *your* strength and be encouraged by *your* encouragement! You will bless countless generations through your tireless example of faith and perseverance." I opened my eyes and saw the beloved face of my Lord mere inches from mine. His dark eyes lit up with warmth and compassion, a serious smile touched his chiseled lips. His rugged features, not classically handsome, seemed to me to be the most beautiful sight in the world.

"I love you," I whispered, gazing up at him.

"I love you more," he whispered back, smiling widely, his eyes

190

crinkling at the corners. Then he kissed me on the forehead where his hand had been. "You've been sealed for my kingdom," he said as he rose and went to pray for the next person.

Ah, the sweetness of that kiss! I don't know how long I lay there, overcome by the deliciousness and significance of the moment. All I know is that it was still dark outside when Shoshana shook my by the shoulder. "Come to bed, Yohana," she coaxed, helping me up. "We need to sleep while we can. Tomorrow we leave for Jerusalem."

I allowed myself to be half-dragged, half-led to the sleeping chamber I shared with the rest of the women. Groping my way in the dark, I flung myself down on my bed, still dressed, and at once sweet sleep descended on me.

TEN

The next day we discovered that word had gotten out that Yeshua was at Elazar's house. Hordes of people trampled over Elazar's finely cultivated property, hoping to catch a glimpse of the Master. We said *shalom* to our gracious hosts, and left, pushing through the crowd, heading for the main road and on to the short walk west to Jerusalem.

The crowd surged around us, buffeting us and enveloping us. It was not the same sort of crowd that I had grown accustomed to from my time in the ministry: no one seemed to desire healing, or deliverance. No, it seemed to be a crowd that had spotted its king and sought to crown him, possibly by force. Yet no one moved a hand to molest us. It was all quite odd.

Another odd thing was the absence of Yehuda. At one point, I caught up to Thomas on the road and asked him what had happened. "He's gone into Jerusalem ahead of us," scowled Thomas, obviously displeased with his fellow talmid.

"Is he still part of us?" I wanted to know.

"That's for the Master to determine, My lady Yohana," answered Thomas.

"But Yehuda was so *angry* last night...," I persisted.

Thomas shook his head. "I know how you feel, but the Master himself told me that he's aware of what's going on with Yehuda. He said to me, *All have sinned and fallen short of the glory of God.*"

"Surely not us, Thomas!" I jested.

"Even us," he replied, with a twinkle in his eye. "Though it's my hope that we'll fall less often as we move forward."

I thanked Thomas for his time and let him go ahead to some of the other men. I felt better now that I had spoken aloud to him my concerns about Yehuda. Still, a vague dread stirred at the edges of my mind. Now, however, was not the time to dwell on it. *I'll talk to Kuza when I see him in Jerusalem,* I decided, and immediately felt relieved. I stepped back and turned around, hoping to see Shoshana, or Miryam, or Rachel, or the Magdalit. Or even Shlomit. What I did see made me stop in surprise.

For some time now, the noises of people walking, shouting, talking, running, had gotten gradually louder and louder. As I faced the crowd, I could see why: hundreds upon hundreds, even thousands, of men, women, and children kept pouring into the street as far as the eye could see. They stretched out behind us like a writhing, pulsating sea of humanity. *Oh, my!*

Wait a minute—what was that they were holding in their hands? All of them were waving palm branches! What was going on?

As I turned to the front again, I noticed Yeshua beckon to Shimon and Andrew. Giving them instructions of some sort, they nodded and then ran off in the direction of the next village. Yeshua rested by the side of the road while the crowd approached him, and in some cases, went a bit past him.

I looked to get near him, but it was just impossible. Too many people. People, people, everywhere! I started to get nervous. I suddenly realized that there wasn't one person I recognized.

Just then, someone grabbed my elbow! It was the Magdalit, her face wisely hidden behind a veil.

"Miryam! I'm so glad to see you!"

"Come with me," she commanded, taking my hand. "We need to get over to the Master and the rest of the talmidim." Then, with even more agility than Shoshana, she led me through the crowd

Yeshua, seemingly oblivious to the mass of humanity that surrounded him, sat cross-legged under a fig tree.

"What is he waiting for?" I asked the Magdalit.

She shook her head. "I don't know. He sent Shimon and Andrew for something."

After what seemed like an interminable period but was probably no more than an hour, Shimon and Andrew returned.

"Make way, make way," Shimon shouted, breaking a path through the crowd. He was leading some sort of animal by a rope. Too many people were in the way and at first I couldn't make out what it was. Only when they got closer could I tell that it was a colt, a young donkey.

Obviously expecting them with the donkey, the Master got up and walked over. Shimon and Andrew draped their cloaks over the donkey and Yeshua got onto its back. He turned its head toward Jerusalem, and slowly it plodded down the road.

Suddenly, the crowd surged forward. Men and women raced ahead, shedding their cloaks and spreading them out on the road for Yeshua to ride on. Spontaneously, people everywhere waved palm branches and shouted, *"Baruch hamelech haba b'shem Adonai.* Blessed is the king who comes in the name of the Lord." The noise became deafening.

"Oh, Miryam," I yelled, straining to make myself heard over the din. "The people have acknowledged him as their king. This is amazing."

Miryam looked worried. "But the Master said that his kingdom is not of this world. Do you think that they intend to make him king by force?"

"I don't know. But he certainly seems in control of the situation."

And he was. Riding the donkey, back straight, posture regal, Yeshua could have been King David himself. The kings ride horses now but, a thousand years ago, in the time of King David, they rode donkeys. And the Messiah *is* called the Son of David and the Root of Jesse....

I could see it, I mused, staring hard at the Master. *I could see him as King David himself.* Only King David sinned and this man hadn't. Not even his birth retained the taint of sin that the sons of Adam inherit as their curse. No. Adonai had taken a virgin and impregnated her by the *Ruach HaKodesh,* the Holy Spirit, so that Yeshua had escaped the curse of sin.

Of course, there had been plenty of opportunity for Yeshua to fall since his birth. Like the first man, Adam. But he hadn't. That was the completely amazing thing. He went through childhood, young adulthood, apprenticeship as a carpenter, leader of a rapidly expanding ministry wherein he had proximity to all sorts of people, *and he never once sinned!*

I knew that whenever Yeshua spoke, his words were as the words of the Lord Himself speaking from His great throne in heaven. Lately his words had much to do with death, so I didn't understand this kingly processional into Jerusalem. It didn't make sense to me. One thing I did know was that events were racing toward a climax at the speed of lightning.

"Come, Miryam," I said, grabbing her arm. "Let's go. We want to stay as close to the Lord as possible." As we ran, we chanted with the crowd, *"Shalom bashamayim v'cavod beem romay al.* Peace in heaven and glory in the highest."

All the way into Jerusalem, the roads were clogged with people waving palm branches and singing praises. Here and there, however, one could see grim, unsmiling faces. Angry faces. Faces that had no right to be part of this celebration of Yeshua's messiahship.

These were the faces of some of the religious leaders.

Rabbi, they hissed. *Rebuke your talmidim! Don't let them say such things!*

And the Lord replied, "I tell you, if they keep quiet, the stones will cry out!"

The angry people left him alone then but gathered together one with another and hatched their evil plans.

"Master, aren't you concerned about them?" worried Shimon Kefa. "Some of these men are powerful and influential."

The Lord looked at Shimon, and his eyes were kind. "Don't let them distress you, Shimon. The only trouble they can cause us is what my Father in heaven will allow. Stay close to Adonai and people will hold no fear for you. It's *He*–" here he extended his finger toward heaven–"who will determine your fate."

When we entered through the gates of the City, Yeshua stopped the donkey. He gazed at the vista of limestone houses and buildings for some time. The crowd grew quiet as it watched Yeshua watch the City. Then tears rolled down Yeshua's face and he wept.

Startled, each man asked his brother, "Why is he weeping?"

"Oh, Jerusalem," proclaimed the Lord in anguished tones. "If you, even you, had only known on this day what would bring you peace, but now it is hidden from your eyes. The days will come upon you when your enemies will build an embankment against you and encircle you and hem you in on every side. They will dash you to the ground, you and your children within your walls. They will not leave one stone on another, because you did not recognize the time of God's coming to you."

"What is this, Lord?" we asked. "When will these awful things occur?"

"Before this generation passes away," he answered us. "This beautiful city will suffer anguish and desolation unlike anything ever seen before."

Once in the City, Yeshua headed directly for the Temple. He sat in the Court of the Gentiles and taught. "I need to be in my Father's House," he declared, impervious to the dangers lurking around him on every side.

The religious leaders who sought his death were frustrated. Here was their prey, in plain sight, but the people surrounded him like a protective coat. They were afraid to risk a riot should they arrest Yeshua in the midst of his followers. "We need to catch him alone," they muttered.

In the meantime, they satisfied themselves with vain attempts to trap the Master with words. They endeavored to make him look foolish in the eyes of the crowd, but they were unable to.

"Tell us by what authority you are doing these things?"

"Is it right for us to pay taxes to Caesar or not?"

"What happens with marriage at the resurrection of the dead?" (This from a sect that dismisses such a thing exists.)

Again and again, the Lord answered these questions in startling ways that showed it was impossible to condemn him by his words. The men who wanted him dead found themselves thwarted at every turn.

"There must be someone among his talmidim who will betray him," suggested one particularly crafty individual.

"Excellent idea!" praised the high priest. "Find him."

"Me?" gulped the man. "How?"

"You'll think of something," the high priest assured him.

So it was that word started in the streets and back alleys of the city that the chief priests and Torah teachers were willing to pay for information that led to finding Yeshua apart from the crowds that encircled him. Little did we know that there was one among our own number who heard—and heeded—that dreadful call.

❧ ❧

The air in Jerusalem that Pesach festival pulsated with excitement. There was no other way to describe it. Even those pilgrims from places outside of Israel who had not yet heard of Yeshua entered the City and sensed the difference. Those of us who had been with Yeshua for some time found it hard to catch our breath. *What's coming? What lies ahead?* We were constantly on guard against the threats of the religious authorities; yet, at the same time, we each harbored in our hearts the awesome but unbelievable thought, *Is he about to establish his kingdom here and now?* Not one of us knew what to expect.

About this time, word got out among the talmidim of a little event that had happened in the very recent past. It appeared that Shlomit, the mother of Yochanan and Ya'akov, had gone to Yeshua in an underhanded attempt to curry favor. Long had Shlomit been alert to the fact that Yeshua saw great promise in her sons. Indeed, all of us knew of the special affection Yeshua had for Yochanan, treating him as a younger brother. Much in the same way, I often mused, that the patriarch Ya'akov's son Yosef must have treated his brother, Binyamin.

It always surprised me that there wasn't jealousy about Yochanan, but Yeshua loved us all, so earnestly and so genuinely, that none could believe himself neglected in favor of another. Yochanan himself never pushed his advantage (which probably contributed to his bond with the Master). There was, I admit, some playful rivalry between Yochanan and Shimon; but the latter considered the former to be one of his closest friends.

So it came as a shock to discover that Shlomit, along with her two sons, had approached Yeshua and requested that each of her boys hold the highest places of honor in his coming kingdom.

The Master had not been happy with this blatant attempt at self-promotion. He shook his head wearily. "You don't know what you're asking," he admonished them. Turning to the brothers, he said, "Can you drink the cup I am going to drink?"

"Yes," they answered confidently, urged on by their mother, not understanding that the cup to which Yeshua referred overflowed with human sorrow and misery.

Yeshua's mouth tightened. "You better believe that you're going to drink from my cup, but it's my Father in heaven who will decide the places in the coming kingdom." He looked at Yochanan then, and Yochanan cast his eyes down upon the ground.

"Forgive me, Lord," he whispered, and both he and Ya'akov knelt down before him.

But somehow or other the other ten found out about this encounter and though there had already been repentance and forgiveness, they all took umbrage at the brothers.

"I can't believe you let your mother push you around like that," remonstrated Shimon to his friend, his eyes troubled.

Quickly, before bitterness and resentment should get a grip on his followers, Yeshua called the talmidim together. "You all know what happened with Shlomit and her sons," he stated simply, eyeing them each in turn.

Various grunts of affirmation, shrugs, and clenched teeth revealed to Yeshua the mood of the group. He sighed. "Look, do any of you understand what it means to be a servant?"

The men eyed each other warily. It seemed to them to be a rhetorical question. Shimon Kefa spoke up. "You do the will of the master if you're a servant," he put forth, not very confidently.

"Let me put it this way," said the Master, not saying right or wrong to Shimon's response. "You all know that Yohana's husband is a servant to Herod, right?"

The men nodded.

"So, does Kuza have proximity to Herod?"

"He sees him every day," offered Philip.

"That's right. Do you, Philip, have access to Herod?"

"I wouldn't want to be near that snake," growled Philip. The rest of the talmidim laughed.

Even Yeshua had to smile. "I appreciate the sentiment, Philip, but you're missing my point. Do you have access to Herod, who, whether or not we like it, has manmade authority in this land?"

"No," answered Philip, graver now.

"That's exactly right. You don't. It's the servant who has entry to the master. And in the world the rulers of the Gentiles lord it over them, and their high officials exercise authority over them. But in the Kingdom of Heaven, that is not how it's done." He shook his head and pointed up. "In the Kingdom of Heaven, whoever wants to become great among you must be your servant, and whoever wants to be first must be your slave—just as the Son of Man did not come to be served, but to serve, and to give his life as a ransom for many. Those who serve in the Kingdom of Heaven have access to the true king.

"Don't hold a grudge against your brothers, but remember that you achieve greatness by serving. If you start playing political games, I assure you that you have already lost." Thus he ended the discussion. Already it was sunrise and time to head to the Temple courts for the day.

For this was how Yeshua spent the last few days before the start of Pesach. Surrounded by crowds, teaching, focused, determined, he poured himself into sharing as much knowledge as the people around him were able to absorb, and then some.

Parable upon parable; story upon story. Yeshua told of tares and weeds; of hidden treasures; of fishing; of lost sheep; of fellow servants; of kings and their sons; of workers in a vineyard; of wedding banquets; of ten virgins waiting for the bridegroom; of a persistent widow; of vicious tenants in a vineyard; and many other things besides.

In everything he did, in everything he said, he strove to describe for the people who God the Father is and what He expects from us. Again and again, he encouraged men and women to seek the Kingdom of Heaven with everything they had; to know that the love the Father had for them was so great as to be without price.

His words penetrated my heart and mind until I was drenched with them, as with the early morning dew. I lay down to sleep at night, and the images from his parables were etched against my closed eyelids. I awoke just before dawn, and words of praise from the Psalms flooded my being. I went about the many tasks of the day, both household and ministry related, and his teachings on forgiveness, repentance, salvation, love, mercy, gentleness, self-control, patience, long suffering—these all flowed through, in and around me. I loved him desperately, but not with the possessive jealous love of the lover. No, I loved him such that I wanted everyone to enter into this love with me.

"You've changed," observed Kuza, holding me tightly against his chest. We had met up at the same rented house we shared the last time I was in Jerusalem. I was so happy to see him, yet all that filled my mouth was Yeshua. *Yeshua, Yeshua, Yeshua.* Bubbling over, my heart bursting with all that the Lord said and did, I started speaking as soon as I saw my husband. It was only when I paused for breath, the next sentence already planned, that he stopped me, kissing me firmly on the mouth.

"Not that you haven't already changed significantly," he added quickly, before I could resume my narrative, surprise and pleasure meeting briefly across my face "But I see that this last season with Yeshua has elevated you to a much higher level."

I basked in the glow of such a significant and well-meant compliment. "It has been a truly unbelievable time," I confirmed.

"Yes," said Kuza, holding me back a bit so that he could look into my eyes. "I see that it has. I must tell you that I'm envious. We've each been off serving a king and mine has been a crushing disappointment." He attempted to laugh but it wound up as more of a snort. "I'm prepared for an emergency exit from the palace at a moment's notice. I believe that my time there is very short."

"Oh, Kuza! Do you think you're in immediate danger?"

"Every moment, Yohana. Since you've left to follow after the Rabbi, it's been borrowed time for us. Only the grace of God has kept me this far. I've made preparations to escape the City. We can only pray that Adonai will keep me one step ahead of Herod."

Wearily, I laid my head against his chest. Then I wrapped my arms around his waist. "Let's make the most of the time we have now," I whispered coyly, or as coy as a middle-aged woman is able to whisper.

"That's an excellent idea," murmured my husband, his eyes brightening.

"Where are we eating the Passover?" I asked Shoshana the next day.

We were sitting in the courtyard of my rented home. The day had already peaked, and now the heat was receding somewhat. In the shade of a palm tree, we delicately bit into dried figs and sipped some watered-down wine. Kuza was at the palace and I wasn't needed today by Yeshua. Shoshana, who was staying at a home a few blocks away, had just come to give me instructions about the feast.

"In this large, beautiful house in the middle of," and she gave me the name of the street. My eyes widened as I heard it.

"That's quite an exclusive neighborhood! How did we happen to end up there?"

Shoshana shook her head. "I don't know. All I heard is that the Master sent Shimon and Yochanan off to meet a man carrying a jar of water. They followed him to this house and told the owner that the Rabbi wants to use the guest room to make Passover with his talmidim."

"And it was all right?"

"Not only that, but the upper room is apparently all furnished and ready to use. We're meeting there tomorrow."

"Tomorrow!" I exclaimed, puzzled. "But the high priest is first starting the sacrifices for the lambs the day after tomorrow."

"Yes, I know," said Shoshana. "Yeshua must believe that the full moon is tomorrow night and not the next one. You know that the Prushim and the Tz'dukim never agree."

That's true, I reflected. The current high priest belonged to the Tz'dukim religious party. Yeshua considered himself to be one of the Prushim. Not everyone concurred on the exact dates of the Feasts, which were regulated by the phases of the moon. The slaying of the Passover lamb occurred at twilight on the 14th of Nisan, at the full moon.

"Since the lambs won't be slaughtered yet, are we still eating lamb at the dinner?" I asked.

"I'm not sure," Shoshana admitted, her fountain of knowledge drying up. "All I know for sure is that we're supposed to all meet up there by late afternoon tomorrow."

"All of us? Can Kuza come?"

"Of course. All the talmidim who have wives and children are bringing them. I expect we'll have a pretty large group."

I looked at her. "Do you think either of your children...?" I left the question hanging in the air.

"No," Shoshana said firmly, with a slight catch in her voice. "I didn't even ask."

"Sit with Kuza and me, my sister. We're your family."

"Thank you," she smiled, a bit tremulously.

"Are we going to help serve at the meal, like we do at Elazar's?" I changed the topic, conscious of the awkwardness of prolonged sentimentality.

"No," responded Shoshana briskly, glad to move on to a new subject as well. "The owner of this house is supplying his servants for the cooking, serving, cleaning up, and whatever else needs done. All we have to do is show up."

"That's fantastic. I'd almost forgotten what it's like to just sit and be served."

"Oh, I'm sure that it will all come back to you," rejoined Shoshana, smiling. "I think we're in for a special time with the Master. It's obvious to me that he has several things on his heart that he wants to share."

I quickly sobered of my mirth. "I'm concerned about what's coming."

My friend nodded. "I am, too. I think tomorrow night will be very telling." She stood up and squinted at the sun. "It's getting late and I still need to act as messenger to Shlomit and a few of the others..."

"Shlomit!" I yelped, interrupting her. "I can't believe how she tried to push Yeshua around."

"Yohana," warned Shoshana. "Forgive her. It's done. They've all repented. Besides, no one's *ever* pushed the Master around."

"*B'seder*, you're right. There's not a kinder man alive, but he will not move from what he knows is right."

"No, *baruch ha Shem*, he won't." She glanced at the sun again. "Look, I've got to go. I'll see you tomorrow."

I kissed her on both cheeks. *"L'hitraot."*

"L'hitraot."

∾∾

Kuza knocked discreetly on the door of the house in which we were to partake of the Passover meal. I stood just behind him, my face covered by a veil. We gave our names to the servant who answered the door, and he allowed us entry. We found ourselves in a large courtyard, which led to another door, this one to the interior of the house. After we had passed through this second door, a well-mannered servant took our cloaks, motioned for us to remove our sandals, and showed us the way upstairs, opening the door to an enormous room.

"Oh my," I exclaimed, looking around me with admiration. This was truly a magnificent space. Silken rugs covered portions of the floor, while other, exposed parts, boasted fabulous mosaics. Mosaics that depicted in colorful and intricate detail glorious scenes from Israel's past. On one I could see Barak charging down Mount Tabor with ten thousand men, routing the Canaanites, while Devorah the prophetess and judge stayed behind to seek the Lord's victory. On another I glimpsed our father Avraham, sorrowfully determined to obey God's voice by sacrificing his son, Yitzhak, only to be stopped by an angel at the last moment. The walls, inlaid with strips of battered gold, brought to mind the opulence of the Temple and its furnishings.

Several long tables covered with cloths of snowy white linen adorned the room. Chairs and low-lying sofas proliferated. The ever-growing buzz of multiple conversations surrounded my ears. I recognized many of my fellow talmidim but did not see the Master. Kuza and I entered the room.

"Kuza! Yohana! Welcome!" I found myself caught up in a crushing hug from Shimon Kefa. His slim young wife, Chana, and their four small sons stood beside him. Well, Chana stood. The boys were in constant motion. It was easy to see from whom they had inherited their exceedingly abundant exuberance. Chana, however, looked exhausted. *She's really had to sacrifice so that her husband can be free to follow after the Master,* I thought to myself.

While Kuza and Shimon exchanged greetings, I turned to Chana. "Have you been here long?" I asked her.

She smiled shyly at me, not entirely comfortable with her current surroundings. "We arrived in Jerusalem yesterday," she confided. "It always astonishes me, to see so many people in one place."

"Well, it *is* Passover," I said. "The whole world comes here for the Feast, or so it seems." Looking around, I changed the topic. "Where is the Master? Have you seen him?"

"Yes. He's in the house somewhere. I expect him any moment."

Just as Chana said these words, I noticed that the conversations in the room had died down and everyone had turned toward the door. I turned to look as well. It was my Lord, come for the Passover. The Master had arrived.

Yeshua strode into the room, a warm golden glow emanating from him. The presence of God palpably surrounded him. All of us who only moments before had been terribly busy *shmoozing* now were silent, our half-formed words frozen on our lips.

Then the moment passed, and all of us swayed toward him, desperate for a touch, an acknowledgment, a word. He seemed to meet all our eyes at once and, mollified but not satiated, we allowed him to move through until he found his rightful place at the head table.

The twelve talmidim joined him; their families (for those who were married) seated at nearby tables. Kuza and I settled ourselves next to Shoshana. Shlomit came to join us, bringing as her companion a tall, gray-haired man with a tanned, weatherbeaten face. He was attractive and looked uncannily familiar.

"Are you...?" I started.

He smiled broadly, revealing very white teeth. "I'm Zavdai."

"My husband," announced Shlomit, proudly.

Kuza stood up, extending his hand toward Zavdai, who shook it enthusiastically. We all introduced ourselves. I made a point of telling Zavdai how much I liked his sons: "We so appreciate your doing without them in your fishing business, you know. They're truly extraordinary young men."

Zavdai's eyes twinkled. "I've become reconciled to losing my two best helpers."

Shlomit grasped her husband's arm and her voice bubbled over with joy. "He's come to understand who the Rabbi really is. He's one of us now."

Zavdai smiled self-consciously while the rest of us warmly welcomed him into our family of believers. Shlomit beamed. A wave of love washed through my body.

Shosh is right, I thought. *We need to forgive one another. I hadn't really given much thought to how hard it must have been for Shlomit and her sons to make a stand for Yeshua when her husband wasn't of one mind. Look how happy she is now! Thank you, Lord, for giving me the ability to love her.*

I was going to say something when Kuza motioned for me to keep silent. Yeshua had stood up and signaled to all of us that he was about to begin the seder. The room quieted down.

Yeshua cleared his throat. We all stared at him, expectantly. He started to speak, but then, apparently overcome by emotion, stopped. Running his hand through unruly curls, in his characteristic gesture, he lifted eyes moist with unshed tears to us and tried again.

"My dear friends." He looked into each of our faces, one by one. I held my breath, all attentiveness.

"I love you all." He paused, meanwhile continuing to look deeply into each person's eyes.

"I want you to know that I have eagerly desired to eat this Passover with you." His eyes met mine. *I love you, too, my Lord,* my eyes said in response to his sweet gaze.

"Before I suffer." A collective gasp went up around the room. Alarmed glances, raised heads. Murmuring started. Yeshua raised his hand and the noise ceased.

"For I tell you," he said, his voice heavy with sorrow. "I will not eat it again until it finds fulfillment in the Kingdom of God."

What does he mean, not until the Kingdom of God?

Is he going to restore God's Kingdom NOW?

Next he picked up the full cup of wine from his place at the table. Raising it high into the air, he recited the traditional blessing, *"Baruch Atah Adonai Eloheinu Melech haolam, boray p'ree hagofen."* Blessed are You, O Lord our God, King of the Universe, who creates the fruit of the vine.

We all drank with him, draining our cups...fearful, expectant.

Then the Master selected a piece of matzah from a stack of three sitting on the table, deliberately picking it out of the middle. Closing his eyes, he held the matzah high above his head and spoke forth the blessing for the bread: *"Baruch Atah Adonai Eloheinu Melech haolam, hamotzi lechem min ha'aretz."* Blessed are You, O Lord our God, King of the Universe, who brings forth bread from the earth. He wrapped the piece of matzah in a cloth, crushing it forcefully against the open palm of his hand. The unexpected noise of the unleavened bread cracking into dozens of pieces in the otherwise quiet room jolted all of us. I jumped in my seat, while Shoshana drew her breath in sharply. Kuza was so transfixed that I wasn't even sure if he remembered to breathe at all.

Yeshua held the crushed and broken pieces of matzah in the cloth. "Come up and take one of the pieces," he instructed us.

Slowly, unsteadily, we all stood and made our way across the room to where the Master remained standing, the cloth in his strong hands.

As each person approached, Yeshua murmured something obviously intended for that person alone. He then handed over a piece of the broken matzah. I trembled as I came nearer, acutely aware of his presence. Off to the side, a musician softly strummed a harp, playing a melody reminiscent of one of King David's Psalms.

Kuza went before me in the line, his head bowed as he walked over to Yeshua. I saw the Master speak quietly to him, then continued to watch as my husband accepted his piece of matzah. When Kuza turned around, his eyes were filled with tears.

Shaking even harder, I went up to Yeshua. I looked into his expressive, fathomless eyes, normally sparkling with life. Now, however, they held a most sobering gravity.

"Yohana." My name, coming thus from the Master's lips, was a summation of my entire existence. Said in such a manner, it showed that my Lord knew me, loved me, understood me, approved of me. "Here," he said, selecting a piece of matzah and fitting it into my outstretched hand. "This is my body, broken for you; do this in remembrance of me."

His body? Broken for me? How? Rarely had I seen such a powerful, dynamic, healthy man. The Master appeared to be in perfect condition, in the prime of his life. *What did he mean?*

I continued to stand there, a questioning look in my eyes, unmindful of those yet in line behind me. The Master met my eyes, gently clasping my hand with the matzah.

"Don't lose faith," he cautioned. "No matter what happens. Stand on what you know to be true." Then he bent over and kissed me briefly on the cheek. Numbly, with tears rolling down my face, I forced myself to walk back across the room to my seat. Kuza put his arm around my waist and I leaned my head on his shoulder.

After everyone in the room received their matzah, we ate it as one. Silence reigned briefly, then Yeshua commenced leading the seder. He spoke, as he always did, about the exodus account of the Israelites leaving Egypt. We shared the different seder plate items: first the hyssop dipped in salt water, reminiscent of the brush used to paint the doorposts of the Israelite homes with the blood of the slaughtered lamb; next the *marore*, or bitter herbs, reminding us of the bitterness of slavery. After that we combined on the matzah both the marore and the *charoset*, a dried fruit/nut mixture drenched in cinnamon, honey and wine. The charoset resembled the mortar the Israelite slaves used to make the bricks in that molten furnace, Egypt. It also served to remind us that even the most bitter things in life are tinged with sweetness.

Tonight in particular, the Master spent considerable time discussing the sacrificed Passover lamb. He stressed that this was a year-old male lamb, taken from the sheep or the goats, without spot or defect. He talked about how the lamb lived with the family, and they grew to love it. He stated that it was only through the bloody, sacrificial death of the innocent lamb that our sins were forgiven and we could come before God. Without the shedding of blood, he emphasized, there can be no forgiveness for sin. When he had finished saying all these things, he straightened his broad shoulders and said simply, "I am that lamb."

"What does he mean?" I asked my husband, as the sounds of others speaking as well brought up the volume in the room.

Kuza swung around to face me and spoke in low, urgent tones. "He's telling us that he's going to die."

"Are you sure?" I gasped.

Shoshana, who had overheard our conversation, looked questioningly at Kuza as well.

"Am I sure?" he replied, speaking to both of us, his forehead creased with lines of worry. "Not completely. But what he's saying doesn't make sense any other way."

Just then, the door to the room swung open and servants entered, carrying trays of food. Fragrant dishes featuring lamb as the main item were placed in front of us. Conversation at our table dwindled as each of us ate our meal, preoccupied with the unusual events of the first half of the seder. Only Zavdai seemed unaffected.

"This lamb is wonderful," he enthused, scooping a generous second helping onto his plate from the platter on the table. "What a nice break from fish. Not that I don't like fish," he quickly added, glancing around lest he had offended any potential customers.

Suddenly I felt like I couldn't breathe. Leaving Kuza to chat with Zavdai, I muttered a hasty "Excuse me" and slipped out of the room. *I just need some fresh air,* I thought.

As I made my way toward the stairs, one of the servants who had been sitting outside the room leapt to his feet. "Is everything all right, madam?" he inquired, with a slight bow.

"Oh, yes," I assured him. "I'm, well, I'm just a little warm and wanted to step outside."

"Come with me," he said. "I will show you the best spot."

Leading me upstairs, and not down, as I had expected, I soon found myself in a small alcove on the roof of the house. "Oh, this is beautiful!" I exclaimed. Potted palms and flowers of many varieties (hard to see what kind in the deepening twilight) made a secret pavilion under the stars. A few chairs and some small end tables provided a place to relax.

"Just come back down these stairs when you wish to re-enter the seder, madam," instructed the servant, bowing graciously as he exited the roof.

"Thank you," I called to his retreating form. Exhaling deeply, glad to be alone, I sat in one of the chairs and leaned my head back so that I could see the stars.

What a glorious night! The full moon, big, bright, and spectacular, was already ascending in the eastern sky. Star after brilliant star glowed brighter as the sky darkened, much as an erratic succession of torches would look if one lit them in tandem. Being out here was a tonic. Already I felt much better.

"Thank you, Adonai," I said aloud to the far-flung heavens towering over my head. "Thank you for Yeshua."

"Amen to that," said a voice from within the foliage decorations.

Emitting a short scream, I jumped up and spun around, my hand at my throat. Before I could speak a word, the owner of the voice climbed out of the shrubbery and revealed himself.

Tall, extremely slender, beardless, a fine, noble profile, and a shock of unkempt hair, the color of which I couldn't ascertain in the dark, all pointed to the likely conclusion that here before me was a young lad, no longer boy; not yet man. I relaxed.

"Who are you?" I demanded, still somewhat cautious though no longer afraid.

"Ah," he drawled. "The question is, who are *you*? Because I am the son of Yosef Mark, who owns this house."

I inclined my head. "Then I am pleased to meet you, sir, and appreciate your kind hospitality. My name is Yohana, wife of Kuza."

He bowed formally. "I have heard of you. You have traveled with the Rabbi." It was a statement of fact.

"Yes," I said softly. I turned aside and walked to the edge of the roof, looking over the edge. "He is my Lord." I turned back. "Do you believe that he is the Messiah?"

"My father does," said the lad. "Before tonight I wasn't sure." He moved restlessly. "But I've been watching him all night. There's something incredible about him, isn't there?"

"More than incredible. He really is the promised messiah, the son of God." My voice rose as my intensity increased.

"Yet," the lad mused, partly to himself and partly to me. "Tonight he spoke of death and being broken. Are these the words of a king?"

Are they the words of a king? A stab of doubt pricked my heart but I willed it away. *He's my lord; I will never forsake him.*

"They're the words of this king," I responded. "If we don't understand, it's not because the words are untrue but because there are things that are beyond our ability to understand."

The lad listened to me, mulling over what I said. I watched him with interest. *What an unusual young man this son of the house appeared to be!*

Impulsively, I laid my hand on his arm. "Come back downstairs with me and meet my husband. The second half of the seder should be starting any minute now."

By the light of the full moon I could just discern the glimmerings of a smile on his face. "*B'seder.* Let's go."

Together, we made our way back down the narrow stairs that led from the roof to the second story of the house. The same servant jumped to attention when he saw me, though I could have sworn that his eyes narrowed slightly at the sight of my companion. The lad flashed a toothy grin at the servant who stared after us as we proceeded back to the main room.

"Oh, there you are," announced Kuza as we approached the table. "Shalom," he said, noticing the lad at my side and standing up to greet him. Zavdai stood as well.

"Shalom, everyone. This is..." I stopped, realizing that I didn't know the name of the boy.

"Yochanan," he supplied quickly. "Yochanan Mark. I live here."

"Well," said Kuza, ever the diplomat. "Then we thank you for your gracious hospitality. Won't you pull up a chair and join us?"

Yochanan Mark cheerily agreed, leaving briefly to confer with a servant about a chair. It seemed to take him a while but soon he returned, looking triumphant. The servant, not the same one as before but with the same hesitant look as the fellow who showed me to the roof, followed carrying a chair.

"Why don't any of the servants look pleased with you?" I asked impetuously.

"Oh," he laughed, waving his hand. "They have this funny notion that I take matters into my own hands way too often. They don't seem to realize that I'm no longer a child."

Kuza and I exchanged glances. Really, this young man was irrepressible but extremely likeable.

"*Sheket*, everyone, *sheket*." From the head table, Yochanan bar Zavdai's voice cut through the noise in the room like a knife. Immediately, conversations died down, leaving behind a lull. Behind me I heard Zavdai grunt.

"We will now resume the seder," said Yochanan. Yeshua stood up then, and Yochanan went back to his seat. But the Lord did something none of us ever expected: he took off his outer clothing and wrapped a towel around his waist.

"What is he doing?" I said aloud; mostly to Kuza.

"Shh," he admonished. "Watch and see."

I looked around the room. Everyone was leaning on the edge of his or her seat, completely absorbed in the Lord's actions. Yochanan Mark sat as still as a Roman statue, but his eyes glittered.

Yeshua took a basin and poured water into it from a pitcher set on the table. A servant rushed over to help but the Lord shook his head, *no*. Confused, the servant reluctantly backed away.

Yeshua carried the basin and set it on the floor next to Thomas. "Put your feet in."

Even from where I sat I could see the surprise with which Thomas looked at the Lord, but he obeyed. Placing his feet in the basin, he sat dazed and immobile while the Master cleansed his feet with the water. When he was satisfied that Thomas' feet were clean, he took the towel from his waist and dried them. We were all stunned that the Lord of us all would do the task of a lowly servant. The servants seemed stunned, as well.

One after another, the Lord knelt down and washed the feet of each of his talmidim while the rest of us watched. When he reached Shimon Kefa, I saw my friend stand abruptly. "Lord, are you going to wash my feet?"

Yeshua laid his hand on Shimon's shoulder. "You don't understand what I'm doing now, but you will later."

"No," protested Shimon, horrified that the Master would place himself in such a servile position. "You shall never wash my feet," he stated emphatically.

"Well, look," answered Yeshua, gesturing toward the wash basin. "Unless I wash you, you have no part with me."

Suddenly Shimon's whole demeanor changed. He threw his hands up in the air dramatically. "If that's the case, then don't just do my feet but my hands and head as well!"

This brought scattered bursts of laughter from around the room. I craned my neck to catch sight of Chana. She was sitting very still, emphatically *not* laughing.

The Lord's reply was very odd at the time, though I understood it perfectly well later. He said, "A person who has had a bath needs only to wash his feet; his whole body is clean. And you are clean, though not every one of you." It turned out that he meant there was one among us who was going to betray him.

After he had washed the feet of the twelve, he turned to all of us and said, "I have washed your feet so that you will understand that you should wash each other's feet. This is an example to show you that no servant is greater than his master, nor is a messenger greater than the one who sent him. Do these things and you will be blessed."

Then he filled the cup with wine, and held it high, again reciting the blessing. "This cup is the new covenant in my blood, which is poured out for you," he explained to us. "Let us drink of it together."

After we all drank in unison, Yeshua said of the wine, much as he had said about the matzah, "I will not drink this fruit of the vine again until the kingdom of God comes."

A chill went through me when he spoke these words. This was the second time in one evening Yeshua had made reference to not eating or drinking again in this world. But an even greater chill went through me when he said, "The hand of him who is going to betray me is with mine on the table."

On the table? The only men at the table were the twelve talmidim! I looked at each man in turn, and my eyes narrowed when they rested on Yehuda from K'riot.

"Yes," continued the Lord. "I tell you that the Son of Man will go as it has been decreed, but woe to that man who betrays him." And he looked with great sadness at the astonished faces before him.

I saw the talmidim all stare at each other. Shimon Kefa motioned to Yochanan, who sat next to Yeshua. "Ask him which one he means," he said.

"Lord, who is it?" asked Yochanan, placing his hand on Yeshua's back.

"It's the one to whom I give this piece of matzah when I have dipped it in the dish," answered the Lord. He handed it to Yehuda from K'riot, who took it and ate. Yehuda refused to meet the Lord's eyes.

"What you are about to do, do quickly," Yeshua told him.

For some reason, nobody seemed to understand that Yeshua was publicly proclaiming, "This is the traitor!" I looked at what was happening in front of my eyes and didn't quite comprehend either. Looking back, I'm appalled at my denseness. We watched Yehuda leave the room.

"Where is Yehuda going?" I asked Kuza.

"Probably to buy something for Yeshua or give money to the poor," surmised my husband, since Yehuda had charge of the money bag. Kuza didn't trust Yehuda, so tended to keep his comments about the man clipped and short.

After Yehuda had gone, Yeshua spoke primarily to the eleven talmidim, but to the rest of us as well. In an intense a fashion as I've ever seen, he shared with us many, many things close to his heart:

> "It is only by your love that men will know you are my talmidim.
> Now is the Son of Man glorified.
> Do not let your hearts be troubled. Trust in God. Trust in me.
> I am the way, and the truth, and the life. No one comes through the Father but through me.
> I am in the Father and the Father is in me.
> Anyone who has faith in me will do what I have been doing. He will do even greater things because I am going to the Father.
> If you love me, you will obey what I command.
> The Father will give you the Spirit of truth to be with you forever.
> Do not let your hearts be troubled; do not be afraid.
> If you remain in me and my words remain in you, ask whatever you wish and it will be given you.
> I have called you friends.
> You did not choose me, but I chose you and appointed you to go and bear fruit—fruit that will last.
> If the world hates you, keep in mind that it hated me first.
> It is for your good that I am going away. I will be able to send the Holy Spirit to you once I am gone.
> I have much more to say to you, more than you can now bear. When the Holy Spirit comes, he will guide you into all truth.
> In a little while you will see me no more, and then after a little while you will see me.
> I tell you the truth, you will weep and mourn while the world rejoices. You will grieve, but your grief will turn to joy."

So many things were shared that night, but it is these shining pearls that stand out in my mind. These words that I cling to.

ELEVEN

After Yeshua had said all these things, he bade us shalom and dismissed us for the evening. He then took the eleven talmidim and went out into the night.

"Where is he going?" demanded my new friend, Yochanan Mark, a frown on his face.

"Probably to the Mount of Olives, to pray," I answered. "There's a little garden there where he likes to go. Why?"

"Oh…" The young man fidgeted nervously, not quite looking at me. He seemed to be struggling internally. I waited. Finally, he looked at me. "Because," he said, "I want to be wherever he is!" This last remark was delivered with an urgent and forceful passion.

Another talmid, I thought. "*B'seder.* The garden is on the right as you cross the Kidron Valley. It's in a grove of olive trees."

"Thank you." Yochanan Mark bowed formally to me and then to Kuza. "This evening has been monumental." He hesitated. "If I need to contact you again, where can I find you?"

Kuza told him the address of our rented house. "It's temporary, though," Kuza warned. "Don't wait too long."

Yochanan Mark then said a gallant shalom to us and to Shoshana, Shlomit, and Zavdai, as well. He turned and quickly left the room, stopping briefly at the door to speak with the servant who had shown me to the roof earlier.

Hmm, that's strange, I thought. He appeared to be arguing with the servant, then someone stepped in front of them and they were cut off from view.

"Yohana." Kuza's voice roused my attention back to my immediate surroundings. I looked at him questioningly. "Are you ready to go home?"

"Yes, I think so." I turned to Shoshana. "Will you walk with us, Shosh?"

My friend smiled a little, droopy smile. "Yes. What a strange and fearful night!"

The three of us walked home. Each was lost in contemplation of the troubling things Yeshua had shared at the seder. It was cold out and I shivered, pulling my cloak tightly against my body. At last we said good night, and soon Kuza and I lay side by side in our bed, my head pounding from the wine I had drunk.

"Do you have anything to say?" I asked my husband.

"No, not really," came his voice from the dark. "I'm very tired. Let's discuss all this in the morning."

"All right, my love. I'm tired, too. *Lilah tov.*"

"Lilah tov."

But despite the lateness of the hour, the wine we'd consumed, and our fatigue, neither of us was able to fall asleep. I turned on my side, and Kuza turned on his. Then I turned back and heard him sigh. We tossed and turned for the better part of two hours, only to find ourselves more awake than when we had first gotten into bed.

"What's going on?" I said aloud into the night.

Kuza roused himself and cradled his head in his hand while propping himself up by his elbow. "Something's terribly wrong."

"But what?" I cried irritably.

Just then a loud pounding on the front door downstairs startled us both. "Should you get that?" I gasped.

Kuza was already jumping out of bed and tying his robe. "Stay here," he ordered, and raced down the stairs.

Thoroughly awake now, I got out of bed and put on my robe. Then I stealthily crept to the top of the stairs and stood quietly, listening. Someone was talking with Kuza in loud and agitated tones. His voice sounded familiar. Listening closer, I realized, it was the young man we had met tonight at the seder! What was he doing here in the middle of the night?!

"Kuza," I called out. "Kuza, can I come down?"

"Yes, no, wait. Not yet. Throw me my cloak, would you?"

Mystified, I did as he asked, then waited a few moments.

"All right," came my husband's voice.

Groping my way in the dark, I reached the bottom of the stairs where Kuza stood with Yochanan Mark. By the light of the moon, I could see our young friend wrapped in Kuza's cloak, shivering uncontrollably.

"What happened?" I exclaimed.

"It's Yeshua," said Kuza, grimly. "Something dreadful has

happened."

"Yes," cried Yochanan Mark. "We need to save him! Quickly, quickly!" His voice cracked.

"What? What?" I felt myself getting hysterical. Taking a deep breath, I tried again. "Tell me what happened."

"Yes," agreed Kuza, the voice of reason. "From what you've already told me, I don't think there's anything we can do right now. Why don't you let my wife know what you saw?"

Agitated, Yochanan Mark looked from Kuza back to me. "*B'seder*. When I last saw you, I decided to try and follow Yeshua and his talmidim after they left the seder, but my father's head servant stopped me. 'You can't run around the city at this time of night,' he said. 'You know your father's orders.'

"So I pretended to go up to my room to sleep, but when I sensed an opportunity to leave I climbed down from the roof wearing only my linen nightshirt. Then I raced to the garden you told me about." He paused momentarily.

"Were they there?" I prodded.

"Yes. But before I even got there, I saw a whole detachment of soldiers."

"Soldiers!" I exclaimed. "Romans?"

Yochanan Mark shook his head. "No. Ours. They were sent from the chief priest. I caught sight of Mattiyahu, one of the higher-ranking officials. They had torches, swords and clubs."

"Oh, how awful!" I cried. "What did the Lord do?"

"He was incredibly calm. That big fellow, Shimon, I think it is, immediately drew his sword and went for what appeared to be the man in charge, one of the high priest's servants. He cut off his ear."

"Good," I said approvingly. "Did that slow them down?"

"It might have," answered Yochanan Mark. "But Yeshua did something amazing. He reached forward and touched the man's ear, and instantly healed him. I heard him rebuke his talmid: 'No more of this!' he said."

"But I don't understand. How did they even know where to find the Lord?"

Yochanan Mark leaned wearily against the wall. "This is the really awful part. He was betrayed by one of your own people! I saw this fellow leading the soldiers and purposely go right over to Yeshua saying, 'Rabbi' clearly and loudly. Then he kissed him."

I felt sick to my stomach. Betray the Lord! Who would do such a despicable thing! Surely not even…"

"Do you know his name?" asked Kuza.

"No," said Yochanan Mark. "All I can tell you is that he sat at the table with the Rabbi, but left early, before the others."

Kuza and I looked at each other. "Yehuda," we said simultaneously.

"Tell us the rest," urged Kuza, his shoulders sagging.

Yochanan Mark sank down onto the floor and leaned his head against the wall. "It was obvious that they wanted to arrest Yeshua," he intoned, his eyes closed, "but they didn't seem to know how to go about it. The Master himself rebuked them, saying that he was in plain sight every day at the Temple, teaching in the courts and they didn't lay a hand on him. 'Am I leading a rebellion, that you have come with swords and clubs?' Then he said, 'This is your hour, when darkness reigns.' "

"That must have infuriated them," remarked Kuza.

"Yes," answered Yochanan Mark. "It did. They sprang into action then, seizing him."

"Oh," I moaned. "Was there a terrible fight?"

"Fight?" In the moonlight, Yochanan Mark's face looked stricken. He shook his head. "No. No fight. Everyone ran away."

They what? Kuza and I looked at each other in amazement.

"Nobody tried to help him?" I sputtered angrily. "What about you? What did you do?"

"Yohana…," cautioned Kuza, placing his hand on my arm. "Don't."

"I'm sorry," whispered Yochanan Mark. "I tried to stay with him, but they came after me and seized me. I wriggled out of their grasp, leaving behind my shirt. That's why I came here without clothes. I panicked and ran for my life. This was the closest place." He leaned his head in his arms and starting sobbing.

The sight of the heartbroken lad crying touched my heart. I repented of my outburst. "I'm sorry," I said, sitting down beside him and hugging him tightly. "I wasn't there. It must have been terrifying to see all those soldiers with their weapons in the middle of the night."

"It was." He gulped, lifting his tear-stained face to mine. "But I'm so sorry that I left him." The tears came again, and he turned his face away.

Kuza had been silent for a bit, thinking hard. Now he spoke. "Look, Yohana. Everything's exploding. I'm going to get back to the palace in case I can use my influence and help Yeshua in any way. Wait until dawn and if none of the talmidim come here by then, go and round up as many of the followers as you can and go to the Governor's palace."

"To Pilate?" I questioned, confused. "Why should I go there?"

"It's obvious to me that the chief priests want to invoke a death sentence on Yeshua," Kuza patiently explained. "That's been their desire all along. They can't kill him themselves, though. They're going to need the Romans to do their dirty work for them. Especially with tonight being the official start of Pesach. Killing Yeshua would render them ceremonially unclean." He gave a sad, little laugh. "I expect they'll be getting Pilate out of bed as soon as they dare. I'll see what I can do with Herod."

My heart constricted in my chest. I nodded numbly. *First Yeshua and now Kuza!* "Just be careful, my love," I begged.

"I'll do what it takes," he said simply. "But before I go, let's pray."

Yochanan Mark stood up, and the three of us linked arms. Kuza prayed. "Lord God, Adonai, our Father in heaven. We come before You asking Your favor and protection on Your anointed one, Yeshua. We ask that You hold him in the palm of Your hand and keep him safe. And we pray that You protect us as well as we go forth into this day, which holds many dangers. Amen."

"Amen," we echoed. I kissed Kuza and let him go, but not without a great deal of unease. When we had prayed for Yeshua, I saw only an unfathomable blackness.

❧❧

Once Kuza left, sleep was impossible. I got dressed and found some of Kuza's spare clothes for Yochanan Mark. He vacillated between rushing right over to the chief priest's house to rescue the Master and alternately being seized by acute fear.

"He's the most godly man I've ever seen," said Mark. "They *can't* hurt him!" He got a frantic look in his eyes when he said this and it was all I could do to convince him to obey my husband's instructions. We sat up in the downstairs room throughout the rest of that long, long night. Once or twice I dozed off, only to start awake. Nasty and hideous nightmares tormented my brief sleep.

When the dark outside finally gave way to a lighter shade of gray, Yochanan Mark grabbed my arm. "Look! It's dawn! Let's go now. Please!"

"*B'seder.*" In the gloom of predawn, the shapes in the room became more distinct. My eyes picked out the chair where I had tossed my cloak several hours before; another lifetime ago.

I wrapped my cloak around me and beckoned to Yochanan Mark that I was ready to leave. I opened the door and started with surprise.

Andrew stood on the doorstep, his hand raised in the air, about to knock.

"Andrew!" I clasped his hand. "Oh, Andrew!" The sight of his familiar face comforted me greatly.

Andrew looked from me to Yochanan Mark. "You were at the garden last night!" he cried, startled at the sight of my young friend.

"Yes," I interrupted. "Which is why I'm aware of the Lord's arrest. We were just heading out to the Governor's palace."

"The Governor's palace? I'm going over to the home of the chief priest."

Quickly I explained to him Kuza's rationale for going to the Governor's palace.

"Sounds wise." Andrew nodded. "But let's first start at the home of the chief priest and see if Yeshua is still there. Where is Kuza, anyway?"

"He went back to Herod to try to do something." Then, "Tell us, Andrew! Tell us what's happening."

He shook his head, shoulders slumped. "We all ran off," he admitted in a strangled voice. "Only Shimon and Yochanan followed, and they carefully, at a distance. The rest of us have been going from house to house telling all the followers what has occurred. Hurry and come with me; I still need to contact Shoshana and Miryam of Magdala."

Immediately, we left the house and went out into the street. The home where the other women were staying was close by. We knocked discreetly, roused them from what looked to be almost as restless a night as I had endured, and told them about the Lord's arrest. Shocked and saddened, they quickly dressed and followed us. We went with Andrew to the home of Caiphas, the current high priest.

As we strode through the silent streets, I heard the soft weeping of the Magdalit. I reached out and held her hand, squeezing it tenderly.

"It is what I most feared," she mourned.

"Don't worry," said I, though distraught myself. "He is the Lord. Nothing can harm him." But we were all terribly, terribly upset.

We crossed the City, walking back over to the spacious, wealthy section, in the same neighborhood where we had spent the seder. The magnificent home of Caiphas loomed ahead, illuminated by the rays of the rising sun. We could see the elaborate courtyard and gardens which surrounded the house. Guards and important looking religious officials swarmed everywhere. Hesitant to get too close, we stood across the street and debated what to do. It was then that we heard it.

'What's that?" demanded the Magdalit, spinning around.

"It sounds like a man crying," Shoshana said.

Andrew listened intently. "I know that voice," he said. We walked a few feet to the left, into a small alcove, following the sound.

What we found shocked us. Curled up in a ball, his back toward us, was Shimon Kefa! I had never seen him cry before, and to see him break down with such heart-wrenching sobs broke my heart.

"My brother!" exclaimed Andrew, bending down to hug Shimon. "What is it? Is it the Lord?"

Shimon's body shook at the unexpected sound of his brother's voice. Slowly he turned and lifted his head, looking at Andrew with red, dejected, pained eyes. "I failed him," he whispered hoarsely. "I denied my Lord."

"Denied him?" repeated Andrew, quizzically. "What do you mean, denied him?"

"I...I pretended that I didn't know who he was. I was terrified! Oh, Andrew! I failed him! Me! Who was willing to follow him unto death!" The tears flowed.

Andrew was silent, but he continued to keep his arm around his brother. "We all failed him, Shimon," he finally said, his voice grave. "We all ran off. At least you and Yochanan had the courage to keep an eye on him. That was more than what I did."

Shimon hiccupped, managing a weak smile. "I still feel like camel dung, but you're a wonderful brother."

"Come, Shimon," pleaded Andrew. "Come with us. We have to see what they're doing to him."

Shimon nodded, pulling himself upright. Andrew gripped his arm and our small group crossed the street, getting as close as we could to the house. What we saw sickened us.

The Master stood within a large contingent of soldiers. He had a blindfold around his face and was being repeatedly struck in the face and body. I saw him flinch as the blows were delivered, but did not hear him cry out. The men heaped abuse at him, mocking his claim to messiah. One burly fellow with a pockmarked face slammed his huge, meaty fist into the side of the Lord's head. "Prophesy! Who hit you?" he taunted, laughing cruelly, before ripping the blindfold off

The Magdalit screamed and lunged forward with her fists in the air.

"No!" Andrew hissed, grabbing her from behind and holding her, hard. "Don't do it, you'll get killed!"

"I don't care!" she sobbed, trying to wrench free. "Let me help him! They're hurting him!" Shoshana and I put our arms around Miryam as well. Shimon stood off to the side, his face a study in despair. Yochanan

Mark stared intently at Yeshua.

It was then that the Lord looked over and saw us. His fathomless eyes, filled with pain and suffering, reached out to us in love and acceptance. Miryam stopped struggling, and gazed back at him. We loosened our hold on her, and she held out her arms toward him, beseechingly. Slowly he shook his head. Stricken, she slumped to the ground, sobbing.

The religious authorities beckoned to the guards then, who grabbed Yeshua, took him (his wrists already bound with strips of leather), and hustled him roughly over to the house. He disappeared from our view in the midst of a detachment of guards.

"Where are they taking him?" I frantically demanded of Andrew.

"I don't know," he answered, helplessly.

Almost immediately, the guards re-emerged. Yeshua was trapped within their midst, bound and chained. Roughly, they hustled him off to the side of the road while Caiaphas, Annas his father-in-law, and many other powerful and important religious officials stepped triumphantly in front. With the high priest leading the way, the guards jerked Yeshua along, directly behind the rest of the procession.

They headed northeast, diagonally across the City, past the Temple. "Kuza's right," I said. "They're taking him to Pilate. I'm convinced of it."

Pilate, the Roman Governor, was currently in Jerusalem. Sometimes he ousted Herod and stayed at the main palace; other times he resided at the Antonia Fortress, a huge barracks-like monstrosity over by the Sheep Gate, off the Kidron Valley. This particular time he happened to be at the Fortress. Only Pilate had the authority to sentence someone to death. The intention was all too clear.

By now the sun had completely risen over the eastern rim of the City. No longer bathed in gray shadow, the City gleamed and sparkled in the early morning sunshine; a mockery of the despair in our hearts. Hurriedly, we followed after the guards, hoping to catch a glimpse of the Master. But we could not. He was obscured from our view.

All of us were silent. What was there to say? The worst thing imaginable was happening and we felt powerless to stop it. All we could do was watch.

It was when we were halfway to the Fortress that I realized how crowded the streets had become since we started out. *What are all of these people doing out and about so early,* I wondered. They tracked with us, heading in the same direction. *Not nice types either,* I decided. All were men: scruffy, ill-kempt and nasty looking. The sort one would hire for dark and secret assignments.

As we were walking, two of the Torah teachers lagged behind the rest of their group and we overheard them talking.

"I still can't believe that he, a mere man, claimed to be the Son of God!" said one.

"It's utter blasphemy!" sputtered his friend. "When he said that from now on, the Son of Man will be seated at the right hand of the mighty God, I almost ran up there and hit him myself!"

"Yes. And when we asked him if he is the Son of God, he replied, 'You are right in saying I am.' What further evidence do we need that he must be destroyed for daring to make himself equal with the Almighty?"

They realized then that they were well behind their associates and, lifting their robes slightly for greater mobility, ran to catch up.

"He *is* the Son of God. He is!" uttered Shimon vehemently. He raised his fists in the air, and then let them fall to his sides, dejected. Several tears ran down his face.

Andrew put his arm around his brother. "*B'seder*, Shimon, *b'seder*. Whatever you did, he still loves you." He glanced nervously up the street, at the backs of the retreating soldiers. "Come on, they're getting too far ahead of us. Let's go."

Quickly, we accelerated our pace and kept as close as we could to Yeshua without attracting undue attention from the guards. Soon enough, we arrived at the Fortress and watched apprehensively as one of the guards went in and requested the appearance of Pilate.

None of the religious authorities entered the building as it would render them ceremonially unclean to celebrate the Passover. So we waited outside, and as we waited, more and more people came up the street, until quite a large crowd had formed. These were the men I had seen on our way here. Unfamiliar faces. Hostile faces. *Paid* faces, I suspected.

It didn't take very long for Pilate to emerge. I had seen him several times in the past and so would have been able to identify him even if he hadn't been wearing the distinctive attire of the governor. His very Roman face, nose flat at the bridge then long over thin lips, short hair and beardless face, was so Gentile. His short, belted tunic and high, laced-up-the-calves leather sandals, combined with a deep purple cape, set him clearly apart from my people. He looked agitated; obviously an emotional crowd outside his window first thing in the morning smelled like a potential riot to him. And Pilate could ill afford another riot.

Flanked by eight soldiers, Pilate strode to the top of the stairs that led to the entrance of the Fortress. He had apparently been briefed by the high priest's guard on the reason for his wake-up call.

"What charges are you bringing against this man?" he demanded, his Hebrew fluent, precise.

Several of the religious leaders shouted at once, "He's a criminal! That's why we've handed him over to you!"

"Take him yourselves and judge him by your own law," Pilate said. The Romans thought the Jewish laws were entirely too complex and attempted to distance themselves whenever possible. When they believed things had gotten out of control, they would step in and massacre people, thus restoring, in their eyes, order.

But the high priests and the Torah teachers had already judged Yeshua. They wanted him dead, dead in as horrible a fashion as possible.

"We have no right to execute anyone," they objected. "He's a criminal. He claims to be a king. He's against paying taxes to Caesar! That's why we've handed him over to you."

When I heard this, I bristled with indignation. *Everyone* who wasn't Roman was against paying such huge taxes to Caesar! *What a ridiculous thing to say. As for claiming to be king, well, he really is one.*

Throughout this interchange, Yeshua stood straight and majestic, an inexplicable peace on his face. Every so often, one of the guards would jerk rudely on his chains, causing him to sway, yet he did not react.

Now Pilate briefly disappeared into the fortress to confer with his advisors. After a few moments he reappeared, beckoning that Yeshua should be brought up the steps to himself. The guards around Yeshua quickly marched him to within ten feet of Pilate.

Pilate looked at Yeshua with undisguised curiosity. I could see him noting the regal bearing of the roughly dressed and bruised man before him. I could see his brain working furiously behind that Roman brow.

Finally, he spoke. "*Are* you the king of the Jews?" A real question. No sarcasm.

And the Lord gave him a real answer. "Yes, it is as you say."

A huge collective gasp went up from the crowd that had gathered at the base of the steps. Angry muttering and shouted curses broke out in every direction. Pilate beckoned to the captain of his guard, who in turn commanded his soldiers. They drew their swords and lunged menacingly toward the crowd. The noise stopped.

Again, Pilate turned to Yeshua. "You are a king, then!"

Yeshua answered, "You are right in saying I am a king. In fact, for this reason I was born, and for this I came into the world, to testify to the truth. Everyone on the side of truth listens to me."

Pilate looked steadily at him for several moments. Conflicting emotions of hope, fear, disdain, disbelief rolled across his face. Then, in a voice lost and weary, he uttered facetiously, "What *is* truth?"

Walking over to the front of the steps, he spoke directly to the chief priests and the people assembled. "I find no basis for a charge against this man."

My scream of delight melted into the collective roar of furious outrage that met this decision. Beside me, the Magdalit dug her nails into my arm, her face white, her eyes hopeful.

"Silence!" roared Pilate. He pointed to Caiaphas, whose face had turned an ugly shade of red. "You can speak."

"He stirs up the people all over Judea by his teaching!" snarled Caiaphas. "He started in the Galil and has come all the way here! He—"

But Pilate cut him off. Hearing that Yeshua was from the Galil was the escape route he had been hoping to find.

"Are you then a Galilean?" he asked, turning to Yeshua. Upon finding out that this was so, which meant that Yeshua came from Herod's jurisdiction, Pilate heaved a sigh of relief.

"Fine, then," he said, pleased. "Take him to Herod." He glared at the crowd. "Dismissed," he barked, heading back into the Fortress, but not without a last, curious glance at Yeshua.

❧ ❧

So the nightmare continued. We followed the surging crowd back across the City to Herod's palace. I knew that it was here I would see Kuza, and my heart beat faster. Could he help? What had he accomplished since he had left before dawn? Had Herod turned on Kuza? This was entirely within the realm of possibility. My blood chilled at the thought. My Lord and my husband, both in peril at once! I grew dizzy and my throat tightened.

When we reached the palace, struggling to keep close enough to the Lord to at least keep him in our sight, I saw that Herod had already emerged into the sunlight. Obviously we were expected. *A good sign*, I thought. *This must mean that Kuza has been successful on some level.*

Herod strode forward when Yeshua was pushed in front of him. Eagerness animated his unpleasant features. He smiled and rubbed his hands together. I knew that he had long attempted to see Yeshua but had failed miserably. Now Yeshua had come to him. He immediately barraged the Lord with questions.

Unlike the direct responses Yeshua gave Pilate, here he afforded Herod no cordiality. He stayed silent, eyeing the king with great sadness. Herod put up with this behavior for a while, going from one question to another though he received no response; going through a litany he must have had prepared for some time:

"Can you really open the eyes of the blind?
Do the lame walk?
Here's a cup of water. Let's see you turn it into wine.
Show me a miracle! Show me, show me, show me...."

After a while, Herod tired of Yeshua's impassivity. He grew less and less genial. He turned his attention away from the Lord and the religious leaders used this opportunity to jump in and attack. One after another, they pleaded their case before Herod, citing their many grievances against Yeshua.

Of course, the biggest accusation the religious leaders had was Yeshua's claim of kingship. Caiaphas, in particular, knew how to taunt Herod with this one: "He says that he is the true king of Israel, your majesty. How can that be, since we all know *you* are God's chosen to rule this land." I don't know which dripped more oil: Caiaphas' voice or his beard.

This latest allegation had the desired effect. "Oh, he's the king of Israel, is he?" Herod sneered. He gave orders to his soldiers and one of them disappeared into the palace. When he reappeared, he carried an elegant purple robe, the type Herod routinely wore.

It was then that I finally saw Kuza. Apparently, he had been standing in the midst of Herod's advisors but I hadn't been able to pick him out from my distance. The only reason I saw him now was because he approached Herod, kneeled before him, and said something. I held my breath, watching as Herod walked over to Kuza, responded, and dismissed Kuza. My husband nodded, stood up, and returned to his place among his peers.

I later learned that Kuza had pled the case for Yeshua's innocence. Herod had agreed that he believed the Master to be innocent of the charges against him, but this did not prevent him from behaving cruelly toward Yeshua.

Herod commanded the purple robe to be draped around the Lord. Then he and his soldiers mocked and ridiculed Yeshua, verbally abusing him. "So you're the king of Israel, are you? Use your power and free yourself!"

Throughout all this, the Lord said not a word, though his regal bearing and noble brow proclaimed him a far greater king than Herod could ever hope to be.

"Why does he say nothing to Herod, yet speak to Pilate, the Roman?" pondered Yochanan Mark, at my side.

"Because," Shimon answered, and we all started at the sound of his voice, so silent for so long, "Herod had his opportunity to understand the Kingdom of Heaven when he conversed with Yochanan the Immerser. Yochanan answered every question Herod put to him. But in the end, he had him beheaded." My favorite talmid shook his head sadly. "The Lord can't say anything that Herod hasn't already heard, and rejected." This brought to mind his very recent denial of Yeshua. Distraught, he turned his face away from us.

What a terrible day this was! An awful day; drenched in darkness and distress. A day when one runs into the safety of one's home to avoid a raging lion, leans against the wall, and is bitten by a viper.

Suddenly we saw the Lord dragged by the guards down the palace steps. Herod watched, then turned and went back into his palace. The crowd surged after Yeshua, angry and unpredictable.

"Where are they taking him?" I heard.

"Back to Pilate," came the response.

Distraught, I looked around for Kuza, reluctant to proceed without him. A man, rough and ill-kempt, bumped into me. "Move it, lady," he barked, shoving me hard out of his way.

Stumbling, I fell against Shoshana, who half-caught, half-braced herself against me so she wouldn't fall as well. "Come, Yohana. We need to keep up or this crowd will run us down."

"But, Kuza," I protested, looking wildly around.

"Kuza will find you. Let's go!"

But Kuza didn't find me—not for most of the day. In the meantime, we walked yet again across the City back to the Antonia Fortress. Mid-morning now, the sun beat down hot on our heads and backs as we trudged along. The crowd around me grew ever bigger. Most of the people looked like paid rabble-rousers, though a few seemed innocent enough, caught up in the excitement. Here and there, I saw the talmidim. Small groups of us swirled in and out, desperate, aching. No one said very much.

When we reached the Fortress, I spotted Miryam, Yeshua's mother. She stood with Yochanan and one of her sons, Ya'akov. I ran over to her, pushing my way through the crowd, the Magdalit behind me.

"Miryam, Miryam," I shouted.

Startled, she turned to look in my direction, her eyes huge in a white, terrified face. When she saw us, her expression changed. "Yohana. Miryam."

She opened her arms wide and we flew into them, holding each other. We cried. Yochanan and Yeshua's brother stood near us, silent, waiting.

I so wanted to offer words of encouragement to Miryam, but they stuck in my throat. I hesitated to assure her that all would be well when I myself agonized over the desperateness of the situation. Before I could speak, however, she did.

"What I feared most has come upon me," she said, emotion thickening her speech. Bleakly, she stared in the direction of the fortress.

"Ema," said Ya'akov, helplessly, seeking to console her but at a loss as to how to accomplish his goal.

Yochanan shifted uneasily. He, too, stared in the direction of the fortress. "He should be here by now."

Just then, Andrew, Shimon, Yochanan Mark, and Shoshana caught up to us. Brief greetings were exchanged. Andrew, Shimon, and Yochanan immediately drew near each other, speaking in low, urgent tones.

"Oh, look!" exclaimed Yochanan Mark, whose eyes were young and sharp. He pointed straight ahead. "There's the Lord!"

He was right. Brought back up the steps of the Fortress, made to look like a mockery in Herod's purple robe, resolute and unafraid, stood the Master. Pilate himself immediately came out, his tone conveying his annoyance at seeing Yeshua brought back.

"Why is this man here again?" he asked. "What did Herod decide? And why is he dressed like this?"

"O Your Excellency," said Caiaphas, from the midst of the chief priests and rulers. "Herod has sent him back to you. You are the one who has the power to carry out a sentence of death against this imposter." Careful not to push Pilate too far, he nonetheless grimaced such that his distaste for Yeshua would be clearly understood.

"It's obvious to me that this man has done nothing deserving death," replied Pilate. "And it's also obvious that Herod did not condemn him. So

I will punish him and then release him."

I breathed a little easier when I heard this, but only for a second. All around me, the crowd sprang to life. Ugly and menacing, people everywhere, as if on cue, started chanting, "Away with this man! Release Barabbas to us!"

"Barabbas!" breathed Yochanan Mark scornfully. "That murderer!"

"Who is he?" asked Miryam.

"A rabble-rouser, Ema," answered Ya'akov. "He's been in prison for an insurrection he started here in the City. A thoroughly despicable character." He pursed his lips and his eyes looked afraid.

Pilate didn't agree to release Barabbas, nor did he agree to execute Yeshua. What he did instead made my flesh crawl. In an effort to pacify the religious leaders without actually taking part in Yeshua's death, he called for Yeshua to be flogged. I expect he hoped that the show of pain and blood would placate the mob. Instead, it fed their hysteria.

I can hardly describe the anguish we all felt at seeing our Lord and Master—the man we knew as the Messiah of Israel, the healer and miracle worker, the one we loved above all else—stripped and flogged publicly. The coarse Roman soldiers laughed as they swung a heavy metal ball with sharp spikes into the Master's back, ripping apart skin and flesh, spraying precious blood.

To my amazement, the Lord still did not cry out. Expelling breath sharply, he fell to his knees from the impact but didn't scream or beg for mercy. I didn't think I could bear another moment of this. Only raw terror at the thought of pain kept me from running and throwing my body between Yeshua and that horrible metal ball. Only the strong arms of Andrew and Shimon kept the Magdalit from doing the same. I felt shame when I saw how little she cared for her own person when her Lord suffered. I agonized but still felt helpless to do more than watch as my Lord endured blow after agonizing blow.

Finally, mercifully, the scourging ended. Yeshua could barely stand, but stand he did. I saw two of the soldiers making something; and then one of them walked over to where the Lord stood and shoved this thing down on the Lord's head. Blood dripped down his forehead and into his eyes. Unable to move his manacled hands, he shook his head to clear his eyes of the blood.

"What is that thing on his head?" I asked Shoshana.

The woman who used to be blind peered closely. "It looks like a crown made of thorns," she replied with a grimace.

Then the soldiers put the purple robe back on Yeshua. They mocked him, bowing down before him, saying, "Hail, king of the Jews!" Every so often, one of them struck him in the face such that his face became unrecognizable.

"Come home, Ema," I heard Ya'akov begging his mother. "This is too awful for you to see. Please, *please*, let me take you home."

Miryam shook her head, the tears spilling out of her anguished eyes. Overcome by weeping, at first she could not answer. Finally, she regained her voice enough to whisper. "No. He is my son. I must be here with him. I must tell him how much I love him."

"Oh, Ema," groaned Ya'akov despairingly. "He knows that! Don't you think he knows that? You've always shown him your love. It's us—his brothers—who have failed to express *our* love." Hollow-eyed, he stared ahead to where his brother endured being brutalized. None of us knew what to say to him. Today, our individual cups of pain overflowed.

Again Pilate came out and spoke to the crowd. "Look, I am bringing him out to you to let you know that I find no basis for a charge against him." Gesturing to Yeshua, standing there adorned in that awful purple robe, the crown of thorns piercing his head, he said, "Here is the man!"

But the crowd, ugly and threatening before, grew worse. *Crucify! Crucify!* they shouted.

Agitated, Pilate walked away and conferred with his advisors. Returning to the crowd, he made a pitiful attempt at a smile. "You take him and crucify him," he said, knowing that the religious leaders lacked the authority to do such a thing. He thumped his hand against his chest. "As for me, I find no basis for a charge against him."

The governor turned to go, but the roar of the crowd rose up like a towering wave. He seemed unsteady on his feet, as if the very vibrations of their noise might topple him. Hassled and uncertain, he turned back around.

One of the chief priest's men spoke up. "We have a law, and according to that law he must die because he claimed to be the Son of God!"

The Son of God! Pilate's face blanched when he heard this! It was one thing to claim to be a king but to call oneself deity! Who was this man, Yeshua? Alarmed, he questioned the Lord yet again.

"Who are you?" he demanded. "Where do you come from?"

Yeshua gave no answer.

Sweating now, Pilate attempted to use his authority to force answers out of Yeshua. "Don't you realize," he said, harshly, "don't you realize that I have the power either to free you or crucify you?"

Yeshua stood there, bloody and battered, his nose broken, teeth missing, the thorny crown piercing his skull, his body mangled, yet with greater authority than Pilate had ever seen displayed even by the Roman emperor. He looked deeply into Pilate's eyes while Pilate, mesmerized, kept his gaze, unable to look away. "No," he said, and his eyes filled with tears. "You would have no power over me if it were not given to you from above. Therefore, the one who handed me over to you is guilty of a greater sin." And he said not another word to Pilate.

Pilate grew frantic. He came over to the crowd time after time, vainly trying to convince them to set Yeshua free. Terribly afraid of being sent back to Rome in disgrace should another riot break out during his watch, he lacked the courage to free Yeshua himself. He wanted the people's approval. This he was not to get.

Just when he was ready to give in, one of his aides handed him a note. Yeshua's talmid, Mattiyahu, came to understand after the fact that this note was from Pilate's wife. She gave testimony to a powerful dream she had that day which convinced her of Yeshua's innocence. This drove Pilate wild.

"Shall I release Barabbas to you?" he asked. Again.

But the people shouted all the louder, "Crucify him!"

When Pilate saw he was getting nowhere, but instead an uproar was starting, he took some water and symbolically washed his hands in front of the crowd. "I am innocent of this man's blood. It is your responsibility!"

The crowd roared back, "Let his blood be on us and on our children!"

Shaken, Pilate released Barabbas but handed Yeshua over to be crucified.

❧❧

What followed next blurred in my mind into one hideous event. I do recall Yeshua's mother moaning and slumping against her son Ya'akov's side when the sentence of crucifixion was pronounced. I saw Caiaphas' face light up in a gruesome smile of triumph. I watched as the Lord stoically and without surprise accepted the verdict. *He's been expecting this*, I thought. I continued to watch in paralyzed numbness as the Roman soldiers took a crossbar of heavy, rough wood and forced the Lord to carry it on his back.

The crossbar weighed so much and the Lord's body was so battered that he instantly sank to his knees. Only his rock-hard inner perseverance, aided by the whiplashes of the Roman soldiers, enabled him to struggle upright and haltingly walk in the direction they pushed him: the execution place outside the city walls, Golgotha, the Place of the Skull.

We followed after him. What else could we do? The women wept and moaned aloud; the men cried as well. Slowly, slowly, we wound our way through the narrow streets. Yeshua stumbled several times under the weight of the crossbar to which his hands would be nailed.

Soon it became apparent even to the soldiers that he had reached his physical limits. They grabbed some poor, unsuspecting fellow on his way into the City from the countryside, and made him carry the crossbar.

At one point, we got close enough so that we made eye contact with the Lord. Turning to us, wincing with pain, he saw our grief and said, "Daughters of Jerusalem, do not weep for me; weep for yourselves and for your children. For the time will come when you will say, 'Blessed are the barren women, the wombs that never bore and the breasts that never nursed!' For if men do these things when the tree is green, what will happen when it is dry?" Slowly, with difficulty, he continued the long, torturous walk to Golgotha.

When we finally reached the dreaded execution place, the soldiers wasted no time. They grabbed the crossbar from the fellow who had carried it and shoved him out of the way. Then, pulling the stake to the crossbar out of the ground (for it stayed at the place of execution), they nailed the two pieces together in the shape of a cross. While this huge cross lay flat on the ground, they pushed the Lord atop it, then took three huge nails, each about six inches long, and pounded them through Yeshua's wrists and ankles into the wood. Oh, the dreadful sound of tearing flesh! The horrible agony of that most shocking of executions! Even now, I shudder and grow pale at the cursed memory.

Still, the Lord did not scream. His body trembled convulsively and he groaned aloud words of forgiveness. "Oh, Father, forgive them for they don't know what they do!"

Before they hoisted the cross to an upright position, one of the soldiers nailed a sign to the spot just above Yeshua's head. It read: *Yeshua of Natzeret, and the King of the Jews.* The sign was written in Hebrew (*Yeshua haNatzeret, v'melech hayehudim*), Greek and Latin. The first letters of the four words of the Hebrew read *yod, hay, vav, hay*—otherwise known as the sacred name of God.

"Take it down!" yelled the religious leaders. "Write instead that he *claimed* to be king of the Jews." That would have changed the spelling so as to not be the sacred name of God.

But the soldiers wouldn't budge. "The Governor himself wrote this sign," said one, aggressively. "What he wrote, he wrote." The sign stayed.

All sorts of people, emboldened by Yeshua's apparent helplessness, came up to the cross and heaped verbal abuse on him.

"You who are going to destroy the Temple and build it in three days, save yourself!"

"Come down from the cross, if you are the Son of God!"

"He saved others, but he can't save himself!"

"If he's the King of Israel, let him come down now from the cross!"

"So you're the Son of God, are you? Let's see God rescue you!"

And on, and on.

Dimly, through my grief, I noticed that two others were crucified along with Yeshua: one on each side of him. Common criminals. One spent his last hours on earth joining in the mockery. The other rebuked his fellow criminal.

"Don't you fear God?" he asked through gritted teeth. "We deserve this punishment but this man has done nothing wrong." Then he said, "Yeshua, remember me when you come into your kingdom."

"I tell you the truth," answered my Lord. "Today you will be with me in *gan eden*."

✜

The air changed. Clouds blew in from the west, obscuring the sun. An eerie and unnatural darkness fell. Although only noon, it felt much, much later. I couldn't quite believe that I really stood there, watching my Lord slowly suffocate as he died an excruciatingly painful death.

Our small group of believers walked through the crowd until we came closer to the cross than anyone else. Miryam, Yeshua's mother, fell to her knees and cried aloud. One of the soldiers swung around and would have beaten her off, but others interceded. *That's his mother.* Somewhat unwillingly, he allowed her to stay.

From far above our heads, Yeshua heard the commotion. Slowly, he looked down. "Ema," he said, wrapping the name in tones of love and tenderness.

Miryam pushed herself up off the ground and raised her arms high in the air toward him. "My son, my precious son," she wept, her voice broken.

"Ema," said Yeshua once more. Every word cost him a tremendous effort. To use his breath meant he had to pull up on the cross, further ripping the wounds in his hands and feet, causing racking pain. He looked beyond Miryam to Yochanan, son of Zavdai, "Here is your son," he gasped. And to Yochanan, "Here is your mother."

The effort of those words cost him tremendously. He looked away from us then, and toward heaven, engaged in a spiritual battle the likes of which made the physical torment pale in comparison.

A familiar hand clasped my arm. I jerked around. "Kuza!" I cried.

My husband stood next to me, exhausted and deeply saddened. He didn't look at me but instead stared up at the figure on the cross. "God in heaven, what have we done?" he uttered, then fell silent.

We stood there for close to three hours, darkness swirling in mists about us on that stony and unforgiving hill. Most of the mockers had fallen silent as well, subdued by the blackness at midday. Every so often, one of the women moaned aloud. The darkness intensified. Then, in a voice so startlingly loud that we all jumped, Yeshua called out, "My God, my God, why have you forsaken me?"

"Psalm 22," recognized Kuza, awestricken.

Up on the cross, Yeshua spoke again. "I am thirsty."

A man I didn't know rushed and plunged a dirty sponge into a jar of wine vinegar. He stuck it on the end of a stalk of hyssop and held it up to Yeshua. Tasting it, Yeshua cried out, "It is finished." With that, he gave up his spirit. He didn't die as men die, but he actually released his spirit, as the culmination to a task completed.

❧❧

As soon as he died, a deafening noise from under the ground roared through, knocking people down. Several screamed. "Earthquake!" someone shouted.

An earthquake! I fell to my knees, panic stricken. What other horrible things could happen today? "Help us, God, help us!" I sobbed.

The Roman centurion who had kept watch in front of Yeshua blanched, his face terrified. "Surely this man was the Son of God!"

The volatile crowd, many of whom had screamed for Yeshua's blood, now beat their breasts in fear. Most slipped away, deserting the execution site.

Since sundown marked the beginning of a special Pesach Shabbat and it would be unclean to leave dead and dying bodies on crosses, the religious leaders asked Pilate to break the legs of the condemned men. One of the soldiers took a large wooden bat and, with a sickening crunch, cracked the legs of the two criminals who were still alive. This was so they would be unable to prop themselves up. Amid screams of pain, they died quickly. When he reached Yeshua, however, he didn't need to break his legs as the Lord was already dead. Instead, he pierced Yeshua's side with a spear, bringing a sudden flow of blood and water. Thus it was that the sacrificed lamb had none of his bones broken, and we all looked on him whom we had pierced.

The soldiers took the dead criminals off their crosses and threw them in the back of a cart, so as to toss them in a common grave. They took Yeshua down as well.

"Kuza!" I cried, clutching at my husband's tunic. "They can't take away the Lord! We must do something."

The Magdalit and Miryam, Yeshua's mother, hurried over to where we stood. Both were frantic, wringing their hands. "Help us, help us!" they cried as well. "Don't let them leave with him whom we love."

Nodding in agreement, already striding toward the Roman centurion, Kuza was intercepted by Yosef of Ramataim. I hadn't realized that the distinguished member of the Sanhedrin had been present. But then, of course, he would have been part of the council hastily called that sat in judgment of the Master.

"Let me go to Pilate and ask for Yeshua's body," he said to Kuza, his normally handsome face lined and strained. "I happen to own an empty tomb in that garden down there." He pointed to a place partway down the hill.

"This is what you want to do?" asked Kuza, aware that Yosef had kept his belief in Yeshua a secret.

"The time for subterfuge is past," said Yosef in response.

"*B'seder*. I'll stay here and guard the body. You go to the Fortress."

With a brief nod, Yosef turned to go, only to come face-to-face with Nakdimon.

The younger man stood there, shaking. "Let me go with you," he pleaded.

Yosef studied Nakdimon carefully. "Will you be all right?"

"Yes, yes, I'll be fine. What can they do to me to equal what they did to *him*? Uncircumcised Philistines, all of them!" He spat angrily on the ground, then wiped his clammy face on the sleeve of his robe.

Yosef looked doubtful, but he took his colleague with him.

Kuza then went over to the centurion and explained that Yosef and Nakdimon were on their way to Pilate to request to properly bury the body.

232

"I better go and tell the Governor that he's really dead, then," decided the soldier. He called some of his subordinates and instructed them to stand watch over Yeshua's body until he gave them further orders. Then he ran off in the direction of Yosef and Nakdimon.

Most of the people were gone by now. Only a few of us still straggled about here and there. I sat down heavily on a rock, completely drained from the momentous events of the day. Kuza came and stood next to me. I leaned my head against his leg, too tired to cry.

❧ ❧

It took a long time until Yosef and Nakdimon returned. In the meantime, Yeshua's brother Ya'akov and Yochanan son of Zavdai tried to convince Miryam to return to her rented room in the City. She would have thrown herself over her son's body and stayed with him indefinitely, but she was not allowed.

"Please, Ema," soothed Ya'akov. "We need you. Your other children need you. Come and rest. It's done here."

Numbly she shook her head.

Shoshana, Shlomit, the Magdalit and myself formed a protective wall around Miryam. "We know you mean well but she's staying," we told the men. Reluctantly they agreed. What else could they do?

Several of the other believers also stayed close to Kuza and myself. Only the Magdalit crept as close as she could to Yeshua's body, continually dodging blows by the Romans as they sought to drive her off.

"Get away, sister!" yelled the man who had hammered the nails in. "We're being nice to you, but don't push us!" He laughed a particularly crude, evil laugh. The Magdalit wavered, her veil loosely about her stunning face, when Kuza quickly came up behind her.

"I'm one of Herod's advisers, men, and this woman is my wife's maid. I'll take her now." He seized the Magdalit's arm and marched her over to us, where she sank to the ground and shook with anger.

"I just want to kill him," she seethed, tears running down her face. "They murdered the Lord!"

"They'll kill you after they rape you, Miryam," said Kuza, brusquely. Then, in a kinder voice. "Stay with us now." And then, "Don't you see, we all killed him. All of us! The Roman Gentiles, the religious leaders, and we Jews. He's the sacrificed Passover lamb. He's the atonement for our sins. If we don't share in the sacrifice, then we don't share in the atonement."

All of us sat, heads bent, hearts weary, and mulled over what Kuza had said.

❧ ❧

Towards dark, the centurion returned. He ordered his soldiers to return to the Fortress with him. They left Yeshua's body.

Immediately thereafter, Yosef arrived, hurrying up the hill. Nakdimon walked a little behind him, next to a servant who had a huge bag balanced on his broad shoulders. The men went over to where Yeshua lay.

As soon as the servant dropped the bag to the ground, Nakdimon ripped it open. The scent that came on the air was unmistakable. *Myrrh and aloes!* Burial spices. By the look of the amount, it had to weigh at least seventy-five pounds.

Soberly, silently, the two men went to work, waving the rest of us away. So we watched while they expertly wrapped the body, with the spices, in strips of linen. This was in accordance with Jewish burial customs.

When they were done, Yosef and Nakdimon tenderly lifted the bound body and, with Yosef leading the way, wound down the hill and into the garden in which lay the new tomb.

The rest of us followed closely behind, wailing aloud, lamenting our dead. I felt nauseated and weak from both the trauma and the lack of food and sleep. I hadn't had so much as a cup of water since last night at the seder and it was starting to affect me. By my side, Shoshana stumbled and I knew that she was reaching her physical limits, as well.

In contrast to the barren, wind-swept execution site we had just left, the garden was really quite beautiful. Ancient olive trees flanked one side while fig trees graced the other. Red, purple and blue flowers, their colors dimmed in the coming twilight, bordered narrow paths. Off to the left, cut into the rocky wall of the hill, like a gaping wound, stood a newly dug tomb.

Yosef, sweating now under the weight of his burden, made right for the tomb. Kuza, Yochanan and Shimon helped, and the five men together carefully maneuvered the crucified Lord into his resting place.

"There's more to be done," fretted the Magdalit. "We need to come back as soon as Shabbat is over."

"Yes," agreed Miryam, Yeshua's mother. I glanced at her in surprise. Not as dazed as only moments before, she seemed to be aware of something the rest of us could not see. In any case, it gladdened my heart to see her stronger.

"That's right, Miryam." I drew my arm around her. "We'll come back at the first opportunity and anoint his body with more spices."

After the men laid Yeshua in the tomb, Yosef showed them a huge round boulder which they could use to seal the entrance. Several of them, grunting with the effort, rolled the stone in front of the tomb.

After that, what was there to do? Discouraged, exhausted, heavy of heart, we made our way home through the deepening gloom.

TWELVE

The next three days were the worst of my life. I fell into such a miserable state of depression and discouragement that I mostly slept. The rest of the talmidim didn't do much better. Kuza spent the two Shabbats with me, the Passover Shabbat and the seventh day Shabbat, but had to be in attendance to Herod on the day in-between.

Hearing about Herod made me want to march over to the palace and strangle him. Highly offended by Yeshua's cold and impervious attitude, he now gloried in the Lord's death.

"What an imposter! King of Israel, indeed!" smirked Herod, fingering his own gold crown.

He taunted Kuza such that Kuza feared for his life from one moment to the next.

"Pray with me, Yohie," he said. "Pray that God would release me from my post. If I just leave, Herod will search for me and kill me. The best thing would be for him to dismiss me."

So we prayed. I confess that my heart wasn't in it. My faith, so strong and vital these last two years, now seemed as fragile as a spider's web. With Yeshua dead, life went from vivid colors to grey.

Three days after the crucifixion, towards the end of Shabbat, the Magdalit came to my door. Face pale, eyes rimmed red from weeping, nose raw, she nevertheless held her head high and her shoulders straight. She came right to the point.

"Yohana, he wouldn't have wanted you to lie around moping like this. We need to move forward."

"Move forward how?" I asked piteously, throwing a robe over my nightdress.

"Tomorrow at dawn several of us are going to his tomb with more anointing spices. Come with us."

"Are you sure you want me to come?" I asked dubiously. "I feel so incapable right now."

"Of course I want you to come!" said the Magdalit sternly. Well, sternly for her. "Miryam, Shlomit, and Shoshana are all coming and you're part of us and we need you."

Miryam! At the mention of Yeshua's mother's name, my stomach lurched. We were all devastated, but *she!* To see the infant you nursed at your breast grow to be an extraordinary man unlike any other, and then ripped to pieces by a brutal and savage mob. I couldn't even begin to compare my pain to hers! And yet she was capable of leaving her bed and seeking out his tomb tomorrow; that holding place for death. Ashamed, I stood up and reached for the Magdalit's hands.

"Yes," I said. "Yes. Of course I'll come with you."

The Magdalit's face lit up with the brilliance of her smile. "I'm so glad, Yohana," she affirmed. "So very glad."

I went to bed early, as soon as Shabbat ended. Waking up while it was still dark, I hurriedly dressed and left for the meeting place a few blocks away. I went empty-handed, as the Magdalit had assured me that she, Miryam, and Shlomit had all the spices they needed. "You and Shoshana just come," she had said as she'd kissed me shalom.

In a very short period of time, the five of us met up and exchanged greetings. Silently, then, we slipped through the gray, predawn streets, heading north out of the City. Shoshana and I took some of the spices the other women carried, so as to share the burden equally.

After a few wrong turns, we found the garden with the tomb. It was difficult, in the hazy, morning light, to find a place we had only been to once before, and then under such harrowing circumstances. But find it we did.

"Oh, no!" whispered Shlomit, pointing. "Look! There's a guard posted."

She was right. Of course! I had totally forgotten that Kuza told me about this. The religious leaders knew that Yeshua claimed he would rise again and so they went to Pilate demanding a guard on the tomb. They figured that this would prevent any trickery. Pilate gave them permission.

"Not only that," said Shoshana. "Who will roll the stone away from the entrance of the tomb?"

We all looked at each other. We hadn't thought of that.

"Do you think the guards would do it for us?" suggested Miryam.

Shoshana snorted. "Them? Who's brave enough to even ask?"

Before any of us had a chance to reply, a familiar rumbling shook the earth beneath our feet.

"Help! Another earthquake!" we screamed, clutching at each other, struggling to maintain our balance.

"Oh, *look!*" gasped the Magdalit.

Descending from the heavens, dressed in dazzling white, so brilliant that we could barely look at him, was an enormous angel! He strode to the tomb, rocking the earth with his footsteps, and, in one swift, easy motion, rolled back the stone. Then he sat on it. Another angel joined him.

The Roman guards were so afraid that they shook and became like dead men.

Frightened as well, we prostrated ourselves on the ground in front of the angel.

"Why do you look for the living among the dead?" asked an unearthly voice, faintly reminiscent of rushing waters. "He is not here; he has risen! Remember how he told you when still with you in the Galil that, 'The Son of Man must be delivered into the hands of sinful men, be crucified and on the third day be raised again.' "

"Yes," said the other angel. "Now these things have been fulfilled. But come, see the place where he lay. Then go quickly and tell his talmidim he has risen from the dead and is going ahead of you into the Galil. There you will see him. Now I have told you."

Shaking, filled with great joy and expectation, we arose and tiptoed into the tomb. The place where the Lord lay was empty! Strips of linen lay there as though a body had been wrapped in them. We also saw the burial cloth that had been around Yeshua's head. The cloth was folded up by itself, separate from the linen. Trembling, we left the tomb, noticing when we emerged into the morning air that the angels had vanished.

Leaving our spices, we ran as fast as we could to the home where the eleven talmidim were gathered. Banging on the door, laughing breathlessly, we practically fell over when Thomas answered the door, rubbing his eyes.

"What's going on?" he asked, amazed at our giddy condition. He himself looked exhausted, desperate.

"The Lord isn't there!" shouted the Magdalit.

"The tomb is empty!" beamed Miryam.

"He's risen!" shrieked Shlomit, Shoshana and myself simultaneously.

Thomas stared at us, obviously convinced we had gone mad.

"Who's there?" yelled a voice from the stairs.

"Shimon!" I pushed past the gaggle of people clustered in the front entrance and ran and embraced my favorite talmid. Startled by my sudden display of affection, he asked,

"What's going on, Yohana?"

"It's the Lord; he's not in his tomb. He's risen!"

Shimon stared at me for several seconds, still as still could be except for a small muscle pulsing under his left eye. Then he sprang into action.

"Where's my sandals?" he roared. "And who's going with me?"

"I am," announced Yochanan, bounding down the stairs with two pairs of sandals in his hands. In no time, the men had their shoes on and rushed out the door. I looked to see who else wanted to go back over to the garden with us, but everyone else seemed skeptical.

"Come on!" shouted the Magdalit, impatiently, her beautiful face pink with excitement. "Let's go also!" She spun on her heel then turned back around. "Oh, I almost forgot! The message for all of you is that he has risen from the dead and is going ahead of you into the Galil." Then she sped out the door.

We raced back to the empty tomb, a little slower than Shimon and Yochanan but still awfully fast for us. When we got there, both men were starting to head back.

"What did you see?" asked Shoshana.

"It's as you say," admitted Shimon, with great wonder. "I don't know what to think." He looked completely bemused. I noticed a spring in his step and a barely contained exuberance. "I'll see you all later." Without a backward glance, he strode off, obviously wanting to be alone to consider these astonishing things.

Yochanan didn't leave as quickly. "How are you, Ema?" he asked Miryam, slipping naturally into his new role as son. Shlomit smiled, proud of this son of her womb.

"I'm excited, Yochanan," answered Miryam, blinking a little in the fresh morning air. "We knew that he was who he said he was, and now to see the angels, and the empty tomb..." Some of the grief and pain of the last few days dropped from her face. Slowly, haltingly, she spoke. "I try to trust in God, and even when I'm not faithful, He always is. And when you see just how extraordinarily faithful He is, and how much He loves us, and what miracles He does for us, His children, well, who has words?"

Who has words, indeed? Like Shimon Kefa, each of us needed some time to be with our own thoughts, and absorb what had just occurred. Yochanan and Shlomit escorted Miryam back into town. Only Shoshana, the Magdalit, and I remained. The Magdalit was a bit agitated. She walked back over to the tomb and stood outside, crying.

"What's the matter, Miryam?" I asked, coming up behind her and touching her lightly on the shoulder.

"Oh, Yohie, I'm so happy I can hardly stand it, yet at the same time I need to know where my Lord is! I need to *see* him." She twisted her hands together nervously and looked at me briefly. "I love him so much. He's everything to me."

"I know, Miryam. I know. Look, Shoshana and I will wait over at the edge of the garden for you. Take your time. When you're ready, we'll go together."

I squeezed her shoulder and walked away, leaving Miryam peering anxiously into the empty tomb.

When I reached Shoshana, I explained what was happening. The two of us sat down, held hands, and spent time praying together.

Meanwhile, Miryam had the most amazing experience. The two angels we had seen earlier were back in the tomb, seated where Yeshua's body had been, one at the head and the other at the foot.

They asked her, "Woman, why are you crying?"

Astonished, Miryam responded, "They have taken my Lord away and I don't know where they have put him."

Turning her gaze from the angels, she noticed a man near the entrance of the tomb. She didn't recognize him and assumed that he must work at the garden, probably as the gardener.

He spoke to her: "Woman, why are you crying? Who is it you are looking for?"

Wildly, stray tendrils of black hair sweeping across her face, she pleaded, "Sir, if you have carried him away, tell me where you have put him and I will get him."

Then the scales fell from her eyes and she realized that the man in front of her was Yeshua!

He said to her, simply, "Miryam."

And she turned to him and cried, "Rabbi!" She tried to throw her arms around him but he eluded her grasp.

"No, Miryam," he said gently. "Do not hold on to me for I have not yet returned to the Father. Go instead to my brothers and tell them, 'I am returning to my Father and your Father, to my God and your God.'" Then he vanished from her sight.

Shoshana and I looked up from our prayers when we heard the scream. Dashing back over to Miryam, we found her jumping up and down, tears rolling down her face. It took her several minutes before she had breath or inclination to speak. Her face, always so beautiful, now held the unearthly radiance of one who had glimpsed heaven itself and would never be the same. Finally, she told us the details of her encounter with Yeshua. Shoshana and I listened incredulously.

We took the by now very familiar path from the garden to the place where the eleven talmidim stay. Yet again that morning we knocked wildly on the door; yet again we were admitted to a place somber with mourning. Yet again we shared of a celestial visitation. Yet again we were met with unbelief.

"But it's true," cried the Magdalit. "I saw the Lord!"

"I know how much you loved him, Miryam," consoled Andrew, putting his arm around her in a brotherly fashion. "Go home and rest."

Frankly annoyed with the talmidim, we bid them shalom and returned to my house. First, though, we sought out Miryam and told her what had happened to the Magdalit. She started laughing and crying at the same time.

"Should we go back to the garden and look for him?" I wondered.

"No," said Miryam, decisively. "He's not confined to the garden. He'll reveal himself to us when he wants."

We spent the rest of the day together in prayer and joyful praise before the Lord. I went home in the late afternoon, anticipating my husband's return. I couldn't wait to tell Kuza about the thrilling events that had occurred since morning.

❧❧

Kuza came back to our rented home an hour before sunset. His terrible upset at Yeshua's brutal death, in addition to living under the cloud of Herod's erratic favor, had all but crushed him. Wearily, he entered, deep circles under his eyes.

He started in surprise when he saw me. Last he looked, I had barely been able to pull myself from bed. Now here I stood: washed, dressed, and hair combed, pouring wine into two goblets. The change, I have to admit, was stunning.

"What are you doing, Yohie?" he asked, softly. "Are you all right?"

I held a cup of wine out to my beloved. "I'm more than all right, Kuza. I'm a forgiven child of God." I took a sip of my own wine. "He's risen, Kuza. Yeshua is no longer in his tomb. Death has no hold on him. I've been privileged to witness the most spectacular event in human history, and right now I'm so happy that I feel as if I'm floating on the very clouds of heaven itself."

Kuza swallowed a mouthful of wine, coughed slightly, and placed the wine cup on the table. He attempted a smile. "Tell me this again. I'm not sure I heard you correctly."

"Oh, you heard me correctly, *motek*," I cried, slipping my arms around him and hugging him tightly. "We have been following the true Messiah who has conquered death! I have seen with my own eyes the proof! I have seen and heard angels tell these very things! Not only I, but both Miryams, Shoshana, and Shlomit." I bubbled over with laughter.

Then Kuza sat down on the couch with me, and ate and drank and recovered his strength. Three times he made me go over my story from start to finish. Finally, he was satisfied.

"God is so good, Yohana." He wept, getting down on his knees. "Come and pray with me."

Together, we lay on our faces before our Lord Adonai, blessing and thanking Him for the provision of His Son, Yeshua.

EPILOGUE

That amazing day when we discovered that Yeshua had risen from the dead, never to die again, marked the end of one story and the beginning of another. Many exciting things happened in rapid succession, leading Kuza and myself to a new life heretofore undreamed of.

That very same night, the first night of the week, Yeshua appeared to the eleven talmidim. He rebuked them for their lack of faith and for not believing that we saw him. Over the next forty days, he appeared several more times before he ascended into heaven, hidden by a cloud.

That year on Shavuot, when Jerusalem filled up with Jews from all over the known world, those of us who believed in Yeshua received a stunning gift. Tongues of fire hovered over our heads in the midst of a violent, rushing wind. When the manifestations passed, we discovered that we were filled with the *Ruach HaKodesh*, the Holy Spirit of God.

Shimon Kefa, along with Yeshua's brother Ya'akov, emerged as the natural leaders of the messianic believers in Jerusalem.

Kuza and I had a truly miraculous escape from Herod's palace. During the forty-day period when Yeshua was appearing to people, Kuza continued to go into work, but with great trepidation. One morning, just before the Feast of Shavuot, Herod suddenly said, "Pack up your belongings and leave the palace. I no longer need your services." Kuza's jaw dropped and he shook with fear, but he realized that this was God's hand of protection over our lives. Quickly, he thanked Herod for his kindness and backed out of the throne room as soon as possible. In a matter of hours, he and Adaba consolidated the possessions Kuza considered worth taking and arrived at our rented home. Kuza felt that this show of favor from Herod could change momentarily, so we made plans to leave the City entirely. We did stay for Shavuot, though, and were with the believers when the *Ruach HaKodesh* came down from heaven.

After Shavuot, we, along with Rachel and Adaba, traveled up to Caesarea. From there, we set out by ship across the Mediterranean to Cyprus. We stayed on Cyprus until the following spring, after which we determined to continue our travels. We sailed to Rhodes, and then up the west coast of Asia in the Aegean Sea. By the end of the summer, we had reached the port city of Ephesus. Both Kuza and I felt led of the *Ruach HaKodesh* to join the Jewish community that existed in the city under Roman rule. Imagine our heady surprise when we discovered my long-lost brother Yishai, his wife, Claudia, and their five beautiful children living within three blocks of us! It wasn't long before they, too, became followers of the Way (as those of us who believed in Yeshua came to be called).

Within a few years, persecution started in Israel. Those of us who loved Yeshua were scattered to the wind, much as a sower sows seed. From our established position in Ephesus, Kuza and I were able to help many of these dear ones begin a new life. To our great joy, both Yochanan and Miryam, Yeshua's mother, eventually made their way to Ephesus and assumed leadership of our community of believers. Miryam and I loved each other as sisters the rest of our lives.

Both Rachel and Adaba stayed with us. Rachel married a dear man from the Jewish community, and he came and worked for us. The high spirits and vitality of their seven children blessed me abundantly. I no longer felt the pangs of a childless womanhood. Indeed, I felt as Naomi must have when the son of Ruth and Boaz was laid on her lap: "Naomi has a son," said the women.

Adaba never married. He worked tirelessly for the Lord, helping Kuza on many journeys and adventures. Adonai enabled him to bring countless souls into the Kingdom of Heaven.

Shoshana returned to her hometown. Her children grew to believe in Yeshua, and they served God together.

The Magdalit never reconciled with her husband. She remained single the rest of her days, serving God in whatever capacity she could. When persecution struck Israel, she vanished into one of the surrounding countries, and I never heard from her again. Often I see her beautiful face before me, and I pray for her, and thank God that He allowed me to know one with such a pure heart.

And what of those who harmed my Lord? What happened to such as they?

Yehuda, seized by remorse though not repentance, hanged himself.

Within eight years, Herod was defeated in battle by his former father-in-law, Aretas, who had long sought vengeance for the insult to his daughter. Three years after that, the Roman emperor Gaius deposed Herod and sent him into exile.

And Pilate? About the same time Herod went into exile, Pilate was forced by Emperor Gaius to commit suicide.

Glossary of Hebrew Terms

Abba—familiar use of the word *father*

Adonai—literally "my lords." Term for God

Aharon—Aaron

Am ha'aretz—lit. "people of the earth." Used to describe the common people

Azazel—scapegoat

Baruch Atah Adonai Eloheinu Melech ha olam—standard beginning for many Hebrew prayers. "Blessed are You, O Lord our God, King of the Universe...."

Baruch ha Shem—lit. "bless the name." Means "praise God!"

Beeti—my daughter

Beit Anya—Bethany

Beit Lechem—lit. "house of bread," Bethlehem

Beit Tzaidah—Bethsaida

Ben Zavdai—son of Zebedee

Beresheet—lit. "in the beginning," Genesis

Binyamin—Benjamin

Brit-milah—circumcision

B'rukhah—blessing

B'seder—lit. "in order." Means okay, all right

Charoset—mixture of fruit, nuts, and wine used at Passover to symbolize the mortar with which the Israelite slaves made bricks

Devorah—Deborah

Dodah—aunt

Eesha, eshet—woman, wife, wife of

Elazar—Lazarus

Elisheva—Elizabeth

Ema—mom

Etrog—citrus-like fruit used in Sukkot ceremony

Galil—Galilee

Gan eden—Garden of Eden, paradise

Gat Shmanim—Garden of Gethsemane

Gavriel—Gabriel

Hallelu Yah—Praise the Lord!

Hanukkah—lit. "dedication"; Feast of Hanukkah

Hoshannah Rabbah—lit. the "great hosanna"; the last day of Sukkot; quite possibly the day of Yeshua's circumcision

Kelev—dog

L'hitraot—a form of good-bye: till we see each other again

Lilah tov—good night

Lulav—sheaves of myrtle, willow and palm branches tied together for Sukkot ceremony

Malach—angel, messenger

Maror—bitter herbs. Symbolic food at Passover seder to represent the bitterness of life

Marta—Martha

Matzah, matzot—unleavened bread. Matzot is plural

Mikveh—ritual immersion, baptism

Miryam—Miriam, Mary

Moshe—Moses

Motek—term of endearment, sweetie

Nahash—snake

Nakdimon—Nicodemus

Natzeret—Nazareth

Ner tamid—eternal flame, or candle

N'tilat yadayim—ritual hand-washing

Pesach—Passover

Prushim—Pharisees

Rosh chodesh—new moon

Ruach HaKodesh—the Holy Spirit

Rosh Hashana—lit. "head of the year"; Feast of Trumpets

Shabbat—Sabbath

Shalom—peace, used for hello and good-bye

Shamash—servant candle on the *hanukkiah* (Hanukkah menorah), which is used to light all the other candles

Shaul—Saul

Shimshon—Samson

Shmoozing—Yiddish term for hanging out and talking

Shmuel—Samuel

Shuk—marketplace

Shvitzing—Yiddish for sweating profusely

Sukkah, Sukkot—booth, booths; Feast of Tabernacles

Talit, talitot—fringed garment worn by Jewish men for prayer, plural

Talmid, talmidim, talmidot—disciple, disciples (m pl.), disciples (f pl.)
Torah—the first five books of the Bible; the Law
Tzadik—a righteous man
Tz'dukim—Sadducees. A religious party in Israel, like the Pharisees.
Tzit-tzit—ritual fringes used to represent the 613 laws handed down through Moshe
Ya'akov—Jacob
Ya'ir—Jairus
Yam—sea
Yehuda—Judah, Judas
Yehuda from K'riot—Judas Iscariot
Yeshua ben Yosef—Jesus, son of Joseph
Yishai—Jesse
Yochanan—John
Yofee—Hebrew slang for "great!"
Yohana—Joanna
Yom Kippur—Day of Atonement
Yosef—Joseph

Bibliography

The Illustrated Bible Dictionary, Volumes I-III, Intervarsity Press, 1980.

The Life and Times of Jesus the Messiah, by Alfred Edersheim, Macdonald Publishing Company, 1886.

The Temple: Its Ministry and Services, by Alfred Edersheim, originally published in 1874. Re-issued by Hendrickson Publishers, Inc., 1994.

Also by
Deborah Galiley

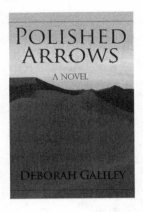

It was a time of great tumult...
and even greater evil.

When the Moavite King Eglon's reign of terror ends abruptly in the fourteenth century BC, the yoke of bondage is at last broken for the people of Israel. Now is their chance for a new start...but will it be enough to turn their hearts?

Devorah, the oldest child of doting parents, has grown up beloved by her entire community. Everyone senses something different about her—that God has specially placed His Hand on her—but for what purpose?

Yael, a purchased bride, is torn from her home and plunged into a life she never wanted. Can she learn to love this man she must now call husband...or is there too much of a chasm between them? And what of her dreams? Has God forgotten her?

Little could these two women guess that their lives would become polished arrows in God's quiver, targeting an entire nation.

A gripping historical tale that transcends centuries and hearts to show that every life...and every life circumstance...has ultimate purpose.

For more information:
www.greatbiblefiction.com
www.capstonefiction.com

About the Author

 **DEBORAH GALILEY** is a Jewish believer in Yeshua (Jesus). She grew up in a conservative Jewish home on Long Island, came to faith in Los Angeles, and has lived in Central New York since 1989. Deborah is a rebbetzen (rabbi's wife—her husband, Steve, is the rabbi), mother of five, author, percussionist, bread baker, and clarinetist. She has been healed of breast cancer in a miraculous fashion and prays for healing in others.

Deborah's first book, *Polished Arrows*, is the Devorah/Yael story from Judges 4. In addition to writing journalistic articles for several publications in the Messianic Jewish Movement, she is also working on a book called *From the Garden to the Heights of Hermon*. These are two short, complementary novels in one volume. *The Garden* is the story of the original Eve, while *The Heights of Hermon* details the spiritual odyssey of an American Jewish girl.

For more information, visit Deborah's website:
www.greatbiblefiction.com

You may write her at:
Deborah@greatbiblefiction.com